HAUNTED FLORIDA

THREE CHILLING NOVELS BY

GABY TRIANA

ISBN: 9781790722839 (Paperback Edition)
ASIN: B07KMLRKDR (eBook Edition)

Book cover and interior design by Curtis Sponsler

Printed and bound in the United States of America
First printing December 2018

Published by Alienhead Press
www.alienheadpress.com
Miami, FL 33186

Visit Gaby Triana at www.gabytriana.com

TABLE OF CONTENTS

INTRODUCTION

Thinking Florida for a lovely vacation? Think again. Florida (Spanish for "flowerful"), known for its sandy white beaches and tourist-filled theme parks, also abounds with unsettling legends and tales of the gruesome and weird. From the bloody history of Cayo Hueso (Key West in Spanish; "Bone Island") to tales of ghost pirate ships doomed to roam the Everglades, to mysterious Afro-Caribbean witchcraft in Miami, it's no secret that Florida is the perfect creepy setting for any book.

Years ago, I longed to read stories set in Florida after devouring Anne Rice's Mayfair Witches series (Witching Hour, Lasher, and Taltos). I thought, hey, if New Orleans can have their own horror novels, why can't Miami? I'd always loved the Southern Gothic aesthetic, tales about haunted plantations, voodoo, and the latent witch powers residing in all of us. This is how the Haunted Florida series began.

So, sit back, grab several cups of coffee, and get ready to read with the lights on, because Haunted Florida Books #1-3 has something for the ghost story lover in everyone.

A HAUNTED FLORIDA NOVEL

ISLAND OF BONES

"A devious mystery with plenty of dark secrets."

Jonathan Maberry, New York Times bestselling author of GLIMPSE and V WARS

GABY TRIANA

From bestselling author of *WAKE THE HOLLOW*

ONE

1951

A weathered old officer from the Key West Police Department stood on my front porch, cigarette clenched between his teeth. "Leanne Drudge?"

"Yes?" I pushed the screen door open, wondering what this was about.

"I'm Officer Brady. This here's Officer Smith." He gestured to a younger man in uniform standing by the patrol car on the street.

"What can I do for you gentlemen?" The shrimp in garlic sauce would burn on the stove if he didn't make this quick.

"Your husband's been in a fatal boating accident." He checked the papers in his hand. "Treasure hunting off the coast of Cuba. On behalf of Monroe County PD, we're very sorry for your loss. We'll need you to come down to the station tomorrow. After you've had a moment to process, of course."

My chest heaved, and my mind erupted into a thousand questions, but I refused to believe him. I gripped the screen door with both hands to keep from falling. "I…I don't understand."

"Your husband's dead, Mrs. Drudge." He spoke with the sensitivity of saw grass.

Yes, I got that part. I just couldn't understand *how*.

Fatal boating accident? Bill was the best boat captain in town. He navigated the seas like he did his wife—carefully. I wasn't the easiest person to deal with, but he listened for the right breezes, searched good and proper for storm fronts, knew when to avoid thick clouds, when to spearhead right through them. He wouldn't have had a boating accident any more than he'd have accidentally forgotten to make my heart and body long for him every day and night he was away.

As the officers waited, an early morning conversation from two days ago haunted me. "Today's the day, Leanne, baby. I can feel it!" Bill had said, excited about his boating trip. He'd been studying the precise location of a lost Spanish galleon, Nuestra Señora del Pilar, for the last seven years. It was his chance to become more than just a lobster fisherman.

But something wasn't right. I felt it in my soul—a darkness.

I hadn't known how to tell him. He wouldn't have listened anyway. "Now, Leanne…" he would've said, "this isn't the time for your mumbo jumbo."

My intuition. It'd always been right in the past, and I should've stopped him from going. Now I looked at Officer Brady without words, and it all made sense.

"I can see you're in shock, Mrs. Drudge. I'll send someone else over, one of the ladies from the station, or—"

"I'm fine." My hand shook on the screen door. My world would never be the same again. What about our dreams? What about Mariel asleep in her crib? What was I supposed to do now?

Officer Brady glanced at the other patrolman by the car who smiled and nodded at him, a silent idea communicating between them. He turned back to me. "In that case, uh…" He removed his cap, pressed it against his chest. Rise of his left eyebrow. Taunting. Pushing limits. "Mind if we come in?"

I gaped at his lecherous brown eyes roving over me. Would the people of this town stop at nothing to judge me? Suddenly, I feared his authority with Bill nowhere near to save me. "No. Thank you for coming." Quickly, I closed the screen and locked the door.

For a long time, I stood there, staring at the door, feeling my world collapse around me. Then, I willed my feet to move and wandered through the house in a fog. I reached my bedroom and the bed's edge, sat staring at my reflection while the baby slept. He couldn't have perished. Not in a boating accident.

No, no. This was wrong, this was impossible.

I stood and moved to the kitchen to pour a shot of whiskey, then took it outside into my garden by the inlet. Downing the shot, I stared at the water. It took a moment, but the wave rising behind my chest finally spilled over. It rose until the tears formed, until I looked at the moon sculpture Bill had carved for me, thought I would die if I didn't let out the pain.

With a wail, I cursed at God. Told him it was no wonder I never believed in him in the first place. What kind of merciful god would do such a thing to a young woman with a baby? A good god would make sure my husband came home. And if he couldn't find that treasure he'd been searching for all his life, then he'd at least trap a few lobster to help pay the bills.

There was no God, just like there was no truth.

And now, there was nothing worth living for either.

Only my baby.

In the coming weeks, Bill's death was a well-publicized "fact" in Key West, even though there wasn't a scrap of evidence. But women like me, we don't take things at face value. We look past the smirks of the fact-people—the reporters, the police. We search beyond the veil. I'd even say we "know" things other people can't explain.

It wasn't no boating accident.

We never saw him again, Mariel and me, and the months dragged by with achingly slow precision. My one-year-old quickly forgot the spark of her father's laugh. She stopped glancing at the door in the evenings. And because my life had been cursed the day Bill disappeared at sea, I even lost my family home.

As a widowed mother with no income of her own, I was forced to sell the only tangible thing I had—*Casa de los Cayos*—the twenty-eight-year-old house where I'd grown up, married my husband, made Mariel out of love. I lost it to Susannah McCardle, of all people.

My neighbor, Susannah, had wanted my house from the moment her daughter, Violet, got married last year. A dozen times she'd asked me when I'd planned to move. She wanted to expand, move her daughter in next door, she told me. Make a family compound of the two homes.

Never was always my reply. This was *my* house, and my mama's before me.

Susannah would scoff and head indoors but always come back out for a smoke. My house needed paint, she'd argue. It needed TLC, a man to care for it whereas that lazy SOB of mine had done nothing but boat and chase gold, and now look at where that had left me. I should just sell it and move to a cheaper key, she'd tried convincing me.

I held on as long as I could—another year. Finally, I couldn't make payments no more. Only so many jars of key lime marmalade sold before the bank account ran dry. Susannah had won in the end. Now, her son-in-law who cut coquina for a living and her hateful bitch daughter, who did nothing but sit on her ass, would live in *my* house.

The shame hurt so bad, it burned a hole in my chest.

With Mariel in my arms, I crossed the gravel front yard,

transporting the last of my belongings, stuffing as much as I could into the old Ford. The little girl from down the street watched me from her cross-legged position on the curb.

From her porch, Susannah watched with that over-plucked high eyebrow of hers. "Told you he would bite the dust out there, leave you like this." She sucked on her cigarette. "Probably ran into pirates or something."

"Shut up, Susannah. Nobody asked you."

"It's better this way, darlin'." She blew smoke into the late summer air and picked tobacco fragments from her teeth.

Meanwhile I tried to make the bicycle I'd bought a few years ago with the money I'd earned waitressing fit in the back. It wouldn't. "You want this?" I asked the little girl witnessing my shame. She stood and gaped, hardly believing I was offering up such a good thing. The bright blue bike was too big for her, but hell, she'd grow into it. Nodding, she took it off my hands.

The mosaic table Bill made me wouldn't fit into the truck either. Even Mariel tried telling me this with her big green eyes. *Mama? Let it go.*

How could I? He'd meticulously placed each piece of glass with his loving hands. I rested my head on the truck door, wanting to sob pathetically, but I quickly collected myself. I would not let Susannah have the glory of seeing me this way. I'd make this table fit in the car if it killed me.

"It's not going to fit, Leanne. Just leave the damn table behind."

"I'll decide what doesn't fit!" I spit. If I could've cast a swarm of flying daggers at her face, I'd have done it.

Damn it, the table wouldn't fit.

From her front porch, Susannah snickered.

Maybe after I got my life together in Plantation Key, I could save money, return to Key West, and buy back my house. "Don't get too comfortable," I told her, reluctantly leaving the mosaic table on the sidewalk. "I'll be back for it soon."

"Over my dead body, you will…"

Panting in the August heat, I paused to look at her. I absorbed her ugliness and toxic energy. The image would never be erased from my memory as long as I lived. Queen Victorious was most pleased now that this simple woman was not only heartbroken, but emotionally decimated as well. Why did she and everybody else hate me so? Because I didn't go to church? Because I felt more spiritual sitting in my herb garden than this town would ever be kneeling in the pews?

Over my dead body…

Yes. Maybe it would take that. But her dead body wasn't up to me. My mother had taught me that we didn't cause harm on others. Karma would take care of that. But I was also tired of living by the rules and getting screwed in the end. Tired of watching others' ships come in when mine was still lost at sea.

I closed my eyes and visualized Susannah McCardle's dead body, rotting, festering in the summer heat. Flies flitting into her mouth laying eggs. The police department knocking on *her* door. My house on the market again. Me earning it back. I could bend my mind around these visions, but I'd never been very good at manifesting dreams, or else my husband would still be here. I could only hope that Mariel would learn my mother and grandmother's ways better than I ever could.

Susannah tapped the porch railing. "Hello, Earth to Leanne." Her crooked smile matched her flyaway, graying hair.

Violet stepped onto the porch in curlers and short shorts, tapping her pack of cigarettes. "What's going on?"

"Leanne's finally leaving."

"About time."

I wouldn't give them the satisfaction of a reply. I plopped into the grass to pet our black kitty. "We can't take you with us, Luna," I whispered. "Apartments don't allow magical creatures." I smiled on the verge of tears. Mariel reached out to Luna, too.

I closed my eyes to visualize.

I imagined no happiness—zero, not a single scrap of it—ever entering *Casa de los Cayos* again as long as I wasn't there to make it happen it. Mariel clung to me, so still, eyes wide. Baby girl knew what I was up to, already learning, showing respect for the craft. Wondering what sorcery Mama was conjuring up this time.

"May this house and all who live in it suffer." My voice shook. "For without us, it is no longer a home."

Blowing out slowly, I envisioned my charged breath traveling, crossing the lawn and curling around Susannah, Violet, and the entire McCardle Family. It snaked over to my property and enveloped that too. As I belted in Mariel and stepped into the driver's seat, cranking on the engine, I stared at Susannah one last time. It was hard to ignore the victory in her eyes.

My lovely pink and white home, like the inside of a conch shell, seemed to sag just then. It called to me, begged me not to go. Not to worry, I would make things right, even if it took a lifetime. I would be back, whatever it took.

"So mote it be," I whispered then drove off down Overseas Highway.

TWO

Present Day

Miles away, Nana fell into a coma, as my boyfriend got down on one knee.

Not to propose riverside at the Museum of Science in Boston, no. That would've been cute and romantic, considering it was where Zachary and I had first met two years ago this very night. It was to pick up my IMAX ticket that had fallen out of my pocket, and the look on his face said it all.

"Ellie, we need to talk."

Ugh, famous last words.

I'd worried about this happening so much over the last month, sometimes I felt I'd caused it. Now here we were, staring at the St. Charles River, and I could almost envision everything he was about to say like a script in a bad, made-for-TV movie.

"This has nothing to do with you," he assured me. "It's me. I think…I think I need to be alone for a while." He wasn't sure what he needed, what he wanted, he added. Some time off would help him figure it all out.

I sat there avoiding the deep hazel eyes I'd never get lost in again.

For two years, I'd given my energy to Zachary when I could've spent that precious time with my ailing grandmother. Two years wasted. When he was done with his monologue, he asked if we could stay friends, and I gave him the middle finger.

That night at my grandmother's bedside, I deleted him off all social media, because who needed Zachary Dum-Dum Bowman condescendingly telling me I'd always be in his heart? Meanwhile he commented on Amada Payne's posts at least eighteen times a day. Didn't know what he needed, my ass.

I took Nana's wrinkled, lukewarm hand and pressed my cheek to it. "You were right. You're always right, Nana." She didn't move or acknowledge me.

Nana always said I'd know when the right man came along. I'd know because he'd adore me the way my grandfather adored her. He'd kiss me passionately before leaving home. There'd be a sparkle to his eye. I was lucky if I could get Zachary to put down his phone during dinner, much less look at me in any special way.

"But no offense, Nana…that kind of love doesn't exist anymore."

I should've been here when she slipped away. I should've listened to her mutter stories about the old days, about that house in Key West, about a mural designed in ocean colors, and an island I'd only seen in one faded photo. A house that'd haunted her dreams until a few days ago when she'd whispered its name in her sleep—*Casa de los Cayos.*

Instead, no thanks to Zachary's sorry ass, I hadn't been at her bedside to say goodbye. I never saw those green eyes again. Nana died in her sleep two weeks later.

When my mother told me that my grandmother had left me a small sum of money, enough to keep me alive a couple of months, I quit my job at the middle school two weeks before classes began. My principal wanted to know where she was going to find a remedial math teacher at this late hour, but I just couldn't deal.

I needed to get over losing Nana, Zachary, my worthless life. To get over how stupid and blind I'd been for two years. I needed a reboot on life, and I was pretty sure how I wanted to start.

Sitting at my mother's kitchen table, I stared at the brown box containing Nana's cremated remains. Inside the box wasn't just my grandmother, but every story she'd ever told me, every memory she'd ever recalled.

"What do we do with all her stuff in storage?" I asked.

Mom unfolded her hands, waved them around. "Keep whatever we want. The rest we sell or give away. She didn't have much, Ellie." She refolded her hands.

"I know." Nana had worked most of her life. First as a receptionist, then as a lunch lady at my mom's middle school in Key Largo, then they moved to Fort Lauderdale, then Savannah, then honestly, I had no idea how they ended up in Boston.

But it was clear she was never the same after my grandfather died, because my mother always talked about growing up with a sad woman who'd always longed for her childhood home. For an idyllic life she'd had with my boat captain grandfather before he disappeared. When I was little, I used to dream about this old life of hers—literally dream of colored tiles and glossy palm fronds, of drinking lemonade on a wooden porch, of a black cat whose name I never knew. I always woke up feeling like I'd actually been there.

"All she ever wanted was to return to Key West." My mother scoffed. "For all the good the island did her."

I stared at the brown box. "Then, let's take her back."

"I don't want to," Mom said, point blank. "She had so many bad memories there, I just can't."

"But it's where you were born. It couldn't have been all bad," I argued.

"One thing has nothing to do with another, Ellie," Mom said.

For years, I'd been trying to get us to visit Nana's old house in Key West. After all, she'd spent so much time reminiscing about it, I was pretty sure she would've wanted to see it one last time before she got worse.

"I feel like the place is cursed, Ellie. I can't explain it," Mom added.

Ugh. I was twenty-six years old and still hearing my mother talk about gut feelings she couldn't explain like they were any kind of evidence.

Mom shook her head. Her frustration was palpable. "Maybe we can send her ashes and hire someone to scatter them for us. I mean, I don't even know where the hell *Casa de los Cayos* even is, and—"

"I'll do it," I said.

"What?"

"I'll go. I'll figure it out. I have nothing else to do."

"But school starts in a few days."

"Mom, I quit."

"You what?" Bright green eyes stared at me like I'd lost my mind. And maybe I had. But I had a bachelor's degree in advanced mathematics, for goodness sake, I could find a job anywhere when I got back.

"Mom," I sighed. "Let me go to Key West. Nana would flip out if she knew you hired some random nobody to scatter her ashes. I'll find the house, I'll scatter them…maybe I'll even connect with Nana somehow."

Connect was a word my mother would understand. She'd been more spiritual when I was growing up, though nowadays, she seemed to be too busy for meditation and incense. She visibly relaxed. "Are you sure?"

"Yes. Positive." I smiled. "It'll be good for me. Help me forget ass-face."

"Oh, Ellie. Don't call him that."

"Mom. Just—don't."

For the first time in a while, I had something exciting to look forward to. A trip to Florida! I hadn't learned enough about Nana in the time I'd had her here. I hadn't asked the right questions, hadn't heard all the tales. I'd been too busy.

Besides, in the last two weeks, my covert OCD had kicked into high gear, giving me night terrors I hadn't had in a long time. This little getaway would be just as much for me as it'd be for Nana. I was on a plane to Miami the very next day, new bikini in my carry-on, Nana's ashes in my bag. Soon, I'd be sipping lemonade in a rocking chair watching the sun go down over paradise.

Tropical vacay, here I come.

THREE

Deep wrinkles covered his leathery face, and though there was nothing particularly scary about him, I wanted to run in the opposite direction. Who was he? The man followed me, crept closer, like he wanted to speak to me, except he wouldn't utter a word.

I felt the familiar sleep paralysis in my chest. I screamed but my cries blended with a pitchy, metallic whine somewhere in the distance. The distance? No, nearby. I jolted upright, swinging at the man's face to get away.

My eyes opened. I was sitting in an airplane, my face wedged between the seat and the fiberglass window. I was on the airplane to Miami, listening to the engines making their descent. The vibration of landing gear signaled that we were almost there. I panted, looking around. I'd startled the older lady next to me. "You okay?" she asked.

"Yeah." I pressed a hand to my chest. "I get nightmares. Sorry."

"My husband does too. Anxiety?"

"Not exactly."

It was hard to explain. I didn't feel like getting into it. Since I was a child, I'd had visions, sometimes awake, sometimes sleeping. Faces, people around me, shadows lurking just outside my peripheral vision. Sometimes I'd hear them speak. In my early teens, doctors told my mom these were classic signs of OCD. Not the same OCD that made people line things up in perfect rows, but *covert* OCD.

This was more internal. I had to line up my thoughts just right to get rid of the chaos, the negativity, the crippling self-doubt. I looked for order, smiles, and pleasant situations to counter the darkness. Probably the reason math and science had always felt good to me. Solid things I could count on. No "mumbo jumbo," as my grandmother called gut feelings. I'd been taking Zoloft for sixteen years now to help. Ever since…no visions, no negative thoughts, just a pleasant evenness.

On some days—numbness.

But ever since Nana died, this one vision had crept his way back into my dreams. He was Native American and harmless, but a moment ago, I'd sworn he was after me. Stupid brain.

"Flight attendants, prepare for landing," a female voice announced.

I pulled my purse from under the seat and plucked out my pill bottle. Only three sertraline left. I'd have to order more when I got to Key West. Breaking one with my fingernail, I figured I could use an extra half right now.

"Headed home or visiting?" My chatty seatmate wanted to know.

I cracked open one eye. "Visiting Key West."

"Oh, how nice! You'll absolutely love it. *Cayo Hueso*," she said.

Opening both eyes this time, I swiveled to face her. "Pardon me?"

"Key West in Spanish." She smiled. "Island of Bones, its original name."

"Oh. I didn't know that." I held my bag close, the one containing my nana's remains—ashes and shards of bone in a box. How appropriate. The plane touched down. "Almost there, Nana," I muttered.

"Changes in latitudes, changes in attitudes, nothing remains quite the same," I sang behind the steering wheel of my rental Prius. Would I have preferred a convertible Mustang like half the cars taking the three-hour trip from Miami to Key West on this gorgeous summer day? Yes, but I also needed to make sure my grandmother's money lasted me at least two months, so I didn't have to hurry back to Boston right away.

As the Jimmy Buffett song suggested, my state of mind completely changed once I hit Overseas Highway, the single lane (sometimes double) road cutting through the Florida Keys. The brilliant sun, bright blue sea, and bite of salt in the air was enough to almost wash away the memories of the last month, like a good, strong gargle dislodging a heavy yuck in my throat.

Mangroves, beaches, and fishing piers rolled by. I tried to imagine Nana and Mom living here when they were younger. Mom had been born in Key West, but they'd relocated to Plantation Key after my grandfather died. Mom said she was too young to remember him, but Nana reminded her often of how much he loved her, played with her, and sang to her in the evenings.

For me, this was another world—a living postcard with brightly painted wooden houses on stilts, giant conch shells notifying passersby of tourist traps, and parrot-shaped windsocks blowing in the breeze. It was hard to imagine this corner of the universe as anything cursed, like my mother had suggested, but then again, the grass was always greener on the other side.

When it came time to drive across the seven-mile bridge, part of me almost pulled over. My fingers gripped the steering wheel. Driving across the Florida Straits with nothing on either side but miles and miles of open ocean—*fan-freakin-tastic.* Behind me, an impatient driver rode my ass. I glared at him in the rearview mirror.

"You can do this, Ellie. Everyone else is."

Picking up speed, I told myself this was just another jaunt on the 495 back home, heading to Martha's Vineyard for the weekend. It was hard to believe that people used to take a train out here in the 1800s, that they even lived this far from the mainland. Hard to believe that anyone in settler times rode their horses and pulled their carts as far as Key West. How had they hopped across the islands without these bridges?

Boats. They traversed in boats, Ellie—duh.

Once I realized I wasn't going to plummet to my watery death, it was easy-peasy the rest of the way. *See? No doomsday.*

Thirty minutes hopping over more tiny isles, and I drove across one last short bridge making it to a traffic light. The colorful sign in the median read, *Welcome to Key West, Paradise USA.*

"I made it," I muttered, checking the time. "Holy shit, I made it."

If I hurried, I could also make it in time to watch the famous Key West sunset while holding a fruity adult beverage in hand. But I hadn't researched the best place to do that, hadn't made any hotel reservations either. I'd figured I could just pop into a Holiday Inn or Motel 6 when I arrived.

Mistake.

Every chain hotel I stopped at either didn't have vacancy or did, but at anywhere from $400-700/night for a basic room, I wouldn't be on vacation for long. I should've come with a plan. I should've thought this through.

I should've, should've, should've.

I stopped chastising myself long enough to find my way downtown to a place called Mallory Square. There I could grab a drink, watch the sun go down, and think about my Plan B. Parking wasn't easy, but the nice thing about a Prius was you could cram it anywhere, so I did between two doorless electric buggies. Getting out, I locked up the car and headed toward sounds of drunk people partying. A fluffy chicken hopped out of nowhere and clucked at me. A big rooster followed her, giving me the evil eye.

"Oh. Hey, chickens," I said, because chickens roaming freely was so normal, right?

Another world, indeed.

At Mallory Square, I bought myself a rumrunner from a street vending cart then parked my butt on a bench to watch the sun descend behind a small island out in the water. Dark silhouettes of sailboats cut out triangular shapes in the tangerine sky, and I let out the biggest sigh ever.

"I made it to the end of the world." That was how it felt, coming out this far south. Lifting my drink to the sunset, I said, "Welcome home, Nana."

Did she and my grandfather ever sail at sunset? Did my mother ever ride on a boat with them? After all, my grandfather had supposedly been a skilled boat captain, though I believe that was also how he'd died. So many things I'd never know. So many things I'd failed to learn about my family, my heart ached.

I soaked in the lazy vibes and party atmosphere, the ocean waves swishing just a few feet from me. Paradise USA was right. *Well worth the drive, Ellie?* I heard my grandmother ask from a distant place.

Well worth the drive. I smiled.

Once the sun sank and the tourists cheered, the nighttime party began. People, vendors, performers on stilts juggling bowling pins all filled the streets making me smile but also feel sad for some reason. Nana had grown up here in the what…1930s, 40s? I did some quick math in my head. She had to have left town in 1952 when my mother was only a year old. Had the island been as touristy back then, or had she lived here during some idyllic era of peace that no longer existed?

Nostalgia for a place I'd never know hit me hard.

The drink wasn't helping either. Everyone had someone to party with, and I was alone with a ghost in my purse and memories of a place I'd never been. How would I find *Casa de los Cayos* on this eight-mile-wide island? I didn't have to find it tonight, I reasoned. Tonight, I only needed to find a place to sleep then start my search tomorrow.

I stopped at a kiosk that sold gelato on one side and vacation timeshares on the other. "Excuse me." I stopped in front of a middle-aged woman with platinum blond hair up in a tight ponytail wearing bright pink lipstick. "Do you know any hotels with vacancies, not too expensive?" I asked. Maybe the locals could point me in a better direction than all-booked Expedia could.

"Did you try up on US-1?"

"Is that the road I drove in on?"

"Yes, the only road in. There should be some places out there. The farther away from center of town, the cheaper."

"Right, there weren't any. But thanks," I said, my hopes slumping. I'd already stopped at those places and they'd wanted an arm, leg, and my spleen for a night's stay.

"Miss?" The woman called me back. The man minding the gelato stand had apparently heard us talking. "La Concha Inn on South Roosevelt. That's the road on the left side of the island when you come in. You probably followed traffic to the right."

"I did. Thank you."

"They might have rooms during summer," she added with a cautious smile. She and the other attendant exchanged glances.

"Great. Thanks again." Walking in the direction of my car, I spoke into my phone. "Find La Concha Inn," I said, while British Siri searched for results. She showed me a location way on the east side of the island about as far from the good stuff a place could get.

Twenty minutes later, I'd arrived at the blue pinpoint on my map. At first, I wasn't sure this was the right spot, as it seemed to be a private home behind a gate surrounded by wild, unkempt foliage. Two stories, wooden columns with porches on both levels, ceiling fans that hung crookedly, the main house had seen better days. On either side were smaller homes like bungalows or cabins sitting in darkness—a compound of buildings. The front lawn had once boasted 70s-style kitschy Florida eye candy to attract tourists—a faded, peeling statue of a conch shell, an equally dilapidated parrot, and a pirate with not only his leg and eye missing, but his power to amuse as well.

I felt sorry for the statues like I felt sorry for the home. It didn't make sense to feel sorry for a structure, but the house looked like an old woman all alone at Bingo Night.

Turning off the car lights, I stepped out, my sandal crunching onto gravel. No big signs, no neon lights, no commercial draw-in of any kind, but the map insisted that this was La Concha Inn and didn't "la concha" mean shell in Spanish? I glanced at the shell statue again. *Yep.*

I grabbed my purse, leaving my suitcase in the car. Pulling back the chain link gate, I walked underneath a thick cover of trees, vines, and coconut palms in various states of growth. A small wrought-iron bench sat rotting underneath the moonlight, and sun-dried plastic toy cars littered the overgrowth. Ahead of me, something reptilian scuttled across the path. *Hello, Florida.*

The main home was poorly lit and needed a few coats of paint and serious refurbishing. It almost seemed to be leaning to one side. I couldn't tell what color it currently was because of the darkness, but it definitely didn't look bright or cheery like other places in town. It also didn't look open for business.

I was ready to call the listed number when the front porch light turned on. My heart pounded when I heard the screen door slowly creak open. A gaunt, braless woman appeared from the darkness wearing shorts and tank top, sallow skin like worn cowhide, cheeks sunken like spoons, and long hair like gray straw. "We're open," she croaked in a voice coated with nicotine.

Clearly, she was talking to me, though not attempting any eye contact whatsoever. "Awesome," I said, unsure that I wanted to proceed. I'd seen horror films that began this way.

If I decided I didn't like the way the establishment looked on the inside, I could always thank her and be on my merry way. There was nothing to this, yet I felt apprehensive heading up the steps. The stress of the last month had clearly spurred old anxieties. It didn't help that I'd traveled all day and been up since five this morning either.

I stepped through the screen door, greeted by a large gray cat with golden eyes who stood perfectly still like a live sculpture. Dusty fake bromeliads filled the small foyer and the smell of cigarettes permeated the air. I refused to believe that a hotel could be this bad and wondered if it was really just someone's ill-kempt house, but judging from the brochures haphazardly arranged in a plastic display case, it was a real place of business.

"You looking for a room?" the woman asked, coming to stand behind a counter to my left. She still wouldn't look at me, which was both rude and unnerving.

"Yes, but I wasn't sure if you were open for business. You should have a sign out front or something."

"Broke during Hurricane Irma. Haven't put a new one up yet."

"Oh, sorry to hear that. So, how much for a night?"

"Two hundred," she replied, "but I can give you a special rate if you stay three or more nights. Hundred-twenty a night." Her fingers drummed the countertop. No smile. No enthusiasm. Behind her, a much older, dark-skinned woman slowly plucked a paper cone from the side of a water dispenser and glanced at me. No smile from her either but then again, she looked like a woman who'd lived a long, hard life.

I wasn't sure I wanted to stay three nights. Maybe tomorrow I could try my luck closer to town and find a more appealing stay. This place looked like it'd seen better days and it wasn't like the innkeeper was doing backflips to be accommodating either.

"Breakfast is included," she added, as if that would seal the deal. The eye contact came then, as though she'd realized she'd have to work a little harder to get my money. There was something off about her dark eyes.

"At what time?" I asked.

"Six-thirty to nine-thirty." Her left eye didn't move. Was positioned differently. It might've been a glass eye, giving her the appearance of a broken animatronic.

I wouldn't be awake until ten-thirty, but I had nowhere else to go, so I bit the bullet. "Let's go with one night to start. If I like it, I'll be happy to pay two more at full price." Even at $200 a night, it was cheaper than everywhere else and staying here would keep me from booking on another island and having to drive here daily.

The woman nodded and clacked at her old keyboard while I picked a few brochures. The Hemingway House, the Southernmost Point, Sunset Spooks Ghost Tours… The big gray cat jumped up onto the counter, scaring the shit out of me.

"Geez," I caught my breath.

"He likes you," the woman grunted. "He doesn't like anybody."

"Well, hello little guy. You scared me." I petted the cat's head. At first, he wasn't sure if he wanted my human hands all over his dusty pelt, but then he leaned into my palm and purred rhythmically. The sound was the only comforting thing about this place.

"It's Bacon."

"Excuse me?"

"The cat's name," she said. "Bacon."

"Bacon?" I coughed a nervous laugh and pet the kitty who rubbed his cheek so hard against my hand, he left a trail of saliva across my thumb. Ew. "Does he show up to breakfast or wisely stay away?" I snorted. "You know…Bacon?"

She stared at the ancient computer screen.

I swallowed and dropped the jokiness. "I've never been much of a cat person," I said. Mrs. Friendly didn't look like she cared one bit about anything I had to say. Just hand over my two hundred dollars. I didn't know why I was being so chatty. I just felt like at least one of us should be filling the silence.

After a minute of taking my information, she pulled a key on plastic ring from a drawer and handed it to me. I'd never stayed anywhere that didn't use a key card. "You'll be staying in Room 2. It's through those doors, follow the garden path to your right, then the second door to your right. Double bed, bathroom, access to the garden, and TV."

"Is there a Wi-Fi password?" I asked.

"You'll get a decent signal with your regular phone service."

So, that was a *no*. "Okay, then." I took the key and tapped the counter. "Thank you so much. What was your name again?" In case I wanted to write a terrible review on Trip Advisor later.

"Syndia Duarte."

"Ms. Duarte, thank you," I said, noting the dour looks from both her and the old woman sitting like a wax figure in the chair behind her. Shaking them off, I turned to go. I was halfway through the living room with Bacon at my heels when it occurred to me that both these women were locals. Either might've heard of the home I'd come here searching for. I turned back around just as she was shutting off the light to her office. "Oh, Ms. Duarte? Would you happen to know where I might find a residence on the island? It used to be called *Casa de los Cayos*?"

She stopped and gazed at me with that glass eye, scrutinizing, analyzing. Did I really expect someone to know about a place that had existed seventy years prior? "It might not be around anymore," I added with a shrug. "Never mind."

It was a long shot, but no harm in asking.

Syndia held onto the counter with both hands, vacant eyes wide. Judging from the way she looked at me—*finally* looked at me—I knew I'd hit a nerve. Her eyelids narrowed over her good eye. "Where did you hear that name?"

Don't tell her, a voice warned. She hadn't liked my question, and I almost wished I hadn't asked. I would ask someone else in town tomorrow. "Uh…a history article about Key West or something. Thanks. Have a good night."

She studied me, everything from my face to my purse containing Nana's ashes, all the way down to my feet. "This is *Casa de los Cayos*," she said. “At least it used to be.”

FOUR

"How does it look?" Mom asked over the phone.

I'd called her to tell her the incredible news that I'd happened to stumble into the right place by total accident. I called from the privacy of my room, of course. Didn't think Syndia would take well to hearing that my family used to live in her hotel and what I presumed was also her house. She seemed annoyed enough as it was.

"It looks…desolate, to be honest," I told my mother.

Sadness streaked Mom's voice. "Is the moon sculpture still there?"

"I don't know. Where do I find that?"

"I don't know either. I'll find the pic of Mom and me as a baby in front of it," she said. "And text it to you later."

"Okay." We talked a little more then I hurried to hang up.

My room was adequate but old with its outdated furniture, and the lights in the bathroom didn't work when I flicked on the switch. Tomorrow, I'd inform Syndia, maybe ask if she could change me to another room. She'd probably be in bed by now and I was so tired, it didn't matter.

Even though it was late, I wanted to get at least one cursory look around the resort before going to bed. From what I'd seen so far, La Concha Inn was a collection of three houses, a centered main two-story building with a living room, dining room, office, and an atrium leading outside. Two houses of one story each flanked the main home, subdivided into three guest rooms. In the center of the backyard was a walled-in scant garden about twenty feet wide with a drizzly half-busted fountain in the center and a giant, creepy tree near the inlet. Enormous vine-root-things dropped from the tree's branches and sank into the ground, giving it the appearance of a massive animal chained by the neck and tethered to the ground.

The rest was too dark to see at this time of night. The whole property must've spanned an acre or so, bordered by long stretch of seawall in the back reaching from one end to the other. The humid August night smelled of salt and rotting coastal plants.

Which building used to be my grandmother's, I wondered? They all looked weathered enough to be original structures. Would anybody working here be old enough to remember? Syndia seemed to be in her fifties, her assistant in the office was even older, and my mom wouldn't remember. I couldn't ask Nana anymore, which burned me.

I headed out for a stroll.

Though it was almost 11 pm, I heard voices coming from the garden. There were other guests here? Why that shocked me, I didn't know, but it did. There they were, having beers in the lounge chairs. As I inched closer to them, I felt like I was sinking deeper and deeper into some land of the lost. The garden was overgrown with wild plants and weeds strangling anything that dared to stand out or be beautiful. The fountain trickled sadly. The gravel walkway had become overrun with stray grasses. Running my hand along the circular rock wall surrounding the fountain and garden area, I paused.

A chill ran through me. Granted, it was late at night and we were situated by the water, but a burst of cold air in the Florida summertime heat felt out of place. I pulled my hand away from the rock wall and moved closer to the people. An elderly couple in matching shorts and polo shirts sat in the extended lounge chairs along with a middle-aged couple about my mother's age. I felt better just knowing other life forms were staying here with me.

They quieted their conversation as I walked by. I waved to show I meant no harm and moved to the seawall overlooking the inlet. Here, I could appear like I was minding my own business while still overhearing their conversations, as they exchanged opinions about the establishment in muted whispers.

"How about you guys?" one woman asked.

"We'll be leaving in the morning. Not happy. Not happy at all, and..." I couldn't make out the entirety of what the wife was saying. "I don't even want to say it."

"She thinks there's ghosts in the rooms," her husband chimed in like a hero for vocalizing what she'd been too scared to say out loud. He chuckled condescendingly.

"Oh, really?" the other couple asked.

Yes, she said. Something about feeling like somebody was watching them in this very garden and last night in the guest room, it felt like a presence had crawled into bed with her.

"Well, at least someone did," the husband cracked, and the other husband cackled like that was the funniest joke ever.

I wanted to tell them that ghosts weren't real. They were fabrications of our minds, that the brain was a powerful organ. That they might even be a symptom of a brain disorder. When I was a kid, I swore ghosts followed me around, until I was diagnosed with cover obsessive compulsive disorder. And then, just like that, with a little pill, the ghosts disappeared. The only ones haunting me now were my own regrets.

I continued to listen with fascination.

"Did you hear about the tropical storm coming this way?"

In my shadowy corner of the garden, I faced them. Storm? I hadn't seen anything about a storm on the news, and the part of my brain that went into worry overdrive perked up at the news. The woman mentioned it could become a Category 1 storm by tomorrow, but it was too early to tell and anyway, it was still out wandering the Atlantic.

"It won't come this way," one husband said. "That's still days away; anything can happen, and from my experience, those things always cut right through the Caribbean and head to Texas."

"Oh, true, true," the other husband agreed. "We should be fine."

"When did you become a meteorologist, Roger?" one wife asked. I could almost see her eye roll in my head.

"It's always the poor countries that need most help after these storms," the other wife said. "I mean, look at Puerto Rico after Hurricane Maria. So devastating."

"Puerto Rico's not a country, hon. It's America."

"You know what I mean," she replied.

Was this true about the storm? Had I really come arrived to town on the worst week of the year? If worse came to worst, I could book a flight home, get out of the islands in time, couldn't I? *Oh, sure, along with thousands of other evacuees, Ellie.* Great, because my OCD needed more negative thoughts to obsess over.

No, everything would be fine, I told myself. One good thing about tropical storms over other natural disasters—you had days to prepare. You could see them coming miles away. Still, I wished I'd checked the weather sooner, or I wouldn't have come until hurricane season was over.

I felt stupid for being impulsive during that kitchen conversation with Mom when I'd agreed to bring Nana's ashes like some family heroine. Normally, I thought things through carefully. This time, it was like a voice inside my brain had made the decision for me. Regardless, I would enjoy my time here as long as I could.

After a few minutes of feeling the ocean breezes waft through the inlet, listening to the sounds of waves crashing below, I got hit with the tireds. It'd been a long-as-heck day, so I headed back to my room, making sure to take a full Zoloft and Ambien so I could get some sleep. I didn't want the native man visiting my dreams again tonight.

Harmless or not, he'd creeped me the hell out, and I was already creeped out enough as it was. Especially when I found Room 2's door wide open, as if someone had just been there, even though there was no one inside and I was sure I'd closed it myself.

"Hello?" I entered the room and scanned around.

Nobody was there, not in the bathroom or closets either. Maybe I hadn't closed the door all the way, or the latch was faulty and wouldn't shut right. Either way, I was perfectly safe and needed to stop obsessing. If only that wasn't so hardwired into my being.

I woke to the sounds of birds chirping and shuffling outside my window. I caught a flash of green. Wild parakeets? The sun filtered through the blinds, lending much-needed light to my room. The bad news was now I could see every crack, water stain, and ancient piece of furniture clearly. I focused on my phone instead.

My mother had texted while I'd slept. She'd sent the photo mentioned last night—a black-and-white faded image of a young and beautiful Nana holding my mother as a one-year-old. They stood in front of a rock sculpture in the shape of a quarter moon.

This is what it looks like, she'd texted. *Mom always mentioned this moon. Dad made it for her out of coquina.*

What the heck was coquina? Some type of rock, obviously. From the photo, it looked like the same rock used to make the garden wall, the seawall, and half the walls around this place. I had a lot to learn about Key West life. Maybe the innkeeper could answer a few questions for me. Would Nana's neighbors still be the owners of the inn? The neighbors she'd mentioned a few times who she swore hated her guts? I doubted it. If my grandmother had been eighty-eight when she died, then they were either just as old, way older, or dead.

If Syndia had recognized the name *Casa de los Cayos,* maybe she was part of the original family. I'd have to ask. I saved Mom's photo in my camera roll, got dressed, and headed out to see if I could locate the sculpture. How cool would it be if the thing still existed seventy years later?

By day, the garden didn't look any better. At least nightfall helped disguise how bad it was, but in full sunlight, the measly water dripping from the fountain was as depressing as the rusted cracks down either side of it. Most plants grew so wild, they lacked organization and made me feel I was staying in a jungle rather than a resort. The lounge chairs where the couples had sat talking last night were sun-faded with cracked plastic straps stretching across rusted metal frames.

The circular rock wall surrounding this center hub looked like it'd been built over many years by different amateurs. The layers of porous rock were different colors, reminding me of all those charts showing layers of earth in science textbooks. Uneven craftsmanship. Not attractive in any way and depressing as hell. The only good thing about the yard was the majestic tree chained to the earth by its own choking roots. Even though it looked like a prisoner in its own space, it was still beautiful in a Frankenstein sort of way.

Banyan…

I looked around.

Had somebody said something?

A cold chill wrapped around me before wafting off, carried by the warm breezes. I shook it off, unnerved that I'd heard what sounded like someone talking nearby. Today *would've* been a good day to find a better resort to stay at, but now that I knew this was *Casa de los Cayos*, I had to stay. I'd come to spread my grandmother's ashes. I couldn't leave until I'd done that.

The closer I got to the inlet and ocean, the lighter I felt. Something about the salty air lifted the heaviness of the garden right off my shoulders. It made me sad to think that Nana's childhood home had fallen into ruins like this. By the property's edge, the water sparkled like diamonds underneath the sun. I thought about the best place to release her ashes, if to release them at all when I spotted it—the crescent moon sculpture.

Tucked away behind wild glossy fronds (were those bananas growing underneath?), the sculpture peeked out pathetically from under the foliage. This might've sounded crazy, but it almost seemed relieved to see me, as if it'd been waiting all this time for anybody to notice it hidden underneath the overgrowth.

I pulled up the photo Mom had texted me and held my phone

up to the sculpture. Same shape, same porous rock, same base, same view of the water behind it. My heart did a little victory dance. How could they let it get covered like this? It was one of the only beautiful things in this garden. I stood beside the sculpture and fired off a series of smiling selfies, then I took a few of the thing without my face.

Another chilly breeze whipped around me. It was a stifling ninety-five-degree heat out. It was strange, but then again, ocean air did bring cool breezes through. I just never realized how much. I texted the photo to my mother: *Look what I found!*

I felt so excited with my discovery that I postponed my plan to run out to Duval Street for sightseeing and spent time with the sculpture instead. I ran my hands over it—bumpy, raw, organic. So this was *coquina.* A quick online search told me it was a type of porous limestone harvested from the shores of Florida, used for building forts, seawalls, and sometimes foundations of homes. Apparently, it could be carved into anything, including quarter moons.

But all I cared about was that my grandfather had carved this particular piece. My own flesh and blood, the grandpa I never knew, had laid his hands all over this rock, toiled under the tropical sun to shape it. He'd fashioned this shape out of love for my grandma.

The only gifts I'd ever received from Zachary had been bought. Easy, whip-out-the-credit-card type stuff, the kind of present anyone could've bought at the last minute. Nothing like this. Nothing special.

"He must've really loved you, Nana," I said aloud, hoping my message would streak across the universe and reach her, wherever she was.

Studying the photos again, I noticed a few had captured beams of light streaking across the moon, blocking its beauty. I deleted those then noticed something else—in the background of a few, depending on the angle, was a woman.

An old woman in a wheelchair.

Hunched over. Ancient.

I moved to the seawall for a better look.

She sat by the water on a lower level of the dock. I shielded my eyes from the glare, watching her. Vacant stare, mouth agape, older than even my nana, motionless as the boats floated along the inlet.

On a nearby bench, the woman from the office sat a while reading from a paperback. After a few minutes, she stood and stretched, placing her hands on the ancient woman's shoulders. "Come on, Miss Violet," she said in a Caribbean accent. She wiped the old woman's mouth and began wheeling her away. "Time for your nap, old girl."

FIVE

Something about the old crone unsettled me. Poor thing, catatonic and unresponsive, just hunched over in the wheelchair. Nana had always said if we had to wipe her chin or change her diaper, then she'd no longer want to be alive. Luckily, she hadn't been in that state for long. She'd left Earth on her own terms.

Combined with the resort's state of disrepair, it was no wonder business wasn't booming. And though I'd come to Key West to spread my grandmother's ashes, I'd also come to get away and relax. So I spent the day down on Duval Street, bar and store hopping, and it wasn't long before I'd sank back three margaritas at Hog's Breath Saloon with tourists who'd come off a cruise ship parked out in the ocean.

I must've made ten new friends while out, though I couldn't remember the names of any of them. One of them told me he was a ghost tour guide in town and showed me where the group departed every night, rain or shine. A woman about my age drank with her friends, celebrating her divorce, and upon finding out I'd recently broken up with my boyfriend, bought me my fourth margarita.

I was so smashed, I couldn't drive back to La Concha. Hell, I couldn't even find my car. I'd have to rideshare back then return for the rental tomorrow morning.

When I got back to the resort, I thanked my driver then entered through the front instead of the side guest entrance I'd seen this morning. Syndia happened to be at the front desk, so I stopped in to speak with her. "Hello, Ms. Duarte."

She stopped eating sunflower seeds long enough to grunt then look up at me through that freaky glass eye. "What."

What? Not *yes*, not *may I help you?* My goodness, this woman needed hospitality courses. I didn't let it bother me. "The light in my bathroom isn't working," I said, allowing her time to respond. No such a thing took place. "I was wondering if you could move me to another room."

"All I have is Room 3," she muttered going back to her sunflower seeds.

"Okay. Is there something wrong with Room 3?"

She looked at me as though I should know. Then, as if suddenly remembering I was the weird guest who'd mentioned *Casa de los Cayos* by name, the one new to town, she sighed. "We don't usually rent it out. It's old, but the lights and water work fine."

Why wouldn't she have rented it to me in the first place, then, instead of Room 2? "Works for me." I smiled to counter the feelings of negativity Syndia was emitting.

"Where did you say you were from again?" Her good eye narrowed. The glass one didn't move.

She should've known this from the info I'd given her at check-in, but I humored her anyway. "Boston."

"Are you the daughter of Mariel Drudge?"

Well, well.

Someone had spent some time digging. After my question about *Casa de los Cayos*, I shouldn't have been surprised she'd taken to investigating. It wasn't hard to track me or my mom down by name. We were both on social media and always linked as mother-daughter.

"I am, though it's Whitaker now," I said. "Not Drudge." Then, figuring since we were getting nosy with each other, I'd ask a question of my own. "Are you related to the family who runs the resort?"

"That side…" She pointed to the half where I was staying, "used to be my home when I was little, where my sisters and I grew up. When my grandparents passed away, we opened the inn on that half, where you're staying now, and moved to the other side of the compound." So, family house on left, guest rooms to the right—check.

"Your sisters live here, too?" I asked.

She took a while to answer, as though the question caused her physical pain. "They're in Miami." She ground the sunflower seeds between her teeth. "They only visit when they need something. My mother and I are the only ones left. Why are you here?"

Hostile, accusing tone. I swallowed and tried to ignore the feeling of pressure on my chest like I was unwanted here. "My grandmother passed away. She'd always talked about growing up in this place."

"Your grandmother being…?" Her question seemed more for her own confirmation. She already knew.

I indulged her anyway. "Leanne Drudge."

Syndia froze, dissecting eyes staring at me. Then, she suddenly remembered to breathe. I thought she would ask more questions, and we'd begin a dialogue about how our families knew each other, but she didn't pursue it. She reached into the drawer and pulled out another key. "Wait an hour for us to get it ready then bring back the other key after you've moved."

"I will. Thanks." Teetering off, I felt dread and anguish all rolled into one come over me. Why would she have been offended to know who I was? And why did I feel like I wasn't welcome here?

My mother's apprehension came to mind when she'd told me she felt this placed was cursed, that Nana hadn't left Key West under the best of circumstances. I hated not knowing the whole story and hated myself even more for not getting it when I had the chance.

Walking through the garden at night brought out the worst of my OCD. Before I knew it, that oppressive feeling of doom I felt in the center hub enveloped me completely. I knew it was a symptom of my disorder, so I ignored it the best I could. Still, it was hard not to imagine every shadow as a person out to get me or every bug that flew past as a spooky orb of light.

Something was following me.

I stopped right then, sniffed the air, and looked around. Nobody. Alright, enough of this. I pulled up my phone, ordering more sertraline from the local pharmacy. I'd have to go without a pill tonight but could pick them up first thing in the morning.

A voice spoke near my ear. *Whore…*

"Excuse me?" I whirled around. "Who's there?"

I scanned the wild landscape but no one was around. God damn it. What was happening? I'd probably heard a guest speaking from one of the rooms or caught a sound byte carried by the water. *You're freaking out for no reason, Ellie.*

"Shit." I wiped my brow in the thick heat and headed to Room 2 to collect my things. Since Syndia had asked me to wait an hour, I took a few more minutes and searched up my grandmother, Leanne Drudge, just to see what came up. Nothing except the obituary we'd printed back home. I added "Key West" to the search, and this time, a PDF result came back. I clicked on it and found her name on a list of residents from 1940-1950 underneath Bill Drudge, my grandfather.

That was it. No other information, which was both a relief and a mild disappointment. Part of me had hoped her whole history would show up, so I wouldn't have to dig for answers or talk to Syndia again.

I took another minute to check the reviews of La Concha Inn on various sites. No surprise that it only had one star, and most of the reviewers said they would've given it zero had the website allowed it. Most of the reviewers also mentioned sensing an oppressive presence throughout the compound, and several wrote full paragraphs about the eerie things that had happened in their rooms, everything from cold spots to the sensation of being watched by unseen forces, to outright apparitions walking through the walls.

Yeah, okay. I laughed. More undiagnosed patients of hallucinogenic brain disorders.

No mentions of weird happenings in Room 3, though, so that was good.

I dragged my stuff to Room 3 and unlocked the room. Musty humidity seeped out, as the space seemed to exhale then draw its first breath in years. I clicked on the light switch, and a dirty yellow glow illuminated the space.

Syndia was right—it wasn't much, but it was better than Room 2 only because everything worked. Besides looking like another cheap hotel room, I could tell it'd also been used as storage, because of the brooms, mops, and buckets shoved inside the closet. The furniture was heavy teak, the kind of stuff you couldn't move once you'd set it down, and I wondered if any of it were original to the house. For all I knew, it could've been around for decades.

The art on the walls were crappy posters that had faded in the sunlight over the years, one of a parrot sitting on a branch and one of a footprint in the sand. Tacky. In the corner of the room, however, with an old lamp on it, was one, unique beautiful piece—a mosaic tile table.

Curious, I walked over to it and ran my fingers along the hand-placed tiles. Cobalt blue, light blue, and white gave the impression of ocean waves. An odd sensation came over me. Had I seen this table before? Of course not. I'd never been here. It looked handmade and had fallen several times judging from the cracked tiles on each corner.

A memory flitted through my mind all of a sudden—of me when I was about twenty, wearing a yellow sundress, happy like crazy that my boat captain fiancé had finally made it back from lobster trapping between Key West and Havana.

Only…I'd never lived in Key West or Havana before.

I'd never owned a yellow sundress before either, nor had a boat captain fiancé. Sinking onto the edge of the bed, I gripped my temples and tried to make sense of the thought. Where had that vision come from? I'd lived my entire life in Massachusetts. Those memories weren't mine.

Something shuffled out of the corner of my eye, but when I turned to face it head-on, nothing was there. Shadows, disembodied voices, a feeling of dread, hallucinations. All symptoms from my childhood days, though they usually affected me in sleep. All indicated deep stress infiltrating my psyche.

Then again, I'd had four margaritas today. That would make anyone hallucinate.

It was time—time to spread my grandmother's ashes then vacate. Split this place. Make like a tree and leaf. I might've felt different in the morning after doubling up on my medicine, but right now, I needed to get this over with. Grabbing my bag, I left the room, making a beeline for the unsettling garden. The moon sculpture would be the perfect place to honor her.

The ocean, I heard someone else's voice.

Nana?

She wanted me to release her into the ocean, I somehow instinctively *knew.*

But it couldn't have been her voice from beyond nor a gut feeling. It was just common sense. She'd lived by the sea. She'd lost her husband to the ocean. She would've wanted to be reunited with him. Fine, I'd spread half her remains at the sculpture and half at the water's edge. When I reached the rocky quarter moon, I placed my flat palm against it, waiting for some cue that it was time.

"Alright, let's do this." I couldn't wait any longer. My mother had been right. This place had a weird vibe about it. The only way to alleviate the discomfort would be to do what I came to do then go as quickly as possible. If that storm was heading anywhere near this place, it'd be the best choice anyway.

Opening the plastic bag containing the sandy granules that had once been my grandmother, I reached in and pulled out a handful of ashes and bits of bone. Did it feel odd holding her charred, decimated remains in my hand? Yes, but oddly, I felt close to her having this control, giving her soul—if there was such a thing—what it wanted.

I closed my eyes and called young Nana to mind. Beautiful,

golden blond Leanne Drudge dancing in the breeze as a child living at *Casa de los Cayos*, pale green eyes staring out at the ocean, full breasts on a thin frame as a young woman, a sight for a weary sailor's sore eyes. Like coming home to pure love itself.

"Rest in peace forever, dear lady," I said, pushing my hand out and releasing her ashes all over the sculpture. I watched the particles swirl and dance on the breeze. I waited for, I didn't know, something magical to happen.

Nothing did.

I only felt sad and nostalgic and as far from peaceful as one might imagine. What had I expected? To feel fulfilled?

"Well, that's that." I began walking away from the sculpture when the wind picked up, or maybe I was imagining one. Not really a wind but not really a hallucination either, but *something* blew up from the inlet over the garden, rattling the plants and leaves. I watched as dust particles twirled in the light of a full moon above. It was probably the alcohol still coursing through me, but I also felt the ground shake just a bit, like a jolly giant from a fairy tale had taken one step before sitting down to rest.

Like the island itself had just coughed.

Taking the path to the seawall, I reached into my bag and pulled out another handful of Nana, holding out my arm and slowly releasing the bits and pieces. The grains fell from my hand like sand out of a funnel all over the dock, getting caught up in the cool ocean breezes, spiraling out to sea.

Finally, a certain peace came over me like I hadn't felt in the two days since I'd been here. Like coming home. Like being reunited with a loved one. Two things I'd never known.

But something new—I felt like I'd just unleashed hell for everyone else.

I wasn't alone. Down below on the dock was the old woman again in her wheelchair, only she wasn't staring out to sea or space. Instead, her head was bent upwards, and she stared blankly, awkwardly at me at an unnatural angle, like her neck had been twisted to look up. Her mouth gaped open, vacant eyes forced out.

What the hell?

Was she dead?

To add insult to injury, I'd just sprinkled human remains over her by accident. Her nurse, the same woman from Syndia's office, sat on the nearby bench reading on an iPad. She hadn't noticed anything amiss, and I wasn't going to be the first to tell her the old woman seemed to have expired.

Catching my breath, I whirled around and bulleted through the garden, back the way I came. This place *was* cursed. *Shut up, Ellie, curses don't exist.* The real Ellie, the rational Ellie, wanted to stay and learn more about *Casa de los Cayos*, wanted to know more about Syndia and her family who'd purchased my grandmother's home. But before the night was over, she'd be dealing with the death of the woman in the wheelchair.

She deserved it.

A male voice this time. Nobody sat in the lounge chairs talking. No other guests whispered in the night from what I could tell. Who deserved it? The old woman? I couldn't wait to buy more Zoloft in the morning and start doubling up, doctor's orders be damned. I had to stop these voices hell bent on talking to me.

Cutting through the unkempt garden, an army of shadows followed me like they'd all woken up at once. I desperately wanted to escape them. I wanted to reach my room and lay down for the night. The banyan tree looked like it wanted to break free of its chains and chase me.

None of it made sense.

I needed sleep. I needed my meds. They'd suppress whatever this attack was on my brain. All I had to do was go to bed and wake up tomorrow, clear my mind of the weirdness. Then, maybe I could stay an extra day, finally relax, sip that lemonade I'd been dreaming of since Boston, then go home. Mission accomplished.

I reached my room and closed the door, relieved to be away from the garden.

And then I saw him standing in the corner—the native man from my dreams.

SIX

The moment my gaze connected with his, the man disappeared.

But I saw him—I know I did. Full body apparition. He'd worn nothing but a loincloth and a beaded red-and-white overlay on his shoulders. His hair had been picked up in a bun, and he'd held a spear. Sun-baked skin. Lots of details for a hallucination.

I didn't know what to think. I only knew I was exhausted as hell. And now, I'd have to sleep in the same room with a ghost. But ghosts didn't exist, or so I thought? They were manifestations of an overactive mind. If my own brain had fabricated him, then why this man in particular? A man I'd never seen before in my life? Was he someone I'd met long ago and forgotten?

He hadn't seemed menacing. More like a quiet observer, watching over me. I didn't get any sense of danger, but I didn't like it either. Maybe this was why they didn't rent out Room 3.

I opened the windows for fresh air, leaving the shutters closed with the slats open. I showered, changed into fresh T-shirt and undies, and climbed into the old creaky bed. Looking around, I could tell I was in somebody's former bedroom from the old armoire, old pine floors with chair scratches near the wall, and perfect view of the garden. If I narrowed my eyes just right, I could imagine myself watching the inlet, waiting for that fishing boat to come back, the one that carried my husband.

What the hell? I pressed my palms against my eyelids.

What fishing boat? What husband?? I needed sleep. I needed my sanity back.

But neither came easy.

He told me not to worry, that everything would work out fine, I would see. I would see, because he'd meticulously planned this trip down to the last detail, and today was the day of its execution. He kissed me goodbye, and when he did, I felt it was the last time I'd ever see him. I wasn't sure how I knew, but I just knew.

The baby in my arms and I watched him go. He waved his hat, jumped into the fishing boat down by the pier, and away they went. "Come back to me," I whispered. "I can't live without you."

Then, the woman came.

Or rather, the creature next door.

She smoked something fierce and liked to watch me plant herbs in my garden from her yard. Sometimes she hung out the window, sometimes stood on her back porch. Soon you'll be husbandless, and I'll take your house. Like hell you will. My husband is working hard for us. He'll come through. The words seemed not to come from our mouths but from some ethereal place like watery echoes. Sure he will, honey, she said. Sure he will.

A little girl kneeled in the weeds, plucking them and putting them in a pile. "Can I get some water now?" she asked, exhaustion all over her face.

"It's 'may I have some water?' And when you're done, girl. You just got started."

Wasn't sure who these people were, and yet…I knew them deeply. Had seen them millions of times.

The man was the love of my life, and the woman could've been a witch from the way she spoke to me with hatred pouring from her soul. A bad witch anyway, like the green-skinned ones only with pale skin and curlers in her hair. The little girl, I had no clue.

We're sorry to inform you, the policeman said.

He was lying straight to my face. How could he?

But your husband is dead.

Something about that statement made him randy. An opportunity had opened up. He wanted into my house. He wanted me for his own...

I blasted awake in the center of the bed, a sheen of cold sweat breaking out over my entire body. Gasping, I gripped the sheets and fought for air. I scanned the room. I could almost see them standing there—the officer, the husband, the horrible woman. How could she have been so cold? I was a young woman with a baby, no threat to her, yet she treated me like I was something to be feared.

"Wake up, wake up, you idiot…" I wasn't any of those things.

I was Ellie Whitaker, unmarried, childless, and twenty-six years old. And I'd been dreaming. I wasn't dreaming as myself. I was dreaming as Nana.

Something had happened here. Something terrible, but not to me.

Outside, a rogue wind blew through the center courtyard, whistling and forcing open the shutters. For a moment, I thought I saw my husband from the dream looking in through the window—Nana's husband, rather—my grandfather as a young man. Standing still, gaping wound across his neck, blood dripping down his sweaty chest.

His wide open eyes watched me through dirt-covered face. He wanted me to know. To see. Jesus Christ, I needed my meds. When I blinked him away, another figure appeared to replace him, that of a cat—a large, gray cat.

"Bacon," I gasped. "What the hell?" I took a moment to catch my breath.

Then, jumping out of bed, I went to the window and opened the shutters, petted the cat's head once before pushing him off the sill into the courtyard. He protested with a loud *mrwow*, and I closed the shutters, this time locking the clasp and the slats as well.

It'd been a dream, a nightmare. I knew this. My brain knew this. My scientific mind could conjure up fifty million explanations for these visions, yet deep in my soul, in my heart where sometimes the only things mattered, I knew that something bad had happened here. Something involving Syndia's family and mine.

My walk to the pharmacy helped clear my mind.

The moment I paid for the Zoloft, I ripped open the package and swallowed back two whole ones. Then I made a note in my phone planner to make an appointment to have my dosage adjusted. My OCD had been under control until Zachary, until the night my grandmother fell into her coma. Since then, my repressed issues had all decided to come to the surface.

Great timing.

As I rounded the street corner back to La Concha Inn under light rain, I slowed down. An ambulance was parked out front, as two paramedics wheeled a covered body into the back. Off to the side, Syndia stood stiff with a tissue at her mouth, her eyes red and glistening. If the woman had looked gaunt and frail when I first met her, she looked ten times worse now. The old woman's nurse stood behind her, sporting a tight-lipped grimace.

"Is everything okay?" I walked through the open gate.

Syndia stared straight ahead. "My mother. She passed away late last night."

"Oh, I'm so terribly sorry." So, that had been her mother.

"Are you?" She cast a hurt gaze at me.

"Excuse me?"

"Are you sorry? You shouldn't say things like that unless you mean them." She held my gaze for a few hateful seconds more then stomped up the steps and entered the house. The two paramedics gave me sympathetic looks.

I felt like I'd been slapped, like I was culpable for what had transpired here. Why did I feel guilty when I hadn't done anything wrong? The woman had been practically a thousand years old, for hell's sake. I mean, I felt bad for Syndia, sure, but it was her time to go anyway. My being here had nothing to do with it.

"People say weird things when they're in pain," one of the paramedics said to me.

I nodded and moved past them. Unable to help myself, I glanced back at the stretcher inside the ambulance. The old woman lay underneath the white sheet, her filmy eyes vacant, her cracked mouth open, saliva drying up. She wheezed, emitting gases and bodily fluids. I gasped, wondering how the hell I could see all that if she was covered.

The ambulance doors closed.

I moved past the woman's nurse, noting the worry on her face and entered the house, hoping to return to my room where I could decide what to do—whether to leave town or stay. Then I saw the other four guests gathered around the dining table watching TV. Amid their unappetizing muffins and bowls of cheap cereal, they chattered as they watched a satellite image of a storm system.

A big-ass storm system.

The weatherman, in his snazzy suit, buzzed about the screen. "Here you see Tropical Storm Mara blazing a trail through the Turks and Caicos Islands, traveling at a speed of twenty-five miles per hour…"

I walked into the dining room and leaned against the wall to listen.

"The bad news for us here in the Florida Keys is that we're close to receiving the dreaded National Hurricane Center Tropical Storm

Warning, but the good news is that storms traveling this quickly tend to be over soon. Last thing we want is a slow-moving storm that dumps rain on us for days."

"A hit and run," one guest mumbled.

Another couple stood, the curly-haired wife with the manicured nails picking up her purse and sunglasses. "We need to get going before traffic gets bad. Well, hope you all get out safely. It was great meeting you," she said to the other couple then headed down the corridor.

"What about us? What do we do?" the other wife asked her husband.

"Let's see what the weatherman says. It might not come."

"Even if it doesn't come this way," I chimed in shyly. "We'll still get those outer feeder bands the weather man was talking about and lots of rain. See them?" I pointed to the swirly outer cloud bands on the satellite image.

"So much for our fun-in-the-sun, tropical vacation!" The husband stood and stretched. "Alright, dear, let's pack this puppy up and take it home. What about you?" he asked me. "You staying?"

"Not sure. I'll check flights out from Key West and decide."

"They're all cancelled," the man said. "We just heard it on the news. All local flights. Your best bet is to drive to Miami and fly from there, if you get out in time. What I'm worried about is the bumper-to-bumper traffic. By the time we make it, the area's under a hurricane warning."

"Right," I said. "I'll have to consider all options." I'd been through bad Nor'easters before, but not a tropical storm. What was the difference besides rain instead of snow? Wasn't it just a matter of hunkering indoors until it passed?

"Well, good luck to you."

"Thanks, you too."

The couple left, just as Bacon jumped onto the table to take scraps of what they'd left behind. As my gaze followed them out of the dining area, it landed on a fireplace in the living room. Above the mantel was a gilded shadow box, something shiny glinting inside.

Bacon rubbed against my leg, asking for more food.

"I don't have anything, buddy," I told him. Checking to see if Syndia was anywhere in sight, I reached into the muffin basket, ripped off a chunk of dry muffin and set it on the floor. Bacon sniffed it but turned up his nose. "Sorry, then. Go kill a mouse or something."

The cat stalked into the living room and stood underneath the mantel looking back at me, almost as if saying, *Come on, come look at this.* He seemed very proud of this room, so I walked over and peered into the shadow box on the mantel. A photo of three gold, round pieces topped a frame article from the *Key West Gazette.* Below it was dated Labor Day, 1951.

The basic gist was this: Key West resident, Robert McCardle, had found a bag of gold doubloons during his shift piloting the Havana Ferry back from Cuba. The bag had mysteriously appeared on the ferry before which he'd dutifully turned it into the police. As no one had come to claim it, the police let him keep the Spanish gold coins. As a result, Robert McCardle purchased the adjacent home next to his to accommodate his expanding family, but sadly, the man died unexpectedly from a massive heart attack the very next year.

My heartbeat picked up. Wait.

Robert McCardle had found treasure in 1951? But I thought my grandfather had been the treasure hunter and fisherman on this property. Shouldn't it say Bill Drudge? It was like my family's name had been erased from history.

"Them only the tip of the iceberg."

I whirled around. Miss Violet's nurse stood there, arms stiff by her side. Bacon hissed at her.

"Hi." I extended my hand. "I'm Ellie."

She took my hand. "Nottie."

"Nice to meet you. What do you mean these are only the tip of the iceberg?"

She stared at the shadow box. "Rumor say there's a lot more gold than that one bag McCardle found." She glanced around nervously, wringing her hands. "He purchased the house next door, you know—your grandmother's house."

"Right, that's what I've heard. Is Room 3 part of her original house?"

The woman wouldn't answer me. "They say he hid the rest so nobody would attack him for it," she whispered. "Robert McCardle did."

Attack, or accuse? "Who would attack him for it?" I asked, trying to imagine a 1950s fisherman hiding his treasure in the house like a paranoid madman.

"Treasure hunters, pirates…"

"Pirates?" I half-laughed. What century were we living in?

"Not the peg leg kind with the feathered hats, but yes," Nottie assured me. "Anyone looking to steal your loot around here is a pirate, you know."

"Got it." I nodded.

"Nottie." The voice was stern and sudden. We turned to find Syndia rounding the coffee table making a slow descent on the poor nurse. "That's enough. You can go now." Her frown told me my informant wasn't supposed to tell me any of that.

"Sorry, Ms. Duarte." Nottie took off faster than a cat burglar under the sudden beam of a cop's flashlight.

Syndia's glassy gaze seemed to accuse me of something I couldn't decipher. "Yes, pirates are a common thing here in the islands. People stealing what's not *theirs.*"

Did she think I was here to take something? I didn't believe the silly little story on the fireplace mantel anymore than I believed some hotels bragged about being haunted, just to attract visitors. Talk of pirates and hidden treasure was a lure for tourists seeking adventure. Especially coming from an establishment that needed more business such as this one.

Syndia already knew I'd heard Nottie's version so I went with it. "Wouldn't McCardle have told his wife where he hid the rest?" I asked. "I mean, why would he keep such important info to himself?"

"Men didn't confide in their wives in those days. Her role was to run the house, not the finances. Besides, he became paranoid after finding the gold. He always felt that someone would take what was rightfully his."

Sounded like guilt to me. A bag of gold suddenly showed up on your ferry and you got to take it home, rich as butter pie? Reminded me of the story of Sarah Winchester, perpetually afraid that the ghosts of those killed by her family's famous Winchester rifles would haunt her, so she built a home with endless rooms, doors, windows, walls, and staircases.

In this case, Robert McCardle had hid his treasure to keep the bad men away.

"Anyway, it's none of your concern. Can I help you with something else, Miss Whitaker?" Her eye stared at me with lifeless intensity.

"So you're telling me this…treasure…is still in the house somewhere?" I couldn't believe what I was hearing. She wouldn't answer, so I looked back at the shadow box, noticing now a brass plaque at the top. Printed on it—*La Concha's Very Own Legend.*

"You better get on the road, Miss Whitaker." Syndia stared at me. On the TV behind her, the 11 o'clock hurricane advisory had just begun, and the weatherman's excitement had just risen a notch. "That tropical storm that's coming? Just turned into a Category 1."

SEVEN

Something didn't add up.

A *lot* didn't add up.

First, how would a bunch of gold just show up on a busy ferry, and only the captain saw it? Wouldn't he have been the most busy person on the vessel? Wouldn't a random passenger have found it first? Second, why would the police have let McCardle keep the gold? Did they take a nice cut of the proceeds for being so generous? Third, if McCardle's family, my grandmother's neighbors, did become rich over all this, why was the place falling apart? Money like that would've lasted a nice long time, wouldn't it?

I didn't know. Like I said, didn't add up.

Apparently, their luck had run out, starting with McCardle's heart attack the following year.

If the story Nottie told me had been fabricated to lure in customers, then why wouldn't Syndia make a bigger deal of it? Why not bill their establishment as one big treasure hunter's wet dream come true? Promote the heck out of the place as a pirate's cove. I realized, suddenly, that was why there were old statues of a pirate out front. And a parrot. And a shell.

They had tried doing just that, but nobody fell for themed Florida hotels anymore. They were relics of the past. Did Syndia seriously think I was here to steal her gold? Enough to ask me if I was Mariel Drudge's daughter, enough to turn pale upon learning who I was and mentioning my grandmother's home by name?

Come on, seriously.

Even if there *were* gold buried somewhere on this compound, how the hell would I find it? Sure, let me just whip out my psychic sledgehammer and tear the place apart. But there were more pressing issues to consider at the moment, and that was whether or not to go with a storm a-comin'.

I took a walk around the compound, checking out areas I hadn't yet seen. Where the other couples were staying, for example, the building looked newer but not renovated. I was hoping to assess how structurally sound the buildings were in the event I decided to stay, but then my mother Face-Time'd me.

"How did I know you'd be calling me today?" I smiled into the phone.

One look at her face, and I knew she was in Mom mode. "Ellie, you need to come back to Boston. There's a storm headed that way."

"It's just a tropical storm. It's not a massive hurricane."

"Ellie, it's a Category 1 storm, and might I remind you you're on a tiny island?"

"So?"

"So, all the ocean needs to do is surge up a few feet, and you'll be underwater."

I hadn't considered the storm surge, but from where I'd stood at the dock's railing, the water level was way below the foundation of this area. It wasn't like the house was on a beach. "You know, this place might not look much from the outside, but I feel like it's safe."

"You can't know that, Ellie," Mom argued. "You're not a hurricane code expert. Just…get on a plane and come home, please. Listen to your mother for once."

I debated whether or not to tell her what was going on here. The stuff I was finding out. Sometimes, when I involved my mother in my decision-making, she made things worse by telling me her "gut" feelings. "There hasn't been a mandatory evacuation yet," I said. "If there is, then I'll definitely leave."

"You're being stubborn. I just don't get why," my mother said, pinching the bridge of her nose.

"Mom, why did you say that Nana had to sell this house again?"

"She couldn't afford to keep it. A single mother raising a small child in the fifties, Ellie. Single mothers didn't own houses in those times unless they'd been left with a lot of money or life insurance, and my grandfather was a poor fisherman. He didn't make sure she was taken care of in the event of his death. He should've used his free time to find a second job instead of go treasure hunting." She scoffed. "Didn't find shit anyway."

But then Robert McCardle came home with treasure, while my grandfather was declared dead, boating accident.

It wasn't no accident, Nana's voice rang through my mind.

You'll be husbandless. The neighbor's words from my time travel dream snaked into my mind. *And then I'll take your house.*

I smelled cigarette smoke. I stopped in the corridor and stared ahead at a tangled mess of wild plants. Nobody was there. No smokers, though smoke could've wafted in from anywhere.

Whore…

Who the hell kept calling me that?

"What is it, Ellie?" Mom asked. "You look like you've seen a ghost."

I kept staring ahead. My mind wandered. "You know I don't believe in that."

"You did when you were little, before we found out what was really going on. Ellie, are you taking your medicine?" It could've been normal maternal concern, but I felt like there was something she wasn't telling me.

"I've been doubling up."

"Good."

"Why do you ask?" I pushed through a section of the plants and stepped deep into the brush. Obsessed. Compulsive. "What would happen if I stopped taking them? It's been a while, so I kind of forgot."

"Your obsessions take over. Negative thoughts attack, and you'll blame it on yourself. You'll hallucinate in your sleep, sometimes out of sleep."

"Are you sure that's all? Is that why I started taking them?" I asked, plants scraping and scratching at my pale arms. What if they hadn't been hallucinations? What if they'd been real visions of real things and all this time I'd been suppressing them?

"Well, yes. Where are you going? What's with all those plants?"

My eyes fell on something rustling in the bushes. "I was just checking something. Thought I saw a cat," I lied. Whatever it was, it made the plants move around like a dinosaur wading through grass.

"Okay, well, look for flights then let me know what you find."

"Okay, Mom."

"Even if you have to drive out of Florida, Ellie. We can get you a flight from Atlanta or something. Just get out of Key West."

"Okay, I'll call you later." I hung up without saying goodbye.

There was no way I was leaving. Too many questions burned my mind, and the same gut feeling that kept my mother at bay from this place lured *me* in deeper. Questions like, what the hell was walking through the grass? I parted the leaves of a massive bush, expecting to see a cat or a raccoon and froze. My heart stopped. There in the grass was a person lying on the ground. A man in a fine-tailored suit covered in dark red blood. Was he real? What was he doing here? I suppressed the urge to throw up, though my mouth filled with warm saliva. Suddenly, it was like an invisible pair of hands lifted the man's legs up and began dragging him through the grass, a little bit at a time with clear effort.

I meant to scream. I needed to, but I was paralyzed. The sound caught in my throat.

"Why are you here, Miss Whitaker?"

I whirled around, my heart pounding through my ribcage. Jesus Christ, why did this woman keep sneaking up on me? Did she not see the dead body being dragged through her property? I looked back again to point it out, but the man was gone. Nothing there but plants and weeds.

"Holy shit…" I grunted out. "Can you…not do that, please? Not come up behind me like that?" I scoffed and backed out of the foliage.

"Answer my question. Why did you come here?"

I snapped. "That's not your business, but since you seem so suspicious of me, I came to spread my grandmother's ashes. Happy now?" I dropped my hands at my sides. "This might be your home today, but my grandma lived here a long time ago. She loved this place with all her heart. My mother was *born* here. Do you understand, Ms. Duarte?"

Syndia stared at me with those mistrustful eyes, saying nothing.

"You don't," I said. "Because you didn't spend your entire life hearing your grandma talk about a place she could never return to. You didn't hear the pain in her voice over losing it. That name…*Casa de los Cayos*…I must've heard it a thousand times growing up. Do you know what it means to me to be here?"

"You're not entitled to anything on this property."

"I know that. For shit's sake, stop saying that."

"Spreading ashes takes a second. You've stayed longer than that. You're curious. You're snooping around my house. I need you to leave, Miss Whitaker."

Was she serious?

I noted the grave expression on her face. She was damn serious and hella crazy too. However, she'd also just lost her mother. "Ms. Duarte, if you think I'm here to find your missing treasure, you need to know that I don't care about your fictitious gold. What I care about is truth. I only want to know what happened to my family.

What really happened."

"You'll never know what happened," Syndia said carefully. "None of us ever will. Our grandparents are gone, and with them…their secrets."

She was right about that.

But if I left now, I'd never have the chance to find out.

I came to connect and connect I would. Storm or no storm, I had to find out what happened here in 1951, why my grandmother carried so much hurt in her heart, why my mother felt a darkness here she couldn't face. Why a bleeding, well-dressed man had been dragged through the trees before my very eyes.

EIGHT

One moment, short gusts of wind were pushing sheets of rain right onto the window panes, and the next, the sun shone brightly like your average happy day. This was the calm before the storm. Hurricane Mara was headed up Cuba in the next two days then would cut right up the middle of the Florida Keys.

At least that was what the Cone of Death suggested on TV.

I spent a good amount of time on my phone checking flights and the traffic situation, just so I could tell my mother that I'd tried. I also did a fair amount of research on the probability of surviving a Category 1 hurricane. According to the articles I read, very few locals ever evacuated the Keys unless a Category 3 or higher was on the way. Tropical storms and Cat 1 storms were playthings to most Florida folks.

Part of me actually looked forward to bearing the brunt of the angry seas.

Part of me also contained the DNA of a diehard sailor.

And just for shits and grins, I researched whether or not Syndia Duarte could kick me out just because she wanted to. Apparently not, as this was my shelter from the storm but also a registered place of business and I'd done nothing to disrupt the peace.

During one of the sunny breaks between rain bands, I heard a car engine outside and peeked through the blinds to see her leaving. It must've been difficult having to run a place of business and prepare for a storm while also dealing with your mother's death. I exhaled, thankful I didn't have to deal with her for at least a little while.

A scratch at my door gave me pause. Slowly, I turned and stared at it. The noise did not repeat itself. Heading over, I opened it only to find a fallen dried palm frond on the ground getting whisked away by a sudden breeze. The new levels of humidity startled me. Moisture stuck to my skin like a thick layer of steam that wished to become a sweater.

Just as I was about to close the door, Bacon meowed his presence and rubbed up against my legs. I could've kicked him out, but what would've been the point? He seemed to like me better than his owner and besides, I could've used the company.

"Hey, buddy. I don't have food." I laughed. "I don't have any bacon for you, Bacon."

The cat waited at the door while staring into the room with big golden eyes. I wondered if he could sense the native man who had appeared here yesterday. If he could, he certainly wasn't afraid of him and strutted into the room anyway. After walking around nonchalantly, examining my bags, my shoes, and my towel on the floor, Bacon entered the bathroom nook and disappeared into a closet.

I followed him.

Behind a modern built-in strongbox, the kind that came with most hotel rooms, was a four-inch space. And behind that four-inch space in the wall was a hole. A carved out hole like someone had taken a crude little saw and made it by hand. Bacon squeezed into the space. A moment later, he curled up by the cat-sized mouse hole and began purring.

This cat had a hideout in this room? "What are you doing in there, bud?" I got on my hands and knees. The cold terrazzo floors were dusty and dirtied my hands.

I reached into the hole and ran my fingers through his thick fur. He purred even louder when my fingers connected with the space between his ears. Jealous that he could see where he was and I couldn't, I grabbed my phone and fit it into his crawl space, snapping several shots in different directions.

Most of the pics were too close and too muddy to show anything, but one showed a rectangular outline on the wall and right at the edge was a small golden lock. Bacon blinked his green eyes at me like a Mona Lisa smile.

"What are you guarding, Bacon?"

I reached into the hole until my fingertips were touching the lock. It was a small lock, like the kind used on suitcases long ago, and when I tugged on it, it didn't budge.

"Be right back," I told the cat and left the room. I was pretty sure I was alone at La Concha Inn, that all the guests had left. Even Nottie was nowhere to be found. Nobody would care if I tested all the doors to see if any were used as a utility closet.

I found what I was looking for by the dining room. A thin closet door revealed a storage unit for cleaning solutions, mops, packages of napkins, take-home containers, a long clear hose with dried brown gunk in it, and shelves holding several basic tools. Grabbing a hammer and pliers, not sure which would work best, I closed the closet and ran back to my room.

Bacon was already outside, looking for me. La Concha Inn's very own watch-cat. "What? I was coming back," I told him. Reentering the room, he followed me inside and stood like a sentinel nearby as I laid down on the floor in the closet and reached into the hole as best as I could with the hammer.

Smacking the lock a few times didn't help, so I used the pliers to grip the tiny lock then twist and twist until the weak, old metal broke free. I pulled open the small compartment and hesitated. Using the camera on my phone again, I took a few photos of the inside of the space.

A cold hand grabbed mine.

I shrieked and yanked my hand back, smacking the phone against the wall. What the hell was that? I waited a few feet back, sweat pouring from my temples, stomach in my throat, waiting for the hand to come out of the hole. "Who is that?" I asked. "Who's in there?"

Nobody replied.

My phone had a crack running through the middle of the screen now. Great. With the video camera on, I pushed it ever so slowly toward the hole again. Once it reached the edge of the hole, I lifted it and moved it side to side, scanning for any unseen presences, but it was hard to do with my hand trembling.

"Somebody there?" I asked again.

The air felt charged with energy. I wanted to lie down and peer into the hole with my naked eye but hesitated. Had the hand been real or another one of my visions?

I pulled the phone back and saw I hadn't captured any significant images of the wall's interior space. Part of me warned to end this right here, but part of me—the stubborn part my mother knew well—needed to see what was in that locked space.

Come on, Ellie. You can do this.

Closing my eyes, I decided to risk it again. Hallucinations couldn't hurt me, and if I kept my eyes closed, I didn't have to see them. Hopefully, I wouldn't feel them either. My fingers felt around the mustiness until they brushed against some papers.

Reaching in, I pulled the stack of small papers out only to find that they weren't papers at all but photographs. Old black-and-white photos. Scrambling to my feet, I peered at them with shaking hands. What I saw, photo after photo, would've been considered risqué at the time. Hell, they were pretty risqué even now. Boudoir photos of a woman. A beautiful woman. On her knees, on the edge of a sofa, breasts bared, legs tightly fused together. I guessed one might call them tasteful.

But the more I shuffled through them, the more I realized that the naked woman in black garter and stockings and heels and pearls, wearing a sexy smile and having a fun time was my very own grandmother.

Those eyes, those cheekbones, that turned up smile.

Bacon meowed.

"No, you may not see these. Oh, whatever." I crouched and showed the images to the cat who only wanted to rub his saliva-smeared cheek on them. I pulled them back before he could damage them. "You led me right to them," I said. "More evidence of the woman I loved. Thank you, buddy."

On the back was old handwriting, the kind of cursive you never saw anymore. Angled, scripty, with long loops. *Leanne, 1949.* My nana would've been nineteen in these. On the opposite corner of the photo was my own grandmother's handwriting: *To my dearest Bill, so you'll always have a thrill.*

Funny, Nana. Very cute.

I smiled so hard, my cheeks hurt. Then, I cried. Because what were the chances of finding a face I loved hidden in these walls? Did the McCardles or Duartes know this was here?

I ran back to the hole in the wall to see what else I could discover, even at the risk of another hand grabbing me, but found nothing. The rest of the space disappeared into emptiness. So, my grandfather had a hiding spot for his nudie pics. Of my grandmother! And the hiding spot was still there after all these years. In fact, this whole room vibrated with a special frequency altogether.

Could this have been my grandparents' bedroom? It would explain the secret hiding spot and maybe the mosaic table that wasn't part of the usual hotel repertoire of furniture.

My mind whirled with the possibilities. I wanted to call my mom right away and show her what I'd found, but I could already hear the incessant questions. I'd work better if she knew nothing.

As I slid my hand back away from the secret compartment, my skin brushed against something taped to the back of the safe. I pulled at the masking tape. A tarnished brass key fell into my hand.

It wouldn't fit into the safe that was too modern. I checked the room to see if any of the furniture pieces required a key, but none did. Dropping it into my purse for safekeeping, I lay myself back against the pillow and stared at my grandmother's photos again. I loved that she felt carefree enough to pose like this. I loved that they'd been done for her husband. My grandparents' relationship was serious goals.

No wonder she'd missed him so much. She'd never even remarried.

It made me angry that Nana had to sell her home. Made me angry that other people moved in and took over. That someone else had found the treasure that my grandfather had tried so hard to find for himself and Nana.

I closed my eyes and tried to see them again. Maybe they would come to me in another dream and I'd again wear a yellow sundress and see my life through Nana's eyes. Instead, I listened to the next feeder band swish against the window panes and fell asleep from mental exhaustion.

The native man tugged at my feet.

He wanted me out of bed. I knew I was dreaming, but it felt real. Lucid. The wind outside picked up, but when I followed him past the door to Room 3, things were not the same. It was Florida alright, but Florida many years ago before it'd earned a Spanish name. No buildings, no cars, no palm trees.

Just beach and palmetto plants and abodes made out of sticks and dry fronds. Chickees, the man told me. This was his village. These were his people.

I looked around and saw many of them—men, women, children, old ones, babies.

They worked together in harmony. The men speared their fish just a few feet into the water and the women cleaned the fish and prepared them for meals. The children helped too, though several of them chased each other around the beach, ignoring their responsibilities. Fire gave the air a scent of sweet smokiness, and I felt like I'd been here before a long time ago.

This is my home, he told me. It wasn't English.

It wasn't any language I recognized, yet I understood him

without him uttering a word. It was my home too, many years ago, before the Europeans. His face sagged when he pointed this out to me, and my basic knowledge of this land's history told me why. But this dream wasn't about history, nor was it about what they were doing in his village.

It was about the fire.

He pointed to it and told me that the women were using it to send messages to the sky gods. They'd burn the herbs and cast their intentions, focusing clearly on what they wanted, releasing their wishes into the ether. I could do it, too, but my mind was focused on the mathematical. The logical.

I didn't know what to tell him.

This wasn't my world and these weren't my practices.

He told me they were and always had been.

Then he disappeared, leaving me in the current day garden, feeling like my life had been empty until now but was ready to be filled.

When I woke up, I had a hard time remembering where I was. Disorientation hit me like a box truck, but then I saw the shutters. They'd been blown open. Cigarette smoke filled my room, even though I wasn't a smoker. Maybe one of the other guests were outside smoking?

I was about to get up and close the windows when the sheets were suddenly torn off the bed. By themselves. Just flew and landed on the floor in a heap. I stood there, shaking, not knowing what the hell to do. Visions were one thing, but visions didn't tear sheets off your bed. Fine, it was perhaps-maybe-possibly possible that ghosts existed. And I had an idea of who'd just been here, who'd come to harass me.

The woman next door who smoked. My grandmother's neighbor from long ago.

NINE

I spent the rest of the day trying to make sense of what was happening. Between my dreams, the photos I'd found, the visions, smells, and things I'd seen, plus Syndia's crazy talk about treasure, I felt rationality slipping away from me.

I also refreshed the National Hurricane Center's website often trying to keep up with everything going on in the earthly world, too. Hurricane Mara headed this way but wouldn't arrive for another day and a half or so. The on-and-off rain had turned into beautiful skies, which one weather lady on TV said was "God's way of giving us time to prepare."

What if we didn't believe in God?

I'd forgotten all about the rental car. It'd probably been towed by now, and I'd have to face a fee. Reportedly, traffic out of the Keys was stop-and-go, and those staying behind were out buying supplies, clearing store shelves of water, milk, bread, and canned goods. Traffic along Roosevelt had increased, and trucks drove by hauling plywood and piles of sand. Everywhere, people helped each other, and it prompted me to go see Syndia, ask if she needed to do anything to prepare.

I followed the garden path down to the main building and entered. The TV with the same weather station was on again, and I heard sniffling sounds coming from the front desk. Syndia sat there, head bowed at her desk.

"Do you need help preparing or anything?" I asked, then realized I should've coughed before sneaking up on her. Not that she ever did the same when sneaking up on me.

She looked up with tears in her eyes. "We've been bringing things in. You can help if you like." I felt bad for her and her situation, but something told me I shouldn't ask about it. I was sure I'd get blamed for it anyway.

"What about shutters?" I looked around. "I don't see any. Isn't that of utmost importance?"

"Utmost importance to me is if you could leave, Whitaker," she sneered, a hard bite in her voice. *Ouch.* "It's hard enough preparing for a storm with a guest like you here. I would kick you out, but by law, I have to provide shelter."

"I'm sorry. I only want to learn more about my grandparents. It's only fair, since they lived on half your property once."

"Well, you picked the wrong week to come. My mother is at a funeral home about to be embalmed, I'm trying to figure out how to pay for her funeral *and* bills if this storm hits…" Her voice built a crescendo as she went on. "And to make it all worse, you're playing detective when my stress is through the roof!" Her jaw clenched tight.

I swallowed. "I only asked if I could help."

"You could help by leaving." She gritted through her yellowed teeth.

"I don't think I can do that." When would I have another chance to come back? What if she sold the inn and turned it back into a private home? Then, I'd never have the same opportunity again.

"Well, I'm fresh out of information to give you." She scoffed, exasperated. "What more do you want from me?"

"I want to know why my grandmother was forced to leave when she loved it here."

"She couldn't pay her mortgage. Simple as that. Why can't you let it lie?"

"Because I don't believe that," I said to my own surprise. What was I saying? That I suspected foul play, and here I was telling the very descendant of those who may have caused my grandmother harm? I needed to quit while I was ahead.

"What do you believe then?" A challenging look crossed her face.

I didn't have much to go on, only hunches, gut feelings, the sort of stuff I made fun of my own mother for having. No facts, only photos of my grandmother young, naked, and happy, and hallucinations by the dozens.

"I believe the truth always comes out," I said. "I'm sorry about your mother. It must be difficult what you're going through." And then I stepped out of the front desk and called a Lyft driver for one more trip downtown, hoping to find answers before it was time to hunker down for Mara.

I needed a historian or a time machine to help me through this. Or both.

The Key West Historic Society had closed for the day "until further notice" and the people at the Hemingway Home were kind enough to let me in, though busy collecting their fifty resident six-toed cats (all descendants of Hemingway's original polydactyl kitty) in preparation for the storm.

I asked one guide there if he knew anything about *Casa de los Cayos* or the history behind La Concha Inn, and he simply shrugged and said that the resort was more full of ghost tales and speculation than actual history. I would be better off talking to Luis Gallardo at Sunset Spooks Ghost Tours, the agitated middle-aged man told me.

I'd heard that name before. In fact…

I reached into my purse and found the business card still there. I'd met Luis—at least I thought that was his name—while out drinking the other night. He'd told me where to meet for the tour, if I was ever interested. He'd said it went on every night, rain or shine.

So I headed that way, stopping first to find my rental car. Sure enough, it was missing, and I jotted down a note on my phone to call the company tomorrow about it. Maybe I could claim storm traffic for my inability to reach it.

I stood on the corner of Duval and Caroline Streets. Nobody was there. It was 8:30 and getting dark fast, as the next rain band started coming in softly. It'd be silly for anyone to conduct a ghost tour on a night like this, I thought, but then down the sidewalk, illuminated from behind by vendor floodlights, was the silhouette of a medium-build man in jeans and straw hat. A cigar stuck out the side of his mouth, unlit.

"Well, well, well…" He clapped his hands once, rubbed them together. He had a charming accent to match his Cuban shirt, the kind of linen shirt they sold in many shops along Duval Street with vertical stripes and pockets at the breast. "Every time I think no one will show up, there's always one adventure-seeker. Like walking in cemeteries in the rain, do you?"

I smiled. "Not exactly."

He arrived to where I stood and stuck out his hand. "Name's Luis. And you look familiar."

I took his hand. "We met last week. Ellie."

"Ah, sí. Ellie from Boston." He smiled an easygoing grin. "I remember you. Are you a believer or non-believer?" he asked, wiggling his jolly eyebrows. "Of ghosts, of course. I always like to ask my guests."

"I'm not sure." I was surprised I hadn't just said non-believer straight-out.

"A healthy skeptic then." He chuckled, patting my shoulder. "I like that. And don't worry, I won't try to convince you that ghosts exists. I know they do and that's all that matters." He winked. "The evidence I'll show you during tonight's tour is all real. All photographic taken by our own guests, and a few EVPs—"

"Actually, Luis," I interrupted him. "Since I'm the only one here, I was wondering if I could just ask you some questions."

"So you're not going to make me do my whole song and dance?" he said, somewhat relieved. Holding up his palms, he tested the rainfall. "Good, because I just showered and wasn't looking forward to getting wet again. Want to go grab a drink?"

"Maybe coffee, if that's alright." I couldn't afford getting sloshed again. The effect could be deadly on my sanity.

Luis was more than happy to take me to the nearest coffee shop, which looked like it was about to close, but he knew the owners, so they let us stay. As we grabbed a table by the window, the harried staff worked to close the place up for the night. Outside, Duval Street looked eerie as locals boarded up their shop windows.

"Why haven't you left town like all the other tourists?" Luis asked. "I mean, don't get me wrong, the City of Key West thanks you." He chuckled.

"I came here for a mini-vacation that turned into a personal mission," I said. I didn't give him the details of how spreading my grandmother's ashes had turned into fighting for her legacy.

The server delivered our coffees, mine, creamy and frothy, in a tall glass and his, dark and strong, in a squat one.

"Sounds intriguing." He placed his unlit cigar back in his pocket in favor of the tiny espresso he'd ordered. It smelled delicious and made me want to trade my latte for some "cafecito," as he'd called it.

"I didn't know about the storm when I booked the flight," I said, feeling like an idiot for admitting that. "But it's okay. Coming here has been the most impulsive thing I've ever done. I guess locals don't freak out over the storms like tourists do?"

He shrugged. "Let me tell you something. Key West has seen its share of hurricanes. Storms are nothing to us. Very few ever set us back. This island has seen hundreds of years of horrors and survived it all. We take a lickin' and keep on tickin', you know what I mean?"

"Kind of like the blizzards up North where I come from."

"Somewhat, somewhat. Do you know how Key West got its name?" He possessed the excitement of a teacher who was about to tell me the answer anyway, whether I liked it or not.

I thought of the woman on the plane. "Cayo Hueso something?"

"That's right. It means Island of Bones in Spanish. See, when the Spanish first arrived here in the 16th century, they found the island covered in bones. Piles of them, and nobody around to explain what happened. Creepy, right?"

"Very."

"Nobody is sure if the Calusa had a battle here or if they simply used the island as a mass grave, but I believe they were forced as far south as they could go by another nation before they ran out of land and all perished here in battle."

"Calusa?" I asked.

"Native tribe from Florida. Fishermen, gatherers, peaceful people."

I nodded. I wondered if these Calusa Indians had anything to do with the native man haunting my dreams. I couldn't see how, since I'd started seeing him while I was still in Boston.

Luis continued. "And since Spanish rule eventually led to English rule in the Americas, *hueso* sounded like 'west-o' to the English, so Key West stuck."

"That's fascinating," I said. "I thought it was because Key West was the westernmost key in the US."

"Southernmost. Ninety miles to Cuba." His light blue eyes lost a bit of their sparkle. "There's actually another island just west of here. Dry Tortugas National Park."

"I saw it," I said. "When the sun was going down."

"Yes, exactly."

As fascinating as this was, I needed to take advantage of Luis and ask the questions that didn't have answers on the internet. "Do you know anything about a house called *Casa de los Cayos* out on Roosevelt? It's a small resort inn now. The owner's name is Syndia Duarte. I was told you might. It's now called—"

"La Concha Inn," he finished for me, nodding. "Of course, I do. I would take my guests there every single tour if it weren't so far out of the way. That place is incredibly haunted."

I could've told him that. If I believed in ghosts, that was.

"How do you know?"

"I've stayed there before. Once. Never heard of it called *Casa de los Cayos,* though." He folded his hands and studied me intently. "Where did you read that? I've read everything there is to know about that place."

"My grandmother lived there," I said. "Long ago. That's what her family called it."

"Fascinating. I did not know that. Did your family speak Spanish?"

"Not that I know of."

"They might have. Many residents here learn it because of our proximity to Cuba. So you're related to the family that lives there now?"

"No, my grandmother came before them. The owners after she left used to be her neighbors. My grandma died last month. I came to spread her ashes, but now it's like I can't leave. There's so much going on, at the inn but also in my head. That's what I wanted to talk to you about."

He lifted his tiny espresso cup and waited for me to clink glasses with him for a toast. "La Concha Inn is one of my favorite topics. And you have me for the next seventy-minutes, Ellie. Ask away."

TEN

"What do you know about the place, about its history? Pretend I'm on your tour and you've taken us out there." I smiled, clasping my hands together.

He slid the dark foamy drink into his mouth, ending with a satisfied grin. "Well, let's see. Captain Robert McCardle owned the place. He used to drive the Havana Ferry back and forth between Key West and Havana. In the early 50s, I believe, he found a bag of gold on his boat and told police about it."

All the same stuff found on the plaque in Syndia's living room at La Concha.

"What else?" I asked.

"But you probably knew all that already," Luis said with side-eye. "You probably want the rest of the story."

"Which is?"

"Which is that Captain McCardle was rumored to have intercepted Captain Bill Drudge's lobster boat at sea after he'd left home on a treasure-hunting expedition."

My grandfather. "Wait, what?"

"I thought that would pique your interest." He bit the corner of his smile.

"Is this common knowledge?"

"Not really, but I've talked to the old folks on this island many years, Ellie. Many years."

"What caused the rumors?"

"The way it happened. Drudge mysteriously went missing days before McCardle came home with a bag of gold when supposedly, he'd been on his shift back from Cuba. How would he have come across that bag on a ferry?" Luis raised an eyebrow.

"That's what I wanted to know."

"Also, records show the Havana Ferry arrived hours late that night. It was supposed to arrive back at 10 PM but finally showed up to port past 1 AM. Drudge's body was never found. Police assumed he became shark food. Soon after, his widow was forced to sell her home—and that became La Concha Inn."

"My grandmother." I stared at him. So strange to hear about my nana from the lips of someone I'd never met who lived so far away from us. "Leanne Drudge."

Luis leaned forward slowly. "Your grandmother was Leanne Drudge?"

"Yes. And Bill Drudge was my grandfather."

His jaw dropped. "You're shitting me."

"I shit not."

"This is amazing. I'm talking to the living granddaughter." He laughed crazily. "Where have you been? Wait, Boston, you told me. And you didn't know any of this until now?"

I shook my head. "My grandmother left Key West soon after her husband died, so I guess she never heard the rumors," I said. "But please, go on."

"Some say your grandmother cursed the place when she left."

I recoiled and narrowed my eyes. "Why would they say that?"

"Well, your grandmother had a reputation for…being different," Luis said, gauging how sensitive I'd be to his choice of words. "Or, for being atheist rather, which, in those times, was practically a sin."

Atheist? She never declared that, but Nana did dabble in natural arts—growing herbs in her garden, astrology, going outside to connect with nature. All when she was younger, while she could still walk. Being outdoors was her religion. I remember her always telling me, *Come look at the full moon, Ellie. It's so beautiful,* when I was little.

But I couldn't see her cursing anyone. "Why would her being atheist make her an outsider?"

Luis shrugged nonchalantly. "Why did they hang women in the Salem Witch Trials? Any woman refusing to take part in a patriarchal religion was considered a witch in those times. In your grandmother's, they couldn't hang anyone, but they could still frown down on them. In fact, the documents from her time were written by churchgoing residents of Key West who believed that a 'wayward woman' lived in that house before the McCardles' daughter moved in."

Her nude pictures. My visions of the witchy neighbor hating her.

"That would explain a lot." I sighed. My grandmother might've been a free spirit who didn't believe in organized religion, but that didn't make her wayward or a witch. I supposed people were scared of anything different in those times.

"You're right. You're absolutely right. Anyway…" Luis leaned back. "About a year or so after your grandfather was declared dead, McCardle died from a heart attack. His son who also worked for the Havana Ferry was laid off when the service closed in 1961, and the old man's wife, Susannah, was said to have gone crazy when she lost her other son to influenza."

"Wow. I didn't know any of this."

"Yep. When the women of the family were unable to maintain the two homes on their own, they converted the compound to a resort in the seventies to try and make a living."

"There were no other working men to support them?" I asked.

"Her son-in-law cut coquina for a living, the husband of Violet McCardle, but as coquina began running low, he had less and less work. Sometime in the seventies, he was found bleeding to death after getting his arm caught in the circular saw."

Violet McCardle. The old woman who'd died on the dock. Syndia's mother. And could the man I'd seen in the garden have been the other son-in-law? I felt like I was going crazy with bits and pieces of information.

"I don't know what happened to the other sister…there were four siblings altogether," Luis continued, "but one of them ended up staying there and running the motel with her children. After a while, I believe her children left, too. The only one left is Syndia Duarte."

"How do you know so much?" I asked.

"Let's just say La Concha Inn was one of the reasons I moved here. I'd read about it in a few primary documents and the part about a rumored hidden treasure always intrigued me." So, he was another treasure hunter lured to Key West by romance.

"Where are you from?"

"Originally? Havana, Cuba. I came to the US as a child through the Pedro Pan Operation in the sixties. I was raised by family members in Miami, but Key West has always intrigued me. Probably because it's the closest I'll ever get to my homeland again."

No wonder his eyes had darkened upon mentioning Havana. I gave him a sympathetic look. "I'm sorry to hear that."

"It was over fifty years ago now." He sat back and rocked on the back two legs of the chair.

"So, what's with this hidden treasure?" I then asked. "Isn't it just a story to attract customers to the inn? You can't tell me it's actually real."

"Well, that's another one of La Concha's 'legends,'" he said using air quotes. "When McCardle came home, he claimed to have only found a small bag of gold doubloons, but then he bought the house next door, fixed it up really nice, and for a while, the place was show-worthy. One of the nicest homes on the island."

"Why does it look so desolate now?"

"The curse—that's my guess. Seems like the family can't catch a break. Things get worse for them as the generations go by."

"Syndia's mother just died two days ago. I was there."

"Violet?" His eyes widened and he made a *tsk* sound. "I hadn't heard. She was the one to live the longest. I'll have to call Syndia and give her my condolences."

"Why don't you come back with me and tell her yourself? We could use another pair of hands putting up the shutters. She has those old wooden ones. I don't feel very safe." I was beginning to think I should've left the island when I had the chance.

"I don't think she'd be happy to see me. Even though they market the inn as a treasure hunting spot, Syndia has never liked having guests there. It's a slam to their pride. She only displays the treasure memorabilia to sell rooms. She wants to find the gold for herself."

"If it exists," I said.

"If it exists." He smiled. "I know I probably sound like a fool for believing such things, but it's not as far-fetched as you might think. People said that McCardle stole Drudge's treasure then…"

"They killed him right then and there," I finished for him, "fed his body to sharks, which is why they never found him. Is that what happened?"

"We don't know. It's all speculation."

Which is what the tour guide had said at the Hemingway House, that the history of La Concha was speculation and ghost stories at best.

The whole thing sounded like pirates to me. 20th Century pirates. My poor grandfather, finally finding the ship he'd been after only for this man to come along and take it from him then claim to have found it himself. Then, to add insult to injury…he drove my grandmother away and took her house.

"This is all so unfair." I shook my head, staring past Luis into the blurry, rainy window. "I didn't know any of this. My mother doesn't know any of it either."

"Your grandmother did her best to forget it, I would imagine," Luis said.

"Was McCardle a celebrity for saying he'd found gold?"

"For a while, this is why he hid it. To keep people from raiding his home and discovering the rest of the gold. Well, apparently, he hid it too well and it remains hidden to this day. That's how the legend goes."

"Why wouldn't he tell anyone where he'd put it?" I asked, agitated. "What if something bad were to happen to him, which obviously did? Nobody would be able to access it. So, he basically drove his family crazy by not telling anyone the location."

"I have no idea, Ellie. If only I were psychic." He laughed.

I stared at him.

Maybe this was another aspect of the curse, if there was even such a thing. Maybe part of their misfortune was not being able to enjoy the gold they'd supposedly found. "What about Room 3?" I asked.

He cocked his head suspiciously. "What about it?"

"Why don't they rent it out?"

"It's haunted."

"How would you know?"

"It's the room I stayed in." He raised an eyebrow. "Cold drafts, shutters opening and closing by themselves, the smell of smoke when no one around is smoking…"

"Yes, the same's happened to me, but who's haunting it?"

"That depends on what you experience. If you're asking me, I think they're all there…plus others we don't even know about. Room 3 in particular is a portal of paranormal energy. Even the cat appears there without explanation."

Well, that one I had debunked. Bacon and his secret room. I smiled to myself and cocked my head. "You're eager to believe."

"Ah, the healthy skeptic." Luis smiled. "Look, it's not just me. Countless of guests have said that ghosts haunt La Concha—McCardle, his wife, Susannah, Bill Drudge, the son-in-law…all of them. Maybe your grandmother will join them now that you've spread her ashes."

He'd meant it as funny, and I probably should've been offended, but I wasn't. Part of me wished my grandmother would join them too, so she could kick the ass of every single McCardle asshole who ever ruined her life.

"I'm sorry. I didn't mean it like that." Luis reached across the table to touch my arm. "Sometimes I get caught up in the lore of these haunted locations. I forgot I was talking to someone who actually knew this family. My apologies."

"It's okay."

These people.

My grandmother.

All my life, Nana had been my mother's mother, my live-in confidant and caretaker, helping my mother raise me when she wasn't able to. She'd cooked, bake, read to me, she'd make key lime marmalade in the kitchen. In later years, she got sicker and less mobile. Ended up in a nursing home. Our job was to keep her spirits up, so she wouldn't think too much of her times here and the life she'd lost. It never occurred to me that she'd have such a complicated history.

My heart ached with a dullness I couldn't put into words. Part of me wished I'd never have opened this can of worms, but now that I had, I had to know it all. Feel it all. Get inside my grandmother's mind. My subconscious knew it, too, hence the visions through Nana's point of view.

"Have you *seen* the ghosts?" I asked.

"I've felt their presence. They appear in photos as orbs of light, ectoplasm, vortices. I'll see if I can find some and send them to you. McCardle is said to haunt the garden and grounds. They sense a negative energy. They feel angry."

"How do we know it's not my grandfather? I would be angry if I were him."

"They see a tall man who fits the description of McCardle. Bill Drudge was shorter and blond, like you, and you're right, he should be angry, but he appears to people as…now this is going to sound crazy, but…"

As he paused, a thought entered my mind. I knew what he was going to say before he said it. My analytical, skeptic mind would never go for an idea like this, and yet I knew it to be true like I knew my name was Ellie Leanne Whitaker.

"The cat," I said.

"The cat," he agreed, nodding. *How did I know that?* "He's wary of everyone. There are reports of people seeing a man's face, then when they blink, it's the cat. This has been going on for years."

"But Bacon can't possibly be that old."

"Is that the current cat?" he asked. "It's been happening with cats on the property for years. Bacon, the tabby before him, and cats before the tabby… For years and years. According to some, it began with the black cat Leanne left behind."

All I could do was sit there and look at him. So many questions, so overwhelming. "Is that everything you know?"

Luis sighed. "I wish I knew more about La Concha, but Syndia makes things difficult. Not exactly generous with family details."

"Sounds like she's hoarding info or protecting something," I said.

"Or someone. Or a multitude of someones. Generations who've all harbored one big secret—"

"The death of my grandfather," I whispered, staring outside at the light rain spattering the street.

"It's a miracle she even let you in her house."

I turned to watch his eyes carefully.

I had so many questions for Luis, but he didn't have all the answers. I felt unfinished and anxious.

However, the ghosts might know. And if I wanted to hear what they had to say, I'd have to be more open-minded. I'd have to acknowledge that they might exist. Maybe all those times I'd seen them as a child hadn't been OCD. Maybe they'd been real, and the meds had suppressed my ability to sense them.

Luis stretched. "Well, I better get going or my dog's going to wonder if I wandered into a bar after work. Not that it's happened before, mind you." He winked. "Thanks for the talk, Ellie. I'll see if I can go by tomorrow and help Syndia prep the buildings."

"There's something else," I said, reaching into my purse. I pulled out the old key. "I found this in the walls of Room 3. Any idea what it might open?"

His eyes lit up with renewed interest. Treasure-hunting interest. He took the key and flipped it over in his hands. "No, but let's suppose I help you find out…and let's suppose it leads to a finding of the gold doubloon variety…will you share it fifty-fifty?"

From his charming smile, I knew he was joking. Mostly.

"Sixty-forty?" He tried again.

But I didn't care about the gold. I only wanted someone to help me find the things that rightfully belonged to my grandparents, so my nana's soul could rest in peace.

I extended a handshake. "Deal."

ELEVEN

Luis disappeared the same way he'd arrived—by blending into the darkness until I could no longer see him.

I stood on Duval Street and looked around in the lonesome night. Only a few residents remained, hammering wood over their shop windows, while all around, blustery breezes ruffled up the palm trees. It was late, and I hadn't thought about how I would get back at this hour. Even the closest Lyft drivers were an hour away.

According to my map, it would take an hour to get back to the hotel if I walked. I didn't have a choice, so I set about in the direction of Roosevelt Blvd and La Concha Inn. I needed to clear my head anyway.

Nana, why didn't you tell me?

Why did it take death to learn about the people we loved? It was eye-opening to know that a woman I'd loved all my life had been harboring so much pain.

The island was still awake with men working on last-minute shutters and women standing by, handing them panels, drills, or drinks to quench their thirsts. They watched me suspiciously, as though a woman walking alone at night the eve before a storm were a strange sight.

The coffee had woken me up somewhat, and now I felt attuned to everything around me—the swishing palm trees, the oppressive humidity, the singing frogs and crickets, the cats that eyed me from their porches, the distant sounds of boat horns. Residents rocked in their rocking chairs, enjoying the late night winds. The island felt like it sat in the front row of a rollercoaster about to take a plunge. I could almost hear conversations inside of homes, wives asking husbands what would they do if the storm hit harder than expected, ways they could earn income that didn't depend on tourism.

Then there were shadows—dark shadows, dancing shadows,

gray in-between shadows, and disappearing shadows. Some shadows seemed to follow me. Some appeared out of dark alleyways only to disappear when I looked at them head-on. Some took the shape of women wearing long dresses with cinched ruffled collars, bustles, and feathered hats until I tried focusing on them.

I rubbed them out of my vision, but after a few minutes, they'd come back.

Soon, the voices began. Muffled, at first. They could've come from second-story open windows or from deep inside the colorful little Victorian homes. But something told me they were around me, following me, begging for my attention.

You are blessed. Speak to me…

"Go away," I told them.

Please…

…if you would only listen…

If I narrowed my eyes, I could almost swear I was a child again, and the voices were bothering me like they did most nights. Men, women, children, people I didn't know, asking me to look at them, to help, to pass on messages. Gripping my head, I almost couldn't take it. I was ready to put on ear buds to drown out the voices.

Then, I paused in my tracks, right there on the sidewalk. Slowly, I put the ear buds back in my bag. He was there again, my native man standing a few feet away, silently watching. Not menacing, just accompanying me. He was a full-bodied manifestation—of what, I wasn't sure.

My thoughts, most likely.

I could clearly make out his near-naked body, cloth covering his hip section, and a net hanging from his waist. A fisherman. Same face as my dreams, as the glimpses I'd caught of him at La Concha. Clearly, he wasn't tied to any one place.

But he was tied to me. "Who are you?" I asked. "Why do you keep following me?"

He wouldn't answer, and I couldn't stand here all night waiting for a silent Indian to tell me what he wanted. I broke into a fast pace, leaving him behind on the sidewalk, but whenever I'd turn around to check if he was still there, he'd be gone. Then, a minute later, he'd appear ahead of me.

"Tell me what you want," I ordered him, feeling more and more anxious. I didn't like this listening to ghosts thing, but if he had something to say, now was the time to do it before I lost my nerve.

I must've been about halfway to the inn, halfway to insanity, when more figures appeared.

Not all of them from the same time period either. I saw Victorian women, modernly-dressed men and women, and a few children. All of them had been hurt. All of them appeared misty and fog-like bearing touches of crimson. Blood seeping through holes in their chests, to red lines crossing their necks. All of them wanted to tell me how they'd been hurt.

"I can't." I shook my head, releasing the visions, and walking a little faster. *Almost there, almost there...* Each time I'd close my eyes and open them again, they'd be gone. I couldn't do this. I couldn't be a go-between to these poor souls, though none of them wanted to hurt me.

I thought I could listen, but this was too much. How did mediums handle it? I felt like I was on the edge of a cliff about to fall into a ravine. Reaching into my bag, I took out my pills and swallowed down two more. No water to wash them down. I tried using saliva to do the job, but there they were, dry and blocky in my throat. Did my mother know, believe that I could see them? Did she put me on meds to protect me from the spirits?

Because I could understand that.

I couldn't imagine spending my life having to go through this.

The full-bodied visions went back to being just shadows. The shadows I could handle. As long as they didn't ask anything of me, I could pretend I was on either side of this psychic veil. Right now, I chose to see them as nothing, so I could get home.

Home.

Hilarious.

After a while, I turned down Roosevelt Blvd. with legs burning and chest heaving. Well, what do you know...I'd gotten the ghost walking tour for free. Now I was almost back, and good thing I'd decided to walk the five or so miles from Duval Street, because I needed to crash hard. I needed sleep, rest deeply from overworking my brain all day.

When I finally reached the gate of La Concha Inn, I found it locked. With padlock and everything. "You're kidding me," I said to no one.

Did Syndia not realize I was out or was she deliberately trying to keep me away? I could've easily jumped the fence, but I didn't want to break any rules or act like an interloper. I was a good guest and would behave like one, despite her making things difficult.

Tamping down the inkling of panic in my chest, I pulled out my phone, ready to call the front desk to let her know, when suddenly, the lock twisted and dropped to the ground and the gate opened by itself. A long, loud creak sounded through the stillness. I was almost sure Syndia would hear it and come out.

A gate had just opened by itself.

I swallowed hard.

Something sat in the walkway leading to the house, something small but big for a feline—Bacon. Golden eyes stared at me through darkness, exactly the way a grandfather would if I'd come home too damn late from partying. Tired and full of parental judgment.

"Oh, hey…uh…kitty?" I walked through the gate and brought down the latch over the post. Was Luis right and this cat really embodied Bill Drudge's spirit? It was silly to think, and yet I sort of loved the idea. "Uh, grandpa." I chuckled.

Bacon turned and sashayed back to the front porch, hopping up onto the railing. He was dusty and dirty, and I loved him. Somehow, he belonged to the house, this dilapidated wooden old house with more secrets than Scotland Yard. I reached over to pet him before heading into the house, when for a moment—I saw him.

My stomach leaped into my throat.

Standing behind Bacon in the foliage below, was a handsome man, the kind of wholesome, sunny face that could only belong to a young sea captain. Only he was hurt worse than the others I'd seen on my walk through the island. His red lines were different. His were everywhere—all over his body—like crackled finish on an old painting, though a large one stood across on his neck.

My heart pounded against my ribcage. I got a good look at him. Long enough to see a resemblance with my mother's face and my own. And then I made the mistake of blinking, a habit I'd been doing all night to ward away the spirits. And so he was gone, vanished into the ether.

"Bill." I spoke into the warm night.

Nothing.

Damn it.

Startled, I entered the house, surprised to find the front door unlocked, and ambled down to my room, feeling like I was going crazy. And maybe I was going insane and this was how it felt—like I walked the hedge between the real and imagined. When I unlocked the room and dropped onto the bed, I spotted the window open again and this time, my suitcase looked like it'd been searched through.

"Seriously? Like my undies and shorts, do you, Syndia?"

All the important items were still in my bag—my nana's photos, the key… I thanked myself for thinking to bring it all with me then tucked the stuff under my pillow before falling totally dead asleep. From now on, I'd hang the Do Not Disturb sign, so no one would come in to clean. I hoped the ghosts would read it, too.

The native man was in my room again.

He stood in the corner, gesturing toward the door.

Outside, a storm was brewing. I didn't want to face it, but he insisted, coming to my bed and pulling me to my feet. In my dream, I was naked. Not boudoir naked like my grandmother in her lingerie but completely naked. Vulnerable and exposed. The native man didn't care. He was used to bare skin and I was the fool to think there was anything wrong with it. The wind blew open the shutters again but this time, I didn't bother to fix them.

Come, he said.

What did he want to show me?

His hand was outstretched. I slid my palm into his and felt the dryness of his overworked skin. From his waist, the fishing net hung, no spear. He tapped the mosaic table, as if to tell me there was something meaningful about it.

Then, he led me outside.

Dark storm clouds rolled over the island, and the smell of fish permeated the air. The ground I walked on wasn't soil or even sand. It was crushed shells. Layers and layers of rough crushed shells, much like the kind in the moon sculpture from the garden. There were no quaint Victorian Key West homes, no cars, no tropical charm.

Simply a quiet island covered in crushed shell. We stood on a beach facing the ocean. Down the beach were piles of white sticks growing in size from smallest to largest. Were those bones? Skulls, femurs, tibias, bones and more bones. The man told me what they were in his language, and somehow, I understood him.

They couldn't bury the bones of their fallen victims on this island made of broken shell, so they piled them. They'd died battling other native tribes. I wasn't sure how I knew this, but I bowed my head in respect. Standing still with southern winds grazing over me, I felt at one with the earth. I felt her pain. I felt the plight of these people.

And I felt my own plight as well.

Mayai.

His name was Mayai, and he'd been my grandmother's spirit guide. He'd been my great-great-grandmother's spirit guide before her, and now he was mine. I only needed to listen, though listening was difficult for me. He understood that—I'd been born in a time of tuning out, he said.

But now it was time to let go of barriers.

Mayai used his hands to motion letting go. And I did. With a handful of ashes and bone fragments, I tossed them into the water, into the salty sea, scattering my worries, giving what was once from the earth and ocean back to its origins. With circular, almost spiritual motions, I returned my grandmother to the island she'd loved, the same one that had forsaken her. Now she could rest in peace.

Mayai told me other things without moving his lips. The Spanish ships would not arrive for another several hundred years. Men would obsess over gold though gold belonged to the earth. In the end, nothing belonged to us, except our energy. I wasn't sure what he was talking about, but I would understand it all soon, Mayai told me.

I came from a long line of light workers, women who connected with the universe. Women were better at connecting than men, he told me. I was ready to learn my grandmother's ways, had been since I was a child. But I'd been suppressed, he said. Barriers…time to let go.

In the distance came shouts, words that didn't fit the new language.

I felt myself being pulled away.

"Ellie!"

Mayai nodded with a smile. It was all right. I could go back. I was ready.

"Ellie!"

The sun and ocean quickly darkened into stormy night skies, and I stood on the edge of a dock looking out. No longer naked, I wore shorts and a T-shirt, clothing that brought me back to the present. Was I scattering Nana's ashes again? I looked down at my hands and found my fingers clutching an empty pill bottle. The new Zoloft I'd just bought this morning.

I suddenly remembered where I was, who I was, when I was.

The ashes I'd scattered—they hadn't been. That was a dream.

In real life, they'd been my pills. I'd just tossed my entire bottle of pills into the fucking sea. When I turned around to ask Mayai why he would have me do this, I faced an old woman dressed in black. Wrinkled, vacant staring eyes, her gnarled hands reaching out for my neck. *You killed me. It was you.*

"No, I didn't. Nobody killed you, Violet. You died because you were old." Was I speaking aloud or still in my dream? I wasn't sure. The veil was thin, and I walked the hedge again.

How could you bring that witch's remains back here? I heard her hollow voice as if from another dimension. *How could you bring back the woman who cursed my family's home? Are you hell bent on taking everything from us?*

"My grandmother didn't do anything," I defended. "She didn't do anything. Everything was taken from her!"

The woman's small filmy eyes disappeared into wrinkled skin. The eyeless, faceless visage seemed to implode until she was only a dark mist hovering in front of me.

"Miss Whitaker!" More shouting, as the winds picked up and the rain slammed down on my bare skin in spiky sheets. The old crone disappeared into a vaporous shadow before my eyes, and behind her, standing on the back porch facing the garden was Nottie, waving me inside. "The bands are getting worse. Get inside! It's not safe!"

TWELVE

The longest line I'd ever stood in my life was here and now—at the CVS.

Because of the approaching storm, everybody needed their backup medications in case transportation to and from the island shut down or the pharmacy became damaged. But now that the sun had come out in between feeder bands, we all came out. Waiting forty minutes already under the boiling sun sucked, especially since I'd already refilled these damn pills once before.

Damn Mayai.

He was my spirit guide, he'd said. He'd been my grandmother's before me, and that was fine. I could deal with a hallucination who claimed to be my own protective ghost. What I couldn't deal with was a hallucination claiming to be my protective ghost who made me throw my pills into the ocean. What kind of protection was that?

Because it was time to let go. Time to connect, he'd said.

He didn't understand. He didn't understand what it was like to be an eight-year-old who woke up screaming in the middle of the night, scared to death from all the shadows around her. He hadn't been there, and he wouldn't know the fear, so he shouldn't have made me do that.

Standing in the queue, I seethed. Gritted my teeth.

Others in line had taken to friendly banter, a camaraderie between residents facing peril together, as they talked about the measures they'd taken to protect their homes and the things they still had left to do. The eye of the storm was now passing over eastern Cuba and within hours, conditions would begin to deteriorate.

"Looks good now, doesn't it?" the woman ahead of me said. She knew I was from out of town based on the "friendly banter" she'd tried to have with me, but I'd been too pissed off at the moment to engage. "It always looks this beautiful hours before a hurricane hits.

You don't hear birds, do ya?"

"Actually, no."

"Most animals have already taken shelter. Humans are the last idiots outside before a storm, doing final preparations until the last damn moment to pick up their medications." She laughed.

I had to get out of here.

I couldn't stand the sun, I couldn't stand the heat, this woman's friendly face, nothing. And I swore to God, I was going to have an anxiety attack right here in front of everyone. Stepping out of line, I bypassed everyone and charged into the CVS all the way up to the front counter.

"Miss, you have to wait in line," someone said.

I nearly shot them a retort in middle finger form.

Instead, I looked the pharmacist in the eye. "Hi. I already refilled these days ago, but there was an accident, and I honestly can't wait. I need my meds now. Please." I had no idea what I was doing. It wasn't like I'd ever been a diva before. I just knew I felt desperate.

The bespectacled man gave me a thin-lipped grimace. "If it's an emergency, go to the urgent care down the street. They'll take care of you there. I'm sorry…next!" he called, avoiding eye contact with me.

I wanted to knock over the stand holding bags of cough drops, but the last thing I needed was to get arrested for disorderly conduct right before a hurricane. Everyone here was waiting, and everyone had to be patient, including me. But it was hard telling that to my OCD brain.

"Yeah, take your white privilege somewhere else," a man muttered as I charged by.

I stopped to take him in.

Speaking of white, he was bone-colored and wore khaki shorts, a Polo shirt, and nice boat shoes. He'd probably just come from tying up his yacht in the marina. Behind him, a shadow form stood hovering over him. It morphed before my eyes—shifting into a large sunburned man with a noose around his neck. Parts of his hands and body had been charred, and he did not look happy.

"Sir, there's a ghost following you around," I said, focused on the dead man's hollow eyes. "Just a head's up, he'll probably choke you in your sleep tonight."

Then I walked off amid gasps and random insults.

Because screw that guy. And screw Mayai for dumping my pills.

Back outside, my phone rang—my mother's happy face smiling in my hand, but I knew she'd betray that façade the moment I'd answer so I let it go to voicemail. I couldn't handle my mother right now. Whatever she had to say, she'd end up texting it anyway.

Reaching La Concha, I again found the gate locked, but this time, I side-swept it and leaped right over the top. Did I care that my shirt got snagged on one of the pointed tips and I scratched the living crap out of myself? No, because I was quickly reaching my limit of zero fucks given.

I also didn't care when I walked through the front door and Syndia, talking to Nottie about the potted plants she hadn't brought into safety yet, paused to look at me. "Where do you think you're going?"

"To my room. Room 3, the room where my grandparents used to sleep. Is there a problem?" I pushed past her when she tried getting in my way. I felt like a rebel and I didn't care. This might've been her property now, but in my heart, it was still Nana's and until I helped my grandfather rest in peace, I would never leave.

Terror shone in Nottie's dark eyes. I could only imagine what abuse Syndia had been heaving on her before I walked in. I tried communicating to her without words that she didn't have to stay here, didn't have to take this abuse, but Nottie was stuck as emotional victims tended to be.

"Whitaker, if you won't be leaving, then I'll have to insist that you do something to help us around this place. We are clearly in harm's way while all you do is leave the premises to do God knows what." Syndia's voice grated on my eardrums.

"You mean reordering my medicine?" I strolled up to the plaque over the fireplace and pointed to it. "And finding out from strangers that everything my family loved was taken from them? Yeah, how selfish I'm being." I probably shouldn't have said that, but I was having a harder time than ever controlling myself without my Zoloft.

Bacon darted through the room upon hearing my voice and slammed his body against my legs in jubilation. Syndia, annoyed that her cat favored me over her, cocked her head and took slow steps toward me. "Everything was taken from *you? Your* family? You can't be serious."

"I'm dead serious."

"What do you think you know, Whitaker?"

"I know enough." I knew—felt was more like it—that something terrible had happened here and my grandparents had been bamboozled out of money, glory, and a happy marriage they'd both rightly deserved.

"Let me tell you about hard times," Syndia said, picking up her hammer that had been sitting on a table where she'd set it down. My mind without drugs imagined her using that hammer to smash my head into the wall right next to the plaque as a warning to other guests. "You booked five days at a Key West resort for two hundred a night. And that's after paying airfare, rental car, and time off from work. Am I right?"

"You don't know anything about me."

"But I do. I'm guessing you've never had a hard day in your life."

"You don't know that." Emotionally but I had.

"I know plenty," she said. "I know you brought Leanne Drudge's ashes here to spread all over my house. I know that you see ghosts."

What? How would she know that?

She giggled at the confusion on my face. "You think you're the only one to see them? They talk to me, too. Why do you think this place is called one of the most haunted spots in Key West? And not in the good, touristy way," she said. "In the nobody-wants-to-stay here way."

"If they talk to you, too, why won't your grandfather tell you where the treasure is?" I asked. "Problem solved." She was bluffing, just like she was bluffing about knowing I could see spirits. "None of this has to do with what happened here in 1951, Ms. Duarte."

"But it does. Your family had enough money to have your grandmother cremated whereas I had to leave my mother with the coroner down at the county. Do you know how much her Medicaid covered?" Syndia slowly encroached in my space.

"I'm sorry about your mother, Ms. Duarte."

"Fifteen hundred, Whitaker." She took slow steps towards me. I backed up, not liking the way she was approaching. "Fifteen hundred, and you know how much a basic funeral costs? You would know. Seven thousand five-hundred. So you see, you ended up better off than I did in the long run. So, why are you here? Can't you leave us alone?"

I felt bad that she and her family had had a hard time all these years, but their choices had been her own. They could've sold this place a long time ago and moved somewhere cheaper, just like Nana had to do.

"You think this is about money?" I spat, backing away. "You keep thinking that. I don't want anything belonging to you, Syndia.

All I want is to find out the truth. My family has a right to know what happened here."

"Your family lost its rights, information included, the moment your grandmother sold the house. You shouldn't have stepped foot in here."

"It was my grandmother's wishes to be here," I said. "Your life is based on a lie, Ms. Duarte. The least you can do is allow me to find the truth."

She scoffed and turned away, sending Nottie into the backyard to finish bringing in the plants.

"This place of yours is built on lies," I told her, entering the outside corridor. "The truth will always come out, and that's been happening since the day my grandmother died." Even more so since I spread her ashes. Maybe Nana's presence agitated the haunting, got all the spirits out of sorts, her return to *Casa de los Cayos* awakening every resting soul on this property.

"How do you know that?" Her voice shook, and that glass eye of hers stared right through me with its lifeless sheen. "How do you know the truth always comes out? Google tell you that?"

"No, your house does. It speaks to me at every turn, tells me more and more each day." I backed off, keeping an eye on Syndia as I felt my way backwards down the hall.

Chewing her bottom lip as she used the hammer to pound a plank of wood against a room door, I knew that Syndia was losing her shit. This woman was crazy. Like I'd lost it at CVS earlier but at a much more psychotic level, because she had more to lose than I did. Even I went home now, I'd be no worse off than when I'd left.

I had to watch myself around her. She stood to lose her home if she couldn't pay it, she'd lost her mother to strangers who would burn her flesh then never return an ounce of her ashes, and now, a storm was on its way, threatening everything she had.

The more I gained, the more she lost.

And that made me her enemy.

THIRTEEN

I was more nervous about Syndia than the coming storm. Which, according to the latest advisory, would be starting very soon, with the eye wall passing over Havana, Cuba by tomorrow evening, putting us in the northwest sector.

I did my best to help her by bringing in loose items from the yard, anything that could become a projectile—empty pots, old yard toys, loose pieces of wood, which I piled inside the living room to use for shutters. La Concha didn't have any of the fancy metallic hurricane shutters I'd seen down on Duval Street that closed shut like an accordion.

No, here, we had to hold the pieces up and drill them into the wooden structure of the house. It was easy to see where former shutters had once been drilled. The holes were still there, and we couldn't use them or the screws would come right out. Hence, Syndia had to drill in new places, which only made the house look worse.

After a couple of hours, she grew tired. The woman might've been over fifty, but she was a beast for having such a small frame. Around five, I sat inside the living room to watch the latest advisory and while Syndia disappeared to another part of the house, saw that tornadoes had been spotted all along the lower keys.

Great. Tornadoes. *Yay.*

I checked my phone and saw at least a hundred texts from my mother and friends back home. I gave everyone the same copy-and-pasted quick reply letting them know I was fine. And then, someone called from a 305 number. Though I hadn't programmed it into my phone, I had a feeling who it was and answered on the second ring.

"Hello?"

"Ellie from Boston!" Luis's cheery voice rang through the line. It was nice to hear a voice I recognized that wouldn't judge me for staying in town instead of fleeing the storm like it was out to kill me.

"Hey, Luis. How's it going?"

"Just finished up helping my landlord with the sandbags, thought I'd check in on you to see if you and Duarte needed anything."

Nottie eyed me curiously from the front office. I sank into the corner to talk privately. "Actually, it's just me and her putting up shutters. The older woman's doing what she can. I honestly don't know if they're going to hold. We're running out of steam here."

"I told you I'd come by to help if you needed it."

"I think we need it."

"I'll be there in thirty minutes. Syndia won't like it, but try to convince her it's for the best. See you soon."

"Will do." I hung up and grabbed a plastic cup of water from a pitcher Nottie had put out for us.

"What is it that we need?" Syndia asked me, coming back in.

"Oh, help with the shutters," I told her. "A friend of mine in town said he would help when he was done with his, so I told him to come over. Hope that's okay."

"It's not okay. I don't have anywhere to put him up during the storm. All the rooms are filled with outdoor furniture and things."

It wasn't true. There wasn't much outside but the broken lounge chairs and a mess of wild foliage. "I don't think he plans on staying," I explained. "He only wants to help. I mean, you want to be absolutely sure that our shutters are secure, don't you? Make sure the house sustains minimal damage? It's good to have a man around for the hard stuff."

It was an awkward, sexist thing to say, but I knew it would appeal to her older woman sensibilities, and it worked. She shrugged, going back inside the office. "But he can't stay."

"No worries there. But I will ask him to," I muttered under my breath. "If I feel unsafe around you."

Before Luis arrived, I texted him to come around the side of the property where he could wedge his way in unseen through the guest gate. I didn't want Syndia turning him away before he had the chance to help.

I was near the spot where I'd seen that bloody ghost, and my nerves were on high alert waiting for a similar experience—the cold shiver up my arms, the frozen spot inside my torso, my inability to move. The rain had started again but it felt good to be outside, absorbing its energy. Somehow, it recharged me, made me feel I could handle anything.

I stood by the back wall of the last guest room, chewing on my nails. If I closed my eyes, I could feel them staring. The shadows. The spirits. Wanting to come near me, wanting to tell me things. *No, no, no…* I shook my head and tried to stay on this side of the veil.

According to Mayai, it was time to let them in. Time to listen and connect, but I just couldn't do it. I kept my eyes wide open, focusing on the smallest of things—the raindrops falling off the eaves, the lines and patterns in the hibiscus bush leaves next to me. Anything but staring into space. That was when they started to come out.

I was scanning the yard, waiting for a sign from Luis, when I spotted something in the corner of the yard. Covered in vegetation, it could've been anything, but the dull gray metal and patches of reddish stain told me it was discarded machinery. Slowly, I stepped through the leaves over to it, only to find it was larger than I originally thought, about six feet wide and four feet tall, a massive thing with gears and dull blades and curved parts to protect the user.

It must've been half a century old.

It was covered in rust and I felt stupid for not being able to identify it. All around me, mosquitoes flitted and landed on my skin, looking to feast. I knew I had to move out of this corner quickly, else become their latest meal. But I couldn't move. I was drawn to this machine and its once-sleek design.

It might've been a strange lawnmower or an old air conditioner unit out here rotting in the wild, but whatever it was, it had taken a hold on me. Lightly, I ran my fingertips along its frame, stopping to close my eyes and just feel.

Them blades will get duller, if you do, then you won't be able to use it no more.

If they do, I'll just sharpen them up again.

Two men talking around me, two men from long ago. One was the operator of the machine. The other was his father-in-law. Hunched over the first man, he watched with great scrutiny, making sure he did everything right. A lot was riding on his ability to perform this task.

On the grass between them was a third man.

Unmoving, lying on the ground. Wasn't a part of the conversation at all. In fact…

I ripped my hand away from the metal. "What the hell?"

"Ellie."

I whirled around. Luis stood there in shorts and T-shirt, looking way more casual than I'd seen him the other night. My head spun with heavy unseen energy. "You scared me."

"I'm so sorry. You told me to come this way, so I did."

"Yes…thank you. I just…"

He put a hand on my shoulder. "Are you okay? You look like you're about to faint. It's damn hot out here, that's for sure."

"Yeah, I didn't expect this much heat. But um…" Ask Luis, my intuition told me. If anyone would know, it'd be him, and something told me he already knew what was wrong.

"Oh, wow, is that what I think it is?" He navigated through the dense undergrowth, stepping over rough-cut stones I hadn't even realized were there. "I've never actually seen one of these before."

"What is it?"

"For cutting stone. Remember I said McCardle's son-in-law cut coquina for a living? This must've been his tool for doing just that. See these rocks all around?" He pointed to the porous gray stones that looked like they'd been eaten by acid. "That's coquina."

"They're everywhere in this yard," I said.

"Yes, the seawall is made out of it too. It stretches all the way down. About an acre wide. Anyway, just tell me where to start." He surveyed the buildings from where we stood. "I see these rooms over here still need shutters. Got any wood?"

I pointed to the pile we'd collected from scattered junk piles, and as Luis headed off in that direction to fetch the planks, the visions returned. I felt the heat stir around me, the ground tilt on an axis, and suddenly, I was there again, watching the two men discussing the machine and its blades.

The third man lay still on the ground. I knew he was dead but didn't want to look at him directly. Whether or not this was my imagination or real, it felt real. Who was he? And what were they about to do? I got a sinking feeling in the pit of my stomach so hard, I had to turn away and suddenly, I heaved the contents of my stomach into the grass.

Bacon came by at just that moment and meowed, sniffing around my feet.

I kicked him aside so he wouldn't mess with the vomit. "Go on, get out of here." I shooed him. He did, only in the direction I didn't want him to—toward the machine. He leaped up onto it, did a circular walk, then growled in the direction of the men I'd seen. Men who were there. Not visions in my mind, but actually there. They'd lived here long ago. Hissing at empty air, Bacon jumped off the machine and ran through the yard.

The last thing I saw was the dead man's leg being twisted like a chicken drumstick by one of the other men. I wasn't sure which because I could barely keep it together. But Mayai would've wanted me to stay calm, open up, listen and connect, so I tried. I tried so hard, but it was taking every ounce of energy out of me. They were tearing this man apart, for crissake.

Then, I saw it—the hatchet coming down, slicing right underneath the knee cap, taking the man's leg right off, pant leg and all. *Skin him good,* the man said. *The less meat, the better.*

I couldn't take it anymore and turned to run, but as I did, I smacked right into a human wall. I screamed, and even as I heard Luis's voice telling me it was okay, to calm down, I still couldn't shake the terror of what I'd seen out in the yard. He put down two planks of wood to hold my shoulders. "Hey, hey, it's me."

I slammed my fists against his chest, pushing away what I thought was the image still in front of me. What had that been? Why was I seeing this?

"What did you say that was used for again?" I pointed to the machine I couldn't look at anymore. The rusted machine out in the corner of the property.

"For cutting coquina," he said, helping me stand straight again. "The shell rock forms naturally over thousands of years, but it's incredibly hard. They used to use all sorts of tools for shaping it. I don't think it's harvested anymore. Real coquina is hard to find these days. A lot of what you see is fake. Are you okay? Did something spook you?"

I couldn't answer. I had to know more. "What else is it used for?"

"That's it, as far as I know. Well..." He raised an eyebrow.

I didn't like the look in his eye. Yes, Luis was an entertainer of sorts, as tour guides tended to be, and he loved the drama of a good story, but I knew what he was going to say next because of the vision I'd seen. And my body chilled up, paralyzing me to my core.

"Some say that human bones are ground up and used to make *manmade* coquina. All mixed up with the shell and limestone. Nobody would ever know because it all looks the same, but that's just stuff we guides tell people on ghost tours to scare them. I've never actually heard of or seen evidence of it."

I had.

Human bones. De-fleshed and ground up.

I'd seen it played out live right in front of me. But I couldn't speak, couldn't tell him what I'd seen. I only closed my eyes one more time and, despite me trying to keep it together, the world went black around me.

FOURTEEN

Mayai was back. We were on a new part of the island.

He showed me the ships, the Spanish ships, that had wrecked on the shore, and the inhabitants, including Mayai, salvaging wood, working together to put them into piles. A new industry for the Calusa emerged—wrecking. This was one of the last times the Calusa would live on this land. Soon, more ships would come, and the tribes would scatter. Many would be killed. Some would flee on boat to Cuba.

It was hard to know who to trust, Mayai said.

Sometimes the Spanish were friendly. Other times, they arrived deranged and ready for war. If it wasn't the Spanish killing the English, it was the English killing the Spanish, and the innocent ones aboard looked to the native people for sanctuary. Many of them lived amongst them for years. Many bred and began families.

I came from one of those mixed families.

I had part European and part indigenous Floridian in me.

Mayai was one of my ancestors.

The blackness in my peripheral melted, as my eyes adjusted to my surroundings. I was in a room, not on a beach with Mayai, and I quickly recognized the space. Room 3. A man was by my side, peering into my face as he hovered over me. "Ellie, you okay? You blacked out. What happened out there?"

"Huh?" I sat up and blinked, head pounding. It took me a

moment then I remembered. "I saw something."

"A ghost?" Luis asked hopefully, childlike wonder in his eyes.

"More like a scene, a reenactment of something that happened long ago."

"A residual haunting." He rubbed his chin. "What did you see?"

I wasn't sure I wanted to tell him. But I felt so alone just then, a world away from my life in Boston with one foot in this new world in Key West that I needed to. Connection. Someone who would understand. "I saw two men operating that machine. And…it wasn't pretty."

"Tell me," Luis said. I got the sense he was more interested to hear my ghostly tale than he was about getting me to feel better. "I mean, if you feel comfortable."

"I don't."

Suddenly, a female silhouette blocked the open doorway. "Who are you? Why are you here?" It was Syndia, filling the frame despite her thinness.

I tried to stand to explain, but lost my balance and sat on the edge of the bed again. My grandmother used to sit on the edge of this bed, too. I wasn't sure how I knew that but the information coming at me lately felt real and trustworthy. "This is my friend who lives in Key West. The one I told you about," I explained. "He came to help us put up shutters."

"Luis Gallardo," she said with a wary, deep tone. "We don't need any more help."

"Hello again, Ms. Duarte. Nice to see you," Luis said, offering his handshake. "She fainted outside, and I think having another hand to help would be beneficial to you."

"I don't care what you think," Syndia snapped, rejecting his handshake. I wondered what Luis had done to make him unwelcome here. If he was anything like me, it didn't take much. "You asked too many questions last time."

"I won't ask any this time," Luis promised. "Trust me."

"The winds are due to arrive by tonight," I said. "We've only covered half the windows. I think you should let him help us."

She glared at us a second more, sizing Luis up. Then, she turned around and left the room. A moment later, I heard the sounds of wood being dragged down the hallway and being plopped down. Banging of planks.

Luis turned back to me. "Told you she doesn't like me."

"She doesn't like anybody," I said. "What did you do?"

"I asked her mother's nurse questions about the family, the ghosts, the gold, because she seemed amenable to answering, and Duarte nearly bit my head off."

"Same thing happened to me. It was like Nottie had said too much."

"Yes, exactly."

"But right now, Duarte doesn't have much of a choice," I said. "I don't see neighbors clamoring to help this woman put up shutters." I rubbed my eyes and worked on focusing my attention, not an easy task without my meds.

We had to finish preparing the house.

I had to pretend I hadn't just seen a dead man's leg get chopped off for what I could only assume was to be fed into a grinding machine. A machine used to pummel shell, not human bones. What horrors had happened in this area since my grandmother left? Who would do such a thing?

"You were telling me about your vision?" Luis asked.

I decided I would tell Luis my story after he'd helped us. Once he'd assisted us with boarding up, I'd reward him. "We'll have plenty of time for chatting later," I said. "Let's get the last of the windows covered up before the next rain band comes through."

Getting up to stretch, my gaze landed on my purse sitting on the mosaic table. It was open and looked as though rifled through. "What the…" I flew over to it and checked inside. The photos were there, but I couldn't find the brass key anywhere. "Where's the key?"

"The what?"

"The key! The key!" I stammered, taking everything out of the purse and flipping it inside out. "Did you take it?" I zeroed in on Luis.

"No. You've seen my whereabouts the whole time I've been here, Ellie. Besides, I don't steal." He was indignant, and it occurred to me how I knew absolutely nothing about the man in my room. He could've been a thief or a murderer, and I'd just invited him here assuming he'd be safe.

No, he's fine and he's safe, I reminded my OCD. The world would not fall apart around me. "I was out for a while, wasn't I?"

"Yes, you fainted, but I didn't take your key."

Then who did? For all I knew, that key didn't lead to anything significant, and here I was panicking for no reason. But something told me that it did, and my intuition, if anything, had been getting nothing but stronger since I'd arrived.

Luis threw up his hands and walked out of the room. "Esta mujer, coño," he said to zero understanding on my part. "You know what? I didn't come here to get accused of stealing, so I'll be heading back now. Good luck with the storm."

"No, wait." I began rushing out then turned back around, placed my purse inside the hole in the wall behind the safe, then stepped into the corridor. "Luis, I'm sorry. I'm not feeling well. I shouldn't have accused you."

"Listen, I'm only here to help you out."

"You're also here in hopes of finding treasure." I lifted an eyebrow. I mean, it was true. "Let's not kid ourselves. You said so yourself. You can see how I might've mistrusted you for a second there."

"Yes, but we had an agreement. We said if I help you find that gold, we'd share it. I wouldn't try and find it myself, I wouldn't take your key without asking, and I sure as shit wouldn't worry about it now when a storm's on the way."

"Fine, I'm sorry. And shh. Don't talk about the gold out loud. You-know-who is somewhere nearby, probably eavesdropping." I craned my neck looking for Syndia, heard banging, hammering noises at the opposite end of the property.

"Fine." Luis pulled planks of wood off the ground and began dragging them toward the guest room without boards up on their windows.

I sighed and rubbed the stress from my face, glancing in the direction of the machine again. Nothing there but shrubbery. But something lingered, something watched from the trees. I hated the feeling that sank deep into my skin.

Following Luis, I again told myself to stay focused, worry about the storm right now. That was top priority, and we'd figure the rest out at a later time. We only had a few hours left to prepare.

The gusts of wind were getting stronger. Palm fronds blew intermittently like long green and brown hair being blow-dried by an unseen force. The giant banyan tree in the center courtyard swished in the wind. I felt chilled even though it was hot outside. Walking through the garden, I again got that heavy feeling like someone was watching, like this center hub was also the heartbeat of the property.

I stopped to close my eyes, sensing my surroundings better this way.

Behind the banyan tree, someone stood near the moon sculpture. Watching me, though there was no one. No one corporeal anyway. I heard Maya's voice near my ear—*they took our land once before. Fight. Don't let them take it again.*

He meant my dream while I'd been passed out. I now remembered it—the ships, the bloodshed, his telling me that I was descended from his tribe mixed with Europeans. "I *am* fighting," I murmured, continuing to walk around the circular stone wall. "I'm here, aren't I?"

I'd stayed on the island fully knowing that a hurricane was on its way, fully knowing that it was crazy to do so, to stay with a woman who was unstable at best.

I stared at the moon sculpture so hard, I felt it would fall over and shatter. Suddenly, Bacon appeared, leaping out through the bushes, positioning himself between me and whatever unseen presence was in the garden. He hissed, baring his sharp teeth and flattening his dirt-filled ears.

Summer gnats flew around his face and occasionally flitted around mine as well.

"What's wrong?" *Bacon, Grandfather, whoever you are…*

Luis called for me, but I was rotted to my spot. Fear and paralysis seized me. I could only stare ahead. I was sure if I waited long enough, something, or someone, would materialize. And as much as I didn't need more distraction, I couldn't look away.

I was about to wrench myself away when the winds kicked up another notch. The blustery breezes whipped the palm fronds high above. *Go away, Ellie,* another voice spoke to me. My grandmother. *Go away, now.*

"Nana? Where are you?"

Go away. Your job here is done.

"No, it's not. They took your house, your husband, your fortune…" I spoke to the emptiness in front of me. My job had been to spread her ashes, but my goals had changed. I wanted to put an end to this messed-up family's reign. I wanted to give my grandmother back everything she'd lost.

If Mayai was right, and we were descendants of this land, then that pissed me off even more. We'd ended up in Boston, for crying out loud, instead of living out our days here in Cayo Hueso at *Casa de los Cayos,* my family home.

My soul filled with anger when I thought about all that might have happened over the years. I took the offenses personally as if they'd happened to me. In a way, they had. My hands balled into fists, and I wanted to scream. Inexplicably. Furiously. I knew it'd cause alarm and Syndia, Nottie, and Luis would come running, so I held it in as long as I could.

They'd taken it all away. Foul play.

I had no evidence. None—zero.

Except for these voices and visions.

Like the one that spiraled into my view this very second. As Bacon continued to hiss, the gnats that had been bothering him before formed a large cloud of even more tiny insects until they took the shape of a man. A tall man made out of swirling bugs with a face, fierce grimace, and everything. Handsome, formidable. Cruel smile. He held a long blade smattered with dark red. The entire vision was comprised of the flying insects.

I couldn't move, couldn't scream, just like my night terrors when I was a child. Powerless to do anything. But I could speak and forced myself to utter a few words.

"McCardle…" The winds shot through the garden as though controlled by the apparition himself. Behind him, the massive banyan tree swayed. Loose, dried palm fronds fell to the ground, one of them nearly hitting Bacon.

Get out of here, the specter hissed at me.

"I will not," I said, feeling my grandmother's hand slipping into mine and drawing me away. But that had to be a desire of my damaged brain, because she wasn't here. None of them were here, and Bacon was merely hissing at the wind. The battle waging was all in my head.

"Ellie!" Luis called from somewhere.

I couldn't reply, though I understood his concern. A force was coming from the inlet, something headed this way. I felt the salty spray of ocean mist cover my face. Whatever it was, it was rogue and wild and spontaneous, appearing randomly out of nowhere.

"Ellie!" I heard Luis's call even closer.

Ahead of me, McCardle's ghost yelled, louder than before—*GET OUT OF HERE!* His voice boomed throughout the garden, just as a pair of warm, humanly arms wrapped around my torso and pulled me backwards. A half a second later, a vortex of spinning water engulfed one of the palm trees and ripped it right out of the ground, sending it shooting through the air and crashing toward us. Its thorns tore long stinging lines through my leg.

Shit.

Luis tumbled to the ground with me in his arms, and we landed underneath the overhang by the atrium. Overhead, the spinning watery tornado cut a course over the house, ripping off a few shingles then it was gone.

"Holy shit…" Luis gasped for air.

"What was that?" I cried.

"Water spout," he said, chest heaving. "The moment I saw those palms kick up and tasted the salt in the air, I knew what was coming."

I forced myself to move, to shake off the shock.

I couldn't imagine how bad the actual hurricane would be if that had only been a precursory waterspout. What had I gotten myself into? But had the spout come naturally or had McCardle caused it? I couldn't believe I was even asking myself such a question.

"Thank you." I sat up and hugged Luis. No, I didn't know him more than a hole in the wall, but he didn't have to save me. He could've let me die then fended for himself. But he didn't. And right now, that made him my only friend on this island.

You should've let her die.

The words were not of this world, and I was getting tired of these ghosts messing with me, their hateful messages echoes of an era left behind. They were ethereal and evil and full of spite, and it was no wonder my grandmother left this town. When I looked up at the cloud of gnats again, I saw the final wisp of McCardle glaring down at us, his wife Susannah by his side.

FIFTEEN

"I'm sorry. I have to go lie down." I rushed out of there as quickly as I could and headed to my room. I felt Luis following me and hesitant to come in, so he hovered by the open door.

"What happened out there?" he asked. "Something's going on."

"No shit something's going on," I snapped back then pinched the bridge of my nose. "I can't explain it."

"You were in some kind of a trance. I kept calling you."

"I know, I could hear you, but I couldn't move. I saw him."

"Saw who?"

"McCardle. I know it was him. I've never seen him, but I just knew somehow. He caused that water spout."

Luis narrowed his eyes a bit. "Ellie, I believe that you saw him. I told you many people do, but that spout…that's a normal occurrence in these weather conditions. He couldn't have—"

"I'm telling you, he caused it!" I snapped again. "You're the one person I know who believes in strange occurrences, and even you're telling me you don't believe in a strange occurrences. Jesus Christ!"

"Alright, look. I believe you, okay? I'll believe anything that happens here. Like I told you the other night, I would bring my tour groups here if Syndia allowed it. Also, if it weren't so…"

"Cursed?"

"I guess that would be the word, yes."

Bacon appeared behind Luis but didn't rub against his legs. He merely looked up as if waiting for an invitation. "Is this Bill Drudge reincarnated?" Luis asked with a laugh.

"I've no clue. Psst, come here, Bacon…" I whistled and snapped my fingers to get him to come in, but he refused. When I got up to pet him, Bacon walked a little further away. When I was nearly close enough to scratch his head, he moved a little further away again.

"I think he wants me to follow him," I said, remembering his hiding spot and my grandmother's photos. "He's led me to objects before."

"Fascinating." Luis crossed his legs and watched as Bacon led me back down the hallway, stopping midpoint to make sure I was still behind him then leading me into the other half of the property. The McCardle-Duarte side of the property on which I'd never been.

"I can't go that way," I told the cat.

"You have to." Luis raised an eyebrow.

"Well, then you're going to have to distract Syndia. Take her to Home Depot or something. Tell her you're out of screws. Anything."

"I'm on it. I'll text you when we're gone." Luis pulled out his keys from his pocket and spotted Syndia coming out of the front office. "Ms. Duarte?" He blocked my line of view, giving me a moment to hide inside an alcove. "Could you come with me to get some materials while Ellie is lying down?" He disappeared into the main house. "She's still not feeling well, and I could use the extra hands…"

Down the corridor, Bacon meowed impatiently.

"I'm coming," I whispered. Nervously, I glanced everywhere and practiced an excuse in my head in the event that Syndia came back in and found me trespassing in her home. "I was just looking for Nottie," I muttered out a fake reason. "Hoping she could give me some aspirin."

Yeah, right.

I prayed to the universe that nobody would catch me in here. The thought that Syndia might have video cameras throughout the house suddenly occurred to me, but then I remembered that Syndia couldn't even afford a new coat of paint, much less high tech.

I followed Bacon to the last room on the left, entered the house, and was not too surprised to find it utterly cluttered. Newspapers, magazines, and boxes covered any view of the walls. More boxes filled with old electronics, wires, and busted light bulbs. Cassette tapes and old headphones, but I couldn't stop to take stock of any of these things. I had to follow the cat.

"Where are you taking me?" I stepped up to a flight of stairs and got a buzz in my pocket. The text from Luis. I glanced at it to make sure I was clear to go upstairs.

She didn't want to go but I said it was imperative. So we're out. Hurry.

Got it, I replied then headed up the stairs.

Bacon meowed again then turned the corner while I thought about all the ways my life had changed in just the four days I'd been here. Here I was, following a cat through a house not my own, out of sheer certainty that he was leading me to something important.

Once upstairs, I caught sight of a gray dusty tail entering a room on the right. Following the tail, I entered what appeared to be a guest bedroom overtaken by more stuff. Boxes and old furniture sat over rust-colored shag carpet. This had to be a breeding ground for fleas. Bacon bumped his side against an old cardboard box.

"You want me to open that?"

Bacon meowed in response.

Quickly, I pulled the lid of the box and found old photos tossed inside. No rhyme or reason. Just a box of random photos, many black-and-white but most of them faded 1970s specials. "I can't take that, Bacon. And going through it would take forever." Still, I kneeled and rifled through the box, jumping at every sound I heard. "Damn it, my nerves."

There were family photos of what I assumed were the McCardles' children and grandchildren in their younger days living in Key West. One after the other. The further I dug, the older the photos got. I had no idea what this cat wanted me to find, and now that I thought about it, I felt even more stupid for believing such a thing.

"You just want attention, don't you?" With my nerves in my throat at the thought that someone could come in any minute, I thought about abandoning this lovely trespassing adventure and returning to my room.

But then I pulled out one particular black-and-white photo—the mosaic table inside Room 3, only it wasn't. It just looked like it but on a grander scale. On the wall was a large, mural-type mosaic covering at least a quarter of the little room. It was hard to tell what the image was, since the photo was mostly gray and had faded even more since it had been taken, but it seemed to be a map of the Lower Keys and Cuba.

I heard a shuffling outside the window. I parted the sticky old blinds and saw Nottie quietly sweeping the grounds. I let out a breath of relief. Did she not know that this place was about to get messy as hell? Sweeping would not help La Concha look any better, and after the storm, it would be even worse. She had to be doing something to get her mind off other things.

Cold air filtered into the room. There was no A/C on. This made the hair on my arms stand straight up. I knew it wasn't coming from anywhere in particular. "Who's there?" I'd almost completely accepted that the ghosts ruled this resort, and I was no one to question their existence.

I heard a car door slam.

Shit. I had to get out of here.

I hadn't found anything spectacular but these photos were interesting. Plucking out as many of the series I could find, I closed the box and hugged them close. A few days ago, I wouldn't have worried about Syndia but now I hated to think of what she'd do if she found me in here.

Hurrying back the way I came, I paused downstairs just outside the door, sweat pouring down the sides of my face. Bacon ran out before me while I hung back in that smoky, nasty room waiting for the right moment to leave. I listened. When I saw Syndia enter the yard, heard Luis's voice, and noticed that I'd missed a text (*on our way back*) my heart shot into my throat.

Shit, shit, shit…

How could I escape this room without Syndia seeing me?

Not only that, but Nottie was still near the door sweeping the sidewalk, talking to herself. In her own little world. From the way she appeared to be lost in thought, you'd have never known that hurricane winds would be starting soon. I could dart out and make a run for it, but that might cause alarm. I could also quietly wander out and pretend like this was all normal. I opted for the latter.

But then, I felt the chill return. Someone was following me—someone in the spirit world. The chill turned into shadows in the corner of my eye, and I knew then that I wasn't alone. I didn't want to see them, though. Didn't want to face them again. Enough ghosts for one day.

Bacon rubbed up against Nottie's legs and meowed loudly.

"What you want, cat? I fed you three times. Fine, let's go eat again." She rested the broom against the wall, and I sank back into the shadows until she'd passed. Nottie was gone for the moment, but now I had to get past Syndia out in the yard looking for more items to bring inside.

As I nonchalantly scuttled down the corridor, Luis caught sight of me and gave me a questioning look, like why was I still on the wrong side of the property. He began to talk to Syndia again loudly, so as to cover up any noise I might make behind her, and I knew that was my cue to get my butt moving.

"What do you have on that side of the yard over there?" he asked her, shooing me away behind her back.

"You said you wouldn't ask questions," Syndia replied flatly.

"I was talking about your famous legend. And your ghosts. This is about your yard."

She sighed, annoyed at Luis's presence. "A few tires. The old shed we don't use anymore. Just another thing to fix." She scoffed. "Let's get these last boards up, so I can rest and you can leave."

"Yes, ma'am," Luis said. "I just need to use the restroom. Would you excuse me a moment?"

I shuffled all the way into Room 3 and closed the door knowing that Luis would be right behind me any moment. He cracked the door open and stepped inside. "Where were you? Didn't you get my text?"

"I didn't notice. I was busy looking at photos."

"Of what?"

"Of this." I handed him the old black-and-whites and stood there, hand on chin, wondering where this mosaic would be today. "Have you seen it here before?"

"Not that I can recall."

"Is it hard to take down a mosaic, you think?" I asked.

"You mean by tearing down little piece of tile by little piece of tile? I would think so, yes. Probably easier just to cover it up. Why?"

I was staring at the wall opposite the bed. It was old and stained and cracked, but that was a beautiful thing. It'd be easier to break apart. "Have any screws in your pocket?" I asked. Glancing at the mosaic table, I went up to it and crouched to the ground, looking up at the underside. A handwritten inscription was there in faded ink: *For my love…1949.*

My grandfather. Another handmade gift to my grandmother.

He reached into his pocket and produced a long wall screw for securing boards. "Am I a handy man, or what?" He laughed. "I have to get back outside before she comes looking for me. We got to Home Depot and when she saw the line for wood, she made me turn around. Didn't want to leave you alone, I guess."

"Yeah, untrustworthy me. It's okay. It gave me enough time." I held up the photo and compared it to the wall. Then, I walked up to the crack in the left third and used the screw to chip away the plaster.

"What are you…oh…you think that mosaic is still under there?"

I didn't just know it. I could see it in my mind. It was colorful and matched the small table etched with my grandfather's initials. In fact, I'd seen it several times as a child. It hadn't been just a dream. It had existed for real. And it was behind this wall.

SIXTEEN

Repetitively, I scratched at the wall with the screw.

It may not have been the best of tools, but it was enough to loosen the chipped sections of the exposed crack. "I bet you anything…"

Bet that this mosaic was underneath this plaster. If my grandfather had made this table, then he definitely made the wall mosaic, too, and where else would it be but in this room? The room Bacon preferred. The room I'd envisioned myself in as Nana. This had to have been their room—my grandparents'. The McCardles and Duartes had tried to cover over it, remove all traces of the family who'd once inhabited here.

My family.

"They used plaster instead of drywall," Luis said, grabbing another screw and helping me chip away. "Why wouldn't they just cover it up in one piece? So much easier."

"Exactly. One piece comes off too easily," I said. My fingertips were beginning to get sore from the awkward scratching of wall with a rusty screw. "If they smeared over the mosaic with plaster, it's because they didn't want anyone to ever see it again. They wanted to cover it nice and good."

This house dripped with oddities. Between the cold drafts, the visions, the mysterious holes in walls, disappearing keys, and a resident cat who knew the place like a former owner would, I quickly learned not to be shocked by anything anymore. Still, I had to find that key. If Syndia stole it back, it had to be important.

Our chipping at the wall created two little piles of white dust on the floor that danced in the vortices of the rogue wind entering the room. We scraped away in silence for ten minutes without revealing anything. Finally, it occurred to me what was wrong—we were working on the wrong wall.

"Stop," I said, catching my breath. "See the way the ceiling boards go vertically?" I pointed out. Taking the photo, I showed Luis the direction of the ceiling boards in the image. "If that's the same ceiling as in the pic, then the boards end at the wall this way, butting up against the mosaic. So, it's not behind this wall. It's behind *this* one." I pointed to the wall behind the bed. "Help me move this."

"Damn. Good catch," Luis laughed.

Together, we heaved the wooden bed frame aside and ran our hands along the wall. Luis knocked on it and tried stabbing another screw into the plaster, but it needed an exposed section like the crack we'd started with. "Ellie, we're never going to chip this off with a screw. Let me go find a hammer or a pick-axe or something."

"I'll go with you. There's a shed in the backyard. Maybe there's tools in there."

"Or dead bodies."

"Not funny."

We went outdoors in search of the toolshed, only to hear Syndia berating Nottie for not being spry enough to help her carry planks of wood. "After this storm passes, we have to reconsider your employment. Now that my mother is no longer your concern."

"Ms. Duarte, I have nowhere else to go. I can earn my keep in other ways. Cleaning the house or maintaining the garden maybe?"

"I have nothing to pay you. Besides, you're no spring chicken anymore. You're pretty much useless to me now." Syndia was so damn careless when she talked to Nottie. What made her think she could just insult a woman like that? A woman *older* than she was?

Luis and I tried to circumvent Syndia, but she spotted us. Hands on hips, she gestured with her chin. "Only one more window to go. It's the large one in the atrium. Should I just cover it in tape?"

"No, I'll find something," Luis told Syndia. "Tape won't help."

"Well, find it quick, because this storm is starting." She scoffed before tying her hair into a tight bun that only accentuated the leathery wrinkles on her face. Behind her, Nottie watched us carefully, and I couldn't help but feel like she was asking for our help dealing with this crazed woman.

"Why tape?" I asked, still watching Nottie. Dark shapes flirted behind her, spoke to her, but she couldn't hear them. I blinked and focused on where I was stepping instead. Bacon ran in my way then trounced into the bushes.

"When there's no wood, covering a window in masking tape is the last option. Doesn't keep it from blowing in, but the tape holds the glass together so the pieces don't go flying everywhere."

I registered the wary look on Syndia's face as her gaze followed us through the garden, now that we were wandering toward her family's side of the yard. "There's no wood left anywhere if that's what you're looking for," she warned us then headed inside the house.

"What are we doing again?" I felt more lightheaded and disoriented than ever, the deeper we ventured into the wildest, untouched section of the property. Here, weeds grew as tall as my knees and even the moths wondered when was the last time they'd seen humans cross through.

"Looking for something we can use to chip away that wall," Luis said. "What's the deal with the mosaic anyway?"

"I think my grandfather made it. He made the mosaic table in that room too. There's an inscription on the underside to my grandmother."

"But I thought you were concerned about your missing key," he said.

"I was. I am. But I couldn't find it and then I saw those pics in a box. They must've taken them when they first bought my grandparents' house. It makes me sad that my grandmother couldn't take belongings with her, like that beautiful work of art."

"They must've taken a photo of it for posterity before covering it up."

"They should've just left it. It looked beautiful," I said. It didn't make sense. Had I bought a house and it came with a gorgeous handmade mosaic mural, I would've featured it, not covered it up.

"Where did you say that tool shed was again?" Luis wiped sweat from his brow. The humidity and fatigue was starting to get to him. I felt grateful to him for helping me out when he didn't have to.

"Over there." I pointed to the end of the seawall which disappeared into a thicket of mangroves. The water from the inlet sloshed into the tangled mess of roots, and the thick scent of rotting wood and algae infiltrated my nostrils.

"God knows the last time anybody came out this far," Luis said, pushing through denser and denser foliage. "You can tell she's had trouble taking care of this place."

"I know. See it there?" I pointed to the little house that finally broke through the greenery, there at the edge of the property. "Could be a toolshed."

"I think that's more like an old pump shed."

"Pump shed for what?"

"For a pool or something electrical that used to be out here. In fact…" His foot kicked at something hard underneath the fallen leaves and palm fronds.

Above us, the trees swayed in the storm front. I hugged myself in the now cool draft, just as the sun hid behind an overcast of clouds. "We should start wrapping this up. I'll find something to use for the wall, my nail scissors, a butter knife, anything."

"Wait, something's under here." Luis pushed at the ground with the toe of his sneaker and lifted up a corner. "It's plywood. Good, we can use this for her last window." He tugged at the corner of wood and lifted it out off the grass. Disturbed ants and centipedes crawled everywhere.

Luis indicated to the other end of the plywood, so I could lift it, but it was in fact three big sheets of plywood all laid on top of each other in sequential order to cover a large area. I helped him lift the first one so we could set it vertically against a palm tree. "There's a hole under there," he said.

The ground gave way to a concave, cemented bowl that was cracked and stained and hadn't been used in ages. "Looks like an old pool."

"Yep, that's exactly what it looks like." He crouched to stare into the dry basin filled with leaves and uneven layers of porous concrete. "Looks like they stopped using it long ago and have been filling it up with concrete."

"It's a weird place for a swimming pool," I said. "The corner of the yard."

"Maybe it was centered back when it was one property, but when they added more land, it got forgotten here in the corner." Luis shook his head and surveyed the area. "So much wasted property. I wish I had the money to buy this place up and fix it up nice. I hate seeing all this go to waste."

"Me, too. Believe me." Especially since half of it used to belong to my family. I walked over to the little wooden house and tugged at the door knob. "It's locked," I said, tugging at the shaky door. I was sure if I just pulled at it hard enough, it would bust open.

Ellie, go.

If that was my grandmother asking me to leave, then I definitely had to know what was inside.

"You okay?" Luis looked at me with concern. "You don't look well when you're here, I have to say. You're a completely different person from when I met you in town."

I nodded absently. "There's energy here that doesn't sit well with me. I never thought I'd say that, but there it is." All this talk of energies and gut feelings and hallucinations had me feeling less like my old self but more like my *real* self than ever before.

He nodded with a sigh. "I feel it too. It's like whatever, or whoever, is here doesn't want us around."

I couldn't deny it anymore. The ghosts—yes, real ones—were everywhere. "But then, I feel good energy too, like my grandparents'." I hugged myself in the wind that was growing harder and cooler by the minute. "A battle between good and evil. It's all here, and I feel like I'm at the center of it."

I was saying too much. I sounded crazy, but then again, if anyone would get it, it'd be Luis. He smiled and rested his shoe against the pump shed door. "A healthy skeptic, huh? Sounds like you knew more than you let on before."

"Hey, I was trying to stay sane before, okay?" I chuckled. Now, there was no point. The only way to get to the bottom of all this was to proceed full force, full crazy, and see where it all led.

"We're all going insane, Ellie," Luis said, reaching for the door handle, getting ready to pull. "Some just get there faster than others."

Then, he yanked—hard.

And when he did, his hand slipped off the handle. So did his other foot. And for a moment, I saw the darkness, the shadow people, heard the grunt, but it hadn't come from Luis. It came from something else, something hidden in plain sight, something just beyond the invisible veil. The entities protecting this corner were watching. It wanted Luis—us—dead. I saw the hatred, the anger, the ghastly offense that we were trespassing in this forsaken corner of the yard as a sheen of black energy washed over Luis's entire body.

Backwards, he slid into the hole that was the old pool…

…slamming his neck on the sharp edge of the other sheet of plywood laid down.

The raw-cut jagged edge severed his neck. His head snapped backwards like a PEZ candy dispenser yawning open, and Luis tumbled into the abandoned pit, blood pooling all around him, spreading into the bumpy ridges of the uneven concrete like spidery veins. His gaze looked up at me for help, but it was too late.

The light had gone from his eyes.

SEVENTEEN

I screamed.

No birds scattered. No cries echoed.

The heavy greenery absorbed all sound. Nothing stopped for me or Luis, yet everything had changed in an instant. One moment he'd been speaking to me, and the next, his body was broken inside a hole in the ground. I tore my gaze away from his helpless, confused stare, a vision that would haunt me the rest of my life.

"Shit…" I pulled out my phone to call 911, but for the life of me, I didn't know how to dial, how to log in with my thumbprint, how to anything. I couldn't think. I could only hear the sound of him gasping as he fell, heard the crack of his neck as it hit the plywood.

"What happened?" Syndia arrived at my side out of breath, hammer still in her hand. Her and her damn hammer. She spotted Luis's lifeless body and didn't so much as gasp or cover her mouth. She stared at it expressionless, inhaling a slow breath. "It was his own fault."

My head whipped toward her. "How could you say that? What the hell is wrong with you?" I wanted to push her into the pool to see how she'd like it and had to bargain with myself not to. "Why do you have an empty pool back here for your guests to fall into anyway?" I shouted.

"I told him not to go back here. I told him it was dangerous," she insisted.

"That doesn't mean he deserved it!" I sounded wild and irrational, though I was the normal one, yet nothing felt normal or ever would again. "God damn it!"

I had to pull myself together long enough to make a phone call. There was some trick to this—pressing the side button, holding down the home button, some shortcut for calling emergency services. I couldn't think of it. My brain simply wouldn't compute. I sank to the ground and rocked myself in a heap. "Jesus…think, Ellie."

"Don't call. He's beyond help," Syndia muttered.

"I still have to call," I growled at her. "We can't leave him here like this."

"The storm is coming in. Emergency won't respond 'til it's over."

"We still have to call," I insisted.

She remained quiet a moment, long enough to remind myself how to dial 911. I was two numbers in when my phone screen shattered in my hand, as Syndia's hammer came down and busted it into a million pieces.

"Are you kidding me?" I shot up and pushed the woman backwards. She stumbled into Nottie's arms, and they both looked at me like I was the insane one. "Why would you do that?" My chest felt like it was imploding, like I'd never take in a full breath again.

"I told you not to call."

"I don't care what you told me, you crazy bitch!" I howled.

"Neither or you listened. If you're not careful, I'll do the same to you."

"What does that mean?" I shook with rage. "Are you threatening me, Syndia?"

I may not have been the start of any problems, but I would definitely end them with violent force if it came down to it. I was stressed and without my pills, and now was not the moment to toy with me.

Taking steps at me with her hammer, she slammed the butt of it into a palm tree, leaving two scars in the tree's flesh. "I told you both to leave," she hissed. "I warned you, but you both stayed. You're not taking what's mine, Whitaker."

"Are you insane?" I yelled. "Do you even hear yourself? You're out of your damn mind, you know that?"

"Of course, I know it. It's why I warned you. Believe it or not, I care."

"You care?" I laughed maniacally. "You just busted my phone, you're threatening me with a hammer, and I'm supposed to believe that you care? You only care about your delusions. If there was a treasure, your grandfather would've left it for you, and his spirit would've told you where it was. Which means you're bullshitting, Syndia. You can't hear him and you only let guests stay here in case they can. Face it, the treasure doesn't exist!"

My words hurt her as though I'd wielded them with daggers.

The rain began coming down in heavy sheets, creating little expanding circles in Luis's deep red blood. Soon, the pool would fill with water, yard debris, God only knew what else the storm would bring, and a precious soul would be covered like yesterday's garbage.

I had to leave La Concha, had to grab my things, and casually walk out of here. As much as I wanted to figure out my grandmother's past, it wasn't worth my life. I wasn't sure that Syndia would try to kill me, but judging from how empathetic she hadn't been just now, I couldn't take the chance.

Rushing past her and silent Nottie, I headed to my room. Not sure where I would go, but the police station sounded as good a place as any. I could tell them what happened, show my phone as proof of a crazed innkeeper over at La Concha Inn, and hope that they'd let me stay for the duration of the storm. A shelter would also take me in, but without a phone to find one in Maps, I'd have to walk in the emerging winds looking for one.

I entered my room, looking back to make sure Syndia wasn't following me. She and Nottie hung back at the scene, getting drenched and staring down into the pool at Luis's freshly dead body. I felt bad leaving him there, but there was nothing I could do for the moment. I couldn't believe I had just witnessed such a horrible death.

As soon as I entered my room, though, something hit me. A clear sense of déja-vu.

The anguish I felt came alive, and I had to pause to catch my breath. The energies were growing stronger. *The elements,* my grandmother's voice told me, *heighten your perception.*

I didn't want rain or wind heightening my perception. I didn't want to see or hear or feel any ghosts around me. I'd seen more than enough of my share since I'd arrived. I'd seen too damn much. All I wanted was to get out of here, get back on my meds, and go home. Yes, my mother had tried to warn me, but I never imagined that the danger would come from Syndia herself instead of the hurricane.

I sat on the edge of the bed, gripping my head.

I couldn't stop the visions from pummeling me.

Nana cried, rocked on the edge of the bed next to me. Was she real? I didn't know anymore, not that it mattered. Her thoughts were my own… How would she live without her love? How would her baby grow up without a father? She'd become one of those widowed young women who few would take pity on. They would say she deserved it. She'd have to fend for herself, work two jobs, but those weren't the worst parts. The worst parts would be the lonely nights without Bill. She'd never marry again, never love again…

"Stop." I gripped my temples.

Cold energy shifted all around me. I heard the rain outside, but I also heard the pounding of my heart, my grandmother's heart, something rhythmic. My grandmother rocked some more, then stood up to scream at the night sky. Yes, it was nighttime outside in this waking daydream. The room filled with sweet scents of rain.

I was dreaming. Hallucinating again. None of this was real.

He wouldn't have left me, she kept saying. *He wouldn't have…*

"They killed him, Nana. They killed him on his way home to you. They took his Spanish gold then used the money to buy you out. It was a shitty thing, but it wasn't his fault," I told her. "There was nothing you could do."

They took what was ours. He never had the chance…

"What chance?" I asked.

He never saw the gold.

A hallucination talking back to me in real-time? Could Nana hear me in 1951? What did she mean he never saw the gold? How else would they have gotten a hold of it? He was the treasure hunter, the adventure seeker of the family. McCardle could only pilot a ferry back and forth along one route, and apparently pirate innocent lobster fishermen.

The pounding in my head grew louder. I screamed to release myself from it.

The vision disappeared but something else replaced it—pounding at the door.

"Who is it?" I called. The police? Syndia, asking to be let in? I couldn't piece together the fragments of dreams and reality fast enough, until it dawned on me. The pounding was hammering and drilling coming from outside while I'd been in a trance.

"No. No!"

Rushing the door, I yanked at the knob only to find it wouldn't budge. In the middle of the wooden door, several screws had been pushed through. The edges where light would've bled in were dark, and I knew she'd covered the door with the piece of plywood Luis had found. Underneath the door, shadows moved back and forth under the rain.

"Let me out!" I banged on the door, my palms turning bright red. "Let me out of here! You can't do this!"

"I can't let you out yet, Whitaker. I can't trust you. I'll let you out once the storm is over."

"Let me out now! I don't have any food or water. You can't do this."

"Drink water from the faucets. You'll be fine." Her footsteps disappeared down the hall.

My heart—I thought it would collapse from the stress this bitch was causing me. This couldn't be happening. She had trapped me in here and all I had were my things, a bed, an empty dresser and my own messed-up situation. No phone, no food, and Hurricane Mara about to hit.

Freakin' great.

Pulling out one of the empty drawers, I heaved it at the door but it only bounced off, causing dents and scratches. I lifted it and tried again, this time opening up the wood shutters and aiming it at the windows, already secured with storm plywood outside. I threw the drawer, cracking the window. All the good that would do me with planks of wood covering it.

One of the drawer's ends split into shards.

"My god, this isn't happening." What would I do for two days inside this room, assuming Syndia would ever let me out? What if something happened to her during the storm and no one would find me here for days? Weeks? Months?

"Nana, Mayai…" I picked up the side lamp and was about to throw it when I realized I'd be breaking my only source of light in this room. I put the lamp back on the nightstand like a good girl.

I had to calm down, or the anxiety would eat me alive. I needed my medicine. I didn't care what Mayai told me about connecting better without them. I wasn't built to be this psychic. I couldn't handle it.

Pacing back and forth, I knocked things to the floor and punched at the mattress to relieve anguish. Searching through my purse, I hoped to find a loose Zoloft somewhere, but only found a headache pill so I swallowed it back dry. The pressure in my temples would form a migraine soon, and the growing low air pressure outside wasn't helping.

I stared at the space where Luis and I had tried chipping away plaster earlier this afternoon. Now he lay dead at the bottom of a pool. A hazardous hole in the middle of the yard. I doubted this establishment ever had their licenses to begin with. Nothing to do but wait for the inevitable. My first hurricane and I'd be spending it as a prisoner.

I could cry about it, or I could keep tearing apart this wall.

Pulling out another drawer, I aimed the corner of it into the wall and slammed it. A tiny chunk of plaster chipped off. I slammed the drawer again in the same spot. More plaster chipped off. Again and again, I used the drawer as blunt force, chipping away at the same spot until eventually, about an inch depth of plaster was gone. Underneath, light blue glass shone through.

My fingertip confirmed it—smooth tile.

The mosaic was there, just underneath the surface. It would take me forever to expose it without the right tools. Luckily, a storm outside began rolling in, I was locked in Room 3 for the foreseeable future with nothing better to do, except chip away at a wall to quiet my raging mind.

A meow startled me. I whirled around to find Bacon sitting up, eyes squinting.

"How did you get in here?" Demanding info from a cat—a new low.

I knew for a fact he'd been outside before Luis had slipped and fallen in the pool. I knew for a fact he hadn't followed me in here. He wasn't a ghost. He was real and solid and made of cat parts, so how…the hell…did he get in this room? I had no idea but I did know one thing—if he'd found his way in, that meant there was a way out.

EIGHTEEN

The good news was that there seemed to be a draft coming from the hole in the wall. The hole behind the safe where I'd found my grandmother's photos. The space probably led deep enough that Bacon used it as a passageway to get through the property, but the bad news was that I wasn't cat-sized and would never fit.

More bad news…

If I couldn't find the tools to help me chip away at this wall, then I'd definitely never be able to bust open Bacon's hidden space. I stood in the middle of the room, taking stock, trying to figure out what to do. It all felt so helpless, and my doom-and-gloom brain wasn't helping. Thoughts attacked me—I would die in here, this was my own fault, I was here because of how stupid I was…

"Stop, Ellie, stop!" I chastised myself.

Outside, the wind picked up, wooing and whistling all over the house. Loose debris flying around scraped the walls and windows, while I tried not to think about how much worse it would soon get.

I took inventory of what I had—not much.

But there *was* a bed, and the bed had a metal frame. With the screw Luis and I had used earlier before he was so freakishly killed by happenstance, I worked to unscrew the bolts holding the frame together. I didn't need to take the whole thing apart, only one long side and that meant five screws, two on either end, and one in the middle bolting down the crossbar.

Just loosening those screws took up two or so hours, and in that time, I cut my fingers into bloody shreds. During that time, what little light filtered into the boarded up house lessened even more, and I turned on the lamp to keep from being in total darkness. Whatever I meant to accomplish, I had little time to do it before the power eventually cut. Pulling out the last screw from the bed frame, I pulled apart the metal piece and held it up.

Like a spear or javelin, it felt weighty and solid in my hand. I wanted to wield it, smash everything in the room—smash Syndia's face if I had to. It was my only weapon in case I needed it. For the moment, however, I rammed it against the wall, over and over again, until the plaster began falling off in chunks, exposing more and more of the colored tile.

As I chipped away, building a rhythm, I fell into a trance.

With little light, all this repetitive motion served to put me in an altered state of mind. Soon, I was hearing voices, as I chipped away plaster. I heard my grandfather's deep voice talking to my grandmother. I heard her laughing and felt him taking her into his arms and kissing her.

Today's the day, Leanne, I can feel it.

Don't go, I heard her thoughts. *Something terrible's going to happen.*

"What happened, guys? Tell me what happened," I muttered.

Light blue tiles turned to medium blues and dark blues. Sometimes, I'd expose a green tile, sometimes white. Sometimes I'd accidentally chip a piece of tile and curse out loud for having damaged it. Eventually, at what might've been one or two in the morning, the entire Florida Straits came into view on the wall. The keys were represented by their own green tiles, and Cuba was comprised of a large dark and light green shape that resembled a hammerhead shark.

Why would my grandfather make his map this way? Why not draw or paint it on paper or canvas like a normal person would? Why make a map at all? Wasn't the information safer locked away in his head?

To manifest…

It was Maya's voice, echoing from a faraway place.

"Manifest? What does that mean?" I asked but got no response. Only more whistling wind and shaking shutters. A darkness seeped into the room that enveloped me like tangled arms of energy. "I hate ghosts," I muttered.

On the map, Northwest of Havana, between Key West and Cuba, was a swirl of white mosaic tiles. It almost looked like a little hurricane right in the middle, but I understood the symbolism. X marked the spot. Bill hadn't made it obvious with a big red X like in pirate movies, but the swirl got tighter with smaller, tinier bits of glass tile, and I knew this was his sweet spot.

The location of the Spanish galleon.

Grabbing my makeup brushes from my suitcase, I used the

blush brush to clean away plaster dust from the tiles. The piece was extraordinarily beautiful, and when I put the little table next to it, I saw what he'd done. The table was a closer version of the swirl design, like someone had zoomed in by pinching out on their phone. Watery swirls, fish, and sharks appeared in on the table version. Details, closer-up.

I hadn't exposed the entire map, only enough to admire it in the feeble lamplight. *Why, though?* I kept wondering. All I could imagine was that my grandfather had been a visual person, an artist at heart. And like many of my middle graders in math, he had to create art with his visions in order to see concepts better in his mind. Maybe this wall mosaic had been my grandfather's vision board, a place to see his dreams clearly.

It humbled me to know that Bill Drudge had stood here some seventy years before and created this masterpiece right in this very room. It pained me to know that Nana couldn't take any of his art with her, that I had to stand here uncovering what time had so ruthlessly tried to erase.

"I'm sorry, Nana. You had to leave it all behind. That must've been so difficult for you." What an unfair start at life. I wished she was here so I could hug her and tell her how much I admired her for starting over with my mother, for living out the best remainder of her life as she could. Because of her, I'd had a good life.

The more I brushed away the debris, the more I could see what was underneath the tile. There was no need to chip the pieces away, since they were made of glass and clear. Right above the tight swirl was faint handwriting on the wall. A set of numbers—N 23° 54' 27", W 83° 37' 54".

Latitude and longitude.

Coordinates?

Coordinates my grandfather felt would lead him to the location of the Spanish galleon. How did one figure that out in 1951 anyway? With no internet, no computer models to help him? That took serious research skills. Even the *Titanic* hadn't been found for another thirty years.

Quickly, I reached for the photos I'd found earlier and shuffled through them. One was a close-up of this exact spot. Who took these pics? A pang of anxiety hit my chest, and I closed my eyes to try and see past the aggravation building in my body, see the answers in my mind.

Open up and access my intuition?

Okay, Mayai, you win.

I'd try it again. I envisioned it, the very moment in time these photos were taken, but it wasn't Bill or Nana who'd taken them. It'd been McCardle's wife—Susannah. Had she broken into their house and taken these photos while they weren't home? Or had Nana invited her in for a margarita…meanwhile, she'd snuck in to take a photo of their private bedroom wall?

I hated the uncertainty.

Bill never saw the gold, because he was cut off at the pass. The next door neighbors had the coordinates to his location. Good ol' Captain McCardle had gone off course to find the spot the same night my grandfather had headed out. Intercepted at sea.

Pirates abounded in 1951. And one of them had been Robert McCardle.

Holy shit, this hadn't just been a case of them finding my grandfather on the way back from his expedition and stealing his gold. No, this had been pre-meditated from the very beginning. They met him at the site.

N 23° 54' 27", W 83° 37' 54"

"Bastard," I mumbled.

I shuddered when the windows began wheezing, gasping for breath. Maybe I shouldn't speak to anger the spirits, considering I was trapped inside a room at the mercy of nature and the paranormal world.

But why the hatred? All because my grandmother had been different? Because she'd been a saucy woman unlike the pious ones who'd lined up to receive communion every Sunday? Because she thought for herself? Did they really want them out of the neighborhood that badly?

It was unfair and infuriating. I sat and admired the mosaic a long time, taking it in, imagining myself in their time. As the only connection to my grandfather, the piece of art felt like a responsibility for me to absorb. I hated the fact that I couldn't take a photo of it now that Psycho Bitch had smashed it with her hammer of deceit.

Outside, the storm had finally arrived.

All my life, I'd thought hurricanes were like tornadoes, beginning forcefully and suddenly. Instead, they crept in slowly, beginning as sunny days, then raining just a little, then a little more until the winds were howling over the roofs, and the planks of wood stuck to the windows rattled with fury. A slow deterioration.

Much like my sanity.

A flash of lightning illuminated the room for a bright moment. I saw the shape of a human shadow in the corner of the room. Someone was in here with me. I scanned the room, waiting for the next flash. On my suitcase, Bacon slept soundly curled up into a ball.

"How can you sleep through this?" I dropped my head against my knees, willing the spirits away. "Please, stop. Enough for one day."

There is nothing in here with me.

There are no ghosts.

It's all in your mind, Ellie.

In my heart, I knew it wasn't true, but I had to tell myself lies if I was going to make it through the night. I crawled into bed, now a mattress on the floor. I collapsed from sheer exhaustion. Each time the lightning flashed, I closed my eyes and imagined the storm going away, imagined the shadows moving to gang up on Syndia instead. But no matter what, I felt them nearby. Someone was haunting me.

"Leave me alone, leave me alone…" I chanted the mantra.

From the scraping, creaking noises outside, the sheer force of the hurricane's winds, and the house trembling with fury, I knew it'd be a while before I saw sunlight again. I may as well try to sleep through it. Perhaps in the morning, it will have passed and all this will have seemed like a dream.

A fucked-up, OCD-infested dream.

I flipped over and covered my head with the sheets like I had as a child when the visions attacked me. A moment later, something jumped up onto the bed, and I flinched, but it was only Bacon wanting warmth. I'd never been a cat person, but I could share the bed with him. After all, he'd led me to the photos and come back to keep me company.

Bacon is my lifeline, I thought.

Within seconds, I fell asleep and was aware of it. I could hear myself snoring and just didn't care to move or switch positions, I was so tired. I dreamed of Luis, trying desperately to pry open that shed door, slipping backwards and falling into the pool. I saw the moment he split his neck open in dreadful slow motion. I heard my own scream and told myself to imagine him as happy in heaven instead, if such a thing even existed.

Lucid, Mayai's voice slithered in.

Lucid dreaming, yes. I'm keenly aware of the changes in my psyche now that you've made me toss my medication into the ocean, Mayai. Thank you.

But in my dream, lucid or not, when Luis landed in the pool, he laughed and got back up. He chuckled and fixed his neck long enough to crawl out of the hole without his head snapping off completely. *It's here,* he said once he'd crawled out, shaken off the dirty leaves, pointing to the shed.

"What is?" I was scared to get near the walking, talking dead man.

The answers. He pointed to the lock, pulled the missing brass key from his pocket, and opened the shed's lock.

Wait. Did he have the key all along? Pulling the shed door back, he showed me the inside of the shed. The stains of caked blood on the floor, the flies laying maggots on the piles of flesh. The shed was floor-to-ceiling filled with dead bodies, and the freshest one on top…was me.

NINETEEN

The house roared like a freight train.

I awoke with a start to find the windows and walls shaking. If the house lifted and carried me into the sky right now, it would've been just as well. A exciting end to an otherwise boring life. Thank you, Key West.

Hurricanes weren't full of rain and lightning like I'd imagined most of my life. They were blasts of wind interrupted by even stronger blasts of wind. Gales piled upon more gales, a constant barrage I thought would never end. For hours, I'd been sleeping. For hours, I'd been hearing the atmospheric train running over the roof in my lucid dreams.

Luis, the key, the shed out in the back…

I couldn't check on any of it.

Stay inside…

Yes, I intended to. Thank you, spirits of the Ellieworld.

Bacon was gone. Probably headed back into his hiding spot. I'd hide there too if I was him. One of the articles I'd read last week mentioned how the safest spots during a hurricane were inside windowless framed rooms, like closets and bathrooms. If worse came to worst, I could hide in the bathroom and put this mattress over my head.

I would survive this.

But first, I had to survive my own mind.

Something sat on the bed with me. Nobody was there, but I could feel it, a female presence. I felt her anguish without having to see her and knew it was my grandmother. Still, I bristled, not liking the feeling of being with someone I couldn't see. In front of the bed appeared a woman. Angry lines, hair in curlers, a handkerchief tied around them. She spoke through the chain link fence.

I saw you posing in your little whore's outfit, Leanne. Through the window last night. Bob saw it too. You go around tempting the whole neighborhood husbands that way? Little tart.

Susannah, Robert's wife. My grandmother hated her, yet she couldn't stop her from harassing on a daily basis. I was pissed for Nana and wanted to tear those curlers out of her head and shove them down her throat.

You're going to pay for it, Susannah said, plucking weeds from the fence line that had crossed over from my grandparents' yard. She shook them at Nana. *Go to church and be saved, witch.* Then, she tossed the weeds back over, as they landed at my grandmother's feet.

The woman disappeared, leaving behind a cloud of disappointment on the bed. "You *were* better off leaving town. Sounds like nobody understood you here anyway."

Bill did. Bill understood me like no other.

When I blinked, it wasn't my grandmother on the bed with me but Mayai, turning to look at me over his shoulder. *Fight for her,* he said.

How could I?

I broke into tears. I was stuck in a cage, a storm raged on outside, and there was nobody left to help me. The only other person in the house was more insane in the brain than I'd ever imagined, a woman on the brink of losing it all. I'd been there too when I lost my boyfriend and my grandmother in the same night.

So had my grandmother.

So had Bill. So had my mother when she went through her divorce.

We'd all been on that brink before, where the world feels about to end but suddenly the clouds break and a silver lining appears. But not all of us went around with a hammer threatening to take others down with us. Syndia, though, was special. Lucky me.

The walls shook again, and for the first time since the storm started, I felt nervous and scared for my life. Luis had said that Key West had endured a lot of storms over the years and came out just fine, but no house on the island had looked as dilapidated as this one. I felt the structure was about to be compromised at any moment.

Maybe I'd overlooked this. Maybe I'd trusted my instincts too deeply, and now it was too late.

I laid myself down and tried going back to sleep, listening to the winds pummel the house, debris flying all around, windows getting hit with loose projectiles. Something slammed into the wall behind me, and I flinched.

"God, Universe, whatever you are…I promise to believe if you just get me through this bullshit," I bargained with anyone who would listen. Reaching over, I tried clicking on the light only to find that the power was out. Must've gone out a while ago as I slept.

The room filled with overpowering energies, like a surge of electricity before a lightning hit.

Just then, the corner of the ceiling lifted, nails ripped out of wooden beams.

"Oh, hell no." Please tell me the roof wasn't about to come off. I climbed off the bed and dragged the mattress into the bathroom alcove where the sinks were, taking the metal bar with me just in case. It was my only implement. Crouching under the mattress, I pulled it over my head and thought about my life. About everything it had meant and everything I still wanted to do.

Nails squeaked, wood creaked until suddenly, there was a pop and the room filled with 140 mph winds. I screamed and held the mattress close to me, using its handle, but the walls around me weren't close enough to hold it in place, and it yanked out of my hands and through the ceiling. I watched the roof yawn open some more, as the palms outside bent to the wind's will.

"Christ…" Using the metal bar, I slammed against the cat's hideaway opening over and over until big chunks of wall came loose. Enough that I could stick my hands inside and rip off big pieces of drywall. Once I'd exposed a big enough hole, I stepped over the safe bolted into the floor and crawled on my hands and knees, ignoring the spider webs and critters scattering at my presence.

Inside the space, I felt safer with all the internal structure and beams around me, but the opening I'd carved still gave the wind a place to blow into. That greedy wind. Didn't it have enough places to invade? The ghosts were nothing now, merely guides and wisps of the past.

I thought of my mother, of all the times she'd sat on my bed and felt my forehead for fevers. Of all the times she'd driven to school to bring me projects I'd forgotten, lunchboxes left behind. All she'd wanted was for me to come home, but I'd been too stubborn.

Now here I was with Mother Nature banging on my door and a crazy woman in another room who didn't care if I lived or died. Who would just as soon leave me outside to rot in a dry concrete pool and threaten anyone who tried getting help for me.

Somewhere outside this wall space, in Room 3, another piece of roof ripped off. I heard it tear then fly away. The only good thing was that its absence let in the tiniest bit of light. Even during a hurricane, sunrise still came. The sun stopped for nobody, no storm. No rays of sunshine invaded, but a dull, cloudy grayness gave me enough light to see that I wasn't just in a wall space but a passageway. And not just big enough for a cat but for a crawling human.

All around me…were things.

Books, boxes, papers bound with rubber bands, drawings of maps, more photos of my grandmother in the nude, plus a big leather book. Using my toe to reach it, I dragged it toward me and opened it. Her handwriting filled the moldy pages. Drawings of herbs, descriptions of their medicinal properties, the garden she was planning to create, a moon sculpture she wanted right in the middle. Next to it, a postscript explaining how Bill had made it for her from leftover coquina in the neighbor's junk pile, how marvelous the universe was that when she asked for something, it gave it to her.

Pages and pages filled with gratitude about her life, her wonderful husband, the beautiful little girl they'd had in later pages. It'd all been here for seventy years. A secret storage room my grandfather had built to keep prying and judgmental eyes away from his family. He'd thought of it all—the location of a Spanish galleon, how to keep his wife happy, how to protect her.

It was a shame he couldn't protect himself.

For the next several hours, as the storm destroyed the world outside, I sat cross-legged in this private space, surrounded by the energies of the people I loved. *Thank you, Bacon.* Thank you, roof ripping off, or I'd never have dug deeper.

My grandmother's book was called a "book of shadows," and it contained everything she knew at the time—about herbs, yes, but also about crystals, their uses, and their properties. Apparently, she put out rose quartz, carnelian, and red jasper every time she wanted to make love with my grandfather and she gave him black obsidian to carry in his pocket each time he went out to sea.

In the last pages, I felt her anger at how some of these things hadn't worked or he'd still be here with her today. She questioned her abilities and started doubting what she had always thought to be true. And then she said something that made me stop—would her daughter have the same abilities? Would she even want to teach them to her for fear of the same persecution? She wasn't sure. If Mariel showed an interest in the occult, she'd warn her of the dark sides. If she was inclined to learn the ways, then she'd assist her, but she wouldn't insist upon it. She'd let her be who she was, witch-inclined or not. Same for any grandchildren she'd have in the future.

Witch-inclined.

My grandmother really had considered herself a witch?

What did that make *me?*

With all my hallucinations and abilities to perceive energy around me, did it run in me as well? "Nana, am I one, too?" I asked aloud. If that was the case, what was I doing here inside a wall space hiding from a storm? I felt so filled with pride, I wanted to walk outside and harness the gales, toss them back to sea, but I wasn't a sorceress, for crissake. A witch was something else.

It meant making things happen, knowing what others didn't know. It was a natural inclination that everyone had, but only a few bothered to cultivate it. Maybe I had that inclination stronger than others.

If Syndia thought I wasn't here to take what was hers, lurking around every corner with her skull-bashing hammer, she was sorely mistaken. Guess what, I *was* here to take it. I would find that treasure. Like Mayai had said, it was time and I would fight for what had been taken.

And the moment this storm was over, that was exactly what I intended to do.

TWENTY

Mara was massive. And relentless.

Every time I thought a break in the action might come, she'd pick up again. Worse, the passageway had begun to flood, thanks to the roof flying off out in the room, so my ass sat in two inches of water. Wet, but safer here than there.

I moved deeper into the tunnel, away from the rising water, and I brought all my family's stuff with me. How would I get all these things out safely? If the hurricane didn't destroy them, Syndia would. Lying on a crossbeam inches off the ground, I put Nana's book of shadows, the photos, and my grandfather's papers on top of my stomach to keep them dry. Then, I listened to the winds, as I clutched the maps tight.

The passageway became a cocoon of whirling psychic energy.

Not only was I stuck here during a strong storm, but these items held long-lost vibrations that spread through me even just touching them. Soon, the rhythm of the winds had rocked me into another trance, and two days without my meds, I'd inevitably see the spirits again.

This time, it was I who traveled to where they were. I was transported to the ocean, a place I'd never been but could see with intense detail as though I'd grown up with it my whole life. The calm waters glistened under the evening sun, and the salt stung my burned cheeks and stubbled face. My boat, *Mariel's Luck*, bobbed up and down on this gorgeous twilight, as the orange ball of fire began sinking to the west. There was still plenty of light left, and I didn't want to go home without my prize. I wasn't me in this dream but someone else—I was Bill Drudge, and this was the last day of my life.

Nuestra Señora del Pilar was the lost Spanish galleon I'd been looking for the last seven years. It'd been part of a fleet of ten others traveling from Havana to Spain, bringing back untold riches, when they were blown off course by a deadly hurricane. The treasure was down there. I had tracked it over years of research.

N 23° 54' 27", W 83° 37' 54"

Those were the coordinates to my destiny. Leanne hadn't asked me not to go, but I could feel her trepidation. She'd slipped me the larger piece of obsidian. Earlier that evening, she'd talked in her sleep, begged me not to leave. But today was the day, I'd told her. I could feel it. Well, that much was true, only the day for what, exactly? A good day to die?

We located the ship and began the dive around noon. After hours of diving, we discovered layers of spilled gold underneath the sand and knew we'd hit the mother lode, but when we surfaced, another ship had met up with ours and our lookout, Martin, was dead on the stern.

The Havana Ferry—McCardle's vessel—empty of passengers.

What the hell was it doing here?

When I climbed up into *Mariel's Luck*, there he was waiting for me. The smug look on his face I'd remember for years to come. Even in death, you remember faces, smells, notes to memorable pieces of music. I told him there weren't no way in hell I'd hand the gold over to him after my years of diligent research, but then he threatened my wife. Said he knew where we lived, laughed, then looked at his co-captain. "She'll have no problem opening them pretty legs to me," he'd said. He'd seen her do it many times before through the bedroom window.

Didn't I know that was one of the reasons Susannah hated her so much? It was my fault, he told me. Mine and Leanne's, for being so obnoxiously in love. It made him horny and his wife resentful because of how often we did it. I could thank Leanne for what was about to happen, he'd told me, because his wife couldn't wait to get rid of us.

I seethed with rage.

I wanted to kill him, but I knew this was the end of the line. After trying to reach for his long knife, my fishing spear and pistol nowhere to be seen—tossed overboard, most likely—there was no way I could win this. I handed him the one bag we'd managed to bring up from the depths. "Promise me you won't hurt her," I said.

"Promise," he said then he twisted my body around and slit my throat.

Everything after that happened quickly. I'd moved into another dimension and watched it all unfold underneath me, as though from a higher plane. I was dead. I knew I was, but no way would I be moving on. I had to see what these bastards did with my gold and my woman. I had to make sure that she stayed safe.

McCardle's co-captain took my body back to the island in a motorboat while my neighbor piloted the ferry back to port. The motorboat arrived right at our home off the inlet where only Susannah witnessed my body and helped the sailor place it inside an empty shed. All the while, I could smell Leanne's cooking filtering through the kitchen screen—shrimp in garlic sauce—hear my baby's laughter, my wife's humming, while I could do nothing to reach them.

No worse agony than that.

McCardle declared the bag of gold with officials, claimed someone had left it behind, then went back a week later to my coordinates to dig up the rest of the *Pilar's* treasures. He'd used photos taken of my map, photos he'd sent his wife to go in and capture at my own home while my wife had been grocery shopping.

The man had everything he needed to take all that was mine. It'd been my own fault for making my visions into art.

Days later, my flesh was dismembered on the dock and fed to the fish, while my bones were placed in a pile next to that machine McCardle's son-in-law had invested in. I was ground up, just yards away from my clueless wife and child. Ground up and mixed in with shells and turned into a porous cement to be used for a garden wall. The circular garden wall that would serve as a center hub for the McCardles when they purchased my home. Just a few months later, their property had doubled in size.

The bitch had planned it for a while.

But Ellie, I was only the first victim of many.

Faux coquina had worked so well to get rid of evidence that Robert and his son-in-law went into the "disposing-of" business with mobsters returning from Havana on the ferry. For a small fee of several hundred dollars, they'd take the bodies off the criminals' hands, run the motorboat back to La Concha and make Spam out of the dead. Some of their clients were pretty big—Lucky Luciano and Meyer Lansky.

They made enough cash, between the rest of the galleon's gold and the blood money off these mobsters, to buy my woman out of our home. They expanded and made their own Camelot, but it wasn't meant to be, Ellie. It wasn't meant to be, because your grandmother employed her unique gifts that day and swore as she left, swore that prosperity and happiness of this family would never thrive.

I heard her the moment she uttered the words.

I helped her carry that intent to the Universe, Ellie, and whatever my woman spoke in those grief-stricken moments came true. That was why I loved her—she was fierce, brave, true to herself. And to be fair, McCardle stuck to his word.

He never did hurt Leanne.

The garden circle is lined with the bones of countless victims. And if you're not careful, you'll end up there too. Wake up. Wake up and forget this foolishness. You have your answers. I have my wife back. You need nothing else.

Water droplets fell on my face from a rafter above, as his voice dropped away into a dreamlike abyss. I sat up and gasped, sucking in lungs full of air, as the passageway filled with more pulsating wind.

I'd dreamed about my grandfather, finder of the Spanish galleon, *Nuestra Señora del Pilar*. His voice had been clear in my soul. When he'd felt the sun on his cheeks, I'd felt its heat. When he'd experienced elation at pulling up a bag full of gold doubloons, I'd felt the same. And when his heart had stopped upon seeing what awaited him on the decks of his ship, I'd felt it too.

"But is there hidden treasure, Grandpa?" I asked.

I needed him to tell me everything. "Is there?"

Yes.

I gasped. "Where? Please tell me where they put it."

The earth will tell.

"What does that mean?"

Our connection had gone. Of course, it had. I would have to return to the sleeplike state to hear him again. I'd have to hold his maps close to me again. I'd have to recreate the same atmospheric conditions again.

He'd given me the answers I'd wanted. He'd given them to me as a full-blown episode of my brain disorder. I'd never see OCD the same way again. What an amazing gift, this channeling of otherworldly energy. He'd done it so I would move on. So I could forget this place and not spend another second here. But what he didn't understand was that I wouldn't go yet.

I wasn't finished, and yes, Grandpa, I was damned stubborn—ask my mom.

If I'd stepped into a house of horrors, and Syndia was the current head of family business, I had things to finish. For Grandpa. For Nana. For Mom, too. Open the shed. Expose the revulsions that had happened here. Give coquina samples to police for DNA testing.

I may have come to spread ashes, but that was almost a week ago.

Now that I knew the truth, I had a new mission—revenge.

TWENTY-ONE

I could alert police and have them begin an investigation into my grandparents' case. That would've been the sensible thing. Just walk out of here unscathed and present solid evidence. Problem was, all my evidence had come in the form of gut feelings, hallucinations, and dreams. They would lock me up in a mental institution before I'd ever see my grandfather's gold.

My other choice was to stay and fight. Bust apart the whole damn property like I'd done to this passageway. Clearly, Syndia hadn't wanted to go that far. She'd chosen to preserve the buildings as much as possible. That was understandable, since they were her livelihood, but what did I care?

When the wind finally seemed to slow down a bit, I ventured further down the passageway. Bacon had escaped through somewhere, I just had to find that exit. If the eye of the storm were going over us, then I should've been able to come out for air. But when I reached the end of the passage, I hit another wall.

"Where did you go, kitty?" I whispered.

As I'd left the area where the ripped roof had been, there was less light. I ran my hands along the walls and kept my ears open for any hints of where I was. Somewhere in the distance, a man was talking—a commercial, announcer's voice. A radio. Someone was listening to a battery-powered radio, and the weather man was explaining how the top recorded winds had been 150 mph at the eye wall, a Category 2 storm, and how the other half wasn't supposed to be as bad as the first. Only a few more hours to go, then they could assess the damage.

"Well, so far we're doing pretty good here," Syndia muttered. Her voice seemed to be coming from the dining room, and I guessed that this wall ended somewhere in the living room.

I jumped when suddenly, a section of the wall near the floor opened and Bacon popped through with a meow. A cat door. He'd stepped through an actual cat door I hadn't seen before with a plastic flap and everything. So this was how he navigated the walls. Unfortunately, I wouldn't be able to come out that cat door, especially not with Syndia standing there.

I decided to lie on my stomach to try and look through the cat door. This way, I could at least see what Syndia was up to and have an advantage over her.

"I think we're going to have some roof damage," she said, "but I can have that fixed as soon as I find the rest of the gold."

Who was she talking to? Nottie, I imagined.

Lifting the cat door ever so slightly, I peeped out and saw a lot of dust on the wooden floor, an area carpet and the side of the fireplace. Apparently, the cat door was in the corner of the living room. From here, I could also see all the plants the women had brought inside, a few legs of chairs, and Syndia's flip-flops stepping back and forth. She still held the hammer in her hand, letting it hang by her knee as she paced the floor.

"But I can't let you in on it, Nottie. I'm sorry but I can't," Syndia said. "I know some people would say I should share it with you. I mean, you are the one person who's stayed loyal to us when even my own sisters left me to fend for myself, but I can't. First of all, you're almost seventy. What would you do with that money? Second, how do I know you're not going to leave me in the dust and take off with the whole thing when I'm not looking, huh? How do I know you're not going to kill me?"

Syndia actually cackled, the first time I'd heard her really laugh, but what was more disturbing was that I couldn't hear Nottie's reply.

"I can't let that girl out either," Syndia added. "I knew she was after it the moment she stepped into this house. She only wants the truth. Pfft." She scoffed. "Yeah, okay." Dirty feet walked back and forth, stopping every so often so Syndia could presumably peek out through the boarded-up window's edges. "Then she brought that tour guide. That man had been here once before, if you remember. I should've taken him out when I had the chance. He's the worst out of all of them. You told him too much, and I nearly fired you there."

Taken him out?

The dead bodies in the shed came to mind, the ones from my dream with Luis. Was "taking them out" a regular thing for Syndia?

"I hated the way he knew so much. Why would you tell him about the ghosts and the machines?" Syndia asked. "Not smart,

Nottie. But you never were the brightest crayon in the box."

Bacon meowed at me and purred. I pet his head and made no qualms when his wet saliva cheek rubbed across my hand, as much as it drove me crazy. The radio turned down slightly, and I had the feeling Syndia was listening.

"Shh," I told the cat and held my breath.

"The good thing about having strangers in the house, though," Syndia added, "is that each one brings a different theory to the table. It's good to hear their view of things, as much as I hate having them here. Like the ghost guide. The ghost guide told a group of tourists once that there was a change in energy around the fountain. I don't know what that means, but maybe it's buried under there."

The gold buried under the fountain?

It would explain why McCardle's ghost had so vehemently protected that area yesterday. Though yesterday seemed like ages ago, at this point. The storm had dragged the hours out and made them seem so long.

"I just didn't want to dig there, because you know…my grandfather had it made for my grandmother. It'd be a shame to destroy it. God, why don't I just invite a metal-detecting crew to come in and find the damn thing then split it with them fifty-fifty?"

My stomach growled. It'd been almost two days since I'd eaten.

Syndia paused. Her feet paused. She took a few steps toward the cat door, while I shrank back. *Don't let her hear me in here.*

"Know what I mean, Nottie?"

Syndia would share the findings with a metal-detecting crew before she'd share it with her mother's faithful nurse? She crept closer to the fireplace. I held my breath and tried not to make a noise. A shadow came near the door and slowly, a woman's hand pushed its way in.

Syndia deposited something on the ground then pulled her hand back. The fleshy piece of meat she'd apparently given Bacon was bloody and made my stomach heave. Was that a tongue? It certainly looked like a human tongue.

Oh, God…

The bile in my stomach rose into my throat. What was more, Bacon actually sniffed it and licked the drops of blood, and for a moment, I changed my mind about the cat entirely and hated him with a passion, but then he turned his nose up and refused the fleshy lump.

I couldn't calm my heart anymore than I could stop my insides from recoiling. What was Syndia doing out there? I imagined a family where getting rid of human evidence was so prominent, such a way of life to them, it just didn't matter anymore what you did to anybody. There were no consequences when you got away with everything. No remorse when one could easily dispose of flesh in the inlet then grind the bones with your rock-pulping machine.

How sick were these people?

Murderers.

When she headed back to the dining room, I again pressed my eye against the crack in the cat door to see what else I could see. A metal bucket by one of the table's legs, and Syndia kept throwing something into it. Whatever it was sounded dull and fleshy. Then, I heard a thwack of something hitting the wooden table, and a hand, black and blue and indistinguishable, fell into the bucket.

I turned right around in the crawl space and threw up close to the ground. Great. Now she would hear me heaving, and I'd be next on her table. Was that Nottie's hand? What had that poor woman done to deserve this?

"Unfortunately, you heard that man mention the energy around the fountain, too, and that's why I had to yell at you. I'm so sorry." Another fleshy body part hit the bucket, and again, my stomach heaved. This time, I couldn't keep it quiet, and a gagging sound escaped my throat.

Bacon sniffed the vomit and recoiled like today was leftovers day at Camp La Concha. He pushed through the cat door and into the house in search of better fare.

Meanwhile, Syndia got down on her hands and knees, and I knew I was shit out of luck. Pushing her cheek close to the cat door so she could take a peek inside, I thought about punching her in the eye, but then she'd know for sure I was in here, and a shit show would ensue.

Apparently, she already knew because the next thing that happened was the butt end of the hammer smashed its way through the wall, opening up two gashes. Two slashes of light filtered in. I screamed and covered my mouth, but of course, that was a moot point.

"I know you're in there, little rat. Not taking what's mine. You hear? You'll die in there eventually." The hammer smashed through the wall again, but this time I took a chance and reached for it, clinging to it with my thumb and forefinger, pulling on it as hard as I could.

I'd pulled in the blunt side and was yanking on it with all my might, while Syndia pulled on the wooden handle with both hands. Our strengths were pretty even, but with my foot firmly pressed up against the wall, I was able to wrestle it away from her slippery, sweaty hands.

"Damn it," she said.

Great, I'd gotten her hammer. Not sure what I could do with a hammer, but at least I could go back to Room 3 and push nails out the opposite way with it. "You didn't have to go this far, Syndia," I told her. "We could've come to an agreement."

"There's nothing to agree on, Whitaker. Nobody takes what's ours. Whoever tries to becomes part of the masonry. It's that simple. This place is built on the souls of all who've trespassed here."

"Too bad I'm not a trespasser," I said, crawling back on my butt and hands. "I'm the one person who actually belongs here."

"Good, because you'll die here."

Grabbing something off the fireplace mantel, she pushed it into the crawl space and dumped it—a bottle of liquid onto the floor. I grabbed the notebook and papers and turned around to book it out of there. Then, striking a match, she tossed it inside and the whole puddle caught fire.

Searing heat engulfed the tunnel, and I bustled away on my hands and knees, avoiding flames which spread quickly, thanks to the airy draft coming from the hole in the wall. They licked at my feet and ignited the corners of my grandfather's papers.

I smacked them against the floor to put the fire out, but Syndia threw another bottle into the passageway and the whole thing began sizzling. Mosquito spray. She'd thrown a whole can of bug spray. Was there no end to this woman's insanity? As soon as the container began bubbling, I knew I only had seconds before it exploded.

I ran all the way to the end of the corridor, to the opening to Room 3 and jumped through with all the papers I could carry close to my chest. An explosion propelled me out and into the intense winds of Hurricane Mara. I gaped at the totally broken room. The roof had been completely torn off, only three walls left standing, leaving me with the challenge of holding onto something or risk being whisked away.

And another prospect entirely—no need for the hammer. I was free. Bad news—I had no shelter.

TWENTY-TWO

I was at the mercy of the elements.

The winds had died down, but they were still strong enough to flail me like a paper bag. Rain settled in, its windblown spiky drops piercing my face. Inside the naked shell of Room 3, I reached for a plastic bag that had blown in from somewhere and put my grandparents' papers and book of shadows in it. My nana's photos were in my purse, but I was sure that had blown out of the room hours ago.

Now I understood journalistic photos of hurricane victims after the storm, walking around, picking at the ground, looking for evidence of their lives in the strewn debris. I moved around the room, reaching for the next corner of the wall or armoire to hold onto. Opening a drawer to the armoire, I placed the plastic bag inside to protect it.

My next milestone would be the big center tree up ahead. If I could reach it without getting blown away, I could hold onto it. Sprinting towards it, I miscalculated the distance the wind would push me and ended up holding onto a palm tree instead. The palm tree was better, actually, not as wide a trunk and easier to wrap my arms around.

Standing outside during a hurricane, hugging a tree, I contemplated my existence. How had I ended up here? Stubbornness, that's how. I had finally gotten outdoors, where tropical storm force winds were the better option over being anywhere near that psycho bitch and her house fire. The smoke carried away quickly, and the flames were dying down, but there was no doubt that the west half of La Concha Inn, my grandparents' half, would sustain significant damage.

From here, I could keep an eye on the back door in case Syndia came outside for me. Now that she'd killed Nottie, there was nothing to stop her from killing me too. Right now, I had to make it over to Luis somehow. If my dream was right, and he had the missing key, I had to take that back. I couldn't risk anyone—Syndia, the police, whoever would find this mess after the storm—getting it. It might not have opened anything important, but it had been important enough to steal.

I reached for the next palm tree, but it was just out of arm's reach. Taking the hammer hanging from my shorts, I used the butt end to reach it and claw the tree to pull myself forward. I did this for several more trees until I'd reached the far corner of the McCardle's yard. The remaining plywood left over the pool had blown away and the empty hole had filled with blown branches and vegetation.

Luis wasn't there.

I had to ignore the deep red stains mixed with the greenery and get down there to look for him.

The pool's depth worried me. Once I reached the bottom, how would I get back up? Luckily, many fallen branches served as bulk on which I could get leverage. The winds were still cranking but the lower I went into the pool, the less I felt the effects due to the pool walls blocking it. My hair whipped around my face, making it difficult to see what I was doing. After tossing several branches aside, I finally uncovered the bottom.

Still no Luis.

"Come on, come on…" I searched everywhere for a body and also the cement for a fallen key. "Damn it." Where had he gone? It wasn't like his wound was one he could've recovered from. The man had definitely been dead.

Frustrated, I climbed the tangled mess of branches and fallen tree trunks back out of the pool and crawled to the nearest palm tree to hold on. Had that key been for the shed, like in my dream, then I didn't need it when I had a hammer. Running over to the shed, I used the wall to block the winds blowing from the opposite side. The shed was more like a small concrete building at the end of the seawall on a solid, concrete foundation. Filled with dead bodies or not, it'd be a good shelter.

The door had an old padlock, but it didn't seem like the kind that would use such an old key. With the hammer, I struck the padlock several times but it wouldn't break off. I put my body weight into it, a hard thing to do when I was being slapped around by winds. I struck at the padlock again, over and over again until the hinges on the bolt came loose, then pulled at the door until the wind caught it and slammed it open all by itself. The shed was empty. Well, not totally empty, but it wasn't piled high with dead bodies.

Sometimes, dreams were just dreams.

I stepped in, closed the door and locked it. Inside, the air was stagnant and musty while outside, the wind crooned and whistled all around. In the center of the building was a long six-foot metal table, like a commercial kitchen table for preparing food, with fish scales littering the floor. It was some kind of cleaning station for bringing back the catch of the day and gutting it before taking it into the house. A hose was coiled off to one side, confirming that this was used for cleaning.

Water still dripped slowly from its valves like it'd been used recently.

Honestly, I was relieved beyond belief. It'd been the first normal thing I'd seen all day, but the moment I closed my eyes and exhaled a sigh, a vision from another place and time flashed through my mind. A freshly dead body lied on the table. All his clothes removed in a heap on the floor. A woman in older clothing was gutting him from chest to groin, eviscerating him completely, removing his organs one by one and feeding them to the fish through a hole in the corner.

She paused and looked at me—Syndia.

I shook my head, gasping for air. "No, no, no…" Why? Why must my brain show me such things? Something in the corner caught my attention. A small closed door in the floor leading to the inlet below. When I removed the latch and tugged on it, the wind whipped up underneath it and slammed it open. Forcefully, I closed it back up.

My heart pounded. This was where they tossed the flesh of their victims—the skin, the meat, the insides—anything that turtles and fish and alligators might love. The hose washed away all blood and bodily fluids, and right there, along the edge of the room was a gutter. I crouched low to examine it. More fish scales but also traces of hair. Brown hair, long hair, silver hair. Still wet with bits of flesh still attached.

Recent, not old.

I felt the rush of my stomach coming up again, but I'd had nothing to eat and dry-heaved instead. This room had been used for de-boning, for cleaning and preparing bodies. Same as butcher shops had done with chickens and fish and livestock all across the world, except with victims over the last seventy years. Human victims.

When I blinked again, the dead man on the table turned his head to look at me with wide-open blue eyes. "Help me."

"No. Stop."

I couldn't stay here another minute. I didn't care if the wind was still going, I would've rather stayed outside than be locked in here with ghosts of a wretched past. It was then that I noticed the walls behind me covered in tools. Knives, some still dirty, some rusted, hand drills, and scoopers, the kind that looked like they were used to scrape the inside of a jack-o-lantern on Halloween.

A few spots were empty. Missing tools. Syndia was probably using them inside the house. Taking a last look at the room in case I had to answer questions during a homicide detective interview, I left the shed but not without going back in a second to pluck something off the wall—a large sharp boning knife.

A flash and the walls dripped with blood. I couldn't stomach anymore and shut my eyes against the vision.

I closed the door. I shoved the knife into my shorts' pocket, slicing through the back. The hammer went into the other pocket. Now all I had to do was get the hell out of here, report this house of violence to the police, and blow this shit wide open. Maybe even get back this house for my grandmother, so she could rest in peace.

So *I* could rest in peace.

But the wind had picked up again, and this time holding onto palm trees wasn't enough. My body got blown back and slammed into another tree, and while I was counting the stars in my head, a large piece of aluminum siding blew past, gashing my forehead. I cried out but held onto the tree. The reality of getting tossed around by a hurricane hit me hard.

I was going to die either way.

"Whitaker, where are you?" Syndia screamed into the wind. "You'll die out there."

She hadn't seen me lying here, but one scan across the property and she spotted me in the grass. Employing the same tree-hugging method, she jumped from palm to palm, bloody knife in her hand, pausing at one to gaze at me, checking to see if I were alive. She wore an apron covered in bloodstained handprints, and her wild hair flew all around her like Medusa.

"Come back inside," she said with a laugh then muttered, "before I lose you."

So she wasn't concerned for my safety; she merely didn't want to misplace my dead body in this tropical typhoon. Didn't want to miss the chance to add the Drudge granddaughter's bones to the family garden wall. Huh, Syndia?

"I can't move." I hoped the lie would get her closer to range. I crept my hand into my pocket, fingers at the ready.

"Good, that makes things easier for me," she said before charging at me.

I acted quickly, pulling out the knife and pointing its gleaming end at her, but the winds had shifted, knocking her off course. She landed on top of me. I felt no pain. She must've gotten her knife stuck somewhere behind me. My blade, however, penetrated her shoulder near the edge of her skin and pulled off a chunk of flesh. Howling in pain, she screamed obscenities, gray glassy eye bearing down on me.

For a moment, I almost felt like I'd seen her this way before—a long time ago. In one of my night terrors as a child. Her arched eyebrow and hateful gaze looking down at me in bed. In my dream, I had hid from her. Not anymore.

"You bitch," she growled.

"Right back atcha," I said, but then she got leverage and, despite Hurricane Mara, despite the flying trees and loose aluminum siding blowing over our heads, despite a million projectiles that could've stopped her, she managed to shove her bloody, dirty knife into my back.

TWENTY-THREE

Ellie, honey, you can let go.

It's alright.

Nana's voice.

I know you're doing this for me, but I'm happy. I'm back with Bill.

Thank you, love. Thank you for bringing me home. You can let go now. Come with us.

She wanted me to release myself of pain, to give into my fate.

Someone pulled me by the hair. Dragged me across a flooded yard. Water sloshed up my nose, sharp edges dug deeper into my wound, and that damn wind hadn't stopped yet. The storm. I was outside in the storm, and the pain in my back made me want to end it all.

But I dared not move.

She thought I was dying—Syndia. And maybe I was, which would explain why I faltered in and out of consciousness, why I couldn't move, even when my mind wanted to get up and fight. She dragged me all across the jagged property. Every so often, I'd crack open my eye and see her struggling, tugging me by both my feet. When she'd hit a rock or a pile of fallen leaves, she'd maneuver me around them. Why wouldn't she just take me back inside the house and wait for me to die there?

Because she was insane, that's why.

I had to stop trying to make sense of her actions—there were none. Syndia Duarte was an obsessed woman who'd lost it long ago, searching for her precious Holy Grail when there was no one left in life to share it with. A woman who'd lost touch with all reality and consequence. And I was about to become another pile of pebbles in her wall.

"I told you to leave, but no. Never tell me I didn't try, Whitaker." She huffed and heaved my body over more rocks and mini rivers that had formed during the storm. "I tried. I definitely tried to protect you. But you insisted on staying."

I groaned.

My fingers blindly felt around for my knife and hammer, but my pockets were empty. I had no defense. The best thing to do was keep pretending I was dead, keep hearing Nana's voice comforting me, telling me it was okay to die if dying was what I decided to do. But I wasn't ready. I still had too much I wanted to do.

A new career in something, I didn't know what yet.

Talk to my mother, ask her all the questions I didn't get to ask Nana, appreciate her.

Get married to someone maybe. Have kids of my own and never, ever tell them that their visions weren't real. I'd tell them their visions were evidence of their power, and the sooner they started learning how to harness it and use it, the better off they'd be. I'd wasted so much time being afraid of mine. The ghosts were awful but they couldn't hurt me.

This bitch, however, was a different story.

I knew where she was taking me—to the cutting machine. I saw them all—Bill, Nana, Robert, Susannah, even Mayai—spirits of the forest, all standing around the clusters of trees in different positions, watching the scene unfold.

Helplessly, they watched while Syndia finally got me over to the machine and threw my legs down in exhaustion. "Damn, you're heavy." She grunted then came the sound of two knives sharpening against each other.

Even if I could sit up now, I couldn't move. The sharp pain in my back made it difficult to breathe. Must've nicked my lung. My foot was lifted, and Syndia's thumb ran across the bones of my ankle. "Pretty feet, Whitaker." She laughed and fished around her pocket for something. "Ready to become cement?"

When she pulled the brass key out of her pocket, I almost shook my head. She'd taken it back herself? I moaned low and tried to push the radiating pain out of my body by imagining it not there.

You're healed. You're made of light.

The body is only a vessel.

Rise out of it, Ellie.

I'd heard my grandmother talk this way a few times over the years, but because I always waved it away as nonsense, she never pursued it. She simply assumed I was another skeptic and stopped banging me over the head with her spiritualism. Now I felt guilty that

I hadn't listened or learned from the master.

You're the master, she said.

You're stronger than I ever was.

The wind knocked the key out of Syndia's hand and she squatted to pick it back up. "I keep copies of this key everywhere. This one was in your bag. You must've found it in the same place as that hole in the wall."

I couldn't reply, but my eyes were completely open now, my gaze on the monstrous dinosaur of metal where I'd had that horrible vision of legs being snapped off like wishbones. She followed my gaze. "Oh, this machine? You're right. They don't make 'em like this anymore. Fact, they don't make them at all."

She pushed the key into a slot, pulled on a lever, and a deep motor turned on, its rumblings resonating over us. It was the kind of machine they made in old days, when levers cranked, other parts whirred, and engines were loud enough to blow your eardrums out. A thing so sturdy not even hurricane-force winds could move it across the yard. An old, dependable beast, functional even in this weather.

"Usually, we clean you guys out first," she yelled over the noise. "Grinding is messy. But I think I'd like pink coquina this time. When I see it in the wall, I'll know it was you. You know, special." She laughed and held onto the machine while a particularly strong gust of wind blew in from the inlet.

Pink coquina. Did she mean…?

Yeah, she did. She meant that my blood and flesh would mix in with the bones and shells and create a unique blend of concrete. That *would* look pretty, but I had bad news for Syndia—she wouldn't be getting her faux pink coquina today.

Maya's voice echoed through my soul—*fight.*

She'd be getting stubborn-ass Ellie.

"Alright, let's get this going," she said, reaching for a bag of sand. Or were they shells? Yes, crushed shells.

When the wind died down again, I kicked up suddenly, wedging my foot deep into her crotch. She cried out in pain, hands gripping my foot, but I managed to wrestle it free and kicked her again. This time in the chin, knocking her backwards. Her shoulder hit against the beastly machine, but the wind was making accuracy difficult, and I didn't get the result I'd hoped for. I tried sitting up, blinding white pain radiating throughout my back.

For the life of me, I couldn't take in a full breath of air. Syndia came at me then to try and finished what she'd started, but I held her at arms' length.

Life slowly seeped from my soul.

Her body pressed down on my trembling arms so hard, I thought my elbows would snap. "Why...won't...you...die?" she screamed.

My lower body, at this point, was stronger than my top, so I hoisted both my feet under her and leg-pressed her skinny ass off of me. Her body went flying and again, she smashed into the machine, but this time I got up and grabbed a hold of her neck. Pushing her head down toward the whirring blades, I made her sweat. Behind her, she kicked out like a five-year-old learning to swim.

"Stop..." she demanded. "Please."

Yeah, that was sweet, watching those beads of sweat pool up on her hairline like that. But the bad thing about having both my hands on her neck was that the rest of her body was free, and in one of her wild swings, she grabbed a hold of my loose hair and yanked on it.

"Ah!" I cried out, as she pulled harder until my long hair was feeding into the blades. I smelled the motor, the burnt parts that hadn't been turned on in a while, the gasoline, and her sweaty armpits covered in dark stubble, as she held me firmly against her hip and pushed me into the machine. "Fuck you. I won't..." I pushed backwards against her. "Die...like this!"

Syndia was strong, but she was over fifty, and the nice thing about being twenty-six years old was that it didn't matter how often you worked out, your body was still newer and ready to work harder than it had all these years. I didn't know where the energy came from, but a boost of adrenaline shot through me, and I managed to push that skinny bag of bones back about five feet.

Grunting, I grabbed the boning knife on the floor and ran with it. No clue where I was headed but right now, I just needed to get away from her. I got about halfway across the property when Syndia appeared out of the outer hallway through a tangle of trees.

"Don't go near that fountain," she said, pointing her hammer at me. "Don't you dare."

I faced her, legs apart, blade in hand, ready for whatever came next. Gesturing to the fountain behind me, I shrugged. "What fountain? This fountain? Why not, Syndia?"

She fumed, blood covering her teeth.

"Because the treasure's buried there? Of course the treasure's buried there. You know why?" I challenged her. "Because your murderer grandfather didn't care for anyone else to have it. Because my grandmother made sure of that through her curse."

"Shut up, Whitaker."

"That's the thing about murderers, they're only in it for themselves. I mean, who does that? Who hides the family money from the *rest* of the family? Oh, wait, your grandfather did. See? No love between him and your grandma. No trust either."

She stepped over a fallen bush to reach me, but I backed into the garden and stood in front of the fountain. "Shut up. Shut up right now," she growled.

"Whereas my grandfather made things way too easy to find. He loved his wife *so* much, he left her a goddamn mosaic mural as big as an entire room proclaiming where she could find the gold in the event of his death. See, *their* gold."

"Leanne was a village whore and everybody knew it," she spat. "Don't try to kid yourself. She didn't love your grandfather—she loved everybody." She laughed, but I knew that wasn't true.

"That's the lie they told themselves to make it okay. To absolve themselves for their sins. Murdering the neighbor, covering the evidence up with that shed over there and with homemade cement, accepting cash once the mob found out about the family business." I stood behind the fountain and held onto it.

The winds picked up again. There was no end to this nightmare.

Behind me, the canopy of the massive banyan tree swayed. Palm trees were perfect for storms with their wispy tops and thin bodies, but banyans? I worried about its roots so close to the surface, about its top-heavy crown. It was a sail-laden galleon catching too much wind, waiting to be tipped over.

Another gust bore down on the island, as I held fast to the fountain while Syndia held onto a lamp post. There was no point in speaking now. She wouldn't hear me anyway. The wind screamed all around, and I closed my eyes. This was a good time to feel its power, the raw energy of Mother Nature herself. It fed me, healed me, and became one with me.

I accepted what I'd always known to be true—all my life, pills had been used to suppress me. That might've been my mother's fault but she hadn't known better. It wasn't meant to be then. Now was different. Now I had control. I knew I couldn't kill this woman the same way she was looking to kill me, but that didn't mean I couldn't turn it around.

Send her own energy back her way.

"I'll tell you why everybody hated Nana," I whispered,

envisioning beautiful young Leanne in my mind. "Because she was the real deal. Didn't give a damn. Didn't care if she was different. Didn't care if the whole town saw her as weird. If being independent and in actual love with your husband, if loving sex was a sin, unlike half those bitches back then, meant she was a witch, then yeah—guilty. They got rid of her because they envied her."

The tree behind me began to groan.

I listened to its lament and told it the same thing Nana had told me—*you can let go now. It's time to die. But don't let it happen in vain. Exchange death for truth and life will go on.* I'd never talked to a tree before, but this wasn't any ordinary tree. This tree knew things. It had watched me from the moment I'd arrived. For seventy years, it had flourished on the life force of the souls who lay here. This tree had seen it all and kept quiet when it had desperately wanted to speak.

This tree would speak now.

One last gust of wind rocked the island, and the whole banyan lunged, groaning as it slowly toppled. Massive tangles of vines and twisted, ropy roots ripped out of the ground, lifting into the air like the stern end of a sinking ship, and I watched the stone wall made of bone mortar, Grandpa's moon sculpture, concrete foundation, the fountain and everything that had been built over its massive network of roots rise into the air with it.

I threw myself at the ground to keep from being in its way and crawled to the side, collapsing against a palm tree. Syndia's gaze was fixated, horrified on the destruction of her beloved homestead.

For a moment, the roots and its stone ornaments all hung suspended against the deepening evening sky like a demented Christmas tree. Then, growing heavier under its own weight, the stone particles collapsed, breaking apart and tumbling to the ground in massive, rocky chunks. Broken dreams. Broken souls. The fallen tree's giant roots exposed dark fertile soil, and something else—bags.

Canvas bags.

Dozens of them. Many had split open, their sparkling contents raining down into the yawning pit of earth. Gold. Spanish gold. The stolen, bloody gold of Bill Drudge, the best boat captain who ever lived.

TWENTY-FOUR

I'd said it several times.

I could still hear my voice inside my head—*I didn't come for the treasure. I came for the truth.* And that still held true. But there was no way I could let this woman take what my grandfather had worked so hard to achieve, his life's goal and dream, his gift to his family.

Not again.

I looked at Syndia's face and could see that she felt the same, that she hadn't worked so hard taking care of this rundown place only to let some newcomer take what was hers. But I wasn't a newcomer. Inside my soul inhabited every single one of my spirit guides—Mayai, my grandfather, Nana, even my mother lived a little bit inside of me—just like I would live a little bit inside my future children.

I'd hoped that Syndia would rush the gold, start picking up the pieces like candy on the ground after bashing a piñata. That way, I could use her distraction as a moment to my advantage. But instead she let out a scream to rival the freight train winds of Mara and came running at me. It was me or her for the gold, and only one of us would get it.

The survivor of the fight, I knew.

I ran with the boning knife, jumping over knocked down trees, heading for the edge of the property. The coquina seawall was there, disappearing into the mangroves. On the dock below, a neighbor's fishing boat had been displaced by the storm and lied sideways capsized against the shore. Next to it were two more boats knocked over like dominoes.

I jumped down onto the dock and sloshed through high water covering it to reach the boat. If I could push off just enough, I'd wade out into the inlet and Syndia wouldn't be able to reach me. Of course, it would be the old man and the sea at that point, but I would take my chances.

The hurricane winds had died down anyway having knocked down the banyan tree as its finale, and now only the rain remained. I could deal with rain. Rain wouldn't suck me into the sky.

I tried pushing the boat out, but it was heavier than I could've ever imagined. I jumped in anyway, hoping to find a gun or something I could use to stop Syndia, but she had already climbed in after me, limping as she dragged her dirty feet through the slick white fiberglass of the vessel.

"Go get your treasure," I called, sidestepping the cabin. "It's waiting for you."

"I will," she replied. "As soon as I don't have to worry about you anymore."

"That'll never happen. As long as you and I are both on this earth, you'll have to worry about me." Behind her, on the inside wall where I'd stepped aboard, was a fishing spear.

"That's why I'm going to fix that right now." She lunged at me over front glass of the wheelhouse and dug her claws into my upper arm.

With my blade, I jabbed against her hand, leaving her deep cut marks and a lot of pain, but she yanked back her hand, digging her nails into my skin as she pulled. I bit my lip to keep from crying out. I didn't want her thinking she had the upper hand in any way, shape, or form. Never in my life had I ever been in a physical fight, and now I'd been in a few all in one day.

She lunged at me again and knocked me off my feet onto my back. While she climbed on top of me and tried to smash my head in with her hammer, I held her wrists up in the air, keeping her hands at bay. Dropping her hammer on purpose, she let it fall, and I tried so hard to move in time, but it bashed my face.

I heard a distinctive crack. My field of vision turned deep purple with scattered yellow stars. I'd never felt pain like this in my life.

"I'm sorry." Her tone was sugary fake. "Did I break your nose?"

Once I'd regained my ability to see, I pushed her torso up high enough to let go of one hand and throw a punch into the middle of her face with the other. All in the same day, she'd tried lighting me on fire, stabbed me in the back, and pushed my head into a cutting/grinding machine.

My fist connected with her cheek.

Her hands flew to her face, and in that second, I rolled out from under her, running to the stern of the boat. My hands grasped the fishing spear, and while I tugged at it, trying to remove it from its bracket, Syndia yanked me down by my shirt. Between the unsteady rocking of the boat, the abating winds, and the rolling of the ocean waves, my feet slipped.

I rolled onto my stomach and reached for a loose life preserver floating around a foot of salt water. As I reached for it, she tugged at my kicking legs, and I swiveled to slap her along the side of her head with the preserver. It wasn't strong enough to do any damage, but it gave me a moment to run to the bow while she figured out what the hell hit her.

When she'd shaken it off and walked toward me again, I was ready. I stood, feet apart, blade in one hand. "Come at me, bitch."

Pausing in front of me, she said, "I've de-fleshed men twice your size, Whitaker. I've ground them up and laid bricks with their bones. You think you're going to do much with that thing? A lifetime, Whitaker. A lifetime of using that same blade in your hand."

"That's sick."

"You call it sick. I call it efficient. Those men were dead anyway. We just repurposed their bodies. It's no different than what we do with animals."

"Except it's murder and nothing to do with animals."

"Tomato, to-mah-to." She shrugged.

"Do me a favor and get rid of yourself, Syndia. The moment investigators see what you've done here, you'll be dead anyway."

"You first, sweetie pie. In fact, that blade works best if you cut your neck here…" She showed me the slanted angle at the base of the neck on the left side. "Blood drains right out. Less work for me. I'd appreciate it."

I stared at her, waiting for her next move. Slowly backing up. Slowly making my way to the spear again.

"You had the chance to leave. Your mommy told you to come home, but you Drudge women, you don't listen. We always have to take matters into our own hands."

"Fuck you."

She was quick when she lunged at me, catching me by the edge of my shirt again and pulling me toward her. Though I gripped at the fiberglass, it was slippery and she was able to heave a blow of her hammer. I ducked out of the way, just as the hammerhead smashed a window in the wheelhouse.

We wrestled, each trying to dislodge the tools from each other's hands, slipping and sliding all the way to the stern again, pushing and pulling, when she swiped her foot under me and knocked me onto my back. Damn it, I couldn't get a break, and worse, she'd swiped the boning knife from my hand and now straddled me, one knee on either side.

"You did it wrong," she said, pressing the point of the blade to my jugular. "It's here. Right here…"

This was it.

I'd done my best, but my best hadn't been good enough.

The spear went rolling against the inside wall of the boat and I imagined my mother at home, worried about me here in the epicenter of Hell. I imagined the little Big Wheel she'd given me when I was a kid, how I played with that thing for months, years. I remembered Nana when she could still walk, still cook and come over to make dinners for me while my mother finished up at her second job.

These women had worked their asses off for me, and all I could do in return was fail.

I'm sorry. I'm sorry…

A bead of sweat dropped from Syndia's forehead into my eye, burning my vision, and at that moment, something swift and instant froze my enemy's body right where she was. Her eyes widened, her body trembled, and thick blood poured from her mouth, dripping off her chin and into my mouth.

I spit the blood back into her face. What the hell?

Behind her, standing on the edge of the boat, holding the end of the fishing spear in her hand, pushing the sharp end through Syndia's neck, was Nottie. Who was not dead. Not in the least. She'd taken a bruising at some point, sure, but otherwise, she was very much alive. Saving my ass…

"I thought…" I couldn't form words. "I thought…"

Syndia rolled off my body and landed on her back like a harpooned starfish, as Nottie yanked the tip of the spear from her neck. I didn't know what in Jesus's name was going on, if I was the next to die, or what. But then, the old woman threw the spear on top of Syndia's chest for good measure and watched as the blood drained from her body.

Here we were, the maiden, the mother, and the crone from my grandmother's drawings in her book of shadows. And the crone had prevailed.

When Nottie sat her shaking body down on the floor of the boat, only then could I draw a breath. "I thought you were dead. I thought you were…" Shock prevented me from forming a coherent thought, but she got the point.

Wiping sweat from her face, she pointed at the cabin underneath the wheelhouse. "I wouldn't help her bring in that man from the pool. She threatened to kill me. She hit me with that hammer, so I run off."

"In the storm?"

"Yes. Been here since this morning."

"In this boat?"

"In this boat."

"But why…why…" I fumbled for words, drawing in my knees. "Why would you help me?"

"Miss Whitaker, for fifty years I worked for this family. Heard the stories. When I began caring for Miss Violet, her senile mind would forget itself and she'd tell me things she wasn't supposed to tell no one."

"What did she tell you?" I asked.

"What *didn't* she tell me." Nottie scoffed. "The more details I heard, the more I knew I was in danger just for knowing them, but I couldn't go. I needed the money." The rain started coming down in sheets just then, washing Syndia's blood like she was one of her fish down by the shed. The bite of salt in the air was strong but felt good. It felt like the storm was over.

"Did you know about their family business?"

"The front or the real one?"

"The real one," I replied.

"I never participated but I knew. They thought it was a secret with all their locked doors but I knew. I cleaned this damned place. Every damn day. The evidence was everywhere. I knew they was operating a house of cards. Only a matter of time before it came down. Your grandma cursed this land."

"So I heard."

"I heard it, too. I was there."

"I'm sorry, what?" I leaned my ear to her.

"With my own ears. I was there. It set off years of misfortune," Nottie said, looking off into the inlet. "But I'll always be grateful to her."

She was there and heard the words? Who was she? "You heard my grandmother?" I asked. "Why? How?"

"Because." She wiped the sweat from her forehead and ran her hand across her skirt. "I was eight years old the day Leanne Drudge left Key West. She couldn't fit her bicycle in the truck, so she gave it to me. It was blue. Nobody ever given me anything before." She looked dreamily at the overcast sky. "I never forgot that."

TWENTY-FIVE

Nottie Francis Parker never wanted to be a nurse.

She'd dreamed of moving to New York City and becoming a ballet dancer. She'd dreamed of singing like Ella Fitzgerald to presidents and dignitaries all over the world and of living in a mansion with great gas lanterns out front and palm trees as tall as a three-story buildings.

But life was tough in Key West for her parents, and she was often alone. While they worked, she played with sticks in the street and chased after her older brother who wanted nothing to do with her and everything to do with the girls from the next street over. She often stood in front of Leanne Drudge's house and stared at it, because it was pink like the inside of a conch shell. Because a baby lived there.

Because the house was pretty.

The thing about being a lonely child, however, was that you saw it all.

She'd witnessed how Mrs. McCardle had talked to Mrs. Drudge, saw the police officer the day he'd knocked on her door to give her the bad news, heard the crying coming from the open window, and smelled the burnt garlic and shrimp.

Sometimes, she'd see my grandmother dancing around in nothing but her birthday suit through those windows, late at night, while playing "catch me if you can" with Mr. Drudge. But it was a playful game between them, and he always kissed her at the end. That always made her smile, since her parents never played that way.

Nottie told me all this while sitting out by the dock a week after the storm hit. Six days after police and investigators tore this property apart after I'd showed them what the banyan tree had revealed. I never said I'd found the gold, because that would've been untrue. They'd told me, because it was legally on Syndia Duarte's property, it belonged to the family. But when they'd contacted Duarte's siblings without giving any details, other than to let them know their sister had died during the storm, nobody wanted anything to do with her.

They knew, Nottie told me.

The siblings knew the horrors and did right to stay far away.

They never wanted part of the curse or the family "business."

The historians came out of the woodwork, however. They all wanted to know. They wanted to meet the granddaughter of the famous boat captain who'd died offshore in 1951, who everyone was almost certain had been pirated by the Havana Ferryboat Captain who'd claimed to find gold that night, though nobody could prove anything. They knew, as Nana had known, that such a captain would never have had a boating accident.

Eight months after my back had healed, after the surgery to repair the tear in my lung, after a few court hearings, the gold rightfully became mine.

I knocked on the door to Nottie's new apartment to tell her I'd share it with her fifty-fifty. After all, she'd saved my life, but she wouldn't accept it. "I'll take enough to live comfortable, Miss Ellie. I'm seventy-five. A simple woman. Don't need to live in a mansion anymore."

And so she'd accepted twenty thousand.

Out of ten million.

A simple woman indeed.

That same day on the bench, she'd told me it'd been Luis's body lying on the dining table. The one I'd seen when trying to spy through the cat door inside the secret passageway. Syndia had gone out in the storm to get Luis and bring him inside before he got buried in debris and disaster relief workers found him. She'd planned on getting rid of his body before the storm was over, same as with my body, but I'd been too stubborn to die.

The inn was declared a total loss. Once the McCardle family signed away rights to it, it also went to the state, and there I was able to buy it on auction. But I couldn't live in it the way it was. Hell no. That place had been hell on earth for so many, but since the day Syndia was killed, there'd been a certain peace on the property.

I'd lingered a while, opening myself up to energy, activity, and spirits.

None to be found.

Though I'd replaced my Zoloft but still hadn't started taking it, the only dreams I'd had had been of my grandparents sharing a kiss out on the dock. Mayai had given me a knowing smile once or twice, but that was it.

No darkness, no evil, no curse.

This house, as from a famous movie line involving poltergeists, *is clean.*

I wasn't afraid to live there. But first I had it razed and rebuilt it over the next year and a half while living in a rented apartment off Duval. Every day I drove over to the new house to watch it be built. I made sure they incorporated my grandfather's mosaic mural right in the dining room as a featured piece, and mason workers were even able to rebuild the broken moon sculpture.

That would go in my garden. My herb garden I'd cultivated using Nana's instructions in her book of shadows. I wasn't sure what to do with them once they'd grown, but I'd learn. I'd made friends with a woman down at a new age shop in town, and she'd told me what all the medicinal properties of the herbs were, how to dry them, make mojo bags, infuse them with intention, even cook with them to bring out the best in my life.

Before this, I had no idea this lifestyle even existed. By some standards, I was considered an eclectic witch by the shop owner's spiritual friends, but mostly, I still felt like myself. Only a new and improved Ellie. A more powerful Ellie.

An Ellie now connected to her true self.

So connected, in fact, that I couldn't get enough information about the island's difficult past and sometimes filled in as ghost tour guide when Sunset Spooks Ghost Tours needed a substitute. I loved taking tourists around spooky Key West at night, telling them all about the weird former residents, the Calusa, the piles of bones, the shipwrecks, and the female ghosts who waited for their seafaring husbands to come home.

No longer the healthy skeptic, I knew Luis would've been proud of me.

The ghosts didn't bother me anymore. They were simply a part of the landscape, their voices in tune with my daily rhythm. I found, if I asked them politely to stay away when I wasn't in the mood to deal with them, that they would.

Key West had become my new home. With its tourists, its history, its roosters running rampant everywhere, its chocolate-covered coconut patties, its key lime pie, its weird but rich, laidback culture, I knew I could live here my whole life. So when the house was finally finished, I didn't rent it out like I'd originally planned, I invited my mother to come down and live with me.

She politely refused, said she couldn't live in a house that'd been built over so much tragedy. She didn't quite get it when I explained that that tragedy had been necessary to release the curse, that now only peace, love, and light lived there.

But it was okay.

She would come to visit soon, she told me.

On the last day of construction, I turned on my gas lanterns, made homemade lemonade and sat out on the front porch on my brand new rocking chair, watching the sun go down in the distance.

Nottie had come to christen the home with me. We clinked glasses and she closed her eyes. "This good lemonade, Miss Ellie."

"I learned from the best." I smiled. Setting the glass of lemonade down on a certain little mosaic table between our two chairs, I stood and picked up the sign I'd commissioned downtown earlier this week. "Want to help me hang it?"

"Sure, I would."

Together, we held up the wooden sign while I hammered a single nail in a column, then carefully hung the wooden plaque over it. I stepped back to look at it. In the evening light with the lantern light casting a warm glow over the wood, the sign was perfect:

CASA DE LOS CAYOS
Est. 1923

The year my great-grandmother had purchased the original home.

Taking a few photos of it with my phone, I smiled, satisfied with the way it looked. Then, stepping back up the porch steps and sinking into the rocking chair, I picked my lemonade back up, sipping as we watched the cars roll by. Bacon purred up against my legs. I reached down to scratch his head. "I got nothin', buddy. Nothin'."

Life was perfect, idyllic, the way it'd been in Nana's tales.

In a way, I guess I'd always lived on this tropical island under the sun, even before my feet had ever touched down on it. My childhood dreams had shown me my future and what could be. My soul had always lived at *Casa de los Cayos*—first as Mayai, then as Nana, now as Ellie Whitaker.

It'd just been waiting to come home.

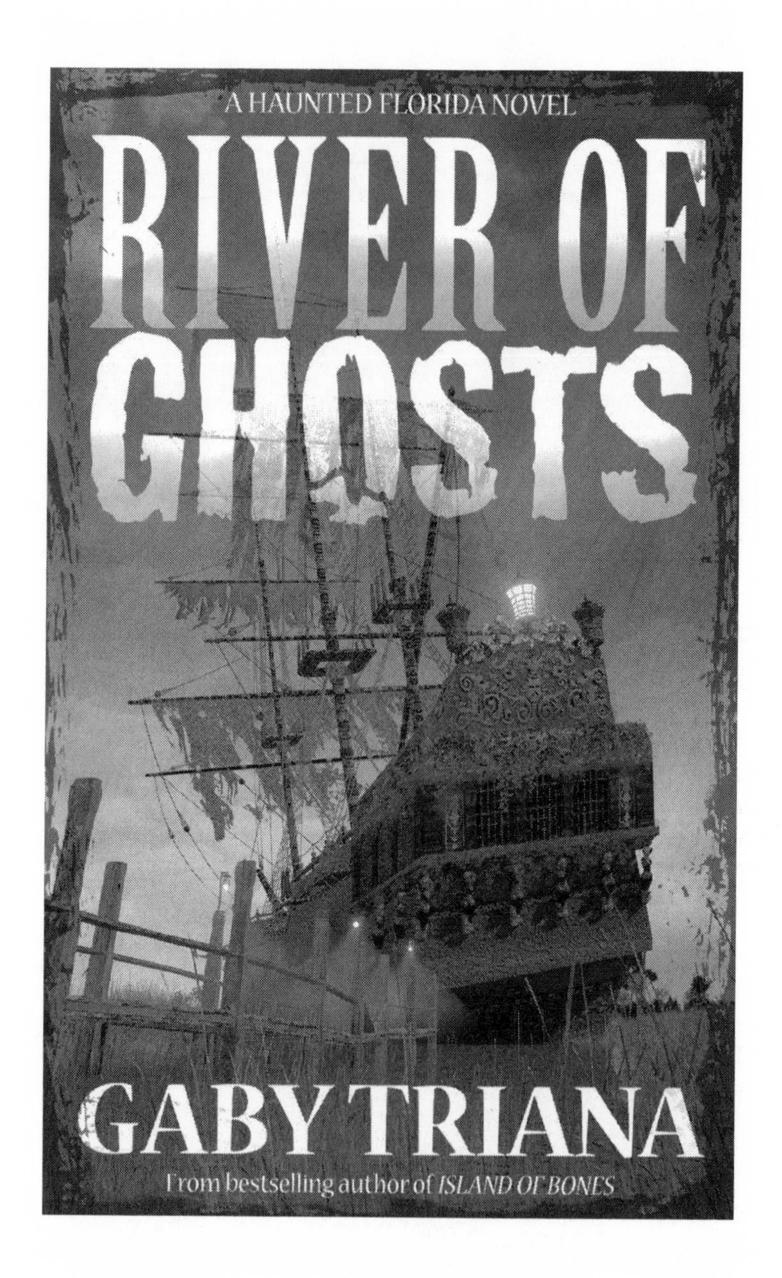
A HAUNTED FLORIDA NOVEL
RIVER OF GHOSTS
GABY TRIANA
From bestselling author of ISLAND OF BONES

ONE

1719

Through his warped spyglass, Captain Bellamy gazed at the silhouette against the setting sun and snorted with disgust. "*Córdoba*! She sails at us!"

"Take action, sir?" Newell asked.

As the sun sank toward tangerine waters, Bellamy gritted his teeth. He couldn't let the *Córdoba* get away a second time. "Prepare to intercept!"

"Aye, aye, Captain."

Bellamy lowered his spyglass to watch his crew, as the deck of the *Vanquish* bustled in preparation for battle.

"Seven bells!" The watch rang out 2-2-2-1.

"Sounding?" Newell called.

One frazzled seaman gathered rope and lifted the plummet. "By the mark of three."

"Shallows, sir," Newell said to Bellamy. "We have the keel, but the *Córdoba* is overloaded. Gold, most likely."

Bellamy peered through his spyglass again, gaze transfixed on the distant Spanish galleon. He pointed northward at the treacherous sandbars of the Floridian islands. "Then it is our duty to relieve them of their burden. We'll ground her there. Come about smartly."

"Aye, aye, Captain. Look sharp." Newell snapped his fingers at the coxswain whose thick arms turned the ship's wheel larboard, cutting *Vanquish*'s hull through the heaves of the shallow straits.

Bellamy dug his fingers into the bridge's rail and waited. Its splintered surface told of his ship's last engagement with *Córdoba* when she'd escaped by the skin of her teeth. "She gave us the slip last. To be certain, she'll not get away again."

He turned back and addressed his startled crew.

"Hear me! No quarter. Tonight, you men will earn your share of gold!"

Cheers erupted, as the lower deck burst into another frenzy of preparation, transferring powder from the dry magazines below and stacking cannonballs.

"Round-shot?" Newell asked the captain.

Bellamy sneered. "Bolas, my friend. Tear her apart enough to cease sail, not to spoil her treasures."

"Aye, Captain." Newell grinned in approval. "Chain-shot, it is!"

"One thousand yards!" the watch called.

Bellamy smacked the rails. "Boom us about. We'll careen her aground."

Córdoba's great sails overflowed with volumes of wind, but she could not alter her course in enough time to escape the *Vanquish*. Bellamy gazed patiently at the merchant vessel filled with treasure that would soon be his.

"Come to me, bilge rats. Come to this watery grave of eternal damnation." He laughed under his breath.

"Five-hundred!" the watch announced.

The captain's nerves sizzled like a lit fuse, as his point of view scanned back and forth along the enemy ship's rails.

Suddenly, he caught sight of an unmistakable shape—a young woman standing intrepidly at *Córdoba*'s bow in flowing green garb. A female aboard a merchant ship? *Córdoba*'s captain truly *did* wish to die an unlucky death. He was nearly asking for it.

The beautiful creature sent a signal. With chin up high and orange tendrils flailing around her face, she lifted two fingers in a rude gesture. Bellamy was taken aback. Damnation, once he eliminated the enemy crew, he would not—*could* not—entertain this woman aboard his ship as prisoner. Such would be bad luck for everyone.

"Very well, sassy wench, you'll be last to die," Bellamy mumbled.

"Two-hundred!"

"FIRE!" Bellamy's command ripped through the decks.

Reflexively, the gunners set their igniters to the cannon fuse, and the blasts rumbled across the decks. *Vanquish*'s eighteen-pound shot shattered *Córdoba*'s weakened sides. The ship wallowed like a sow in mud and lurched at every iron punch. Chain-shots burst from cannon muzzles twirling skyward.

Direct hit.

Each of *Córdoba*'s three masts buckled and snapped, her tattered sails billowing like death sheets over the ship's broken body.

More chain shots blasted from *Vanquish*'s formidable cannons. The engagement lasted but two minutes, a stark contrast to the hour of last encounter. Marksmen, high in the ship's rigging, eliminated most officers, even piercing the cannon ports, felling gunners and loaders. Sulfuric clouds transmuted into an ominous fog, plunging the Spanish ship into a suffocating curtain-fall.

Bellamy held a hand in the air to cease fire, for he was not a brutal man.

He waited to assess the damaged ship. He did not wish the enemy vessel sinking below the water, or all would be lost. Silence settled over the straits. The ringing in his assaulted ears lingered.

Suddenly, the fiery glow of the setting sun gave way to blazing tentacles of *Córdoba*'s powder magazines. The enemy crew abandoned their doomed ship, leaping into the water, flailing, screaming curses, begging for life, many impaling themselves on splintered debris in misguided efforts to avoid capture.

Bellamy smiled. "Scramble aboard and save what you can. Run out the plank!" he ordered, turning to the helm. "Where's my boatswain? Where the hellfire is Knox? Do not let that ship go down!"

Knox grimaced, a disheveled man in a blue and red jacket with stolen Commodore rank markings. He scrambled up the aft steps holding a shimmering sabre. "Here, Captain. Me and Smith…we was down below. We, eh, knew you'd want this sharp and handsome."

The captain took the sabre and spun it about in quick swings, testing its aptitude. Abruptly, a massive impact shook the *Vanquish*, sending several men tumbling to the deck as the captain hung onto the railing. "What the devil is it now?"

A black cloud rose starboard side. Embers fluttered like fireflies in a field of soot, the glow of the blaze spreading across the water's surface. From the charred remains of the *Córdoba*, crew members of the *Vanquish* worked diligently to save the merchant ship's cargo.

From his own lower deck, a seaman called up to Bellamy. "Sir! *Córdoba*'s captain set her magazines—and his self—ablaze. These are all who survived."

Shouts of anguish and rage filled the pungent air, as Bellamy glanced down to see fifteen Spanish crewmen, and that one blasted woman, staggering across his deck, chains and shackles weighing down their hands and feet.

"And the gold?" Bellamy asked.

"Has all sunken, Captain. But these are shallow waters, and—"

"I know that, fool!" Bellamy shouted.

Blasted cannons. He hadn't intended to rip them apart. Whose fault had it been, though, for giving *Vanquish* aggressive chase on their previous meeting? He would have to return at sunrise to salvage the sunken treasure. And here, he'd hoped to sail back to Port Royal tonight, victory under his plumed hat.

Bellamy pointed his sabre at the unlucky lot. "Line them up on the larboard rails, then put a league between us and that scow." He frowned at the crew, especially at the woman whose wet, ginger locks reflected the fire emanating off the waves. "You will pay for this trouble."

Blasted woman.

His quarter master and boatswain scrambled from the helm, lining the weary prisoners against the rails. All manners of odor spoiled the fresh ocean scent, from stale sweat of the damned crew, both his and his captives, to the sulfur of cannons.

Bellamy strolled the length of prisoners from his high position of the upper deck. "You gave us trouble once before," he told them. "And again tonight. Now look at the result. I assume it wasn't worth it?"

His heavy boots descended the bridge ladder, as his gaze followed the smoldering carcass of the Spanish galleon sinking into the straits. A bright flash washed over the *Vanquish*, and Bellamy flinched in preparation for the *Córdoba*'s final concussion.

Yes, they would return to retrieve the gold in the morning, though it would have been infinitely simpler to carry it ship-to-ship, rather than sacrifice his valuable crew to the bottom of the sea like shark food.

Bellamy paced before the sixteen fearful prisoners, but only one dared to stare into his gaze—the same wench who'd given him rude gesture aboard her master's ship. Gauging from her fine threads and features, he gathered she'd been the captain's wife. He paused, slipping the point of his sabre underneath her chin.

"*¿Quién eres, diablo*?" the woman asked.

"Pardon, madame, but I seem to have left my Spanish dictionary in my cabin." Bellamy laughed, examining her facial features. Proud nose, bright green eyes, lovely lips. A fine creature indeed. Shame he would have to dispose of her.

"Who are you to declare war upon *Córdoba de España*?" Her English was quite good to his surprise, and her accent sent a thrill through his loins.

Bellamy reached into his coat and held up an envelope sealed with red wax and royal impression. "By the word and seal of His Majesty King George the First, I hold this letter of marque."

He approached the woman and waved the envelope at her face.

"So *I* ask—who are *you*, woman, to query?" He put the letter back in his coat then lifted his sabre, its point shifting aside the hair obscuring her delicate face.

"*Mi nombre es* María Pilar Carmona, wife of Capitán Agustín Lara of *Córdoba*." She spoke in heaving breaths, her voice laced with heartbreak, eyes rimmed with tears. "Why would you lay waste our ship, my husband's life…why, *capitán*?"

"Well, if it pleases you…" Bellamy suppressed a smile. "I'll have his remains raised alongside the gold tomorrow morning."

The woman's eyebrows drew together. "Gold? *Córdoba* carries no gold or treasures of worth. Any precious cargo sank in the fog of México during the storm we encountered. We were simply making our way back home." She began cracking a laugh then held it back, as if realizing the mistake too late.

Bellamy's chest filled with ire at her mockery. He was a good captain who tried to be kind. After all, he'd saved most of the enemy crew, including the bad luck charm herself, had he not? And here she was, making a fool of him?

Without another thought, he brought down his sabre and sliced off the wench's ear, sending the fleshy appendage spattering onto his pristine deck. A crewman picked it up and tossed it overboard. The woman cried out in agony, pressing a pretty hand to the side of her head, as blood splashed across the faces of the men chained beside her.

Mockery! He would have known of this storm, as most wended their way west from the eastern reaches of the ocean. She spoke of a storm borne from curse.

Bellamy was many things—a fine captain, a kind man, and a brother when needed—but one thing he was not was tolerant of witchcraft.

"Do not play with me, sorceress. Your life is forfeit, worth less to me than a full spittoon." Bellamy jabbed his sabre between her breasts. He did not trust women, especially ones who cackled at his misfortune. To the prisoner beside her, he asked, "This be true? The gold was lost at sea?"

He moved his sabre to the man's neck.

The poor seaman shuddered as if caught in winter's blizzard. "*Sí, capitán.* It is gone. The storm, it bore down on us, and—" Bellamy plunged through his flesh, lacerating his neck, as dark blood sprayed across the witch's voluptuous figure.

She covered her face. "*¿Diós mío, pero por qué?*" she screamed.

Bellamy could not contain his patience any longer. First, *Córdoba* had given him heavy chase, then they'd returned to taunt him with no pleasures for the taking. Now, her crew mocked him.

"I condemn you all to die this night." He shook with rage and slapped the woman's cheek with his blade. "And you, sorceress, shall watch them, one by one, and be the last to die."

Her tears carved rivers through her blood-stained face, as emerald eyes burned with scorn. "In this case, you shall suffer before dawn," she said in a hateful tone. Had this woman no remorse for her actions? "As above, so below, and within…you shall suffer and never see the sun again."

"Quiet!" he shouted, enraged for losing his patience. But her curse echoed in his mind, and for a moment, Bellamy wondered if truth might exist in her words. He wasn't normally a superstitious man, but when it came to women…

He thought of tipping her chin up with his fingers but reconsidered the touch. "Strong words coming from reptile food. What be the time?" he called out.

"By the bell, a half-and-twenty." A crewman struck the bell 2-2-1.

"Take us to the corals of the bay," Bellamy ordered Newell.

"Aye, Captain."

The great ship cut starboard, due north, toward the mainland.

He turned back to the Spanish woman—the Red Witch, he would always remember her. "You have one bell to make peace with God before eternal slumber welcomes you."

"I know no God." She glared at him, as he turned back to his bridge to watch the spectacle unfold. *No God? A witch indeed.*

The half moon loomed in the twilit sky casting a bloody pall over the seas, as the *Vanquish* sailed into the shallows. Crows and gulls swooped in great arcs above the masts, vultures of the sea waiting to gorge, and Bellamy was in a generous mood to feed them.

Soon another bell rang out, and the captain readied to discharge the prisoner's sentence. He pointed to the seaman standing beside the slain prisoner. "You. You shall be first to walk. Go, then."

The prisoner spoke through his tears. "*Pero, señor, por favor…*"

Bellamy rolled his eyes. Must they always plead for their lives? Was it not better to walk silently and with dignity? "Keep the corpse chained for *dead* weight," he instructed his crew.

"HA!" Knox pulled the prisoner from the line and dragged him, attached to the dead seaman, to the gape where the wooden plank jutted over the sea. Knox pressed his cutlass to the shivering man's back as he shuffled him toward the edge. "Any last words?"

The man closed his eyes. "En el nombre del Padre, y del Hijo, y del Espíritu Santo…"

Knox pushed him off before he could finish his trinity prayer. A loud splash sounded below. Bellamy loved the commotion more than he cared to admit.

"Green stars approach!" Newell called, Bellamy's first mate's favorite expression for the hungry sparkle in a crocodiles' eyes. Tossing bodies overboard had attracted reptiles of the brackish waters before, thus they arrived quickly.

"Next!" Bellamy ordered.

One by one, he watched the lineup disappear punctuated by a Red Witch at the end of the line, one who would not weep, even as she awaited her fate. Nothing irritated him more than a woman who would not submit.

With shouts of protest, the men shuffled back on their heels, while Knox shoved them off the plank with a kick centered on their backs when they would not jump willingly.

The prisoners plunged toward the eager reptiles, happy for the rare delicacies. One by one, they ripped their flesh to pieces, much to the captain's delight. *See now, those are grateful creatures,* he thought.

Soon, the feeding frenzy had turned the orange waters deep purple. Fourteen became thirteen—became three, two, then one. Finally, as promised, the enemy captain's sorceress wife was the last to walk.

She stood still as a marble statue at the plank's edge, chin lifted high in resolute pride. Her blood-stained green dress wavered in the salty breeze, and for but one moment, the captain considered keeping her for himself to distract him from long nights.

But no—women aboard vessels, they be bad luck, and she had already proven this to be true. Rogue storms did not appear out of nowhere to sink loads of gold amid calm waters. She had been *Córdoba*'s downfall from the beginning—not the *Vanquish*—and he could not allow her to become his as well.

"Prepare to join your husband," Bellamy said, taking slow steps toward her. This fall he wished to watch from a better vantage point. "Any last words before becoming a croc's sweet ending course?"

The ginger wench stared at the horizon and quarter moon, a peaceful expression across her cheeks. She turned a rebellious gaze on him that filled him with momentary dread. "To all who sail this ship, may the waning moon's light condemn you to an eternity of grief and pain..."

Bloody hell? Was this blasted woman actually delivering a curse on his very deck?

"Get rid of her!" Bellamy shouted, a shiver of repressed fear running through his veins.

The woman went on, as Bellamy's crew paused in rapt attention. "…forever to wander, marooned on land between life and death. You will never know peace again. So mote it be…"

Seeing no one exterminating the wench, the captain lunged at her, determined to push her off himself, but the woman stepped off the plank and plunged into the seas on her own terms, irons dragging her to the sandy bottom. When one crocodile moved upon her then floated belly-up, the captain knew he was doomed.

Bellamy watched the rest of the crocs retreat and the woman's body sink, her last breath rising as bubbles to the surface before exploding like dying stars. As Moses' staff turned the Nile to blood, each of her bubbles ruptured into black tendrils spreading toward his ship.

Vanquish's men gasped and scattered to hide.

Bellamy stared into the water. "A demon be upon us..."

The poisoned mist whirled toward him and the waters receded, exposing a jagged seabed, as if the Devil himself had taken a deep breath before exhaling. Low on the horizon, a wide green mist tumbled toward them, bringing lightning and rumbling dark clouds.

"Rogue wave!" the watch shouted.

The seabed trembled. A folding wave of green water rose then raced towards them.

This was it…

"Lash yourselves!" Bellamy ordered. Never had he imagined waking upon calm waters this morning, that he would be condemned to a watery death by a wicked woman.

The crew scattered for rope and threw themselves against the rails. They tied the rope tightly and prayed to the last. Some men abandoned ship, but Bellamy would not leave the *Vanquish*. He lashed himself to the helm and held his arms wide at the inbound wave, challenging it to take him.

The wave struck mid-ship, lifted *Vanquish* high on its peak, tossing her inland where ravenous crocs, serpents, and God knew what other swamp creatures awaited to feast on them. Bellamy knew how to sail the ocean, not a river of grass. The very idea of wild lands frightened him.

The grasses would serve as a prison from which the ship would never escape.

Vanquish rolled from keel to deck, pushed ten leagues north of the bay deep into the marshland. Her masts and bulkheads crumpled and snapped like bones in a wolf's maw. All of Bellamy's crew drowned or were crushed, slashed to bits through the sawgrass and coquina crags.

As for the captain himself, the green mist rose and enveloped him, as he cast his last words into the night. "This be witch's work. Nigh be time to die."

TWO

Present Day

"And that, ladies and gentlemen, is the tale of the legendary pirate ship doomed to roam the Florida Everglades forever."

The setting sun cast its perfect palette of orange and purple shadows over the sawgrass seas, and my work day was done.

"I hope you've enjoyed my airboat tour of the River of Grass. Any questions?"

A small child of about seven raised his hand high in the air. "Is that a gator tooth on your necklace?"

I pinched the charm between my fingertips. "Yes, you like it?"

He nodded. "Is it from the crocodile that ate the people?"

"No," I laughed, leaning into the boy. "That was just a spooky story I told."

A spark of curiosity twinkled in his eyes. "But can we see the pirate ship?"

"You mean, does it still exist?" I asked. He must not have understood that my tale was a famous Everglades *legend.*

He nodded, his proud parents taking pics and videos behind him.

I crouched, looking at the boy straight in his dark brown eyes. "What's your name?"

"Nathan."

"Well, Nathan. They say that on dark nights when the moon is only a sliver, you can still see the doomed ship sailing along, searching for a way out, its ghostly crew trapped in a prison of watery grass."

"The River of Grass." The kid parroted the nickname I'd used throughout my tour. Most tourists mistakenly thought the Everglades were a stagnant swamp, but I always made sure to clarify that it was a wide, slow-moving river. It overflowed from Lake Okeechobee then headed south until it emptied into Florida Bay.

"You were paying attention. I like that." I smiled.

"Are there other ghosts out there?" Nathan's mouth parted ever so slightly, hesitation at his lips. His parents' enthusiasm dampened slightly.

I could have told him no. Or that my tribe didn't dabble in the paranormal so I wasn't sure, or that because of my culture and religion, I wasn't supposed to speak of such things. But I knew ghosts were real—I'd seen them.

I didn't want to lie to the boy. "Some people say there are," I answered carefully.

"Have *you* seen them?" he asked.

Everyone in the airboat, not just Nathan or his parents, watched me, hinged on my reply. Nineteen people stared at this thirty-one-year-old Miccosukee woman, and I knew what they wanted. They wanted thrill. Entertainment. It was why they had paid for my airboat ride, besides to learn about the *Kahayatle's* ecosystem. They wanted a good time, a story they could post to their Instagrams.

I nodded. "I have."

Maybe not the pirate ship, per se. But I'd seen spirits. My little brother's, for instance—the day he passed away—but that was one ghost tale I would never tell again. Not to anyone.

Nathan leaned back to sink into his mother's arms, as she whispered that it was just a story, nothing to worry about. A shadow of blame cast over her steely-eyed gaze at me.

I left it at that—didn't want to spook the child anymore than he already was. But the Everglades were most definitely filled with the spirits of many who'd refused to move on. Most nights when I sat outside, quietly meditating over our camp, I could feel them, see their silhouettes in my mind's eye. Lost souls crawling their way out of forgotten memories, begging to be acknowledged, wishing to walk again.

Pushing the thought from my mind, I navigated the airboat back to the Miccosukee Indian Village, our camp out on Tamiami Trail thirty miles west of Miami. The village was a roadside stop where people could get to know our culture, watch alligator wrestling, or buy colorful necklaces made by one of my tribe members. Tomorrow was Gale's turn to do airboat tours, while I'd sit with my grandmother to make beaded craft parrots and gators.

Day after day.

Sun up, sun down.

Make fry bread, beaded animals, put in hours at the daycare, give airboat rides to tourists. Sometimes my life felt like an endless cycle of rote existence, like a residual haunting caught in a replay.

I enjoyed my life—it wasn't that I didn't. But I was past thirty and not much had yet happened. Our family was traditional, so we wore traditional clothes, ate traditional foods, and lived in a traditional way, in our camp instead of in the city like many of my cousins who'd distanced themselves from the camp lifestyle. We weren't as hardcore as the traditional Miccosukee who refused to live on the reservation, though. To them, we were sell-outs.

It wasn't true.

All of us on the reservation were committed to preserving Miccosukee culture. As my uncle had told me a million times: with every passing year, our way of life was disappearing. It was up to us to maintain it. Forget the modern world and focus on our established ways, otherwise one day, all six hundred of us would become three hundred, and three hundred would become one hundred. Before we knew it, the Miccosukee Tribe of South Florida might become another extinct culture. Our blood would continue, the *Kahayatle* would continue, but our lifestyle would perish.

It made me sad to think, but it also left me longing for more.

What if I didn't want to live this way, day in, day out? What if I wanted to move to the city, buy a nice car or big house like many of my cousins? The casino down the road made enough so I wouldn't have to give airboat rides if I didn't want to, but that wasn't the point. The point of the shows, the tours, the festival every year after Christmas Day was to share our art, music, and activities with the world. So they wouldn't forget. So they'd know we were here and continued to be.

To leave our mark.

I did my part to keep things going, but every time my boat arrived back at the dock, and my tour group hopped out, and some of them handed me dollar tips like they did now, and they took their selfies and returned back to the parking lots…sometimes I wished I could go with them.

Get me out of this place, my heart would scream. *I want to see the world.*

I reminded myself that the grass was not greener on the other side. Lots of people with complicated lifestyles wished they could live in a simpler way like mine, telling spooky stories on the airboat, enjoying the sunshine, a life with few bills to pay, pointing out flora and fauna before returning to the village to discuss the day with family. I'd remind myself that life was good, even if I didn't wholeheartedly feel it.

Still, I wanted to feel it.

"*Gracias. Muy amable*," I told a woman who made her teen daughter give me a five-dollar bill. I had heard them speaking "Spanglish" during the tour. "Thank you. Thank you so much." The last family handed me two crumpled dollar bills for my two hours of carefully disseminated information.

Good thing I didn't depend on these tips. I cringed to think how others survived in the modern world on these meager earnings. "Drive safe. Careful with those speed bumps."

The white family turned their faces over the shoulders to giggle at my joke. On the tour, I'd mentioned moving speed bumps, otherwise known as alligators sunning in the middle of Highway 41.

"Thanks for the great tour. What was your name again?"

I turned around.

Two of my tour passengers—a man and a woman—stepped up to me. They were a couple, judging from the way the woman had her arm slinked through her boyfriend or husband's the entire tour like her life depended on him.

"I'm Avila Cypress," I said, shaking the man's hand.

"Pretty name." The woman tapped it into her phone.

She was fair-skinned with luxurious long black hair pulled into a thick ponytail. Her nails were painted a bright blue to match the hull of the boat, and her khaki shorts, green polo, and white visor told me she'd carefully planned this as her "Florida Adventure" outfit.

"Avila," she said. "I am going to write a review online of that presentation because it was just that wonderful. Thank you so much."

"Oh. I'm so glad you enjoyed it." I was relieved. I never knew how people would react to the airboat rides. Generally speaking, people found them to be either extremely interesting if they loved nature, or extremely boring. Hence why I added the spooky tales. Throw a little excitement in there.

"We did," the man said, a handsome black guy in his forties, I would guess. "In fact, we're familiar with all those legends and ghost tales you talked about. We heard about your tour and were hoping you'd mention Villegas House."

My ears burned.

A tremor shuddered in my chest.

How did they know about Villegas House? Very little was written about the dilapidated old depot out in Big Cypress that'd once belonged to a famous environmentalist. They must've read about it on that crappy *Deadly Florida* website that'd been circulating the internet a few years now, because as far as I knew, only locals knew about Villegas House, and God knew, it was taboo to even discuss it.

"Was it something we said?" The man cocked his head.

"Sorry." I blinked. "It's just, nobody ever mentions that house."

"Ah." The man reached into his pocket and handed me a twenty-dollar bill. "Well, we're Kane and Eve Parker. This is for today's tour, but we were hoping you'd be available to give us a private tour of Villegas House in your free time. It has a reputation for being haunted."

"Yes, I know. That's why I didn't mention it." And it would take a lot more than a twenty to get me to even consider going to that place.

"Why? It fits right in with your other ghost tales." Kane cocked an eyebrow. "Doesn't it?"

"No, it doesn't." I folded the twenty and slid it into my bag. "Villegas House is an actual place with actual history, not good history either. It's not a campfire tale, Mr. Parker. Besides being haunted, it's a rotting death trap. No one in their right minds would go there."

"Well, you see…that's just it." Kane looked at his wife and chuckled. "We're not in our right minds." He adjusted his baseball cap. A flashy Rolex told me that twenty-dollar bill was chump change to him. "We're interested in seeing it and were told you're the only one who knows where it is."

"Who told you that?" My eyebrows knit together.

It wasn't true. Many of us knew about it. We just never mentioned it.

"Sources." Kane smiled a row of perfect teeth.

The only person I knew, besides me, who had a fascination with Villegas House was John, our airboat tours manager, so much that he'd gotten in trouble with my uncle once for mentioning it to tourists. Miccosukee folks avoided the place like the plague. Not only were we traditional but also Christian, so venturing into a haunted, condemned house was not our idea of a good time.

And so, we stayed pretty much silent on the topic. But that didn't stop me from thinking about it. Or having nightmares about the place since I was a kid. In them, I'd see them lying all over the forest floor. *The bodies…*

"Hello?" Eve peered into my lost gaze.

I looked at them again. "I'm sorry. Nobody in my camp would ever set foot in that house, and nobody has gone out that way in years."

"Does anyone else, besides you, know where it is?" he asked.

"No," I lied.

Uncle Bob knew, John knew…I was pretty sure at least ten people in my camp knew. I only knew because of my dreams. In them, I'd follow the river upstream to Big Cypress, turn right into a dense cypress island, then end up smack in front of the old two-story, hand-built home.

"Maybe the Miami-Dade Police Department?" I added. "They might have records of the place. Because of what happened there."

"Something about murders?" Mr. Parker asked.

"I'm not at liberty to discuss it."

"Avila, we would so appreciate it if you could show us where it is," Eve said.

I shook my head. "You don't get it. The place is dangerous. It's falling apart. It's a huge liability. I could go on and on."

"We'll sign forms," Mr. Parker said. "Releasing you and the tribe. No worries there."

I sucked in an impatient breath. "It doesn't matter how interested you are in that house, it's bad news. Besides, it's in the middle of a delicate ecosystem that's been undisturbed for fifty years. You'd get eaten by mosquitoes, not to mention pythons who snack on alligators."

I employed all the monsters I could think of to keep them away.

"The spirits there aren't the happy kind either," I added. "They don't want to move on to the other side, they don't care how peaceful the Light is, and trust me, they don't believe in God."

A stare-down took place between the Parkers and me. Something told me they weren't going to back down. They were used to this sort of thing, and my words meant zero to them. One way or another, they would get their wish.

"Perfect. Exactly what we're looking for." His charming smile unnerved me, and I envied his determination. If only I had the courage to insist on the things I wanted the way Mr. Parker did. "Alright, I get it…"

I watched as he reached into his pocket and pulled out his wallet.

Hundred-dollar bills shuffled out. Two, then three, then five, then a few more, all in the palm of his hand. With a smooth motion, he folded the money between his fingers and held it up. Tangerine-tinted bills flashed in the light of the sunset. "Would a grand make it worth your time?"

Good Lord, this man.

"I wasn't quiet because I wanted money. I was quiet because I can't take you. End of story." Part of me hated the fact he was trying to tempt me with money and another part of me…hated myself for saying no.

The truth was, I itched to see Villegas House for myself. I could face it once and for all. Get it out of my system. Shelf that obsession away forever.

A thousand bucks right there in his hand, but that wasn't the possibility that buzzed in my ears. It was opportunity—to see something new, to finally meet the old creepy house, to hang with new people, for once. It didn't have to take long. All I had to do was airboat them out, show them the error of their ways, and call it a night. Show myself there was nothing to be scared of, then go home.

Speaking of home, it was getting dark out, and tonight was my turn to make dinner. "I appreciate the offer, but I can't. I'm headed home now. Thank you for the gratuity." I smiled and moved past them, bustling toward the rental shop before I changed my mind.

From the slow crunch of gravel, I could tell they were casually following me. "We're staying at the resort and casino," Eve called out. "We'll be here 'til Monday. If you change your mind, just give us a call."

Kane and Eve Parker were different from other families on the boat—more put-together, polished, rehearsed. They'd done this before.

I faced them. "Thank you both for the offer. But I can't take you. It wouldn't be right. I'd be in hot water with my tribe."

Mr. Parker's gaze connected with mine again, as though sending silent messages to try and alter my decision. His wife handed me a business card—ShadowBox Productions with an old-style television set for a logo.

"I think I've insulted you, Ms. Cypress." He reached into his wallet and pulled out more hundreds. "Two thousand. Your time and trouble is worth more than my original offer. I apologize."

I stared at the bills in his hand. They really wanted to see this house, didn't they?

THREE

Worse than staring at two thousand dollars was someone *watching* you stare at two thousand dollars. Kane and Eve Parker clearly didn't realize that I didn't need their financial assistance, but I may as well have been a hungry dog salivating over a nice, juicy steak from the way I stood there, staring at the money.

The casino profits gave us more than enough. We lived modestly and worked at the camp every day, but make no mistake—we were set for life. This wasn't about money. This was about me selling out to a different lifestyle, something my family would frown upon and would send our most traditional members into a moral tizzy.

"Only one day." Kane Parker raised an eyebrow.

The "what ifs" snuck into my mind again. What if I wanted a career? What if I didn't want to live this way anymore? Kane Parker may as well have been holding a ticket to freedom in his hand.

"Your call," he said. "We do a show on Netflix called *Haunted Southland.* Maybe you've heard of it?"

Haunted Southland? I watched it all the time. Was that where they were from?

The host was an older woman with a deep Southern accent named Sharon Roswell from Atlanta, Georgia. Their investigations were always at the coolest homes and cemeteries, and I always felt a pang of envy when they explored these beautiful locations. Their equipment was modern, and I appreciated the way they respected the spirit world. Most of the time. Sometimes, Sharon could push the envelope to try and get the spirits riled up.

I nodded. "I've watched a few episodes."

Parker's face lit up. "Yeah? Nice. Well, we've explored all the antebellum plantations, haunted gardens, and battlefields we're ever going to see, and this time, we were hoping to shoot a unique Southern location for once. Somewhere exotic. That was when one of our staff mentioned Villegas House in the Everglades."

Exotic was not the world I would have chosen to describe Villegas House's crumbling structure. "It *would* make a cool episode. Too bad I can't take you."

He smirked and withdrew the bills, pressing them back into his wallet. "It *is* too bad. We were hoping, if we liked you, maybe you'd like to join us on a few more shoots. Go on a few expeditions with us. Our ghost consultant is about to retire."

Ghost consultant.

They were scouting me to possibly hire me.

While it was nice that someone finally appreciated my talents and was willing to pay me for it, at the end of the day, being a "ghost consultant," if that was such a thing, wasn't who I was. Watching ghost shows in secret was who I was. I enjoyed learning about the paranormal from afar. And that was the way it had to be if I wanted to avoid dishonoring my family.

"I truly appreciate it, but hopefully you'll understand."

Mr. Parker and his wife exchanged quiet looks. "Then, we're sorry to have taken your time. Thank you so much for the tour. It was entertaining, definitely a pleasure." He tipped his hat and tacked on that wide smile again.

"The pleasure was mine. Thank you for visiting the Miccosukee Village."

That's it, Avila. Walk away. Your ancestors would be proud.

"Again, if you change your mind, we'll be at the hotel and casino a few more days," Mrs. Parker called out. "The number on the card is my direct line."

"Got it," I said, holding the card up in the air. I wondered if they would continue their hunt for a tour guide, or if they'd go home empty-handed now that I'd turned them down. My guess was they'd somehow make it to Villegas House anyway—they'd just find someone else to take them. Deep down, I hated that.

I trudged toward the rental office. Entering the chickee and heading toward John, I waited until the Parkers had driven off in their Rove Ranger before tossing their card in the trash bin and letting go of the biggest exhale ever.

"What's up?" John shuffled through a stack of envelopes. "More customers who think the sawgrass wasn't exciting?"

"Nah, they were fine," I replied. I wasn't about to share what had just happened with John in front of Charlie Cypress, eavesdropping from the back office. The man was good friends with the General Council's Assistant Chairman—a.k.a. my uncle. He would only tell me I'd done the right thing by turning them down, and I wasn't so sure.

John handed me my paycheck. "Have a good weekend, Avila. Say hello to your mom and *pooshe* for me."

"I will." I ripped open my envelope and stared at the meager earnings that were more a token than a salary. For a moment, I entertained the idea of waving down the Parkers' truck. I wanted to see the house that had haunted me my whole life, the crumbling structure I had dreamed about, the place of terrible stories I'd heard.

The location of my grandfather's death.

That was the main reason nobody spoke about Villegas House. The land was sacred, the final resting place of our head of council—Robert Cypress. Villegas House terrified me so deep in my bones, I never mentioned it for fear that it would come for me just by using its name.

But I didn't chase after Kane and Eve Parker.

I went back to the garbage bin and pulled out the ShadowBox business card. Then, I climbed into my truck and went home.

Just like I did—day in, day out.

After a shower, I went about preparing dinner, grilling bass, and setting the table. My mother looked up from her chair where she sat sewing a new patchwork skirt of blue, red, yellow, white and black. "Set the table for four, Avila."

"Uncle Bob?"

"Yes."

Inwardly, I groaned. Why did Uncle Bob have to come tonight of all nights? It was bad enough I was still reeling from having turned down a once-in-a-lifetime opportunity. I didn't need tradition shoved down my throat, too.

Pooshe strolled into the kitchen to help me flip the fish in the pan, as though I were a child incapable of doing it myself. In *elaponke*, she told me how her own mother used to prepare and cook deer, but never while on her monthly period, as it was considered a sacred act.

I listened politely but my thoughts wandered as she talked. I'd heard all these stories before. She recounted them so I could pass them on to my own kids one day, but that would never happen if I didn't get out of this place and meet someone.

Uncle Bob arrived right on time—as usual.

"*Eelechko*," my mother greeted.

"*Chehuntamo*." Uncle Bob sat at the table, ready for his meal, legs apart, elbows wide. "And there she is…" Something about the way he looked at me made me nervous. My stomach hurt without even knowing why. "Avila Cypress, wannabe ghost hunter."

"What do you mean?" My stomach sank. Why did he have to do this in front of my mother and grandmother?

"We received another complaint about your tour today." He chugged his water and set it down again.

"What?" I stared at him. "About what?"

"About the extra garbage you add to your tours. Spirits? Pirate ships? Avila, you're scaring children now, and people don't sign up for a haunted storytelling hour that has nothing to do with the Everglades. Take them out, show them alligators, tell our history, talk about genocide that must never happen again. Return home. End of story. Can't you do that?"

"I *do* do that," I muttered. Great, another Avila-does-everything-wrong dinner. I was thirty-one and still listening to this crap. "Look, I only add a few mysteries here and there to spice the tour up. People like it when I say the weird tales. It's not hurting anybody."

"Yes, it's hurting us," my mother chimed in. "It's not who we are. When people pay for an airboat ride, they're expecting animals, scenery, photos, history, Miccosukee traditions. Not ghosts."

Uncle Bob gave me a stern look. "That's right. We expect you to tell them about how life is changing. We can't drink the *Kahayatle's* water anymore. Crucial elements of our life are no longer possible. We're fighting to keep these traditions alive. We don't expect you to talk about plane crash victims."

"Flight 411 was an actual event. It's history," I countered. "Maybe not the history you want me to talk about, but history of the Everglades nonetheless. You want me to stop that too?"

"Avila…" My mother eyed me.

"Fine, I'm sorry."

I knew I sounded childlike, but this was only the second time someone had complained, which was unfair, because people complained about the airboat rides no matter what. *They're boring, we didn't see enough, I only saw one alligator…* At least my airboat rides were entertaining. Because of me, we had a 4.5 star rating on TripAdvisor.

"We need you to stick to the script, Avila." Uncle Bob's forehead crinkles warned me not to challenge him. He was my elder. My job was to listen, respect, and promote our ways proudly. As part of the General Council, his was to tell me what to do.

"Avila, we have talked about this." My mother set down her needlework and sat at the table. "You know very well how I feel about all those shows you watch. Ghost this, ghost that. You're inviting dark spirits into your life every time you watch that."

"Really, Mom? By watching TV? Look, I'm not inviting dark spirits in. I'm not playing with a Ouija board or anything. I'm not into the occult, if that's what you think. If I mention ghosts in my tours, it's only for entertainment value. I'll stop, okay?"

"You will," my uncle said. "Or we'll leave the airboat tours to Gale."

"You don't need to do that." I gritted my teeth then slapped on a fake, grateful smile. I liked the airboat rides. I liked the peacefulness and the fact it was the only way I got to interact with people outside our camp. "Now, can we eat?"

Stick to the script. Smile and accept the tips.

Got it.

From the time I was little, we were encouraged to learn traditional ways but also non-Indian ways as well. It was the reason we went to private schools who employed all kinds of people from all different races and backgrounds, so we could harmonize with the outside world, not be isolated from it. Well, guess what? The outside world held a fascination with the supernatural, and so did I.

"We just don't want you misrepresenting our culture," my uncle added, as my grandmother silently set the fish and fry bread on the table. We gave thanks to God for this bounty and ate in silence.

I had nothing else to say, nothing to add. More than ever, I wanted out of there, to drive down the road to my cousin Kellie's in Miami and watch movies, to get away for a while. We might even watch *Haunted Southland* on Netflix, now that I'd personally met the producers. I could tell her about the money I was offered without getting an earful. I could be myself without feeling like I was being judged and that "me" was a mix of tradition and modern ways.

After dinner and cleanup, I sat in my room and picked up the faded photo of my grandfather. Long hair pulled into a ponytail, crinkly eyes, handsome smile, wearing the same gator tooth necklace I now wore. Having died long before I was born, I'd never met him but always felt close. When I was little, I'd get into trouble, pick up this photo, and imagine myself talking to him, telling him my woes. He'd always tell me to hang in there and fight another day.

Next to it was the card Eve Parker had handed me—ShadowBox Productions.

Being around a TV crew might be good for me. God forbid I should learn a new skill. Hiring me as a consultant would mean getting to travel around the country, investigate cases, and I got goose bumps just thinking about it.

Yes, I respected my family and tribe, but what about me?

I needed to live my own life.

My little brother had died on the side of US-41 at the age of six in a truck crash we'd been involved in. Minutes before, he'd asked me if he could ride in the front for once, and I'd switched places with him while Mom drove. He'd been the same age as that little boy on the boat today.

He'd died so that I could live.

That terrible night, I watched a wispy white light rise out of his chest and disappear into the ceiling only moments after he'd drawn his last breath. About a year later, he visited me while I was in bed. Scared the living shit out of me. Appeared as a filmy gray apparition by my bedside. I never got to talk to him, because lurking behind him had been an ominous, dark energy.

Immediately, I began praying to make him go away.

He did. So did the cloudy darkness.

I'd been praying for them to stay away every night ever since.

Billie never had the chance to do more with his life. Neither had the passengers of Flight 401 who perished out in the Everglades. Neither did any of the people killed and made to "disappear" out in the *Kahayatle*. But I did. And I'd never shake the guilt of surviving either. I carried it with me like a cross.

My mind whirled with the possibilities. For the first time in a long time, I felt like there could be more for me.

I waited until my mother was asleep before calling the casino resort and leaving a message for Kane and Eve Parker to call me in the morning. I said my prayers, told my brother I loved him like I did every night, and fell into a dreamless, peaceful sleep.

FOUR

Sunrise over the Everglades was the most beautiful thing about living here. I didn't see the early morning sight often enough. Today, though, as I waited by the side of the access road that would lead us deep into Big Cypress National Preserve, I soaked it all in—the golden rays filtering through the cypress trees, the reflection of blue sky over the water, the anhinga quietly perched on a log, spreading his wings to dry.

So much magnificence and stillness.

Yet ShadowBox Productions wanted to see the ugly parts.

I'd taken the offer. Two weeks ago, I'd spoken to Eve and told her I'd escort them out to Villegas House after all, but they could not mention it to the tribe. She couldn't have been more delighted that I'd changed my mind, and the more we talked over the phone, the more I liked her and felt this would be an exciting opportunity for me, especially if they were considering keeping me on for other projects.

Eve told me they'd return to their home base in Atlanta, plan the Everglades episode, then come back to South Florida in two weeks with the crew. That should give me enough time to prepare.

For two weeks, I thought about how to tell my family that I wouldn't be home for a day, possibly two, because I'd taken a tour job to Villegas House. In the end, there was no good way to do that. For the first time in my adult life, I'd lied straight to my mother's face. I'd told her I was going fishing with Kellie, and though my mom had thought that was strange, she'd shrugged and told me to have a good time.

That might've made me a liar, but I couldn't do it.

Especially after the talking-to I'd been given during dinner that evening, which only reinforced why I felt stuck. Perhaps if I ended up with a job consulting haunted places for the production crew, they might be proud of me and understand why I had to do it. But I had to tell them eventually. I wouldn't be able to live in good conscience otherwise.

Taking in the last few moments while waiting for the crew to arrive, I thought about what might happen at Villegas House. The place was built in the 50s by Roscoe Nesbitt, the father of the two gladesmen brothers who taunted the new residents there in 1967. I knew this because I'd overheard my uncle talking about it to councilmen when I was a kid, though nobody was supposed to know what happened there.

I know that Gregory H. Rutherford, an English environmentalist and avian expert, moved into the deep Everglades cabin a decade after Roscoe moved out and claimed it was uninhabitable due to its haunted nature. The place served as his home and rescue center where he, his Cuban wife, Elena Villegas, and two biologists all lived, studying the natural habitat and rehabilitating injured animals.

As soon as he moved in, bad stuff started happening.

William and Richard Nesbitt began coming around telling Rutherford and his crew to leave; it was their father's house, even though no permits had officially been pulled to build it. They got into arguments that lasted a couple of years. Besides quarreling over the property, they argued over hunting. Rutherford opposed the shooting of some of the most endangered species in the Everglades—panthers and snail kite—and the Nesbitts argued it was their right to hunt.

I'd always understood both points of view.

What happened next depended on who told the story. I'd spent years trying to decipher the truth. So far, the truth had eluded me, but the gist was this—the Nesbitt brothers went berserk and killed everyone during an argument, including my grandfather. Knowing they'd never get away with murdering a high profile scientist or leader of the Miccosukee Tribe, they killed themselves.

Seven people in total.

Down US-41, the caravan approached. They came in two vans, one of them hauling an airboat. I wasn't sure where they'd rented it, but I hoped it was one of the newer models I felt comfortable driving, since they were pretty tricky to handle, especially in marshy Big Cypress.

A ball of nerves coalesced in my stomach, as I watched the caravan slow down upon seeing me standing by the side of the road, waving my arms. This was it. They were here, and soon, we'd drive up the access road until we couldn't drive anymore. Soon, we'd switch from van to airboat to make our way up the River of Grass. I was crazy—pure crazy to do this. I could already visualize something bad happening and my mom telling me, *en maheem*—I brought it upon myself.

Still, I couldn't wait.

The vans slowed, tires crunching over gravel. They came to a full stop, as new people began stepping out, including the Parkers. The group looked out of place, and I suddenly felt guilty bringing strangers into my homeland.

"The crack of dawn, Cypress?" Mr. Parker joked, coming over to shake my hand with that big smile he wielded so well.

"It's a long journey to where we're going, Mr. Parker," I said. "Trust me, you don't want to boat when the sun is boiling or in the afternoon when the storms begin. Follow me down the road. We'll put the airboat in the water about a mile north of here."

"Listen, call me Kane. Mr. Parker is my father, and by the way, these are my crew. You already know my lovely wife, Eve. That over there…" He pointed to a tall, gangly white man in his late thirties with sandy brown hair hanging over his eyes who'd begun taking photos. Serious, not very friendly, he would soon be sorry he wore a long-sleeved flannel shirt to the Everglades at the height of the steamy wet season. "That's Quinn, our cameraman. BJ Atkins is our tech."

An overweight white man with cropped black hair and black glasses waved at me out the front seat of Kane's rental. I waved back, feeling bad for how obese the man was given how young he looked. Our airboat needed to be delicately balanced between all weighted persons and objects.

"You know our host, Sharon Roswell." He pointed to the blonde woman I'd seen guiding viewers through crumbling sanatoriums and haunted theaters. She stared at her phone, detached, unaware that Kane was introducing her to me. Then, he pointed to another woman, an elderly lady with light auburn cotton candy hair. "And our ghost consultant, Linda Hutchinson. She prefers the term medium." He chuckled.

"Hello!" Linda waved from the window.

"Nice to meet everyone. I'm Avila Cypress. I do the airboat tours on the reservation. I hope you brought sunscreen and plenty of water. We should get moving."

Tapping the hood of my truck, I quickly climbed in behind the steering wheel, just so I wouldn't have to talk anymore. Though I was used to giving tours, being in front of a real, live production crew for a show I actually watched made me nervous.

As I drove up the access road, I tried to figure out if I was scared for good reason or simply because my family had put the fear in me about the place since I was little. A memory of Uncle Bob chastising John for attempting to visit Villegas House one time came to me.

My father didn't die in vain so we could make a mockery of that spot, Uncle Bob had told him. *It's a burial ground now. No one is to ever step foot there again. Last thing we need are gladesmen breathing down our backs.*

He'd meant we didn't need more confrontation with the area's hunters. The weird thing is, gladesmen and traditional Indians weren't all that different. We both lived in camps, migrated according to the season, rode our airboats, hunted and fished, though many of my tribe refused to eat fish from our mercury-tainted waters. Gladesmen passed their way of life on to their young ones just like we did. Some called them rednecks or Cajuns of South Florida. Some called them sawgrass cowboys.

Gladesmen invented the airboat to navigate the marshlands when the Miccosukee were still using dugout canoes. They existed today in much the same way Miccosukee did—marginally—growing more frustrated with their diminishing existence. I'd never known any personally, but I'd run into them before. Always felt intimidated when I'd seen them in town or passing by on my airboat.

I believed my grandfather had tried going up there to ease tensions, using diplomatic tactics to settle the score between the two groups. But the gladesmen weren't having it and killed Rutherford, his wife, his two assistants, and my grandfather. Murdered in cold blood for no good reason. When county police arrived to investigate, they found *seven* dead. The two gladesmen brothers were dead too, their bodies rotting away, as alligators and turtles lingered in the perimeter.

For some reason, police left without concluding their investigation, and area locals had to come bury the bodies themselves. What lived in Villegas House that made them vacate as quickly as they'd arrived?

My brain tingled with nervous excitement.

As we arrived at the edge of the waterway, I cut off my truck's engine. *Nothing bad is going to happen,* I kept telling myself. Cameras might capture an orb or two, they might get a few words on their ghost voice box, but mostly, the wilderness would provide most of the entertainment. I'd get paid, we'd all go home…no harm done.

The party bustled to unload, drop the boat into the water, and get everything aboard. It was a large airboat used for tours, the kind with two levels of seats—five on the upper, five on the lower, with an area underneath the elevated scaffolding to hold all cargo—cameras, black boxes containing tech stuff, tripods, and backpacks.

As everyone carefully stepped in, my worry stuck to the big dude. I didn't want to offend him, but he was going to have to sit in the middle two seats to keep the boat balanced. An airboat was nothing more than a motorized skiff, flimsy enough to skim the surface and cut through tall grass. Choosing a nice sized wading stick off the ground, I thanked Mother Earth for it then threw it into the boat, pushing it to one side.

Once everything was settled, I passed out life vests and ear protection and then Kane stood, propped one foot up on an empty seat. "Alright, anyone have any questions?"

"What do we do if we sink?" Sharon asked. Everyone laughed nervously, shooting looks at her, as if they knew she'd start acting up.

"You swim for the nearest edge," I said.

All eyes fell on me.

"But you won't sink. You got yourselves a decent airboat here, and I'm a certified operator. Just keep a few things in mind: airboats have no brakes. If I see something coming toward us, I can only release the gas and veer off to the side. That's why I won't be driving fast. Better to take our time. Also, keep your hands inside the boat at all times."

"Because…why?" Quinn asked.

"Because gators." I shifted my gaze to his skeptical face. "They jump."

"Good Lord, what do you mean they jump?" Linda pressed a manicured hand to her chest.

I raised my eyebrows. "I mean, they jump. Out of nowhere, sometimes. See the guard rails? They're your friends. The Everglades are beautiful but don't be tempted to stick your hand in the water. Any other questions?"

Nobody spoke up.

"Alright, Kane, I think we're good."

"Let's do it." Kane clapped once and rubbed his hands together with excitement, like a kid getting ready for a big race.

I sank into my seat, put my ear gear on, and turned on the

engine. The airboat roared to life, as a few egrets rose into the air and flew away. My passengers all exchanged excited glances. I felt their exhilaration. Today, everything changed. Today, I conquered old fears.

I allowed myself to take in the moment. Be present. Release all guilt.

The warm morning air, sun on my face, brackish water and sawgrass all calmed me. This was my home turf. I was in my element. In about two hours, we would arrive at Villegas House. I couldn't wait to see it, rotting and all. I had to hand it to Kane and Eve—it was the perfect setting for an episode. As long as we got past the front steps, everything would be just fine.

FIVE

Big Cypress—vast wet wilderness.

Still pristine, still ancient.

One of the only places left in the world where you could drive a buggy or an airboat for days and days and never see another person. Even though these lands were protected as part of the national park system, its inhabitants' lifestyles was protected too—the Miccosukee, the Seminole, the gladesmen—and that made us just as vital to life of this ecosystem. This mosaic of cypress trees was our canvas, and the creatures living here were God's works of art.

I wasn't sure anyone else on the boat saw the watery grasslands the way I did. They probably saw an overgrown wasteland. What they didn't know was just how delicate everything was underneath the surface. Life depending on life, depending on water cycles, and to think of the number of times in history where that delicate balance almost went to shit thanks to government.

As my guests and I delved deeper into the glades, we saw the familiar clusters of cypress trees popping up like domes, an above-ground inversion of the rain-filled basin from which they grew. We saw dollar sunfish and large mouth bass, catfish and yellow bullheads. Flying overhead were wood storks, roseate spoonbills, and egrets. I pointed out the various landscapes, such as prairies, hammocks, pinelands, swamps, and estuaries.

To me, they were beautiful. But studying my passengers, I worried for them.

What would happen when it rained, because it was summer and did every day? I hoped they brought ponchos like I'd suggested, mosquito repellant for their delicate skin, and boots for slogging. I hoped they weren't scared of a little lightning in the afternoons. If they were, this would surely suck for them.

But the women on this expedition wore shorts instead of jeans to protect their legs, and the men wore sandals, because visiting Florida, they must've thought that was the thing to do. I sighed to myself and heard my mother's voice in my head telling me that I failed these people.

The sky became overcast. I pushed the airboat along a little faster so we'd have enough time to settle in before the rains came. I cut through water lilies so fast, pig frogs leaped out of our way. Up the river about thirty or so miles, the cypress trees became more dense. We hit a watery fork in the "road," and I knew I'd see it soon.

And isolated cypress island.

In my dreams, Villegas House always emerged from the fog before the sun had a chance to burn the mist away. I wondered if it would appear the same way today. Right when the trees became denser and the waterway more narrow, I knew we were getting closer. I slowed the skiff so we wouldn't miss it, then turned off the engine altogether.

The airboat's vibration ceased, and then, everything went dead quiet.

Only sounds of crickets and mosquitoes echoed over the river.

If I didn't know where we were headed, I would've said the air felt peaceful. Tranquil. A religious silence. I was almost sure everyone could hear my heart pounding through their ear protection. Our boat drifted underneath mossy overgrowth.

Kane leaned back from his seat. "What are we doing?"

I took off my ear protection and picked up the stick I'd brought. "Wading." I sank the end into the water and used it to push us through just my ancestors had been doing on dugout canoes for centuries. "We're approaching your beloved destination."

He jerked his head at me and gave me a playful, scorned look, but I hadn't hurt Kane's feelings. The man was happier than a squirrel in a pile of acorns now that we were almost here. Finally, he could gaze upon the legendary house he'd so desperately wanted me to show him, so much that he would offer two thousand dollars and the possibility for more.

Everyone slid off their ear protection and slowly looked around. The cameramen aimed their cameras in the new direction of the tree-lined tunnel. Slowly, we waded down a pathway growing more dense with trees and hanging moss. Spiky palmettos stretched across the marsh, reaching to scratch us like jagged fingernails. Kane stood, took a bowie knife off his belt, and cut the longest fronds to get them out of our way.

I bet he'd been waiting all his life to use that knife.

The closer we moved toward our destination, the quieter things became. A sense of foreboding sifted through the sawgrass, like the land itself was waking from a long night of unsettling slumber, sighing at our presence. Nobody dared move or say anything. Only the clicks of the camera shutters broke the silence. Linda occasionally bat at her legs, slapping at mosquitoes, and Sharon bounced her knee nervously, as she sat staring at the right bank, waiting for the house to come into view.

Finally, a dark mass inched through the morning mist, peeking through the foliage like a giant-sized human prisoner crouched in a corner, wasting away, simpering, wondering if his punishment was yet over. Riddled with holes, broken timbers, a sagging wooden roof, and busted windows, half of which were missing, the house seemed ashamed to see us. It front door yawned open like the last person to leave knew nobody would ever return to chastise them. The horizontal planks of the house were dark brown to black, covered in patches of bright green moss in some spots, in others penetrated with rogue, swirling vines. Jesus—it looked as though the earth itself was a python slowly unhinging its fangs and swallowing the thing back up.

In the pit of my stomach, a knot tightened. It was too late to turn back.

I pulled the airboat as close as I could to the island, but there was no shore on which to bank. There were cypress trees and palmetto trees and thick mangrove roots we had to navigate before stepping onto firm land, hence the slogging we were about to do.

"Is that as close as you can get?" Sharon glanced at me over her shoulder.

I cast side-eye at her. I wasn't the only one. I definitely saw a few eyerolls from the rest of the crew. "Yes, ma'am. Until this boat grows legs anyway," I said.

I hadn't meant for it to sound snippy, but for a woman who hadn't said two words to me since she arrived, she could've asked more politely. I knew, though, that tensions were high now that we were here.

I turned to Kane. "This part is tricky. There's no definition between water and land, so we're just going to have to slog."

"What does that mean?" Sharon asked, sharp blue eyes accusing me. "Slog?"

"Roswell, remember in the meeting, I told you all to bring boots?" Kane asked, nodding. "Well, it was for this. I just didn't know we needed them now."

"Yes, you need them now," I said. I should've asked them to change shoes while still on land, but I wasn't used to leading a slogging experience.

"Let's go, guys. Get them on."

"Move slowly, please!" I called out, so everyone wouldn't move at once. Smartly, BJ let everyone shift about the boat first while he stayed anchored in the middle.

"You want us to go in the water?" Sharon asked calmly.

"It's the only way to get to the house," I said. "There's no dock here. It's not deep. You just wade a few steps until you get to the bank, then you climb over the roots."

"You say that like this isn't Florida."

She was making it a big deal by not trusting me, but I supposed this could look pretty intimidating to anyone who'd never done it before.

"What if there's gators or snakes?" she asked.

"There could be, but you all wanted to come here, not me," I mumbled under my breath. Most heard me and gave me wary glances. Kane and Eve gave each other silent looks.

"Great spot, guys," Quinn said sarcastically, getting on his boots.

"Alright, look, don't worry," I added. "We're going to move quickly, and if there was a gator, you would see it coming. The water is crystal clear, see?" I gestured to the water that was, in fact, pretty darn beautiful for being marshland. People thought swamp water was mucky or putrid, but it was absolutely vibrant, since it was actually a river.

"Everyone grab what they can," Eve ordered. "So we only have to do this once."

One by one, the production crew got their proper shoes on, dropped into the water up to their knees, and pulled off bags from the skiff. Hoisting boxes over their shoulders, onto their backs, they handed them to each other and worked like a team.

BJ looked at me for permission. "Go ahead," I told him. A captain never abandoned their ship until they were the last, so I stayed onboard and kept an eye on the water in case any curious moccasins decided to swim by right as BJ struggled to disembark.

Only when everyone had pulled themselves onto firm cypress island did I jump into the water with the remaining bags and wade toward the island as well. Climbing up using the walking stick, I bent to catch my breath. "You all might want to find a stick, too. They come in handy." Facing the house, I gestured and my hands fell by my sides. "And there you have it—Villegas House."

Except for the occasional "damn" or "holy shit" muttered under their breaths, the group hushed to study the decrepit old cabin. I called it a cabin, though it was really a large, two-story house built crudely without permits. Rotten and even more decayed the closer we got, the house just felt…forsaken.

I shouldn't have come here.

I shouldn't have brought these people.

If my tribe had asked us all to stay away, there had to be a reason.

No, Avila. It's fine. It's just old.

As Quinn and BJ took photos, Sharon stood taking it all in, and Eve stuck tightly to Kane's side. They soaked in the monstrosity they'd asked to see.

"We've seen some crazy shit, guys," Kane said. "But this is the craziest ever."

"So true, baby," Eve said, taking photos. "But it's beautiful."

Linda, the medium who'd been standing off to the side quietly, stepped over to me. "It's dark," she said. "Much darker than I imagined."

"Yes, it's the wood," I told her. "Probably Dade pine that's rotted through…"

"No, I mean its aura."

I looked at her. "Excuse me?"

"The house's aura. It's dark, like a gunmetal silver. I don't like it." She stared at the house with narrowed eyes. I could see she felt it was a mistake to come here. If the medium of this expedition was having second thoughts, that didn't fill me with confidence of any kind. She glanced at me. "Your aura is bright, though. Are you spiritual?"

I was a bit taken aback. "Mine?"

"Yes, it's beautiful. Bright blue with a silver lining to it. Do you have psychic gifts?" Her fluffy reddish hair shook, as she tilted her head to examine me from a few more angles. I stood still in case her studying my aura required me to remain motionless.

"Not that I know of."

Yes, I had psychic gifts, but I'd worked too hard to suppress them to have her bringing them out into the open again.

From the day I'd seen Billie's spirit rise, to the day he visited me in my bedroom, to seeing the dark entity hovering behind him, I knew I was psychic to some degree. But like any skill, it could die away from atrophy if uncultivated, and that was exactly what I'd tried to do all my life. I wasn't strong enough to deal with real spirits. I didn't know how people like Linda did it. I didn't mind knowing the ghosts were there, and I loved telling stories about them, as long as they left me alone.

Linda's Mona Lisa smile hinted that she didn't believe me. "Well, you should be," she said. For an old woman, she was beautiful but also seemed to have gone through a lot in her life. Melancholy lingered just inside her eyes, and the laugh lines outside of them seemed to weep.

"What do you mean by the house has an aura?" I asked. "I always thought auras were the fields of energy surrounding *living* things."

Her almond-shaped brown eyes focused on Villegas House. Lips pressed together, she nodded like saying it out loud might make it true. "Exactly."

SIX

A house as a living thing. With its own dark gray aura.

Great.

The very thought sent a spike of unease through me, but it was too late to leave now. Here we were, and here we'd stay until this job was done or one of us got swallowed by the house's aura, whichever came first.

Calm down.

I was surrounded by people. What could happen surrounded by so many people?

Kane's crew got to setting up tents, opening backpacks, cracking open equipment cases, running cables, and starting a generator. Its rumbling ripped through the tranquility, and I thought of the animals that lived here and what they'd think of us for disturbing their peace. The ghosts, too.

Were they watching us now?

As it turned out, I would be sharing a tent with Linda. Kane and Eve would be taking their own, the two tech guys, Quinn and BJ, were sharing, and Sharon had apparently requested her own tent, which was fine, since her ego needed a big place to sleep. I felt more comfortable sharing with Linda, anyway, even though she didn't seem to want to be here.

Once we'd set up camp, the crew stood facing Villegas House, taking photos and talking about what they'd do once they went in. I realized they weren't entering, not because they were scared to, but because they had an established methodology for doing these investigations. Everything was recorded, so it wasn't until cameras got rolling would Sharon or anyone set foot inside.

I was itching to find out what would be inside the crumbling rotten structure but grateful that the *Haunted Southland* crew would be finding out first. I'd be waiting outside. By the tent. In the safe area.

BJ had set up a couple of monitors which connected signals with their video cameras, so anything that Quinn taped while inside, we could see it out in the "tech tent." They did a test run on lighting, Sharon's voice and movements, and a few other video tests I didn't understand because I didn't speak TV production. Everyone was too busy to explain what they were doing. I liked the buzz of it, however—the energy this team created. They worked cohesively, like a well-oiled machine, and I felt envious of their chemistry.

Mosquitos invaded after noon, so I made myself useful going around, spraying repellant on anyone who would let me. We didn't use repellant in our camp, but anyone not used to mosquitos definitely needed it.

A female presence sidled up to me and spoke in a southern accent. "What can you tell me about this place, Cypress?"

It was Sharon, hands on hips, chin gesturing to the house. She was taller than I was, statuesque, and though she was in her mid-40s, it was easy to see that she had once been a beautiful twenty-something with a career in television. I'd read somewhere that she'd used to be an NFL cheerleader turned soap actress turned ghost investigator, a smart move if you asked me, because youthful beauty did not live forever.

"Honestly, I don't know much. Only that a gladesman elder built the place in the fifties. He left almost as soon as he finished it. Later on, his sons would get into one altercation or another with an environmentalist who moved in, then one day, there was an accident."

"An accident, or a murder?" She raised an eyebrow.

"Nobody knows for sure. I mean, we know it ended in death, because they came out here to investigate. There's photos online of decomposed corpses lying around, but that's all they have. They didn't stick around long to find many facts."

"Could it have been a natural death? Like an animal attack?"

I shrugged. "I don't know of any creature that would do that. The Everglades has its mysterious Skunk Ape, kind of like a Big Foot, but it's peaceful—if it's real, that is—not something that would kill seven people."

"What about panthers?" Sharon faced me. I could almost envision her as a police officer with uniform, badge, gun in holster and everything.

"Florida panthers are shy. I doubt a panther would've killed everyone that day, especially hunters who would've ended it with one shot."

"Were there any women here?" Sharon asked.

"Women? Um, well, there was Rutherford's wife, Elena. Plus I believe one of the assistants was a woman. Why?"

"Just curious. What about the Nesbitt brothers? Were either married or were their wives part of the confrontation that took place?"

"Thing is, I don't really know. Everything I've learned has been passed down orally, and you know how that is. Details change from year to year." For being considered for ghost consultant, I really didn't know much, did I?

"What happened after the killings?" Sharon asked. "Did anyone come back and experience anything strange? What's the haunted history like?"

Sharon's questions were starting to bother me. Not because I didn't have the answers she wanted, or because she seemed to think I was the Wikipedia of Villegas House, but because she seemed to want them for her own. Kane had told me that we'd have a meeting once we got here, where I'd share all I knew about the house, but Sharon had isolated me and interrogated me. Just a little Avila-Sharon session.

"Ms. Roswell, I know very little about its haunted history," I said, staring at the ground, a mix of grass, sand, but also shards of wood. "I only know that my tribe stays away from here. They consider it bad luck. They've told stories of men who've come back to the village changed, never to be the same after visiting. It's a legend because no one knows what really happened. The Everglades has a habit of blurring the past that way."

Sharon frowned. "I thought you were the hired historian, but you don't know shit."

"I..." I tried not to feel rattled, but my pride was hurt. Who did she think she was? "I'm not an historian. There is no historian about this house. I'm only here because I guess I was the only one naïve enough to bring you."

Sharon's bright blue eyes scanned over my face, as if she could read my intentions and find out if I was lying. She didn't trust me, but that was okay—I didn't trust her either, and I hadn't come here to make friends.

"You were the only one, huh?" She smirked then turned to

watch the crew setting up. "Well, we'll have to use Linda as much as we can then. She's the reason I'm here."

I looked at the aging medium sitting in her camping chair outside out tent, doing a crossword puzzle. She stopped, fished the ground for a piece of wood and held it with eyes closed. She seemed underappreciated, as though she saw herself as an older woman of little or no value. Which was sad, because so far, she'd been the only one who'd provided any useful information about Villegas House.

As curious as I was, I didn't want to continue engaging with Sharon any more than I had to. Talk about the real person being completely different from the celebrity. She skulked off to my relief.

I took a seat next to Linda

She handed me the bark. "Look at this. What do you think?"

I took the shard of wood and flipped it over in my hands. It seemed to be from the house, same color, same type of wood, and everything. "Probably a broken piece from the house. Why, what do you think it is?"

"I know it's from the house. That's not what I mean. Close your eyes. Tell me what you feel." She closed her hands around mine with the wood tucked in my palm.

I closed my eyes and felt the wood, its density, the smoothness of its surface. It wasn't Dade pine, and it wasn't Cypress, so it may have been any kind of imported wood from the days when Gregory Rutherford lived out here, but none of that mattered or was why she'd asked me to hold it.

The only thing that mattered was that my chest hurt. Breaths became shallow, as though I'd run a marathon, and my side cramped, yet I couldn't drop the stupid piece of wood.

Its effect had taken a hold of me like an electrical current. I gasped and finally threw the piece of wood on the ground. "What the hell was that?"

Linda nodded, satisfied. She sat back in her chair, as though her suspicions had been right. "You're like me, Avila. You see beyond the veil."

SEVEN

Of course she knew.

She was bloody psychic.

I dragged my gaze away from her, hoping she wouldn't mention it to anybody, but my silence was admission enough.

"Alright, everybody. Over here, let's talk." Kane clapped his hands together once and swung his arms, waiting while everybody made their way to the center of camp. He sat on top of a crate and swung his baseball cap backwards. "We're ready to do this. Avila," he said. "First and foremost, thank you for bringing us here. We know how hard it was for you, but do know that we really appreciate it."

Everyone looked at me. Only Eve and Linda smiled.

"No problem," I said. Actually, big problem. But that was my burden to bear, one I'd deal with when I returned home. I appreciated his acknowledgement, though.

"Also, thank you, Linda. I know it's not always easy for you, doing what you do, but we appreciate you being here, as always."

"I'll be here if you need me, sweetheart," Linda said in a melodious voice. Turning to me, she mumbled, "My work comes later."

"We like to receive impressions without her in the beginning, then bring her in afterwards," Sharon clarified for me, as though Linda's explanation hadn't been enough.

"Yeah, for the heavy lifting." Linda smirked. "Which there will be. I can tell."

Sharon ignored her.

I nodded and focused back on Kane. Next to me, Linda fanned herself with a folder. The woman did not look well, and the heat and humidity were pretty oppressive, even for me.

"Avila, this is for you, since we know it already. Keep everything dry, cell phones off, loose jewelry taped or put away. Like what you've got there…" He pointed to my neck. I instinctively touched my gator tooth necklace. "Not that it looks noisy. In case you're in any of our shots, Sharon's our host, so we don't do, say, or touch anything without her OK. She's the one who guides this whole process onscreen."

A slice of panic cut through me. "I'm going to come out in this?" I thought I was just here for the ride, quietly hiding in the background.

"We don't plan on having you in any scenes, but you never know. Sometimes spirit activity affects the crew in different ways, and people end up on screen."

"Okay." Last thing I needed was to come out on *Haunted Southland* and have my family see me escorting strangers to Villegas House before I was ready to tell them. Though eventually, word would get out that a show had been taped here.

Kane went on about technical things. He may as well have been speaking a different language. "We'll need to boost the gain," he told Quinn and BJ. "Check the batteries, I don't want to break the stream."

"Do we go with a ring light?" Quinn asked. "Or softie?"

"Ring light," Kane answered, launching into a discussion about more editing things. I took the time to hear them all speak, get a sense of what kind of people they were.

Quinn was the consummate professional, BJ was quiet and meek, Kane was definitely in charge, Eve was there to make her husband look good, and Sharon listened but I could tell that she would challenge authority from the way she shook her head at stuff Kane was saying.

"Great, another cave to shoot in," Quinn said, adjusting his video camera.

"Don't worry, we'll fix it in post," Kane replied.

"I *am* post." Quinn laughed.

"Overall, respect the house," Kane said. I felt like maybe he was saying this for my benefit, since I'd told them the ghosts here didn't mess around. "Respect the spirits. If we want to get anything, we want them to invite us in. Got it?"

"Got it," they all mumbled then got around to getting ready. Eve blotted her husband's forehead of sweat then came around with more wipes to make Sharon camera-ready. Watching them work was fascinating, but I couldn't help but feel like this wouldn't last long.

Eve passed by me, stopped, retraced her steps, blotted my forehead with a smile and said, "You don't need this. You always look fabulous."

For the first time since arriving, I cracked a smile. At least there was Eve.

"Let's get an opening shot," Kane said, crossing his arms. All eyes were on Sharon. "Steady…roll tape in three…" He counted down on his fingers…two…one.

"Hello, I'm Sharon Roswell, and today we come to you from one of the deepest, darkest secrets of the Everglades—Villegas House. Built circa 1955 by local gladesmen, this two-story plantation home situated on a cypress island later became home to environmentalist Gregory H. Rutherford and his wife, Elena Villegas, after the original builder abandoned it due to unclear circumstances. Is Villegas House haunted? We'll soon find out."

She went on to explain how the couple rehabilitated endangered species injured from hunting then released them back into the wild. How Roscoe Nesbitt's sons, William and Richard, harassed the new residents on the property and how the family feud lasted a couple of years until 1967 when everything went horribly wrong and police found six dead bodies, the seventh death happening in a nearby hospital.

I wondered where she'd gotten her information. It seemed she had studied it previously and only asked me for my version to verify it.

"Locals say the house is so haunted, nobody gets past the front door. Well, we're going to change that today, aren't we?" Sharon asked dramatically. Suddenly, right in the middle of filming, a loud noise, like a bang of wood, crashed inside of the house. "Did you hear that?" Sharon's eyes scanned the area, the camera following her at every expression.

Kane and BJ exchanged looks, and Eve seemed happy that things were already starting to happen by the way she silently clapped her fingertips together.

"Let's go inside and take a look…"

Sharon walked up the disheveled steps of Villegas House and touched the front door, which was wide open, with her fingertips.

"Shit. I don't know, you guys…it feels oppressive in there." She looked at the camera and shook her head. I knew this was part acting to create suspense viewers would eat up, and that "shit" would get bleeped out.

What we'd all heard was more than likely pieces of wood falling, literally rotting away, as we stood here, and if anything happened to Sharon Roswell, it would be nobody's fault but ShadowBox Productions' own.

Still, I stared at the house, drawn to it, as the sounds around me fell away. Something seemed to call to me, made my stomach clench and my heart palpitate. Were those whispers, telling me to stay away, other voices asking who I was, who we all were? No, it couldn't have been. I shook it off. My nervous brain was messing with me.

Behind me was Linda, still sitting in her chair, holding a clipboard and a pencil, still doing her crossword puzzle, but she looked far from entertained. The woman shook her head. "We shouldn't go in there," she mumbled.

Her voice sounded deeper, not as melodious as before.

Kane shushed her with two fingers held up. He continued to watch, as I did, the two big monitors BJ had set up showing Sharon and Quinn walking into the condemned house.

"But I understand," Linda mumbled again. "All in the name of research."

I got a sense of dread hearing Linda, the one woman they should all be listening to, telling us that we shouldn't go in there.

"It's why we came," Kane told Linda then looked at me with wide eyes, silently communicating that sometimes, things got tense on the set.

I could see how a medium's impressions might interfere with a smooth production. Eyes back on the house, I watched as Sharon slowly made her way inside, then within seconds, she and Quinn had disappeared into the gloom. My eyes shifted to the monitors, which changed to the grainy image I often saw on TV when they were filming in the dark. Suddenly, the screen turned black with only white lines breaking up the darkness.

"What's going on?" Kane asked BJ.

"We lost connection."

"Damn it. Keep rolling. Quinn, Sharon, you all right?" Kane asked.

A few moments later, the host and the cameraman reemerged from the house, shaking their heads. Sharon wiped sweat off her brow and gave Eve a look like that didn't go well, while Quinn walked all the way up to the tech station.

"Camera's dead," he said.

"What do you mean?" Kane asked. "Dead-dead, or?"

"Dead," Quinn replied. "It just turned off while we were walking through the first room. I tried turning it back on, and you know I charged the shit out of it before we started, so I don't know what the hell's happening."

"What's happening is the spirits don't want you inside."

Linda again.

We all looked at her, dark eyes gazing ahead at a spot on the ground in front of her, unfocused. Her hand holding the pencil skittered across the page, scratching out on the paper. Something about her looked…off.

"She's doing it again," Kane mumbled to his wife.

"They don't want you," Linda mumbled. She scribbled harshly now, ripping into the paper. Quinn took hold of a different camera and rushed over to stand behind her. I shifted my spot to see what she was writing as well. She held the pencil in a fist, child-like, trance-like, staring straight ahead, as though someone else were writing messages through her.

And there, in large chicken-scratch letters was the word—DIE.

EIGHT

"What is that supposed to mean?"

"Did she just write DIE?"

"Did you catch that? Did everyone see that?" Sharon spoke dramatically into the camera as it filmed Linda.

I'd seen enough episodes to know how this would end up in post-production. These were the snippets when the host, in a voiceover, said things like, *Suddenly, our medium, Linda Hutchinson, who'd been sitting peacefully at our camp, began channeling messages from beyond the grave…*

But Linda didn't seem to be acting to me. She continued to scratch the paper with her pencil point following the same grooves, over and over again—DIE, DIE, DIE—her eyes wide and full of a panicked emptiness.

Sharon reached out and placed her hand over the paper to get Linda to stop. "Linda? It's okay. Come out of it, dear. We're all here," she said then louder into the air, "You want us to die, spirits? Is that what this message means? Well, we're not here to do that. We're here to find out who you are and what happened here in 1967."

If they asked me, the spirits did not care to discuss why they were trapped here or what happened to them. My tribe members had said it many times before—the restless souls at Villegas House were not eager to go into the light. They were eager for us to join them.

I shook my head and told myself that all was fine, that the poor woman obsessively scribbling the word DIE on the piece of paper was not in any way freaking me out whatsoever. I needed to get out of here a minute and clear my head space.

Walking toward the airboat, I briefly imagined taking off in it all by myself and leaving them behind. I could never do that, yet I couldn't shake the image. I shouldn't have come here. I shouldn't.

"Avila?" It was Eve calling to me.

I held a hand up while walking and stopped to catch my breath.

A moment passed, and she muttered, "She just needs space. It was too much for her."

Maybe it was. I'd never seen such a thing in all my life. Had that been real-life possession or acting for the camera's sake? Who would tell us to *die* like that?

Once at the riverbank, I stopped cold. Lined up near the airboat were three alligators—large, perched on the mangroves, black bumpy snouts with mouths open, hissing the moment they saw me. It wasn't unusual to see alligators in the Everglades—I saw them every day. What was strange was that they kept their distance. Alligators loved to climb up onto the land to bask in the sunshine when they were tired, but these gators seemed to want nothing to do with the house and remained resting half in the water, half on the cypress roots.

It made me think about how police were surprised to find the dead bodies here untouched by alligators after the massacre.

"I don't blame you," I told them. The hissing stopped, but they continued to keep a wary eye on me. If they could get past their fear of Villegas House, they would be all over our camp. After a few minutes of clearing my head, I trudged back and informed Kane, "We need to move closer to the house. At least four feet above the water level."

"Why? What's wrong?"

"Gators. But don't tell the others. Trust me."

Last thing these people needed was to know that predatory reptiles surrounded the airboat a mere thirty yards from camp. They weren't hurting us and didn't seem like they would come nearer. Still, non-Florida people always freaked out about alligators, and we didn't need more alarm. After seeing Linda channel the word DIE from an unseen spirit, assuming it hadn't been theatrics, it was better that way.

By six o'clock, the crew had not yet re-started filming, and I was beginning to think we would stay the presumed "last resort" night over.

They'd spent the better part of the day trying to get the faulty camera working, only to discover their interior spare not turning on either. The last camera was for exterior shots, which they refused to take inside the house. I could feel Kane's frustration growing the more our daylight sank beneath the horizon.

Staying out of the way for most of it, I decided Linda looked like enough time had elapsed to approach her about what had happened. I pulled up a camp chair next to hers where she sat reading a book. "No pencils this time, huh?" I asked.

She gave me a sheepish look. "Sorry if that scared you."

"Hell, yeah, it scared me. I've never seen anyone do that before. Was that you writing?"

"It was me, my hands, but no, that wasn't my message."

"Were you aware of what you were writing? It almost looked like you wanted to kill someone the way you were stabbing that pencil into the paper."

"I wasn't aware at that moment, no. It's like meditation when you're in an alpha state. Have you ever meditated?"

"Not in the yoga sense, but I do zone out on the boat sometimes. It's my sacred space."

"You see and hear what's going on behind a sheet of glass?" she asked.

"Yes." That was a good way to describe it. But I didn't want to talk about the way I sometimes tapped into the other side, because it scared the shit out of me. I switched focus. "Linda, who was telling you to write 'die?'" I asked, picking up a blade of sawgrass and running my thumb along its jagged edges.

"Something dark. I don't know *who* it is. It's in charge of this house, maybe of this whole island. We do many of these investigations where I warn them about an evil presence, but it's their job to proceed. Still, I can't help but wonder if one of these investigations won't be their last."

The lines around her eyes told of years' worth of witnessing odd things. Even though I didn't envy her job, I envied how many places she'd been and the world she'd seen. And if I zoned out and looked at her hard enough, I saw something else…

Disease…

I sat back in my folding chair and stared at her.

Where that word had come from, I didn't know. But there it was. I looked at Linda. Linda looked at me like she knew that I knew something about her. Until she mentioned it, though, I wouldn't. Still, it did make me wonder why she was here to begin with if, in fact, she was ill. Her dark, kind eyes reminded me of someone I couldn't place.

"That's why I've never come here before. I have too much

respect for the other world."

"I do, too, Avila. But something about having me here makes them feel better. The messages which come to me corroborate their findings. They get hunch feelings that dark presences exist, and I verify them."

"Then, why bring you on at all?"

"Sometimes they have trouble communicating. Their Ovilus III will stop working, messages won't come through, they need somebody sensitive." She scoffs. "It's funny. Any one of them could do what I do. It takes years of meditation and practice. We all have psychic ability to varying degrees. Still, they prefer their techy things."

"It's easier," I said.

"And faster. But you…" The waning light had turned her eyes a shade of golden amber. "You could do what I do."

I shook my head. "Oh, no. I can't. I'm too chicken shit. I mean, I love *telling* ghost stories. I love ghost lore from afar. I could never be hands-on involved with them, day in, day out like you."

I said the same thing about giving airboat rides.

What can *I do day in, day out?*

At least Linda employed her talents by helping others, warning them, facing the unknown. When I reached her age, I hoped to be as useful to others, but the way my life was going, I didn't see that happening.

"You're young, Avila," Linda said, glancing at me. "I didn't develop my skills until much later in life. Middle age has a way of making you face things you never wanted to face. You're better off in the end, though."

She closed her eyes for a much-needed break, and I got up and walked toward the woods, hoping to ground myself again. Being in the camp made me feel claustrophobic. Normally, I'd love spending the day on a cypress island, checking out wildlife, searching for animal tracks, observing nature at its finest, but this particular island felt devoid of life. Oppressive. Something stagnant in the air sucked the vitality right out of it. It felt like it needed a good sage energy clearing.

As I felt the first drops of rain, the air cooled down significantly. The storms had come late today. Afternoon rain in the Everglades were an everyday occurrence in the summer. With so much heat, marsh water evaporated when the sun was at its hottest, then the clouds, unable to contain their fill, spilled every afternoon. Sometimes it fell in torrents, and tourists would ask if this was normal.

It was.

Except as the droplets began falling, I could tell this would be a hard torrential rain. I could hear Kane giving orders to put all equipment into the cases and bring them into the tents for the duration of the storm. Even with all the hubbub around me, I felt myself distancing from the rest of the team. I walked toward the edge of the property where the denser woods began.

Something was in there.

Someone was…

…calling me.

Most likely, it was in my mind, but I heard my name echoing from a distant place. When I paused to listen with closed eyes, I felt my whole body trembling—no, vibrating—gently. It could've been the earth underneath my feet, spiking energy through me, especially with the rain pounding, soaking my patchwork blouse, the elements coming together to amplify sensations. But the vibrations got stronger until I felt they were coming *from* me.

Avila.

I opened my eyes, stared ahead. The cypress trees with their long, thin trunks and bulbous roots reaching into the watery ground looked like people standing there, legs apart, facing off with me. Cognitively, I knew they were trees, just like I knew this was rain falling, but I couldn't help feel like they were alive. Of course they were alive, Avila, but alive, in the human sense, as though they were watching me, inviting me in.

Get away from those people. They are not like you.

They want to exploit the house, this land, but you respect it.

Come with us.

I didn't hear these words like I'd hear normal words. They coursed through my veins, whispered to me suggestively, like a flowing river or an electrical current.

People.

The trees looked like people, and the darker the sky got, the heavier the rain, the more insidious their shapes appeared. Hunched over… The more the gray clouds took over, creating a hazy neutral tone over the woods where it was difficult to tell what was what.

Avila…

Was that…

My brother?

I knew that voice. I'd know it anywhere. I'd heard it at least a hundred times a day when I was a kid. I'd even wished he'd stop calling me so often, as older sisters often did wish their pesky little brothers would go away. But at this moment, I felt myself wanting to hear him again.

"Billie?" My voice shook. Was it really him?

If it was, would the dark energy be with him? To this day, I still didn't know what I had seen lingering in the background the night he visited me in my sleep, but I always imagined that I'd see it again if Billie returned.

I waited.

It definitely sounded like him, but why would he, or his spirit, be in this place? Billie had died on the roadside of US-41, and I always thought ghosts lingered wherever they were known to have passed away. Maybe he was a figment of my imagination.

"Billie, is that you? I'm sorry for what happened…" I said, my voice cracking. "I'm sorry I let you sit in the front seat. I shouldn't have switched with you." It should've been me on the other side, not him.

The trees continued to be nothing but trees while channeling human energy at the same time. I knew I wasn't alone, had never been out here or anywhere. No matter where I went, someone was always watching. From the moment we'd arrived on this island, they'd been watching us from the woods.

They're out there—the dead.

It's not fair…

"What's not fair, Billie?" I narrowed my eyes so my vision could focus on one particular tree that seemed to move, take slow steps, until a little boy came around the bend, emerging from the shadows. A little boy I had loved so much, my heart ached every day just knowing I'd never see him alive again. He wore the same clothes as the day of the accident—blue jeans and the sewn traditional top my mother had made him.

You got to live.

I knew it.

My head dropped. The tears came.

"Yes, Billie. I got to live while you had to die. Damn it. I'm so sorry for that…" It'd always lingered in my mind—the debilitating guilt that I'd survived the crash. Sometimes I wondered if I really got the better deal out of it, though. My life hadn't meant much so far, whereas he got to explore the cosmos, Heaven, wherever he was.

When I was finished feeling sorry for myself, I opened my eyes again, but this time, it wasn't Billie I saw coming around a cypress tree like a slithering wisp of fog. For a moment, I worried it was the dark energy that had accompanied him long ago.

Instead, a young woman stood in the middle of the woods staring at me, long reddish-brown hair hanging down either side of her face. She was beautiful with smooth pale skin, like a porcelain doll made from bone china. My heart raced, not only because this spirit stood there studying me, but because I knew her.

NINE

I shouldn't have recognized her.

I'd never seen her before, and yet I felt like I'd known her every day of my life. Her hair was long, flowing. Eyes bright and understanding. I knew the way she moved—fluidly, like underwater—the way her dress poured out behind her. She stepped out of the trees toward me, and once she hit the rain, was gone.

She looked like a much younger Linda. Could I have been seeing a projection?

Disease…

Suddenly, I feared it was her. Was Linda okay, or was I seeing a form of her ghost?

I bolted back to camp, tripping over logs, scampering through the cypress trees. She hadn't been looking too well all day, and I had an impression of her being sick. The moment I arrived back at camp, Sharon asked where Linda was. I didn't want to mention just having seen her in the woods as a young woman, so I kept my mouth shut and helped look for her.

"She was here half an hour ago," Sharon said.

"We have to find her," I said urgently.

Sharon gave me a cursory look. "Why do you say it like that? Is she okay?" She broke into a faster hustle, searching in each tent and around the house. "She wouldn't have gone inside the house, would she?"

Kane stepped up to us. "You guys looking for Linda? I thought she was with you."

"I thought she was with you," Sharon said.

"Crap." Kane, Sharon, and I split into different directions, and I found myself hovering near the cypress trees again. I felt drawn to them, though my nerves were shot knowing that one of us would probably find the old woman dead at any moment.

Out of the corner of my eye, I saw a flash of white and saw a shirt, an arm, a leg scuttling on the ground, like a roach on its back trying to get up from a pile of dry brush.

"Linda!" I ran to her. She was down but not dead. As relieved as I was, seeing her struggling to get up also left me confused. Who, then, who had I seen out in the trees? "Are you okay? Guys, she's here!" I called out.

Sharon and Kane ran over while I helped Linda to a sitting position. She'd had the wind knocked out of her. "Something led me…" Linda struggled to breathe. "Something called me out here."

"Something called me, too," I said. I gave her both my hands, as Kane stood behind her, placing his hands on her middle back. Sharon and I hoisted the woman to her feet. "A young lady. She told me her name, but now I can't remember it."

"Did you fall? What happened?" I asked once she was on her feet.

"I don't know. I…lost consciousness."

"Let's get her to the tent and aim a fan on her," Kane told us. "We'll plug the one that's on the tech onto her directly, so she can get some fresh air. It's stifling out here."

We carried Linda to the tents and sat her down, positioning one of the two small portable fans directly on her, so she could catch her breath. Bringing her a bottle of cold water from the cooler, I twisted it open and handed it to her. It only took a minute for her to regain her color.

"You scared me," I told her. I really didn't know what we would've done had Linda passed away out here, and I was at even more at a loss to explain the ghost woman in the forest if it hadn't been her. I might have witnessed the spirit of either of the women who'd been murdered here in 1967, but I was pretty sure, having seen photos of Elena Villegas on the internet, that she'd been olive-skinned and dark-haired.

"I'm sorry," Linda said, eyes closed, water bottle in hand. "I can feel it, though."

"Feel what?" I asked.

I knew her answer before she even said it. I knew because some kind of shift had been happening to me from the moment I arrived here, one that opened me up to currents of information to which I shouldn't have been privy.

"My time," she replied. "It's coming."

In the evening, after an unappetizing dinner of canned pork and beans heated on a portable burner, Kane announced we'd be spending the night. They'd gotten very little done during the shoot today thanks to the faulty equipment but he hoped that tomorrow would be better. If they continued to have issues, they'd cut the expedition short and call it a loss. If anyone wasn't feeling up to snuff, Kane also said, now was the time to say it so we could return to the village and part ways.

I asked Linda if she was okay enough to stay. "You sure?"

"I haven't felt well in years, dear, but I'm not going to leave. They have work to do in that house," Linda said, going back to her crossword puzzles. "They don't make their investment back, they don't get paid. Kids don't eat."

"Kids?"

"Kane and Eve. Got a boy back home, a girl just started college."

"Ah."

It must've been difficult for her to come along on these investigations, be the one person who connected the most with psychic energy, but remain neutral on the decision-making part of the process. Linda Hutchinson was their puppet. And their trooper.

Kane looked at me inquisitively since I was talking to Linda, as if asking for a report on how she felt. I gave him a thumb's up to express that Linda seemed fine. "Alright then, hope you all get some sleep. Anybody need anything from the food tent before I close it?"

"I do." I scrambled over to the big plastic tub containing the dry packaged foods and cans and grabbed a granola bar. The pork and beans hadn't done it for me. As I was heading out of the tent, Kane held onto my arm.

"Did she seem okay to you?" he asked, worry lines on his forehead.

"I think she's a little worn down, but she seems okay now."

"You sure?"

"I think so. She's in good spirits, doing her crosswords."

Kane laughed a shallow laugh in his chest. "Yeah, she loves those. Alright. Since you're sleeping in the same tent as her, keep an eye on her, will you? Linda's been with us too long, and I'd hate for her to feel sick and not tell us. She's done it before. Kind of a martyr, if you know what I mean."

"Sure. I get it." And with that, I headed to bed, knowing I wouldn't get a wink of sleep. Hoping to God that nothing would visit me in my dreams. I unrolled the sleeping bag the crew had brought for me and lay on top. It was too hot to get inside a flannel-lined cocoon, so I lay over it staring up at the apex of the tent ceiling.

"I'm sorry if I scared you out there," Linda said from her chair by the open flap of the tent. "I'm afraid this place is affecting me more than any other I've been in recent years. I used to be affected quite a bit when I first started coming along on investigations, but this one…this one is different."

"Different how?" I rolled up the top side of the sleeping bag to form a soft pillow and readjusted myself until I was somewhat comfortable.

"The entities here are older than most houses. More primitive and powerful. I told them in Atlanta that coming here wouldn't be a good idea."

"They said it was a unique location."

"Is that what they said?" Linda harrumphed, closed her crossword puzzle book, and slowly stood. She moaned in the typical way older folks did about their aches and pains and joints upon standing. "Goodnight, everybody." She waved to the tech crew that was still doing some work out by the lantern.

Everyone bid her goodnight, then she lowered her head and came into the tent. Eve had been nice enough to double up sleeping bags for Linda, and I would've given her my own for a third if I didn't need it myself.

"You know," she said, out of breath, lowering to a seated position on the ground. "I do these for another reason too."

"What's that?" I asked.

"When I was younger, I didn't fully accept my gifts. I wanted them gone." She spoke as she got her things ready for bed. "There were so many people who would've given an arm and a leg for my abilities, but here I had them and wanted nothing to do with them."

Linda pulled a small bottle out of her bag, uncapped it and placed a tiny pill onto her tongue before taking a swig of water from her bottle.

"As I got older, I realized this was why I was here. I'd been given this gift for a reason, and that was to help people. You shouldn't be afraid of your gifts either, Avila."

Looking at Linda, I saw the honesty in her face, the exhaustion in her eyes. She'd lived a good—what—sixty or seventy years? I couldn't tell, but it had been long enough to accrue the kind of wisdom I should definitely listen to. I just wasn't sure "gift" was the right word.

"But I *am* afraid of them," I said.

Linda rested her head on a small pillow. "That will either change with time or with circumstance," she said, turning off her flashlight. "Whichever comes first. I do think this will be my last, though."

"Why do you say that?"

"Look at this old lady getting into a sleeping bag, Avila. But I came to help someone find closure, so I want to make sure she gets it."

Sometime in the night, I awoke to a revelation.

Panting, catching my breath, I'd been dreaming about Sharon and why she'd asked me all those questions the day before. It wasn't for the show. She wanted to know for herself. She had a personal connection to Villegas House, and Linda had told her that I would take her here. That was why Kane and Eve had sought me out. She said a Miccosukee woman would know about the house, and when they'd done their research, they'd found—me.

Why did Sharon want to find *this* house, of all houses? It couldn't have meant anything to her. Around me, the silence felt unsettling. A quick look at my phone told me it was 3 AM. I'd been asleep several hours.

Linda had told me I shouldn't be afraid of my gifts, and that was all I could dream about for half the night. No matter what images my brain had conjured up in the night, I could hear Linda's voice in the perimeter telling me it was useless to be afraid. The spirits could be menacing, but they couldn't hurt me—not physically anyway.

I wasn't so sure.

I'd seen episodes of their show where Sharon would get scratched, or finger marks would press against someone's throat. Right now, the crickets had quieted, and that, in and of itself, scared me. Did something walk outside the tent? The more I drifted in and out of sleep, the more I felt it was something physical, of this earth.

Feet scuttling, hands grasping.

Whispering.

I sat up on my sleeping bag and listened. I might have been dreaming. My mind may have been playing tricks on me, but sure enough, I heard hushed voices and twitching sounds. The voices were not familiar, or even human, and then I heard the crunch of plastic and metal being hashed around. Was someone messing with the equipment?

I wouldn't be able to sleep again until I knew.

These wild areas of Big Cypress could be dangerous if you weren't vigilant. I didn't want to find out too late that a wild hog or kowi—panther—had been on the prowl near my guests. Shuffling to my feet, I crawled to the tent flap, unzipped it open, and went outside. Just in case, I grabbed my phone, turned on the video, and got it ready.

TEN

Surrounded by tents, camp chairs, coolers, and our makeshift kitchen, I stood in the darkness and listened. Not a single movement. Not a shift of branch or leaf coming from the woods. In the stillness, I closed my eyes, detecting the very normal, very human sounds of loud breathing and snoring.

From the trees came a silence that permeated my soul.

Even nature wasn't that quiet.

The heroic part of my brain wanted to explore, assure the security of the crew's safety as they slept, make sure no panthers were prowling, but the other part of me, the part that had been imbued with fear of the unknown since a young age felt paralyzed.

Evil was out there, like the things I'd seen long ago.

I felt them.

What if ghosts watched us from the perimeter? What if they'd been waiting for us to fall asleep so they could invade our dreams, take our souls? Then I'd capture them on video, hand the footage over to the crew, and get the hell out of here. Scanning the camp, a million scenarios ran through my mind, not a single one of them practical or reasonable.

Avila.

No. No, I'd seen this movie before, the one where the unsuspecting scream queen followed the sound of her name being called, leading to inevitable danger. There was no way I'd follow. No way, except the voice sounded like Billie's, or the way my brain attempted to piece together the memory of Billie. Why would my little brother be here in the middle of the Everglades? Maybe he was always with me, and only now did I notice.

"Billie?" I watched the darkness through the staticky phone

screen.

The glades' heat and humidity did nothing to quench the chills on my skin.

"Billie?" I called again.

Whispers carried through the humid air.

My skin pricked with goose bumps.

I floated through the camp in an out-of-body experience, except I *was* walking. I felt the peat moss and cool moist dirt on the ground beneath my feet, the vibrations of the ground rising through my legs, the phone trembling in my hand. All reminded me I was alive. Mortal. Made of flesh, unlike whatever stalked the swamp. In fact, I'd never been more alert in my life, more tuned-in to the world around me, but which world—which dimension—did I walk?

Villegas House—the wood, the sagging roof, the shingles—existed on one plane.

Its heart and soul existed in another.

And it watched.

I stood facing the house. If I squinted just enough, the windows looked like manic eyes carved from a jack-o-lantern and the eaves looked like disheveled eyebrows, and that front door… I shook my head. This was nuts. There was no way the house was alive or real or looked like a face, or looked like it was grinning, or calling me, or any such imaginings. It was 3 AM, damn it, and I was under the influence of sleep with the sharpness of a woken mind.

Avila…

"No." I shook my head, tried to squeeze the voice from my head. "No, Billie. You're not here. You're in my memory. This house is just trying to get me to come in."

Above me, a pair of shutters slammed together and wavered back and forth in the breeze. I ripped my gaze away from the slumping structure and looked at my feet to make sure I wasn't dreaming. Bare, dirty feet firmly rooted in the grass. The house wanted me to stare it down, challenge it, step inside, but there was no way I would.

I was about to turn off my video when to my right, I heard the whispers again, only this time they didn't sound like people discussing in hushed tones. They didn't sound human or ethereal either. Taking steps toward the camp's supplies tent, I paused to listen. Skitterings, if that was a word. Scuttling and discussion and scheming. The tent shook gently, stopped, then shook again. Half my brain knew it was critters, more than likely, but the other half…

Come into the house, Avila.

We need you.

"No," I told the voice. There was nothing special about me. I was an ordinary woman with an ordinary life. No way did ghosts know my name or need me. This was my brain, my sick, deluded brain playing tricks on me. "Go away."

I could do this.

Coming around the side of the tent, I spotted it—the perfect cut-out window in the nylon siding and immediately knew what was going on. I crept up slowly, because what if it wasn't? What if something besides critters were inside that tent?

Avila, you're psyching yourself out.

I had seen this same scenario before. Anyone who lived in a natural habitat had. Swallowing my dread, I pushed aside my nerves and let the rational side of my mind take the reins. I pulled back the loose piece of nylon wavering in the minimal breeze, and peeked inside.

Several sets of beady little black eyes looked back at me, frozen with guilt.

A tsunami of relief washed over me so hard, my knees buckled. Raccoons I could deal with. Raccoons were of this world. Raccoons were harmless.

"Shoo! Get out of here," I ordered the creatures. Little trash pandas had ripped a perfect incision into our supplies tent, opened the Rubbermaid containers with their nimble hands, and were chowing down on granola bars and raw hot dogs.

The raccoons shrieked then scattered. They jumped out of the tent and left a mess in their wake. They bolted into the woods, bouncing and criss-crossing each other in panic while I stood there gripping my freaked-out heart. "Shit."

In the night and darkness, they'd sounded like bandits. I wasn't the only one awake now, as I tuned into real human voices crossing the camp. Familiar figures emerged from the dark and joined me at the scene of the crime.

"What happened?" Quinn, fully dressed, and Kane, in only shorts and no shirt, crawled up to me. I averted my eyes from Eve's shirtless husband and looked at Quinn instead. In his hand, he held a shotgun aimed at the ground.

Seriously?

"Raccoons got into our food," I said, gazing at Quinn's weapon. What was he doing with that thing? Nobody told me there'd be a gun at this camp. Shouldn't there have been full disclosure of that at our initial meeting?

"Wasn't it closed up?" Kane whispered.

"Doesn't matter," I said. "Knowing how to get to food is their specialty."

Kane peeked past me, craning his neck to view the carnage. All inside the tent floor were open wrappers, container lids, and punctured sports drink bottles. A soupy, nasty mess. Quinn peeked in as well, shaking his head. "Little shits."

Yes, they were, but raccoons weren't the problem. Besides a perfect stranger toting a weapon around me, about ten feet away lying motionless on the ground was a small four-legged plump furry body. "Look there."

Kane stepped closer to the corpse already abuzz with angry flies. One raccoon hadn't fared as well as the others. It'd been ripped open, its black and brown body torn to shreds, entrails everywhere, a pudding cup still in its dexterous little hands. "What the hell?" Kane covered his mouth.

Quinn got in close to examine the raccoon then began checking for tracks. "What could've done this? Panther?" He aimed the gun into the woods, a cowboy ready for anything.

Kane must've seen the worry on my face, because he touched Quinn's arm and made him lower it with a quiet shake of his head. "Not now."

"Then when?" Quinn retorted.

I looked past everyone at the woods. "A panther wouldn't have mangled it. Panthers hunt and eat, not murder for sport." The animal hadn't been eaten. Instead, something had torn it apart without taking any of its meat.

"Then, what did this?" Kane asked.

"I don't know." We could crawl back into our tents, but the thin nylon walls would provide us with zero protection. "Maybe we should leave the island."

He looked at me, hands on his hips, lips pressed together. What was going on in that man's mind? Something to do with ratings, viewership and lost investment, most likely.

"Let's get this cleaned up," Kane said, looking around. "Quinn, help me put the animal in a garbage bag. We'll double-bag it and hope the smell doesn't attract anything else."

Kane gave me a knowing look. He knew about the nearby gators, because I'd mentioned them, but this wasn't made by a predator.

"Guys," I said. "Something mangled that raccoon, something that didn't even want to eat it. I don't know any animal that would do this, and I've lived in this area my whole life."

The men listened but ignored me for the most part. It was clear they had no plans on leaving any time soon, certainly not in the middle of the night, and not until they'd captured something that could be minimally produced into an episode.

Maybe I was freaking out for no reason. A wild hog could have ripped apart the raccoon, one that had been thwarted when I came to investigate. Maybe I was wrong and panthers were hunting tonight. I had to calm down.

"Should we shoot this?" Quinn hoisted the shotgun over his shoulder.

It took me a moment to realize he meant shooting footage.

"Yeah, go ahead," Kane said. "Get the camera. A few good angles and pics for studying later. I don't know how to approach all this, I'll tell you that much."

"It's been more about the living than the dead," Quinn added.

In hushed tones, they talked about the show and how to package the shots they'd taken so far. Here I was, worried about whatever was in the house that wanted to harm us, and these guys' minds were still on the show.

I realized my own video had been running, but I'd had it aimed at the floor for the last few minutes. Turning it off, I put the phone back in my pocket and slowly backed away from the men.

The house looked at me again. I stared back at the monster.

I won't go inside, I told it.

Looming in the darkness, its mouth—the front door—yawned wide open.

We all looked at it.

What did it want with me? Why did it taunt me? I might have been losing my mind. A raccoon had been torn to shreds a few feet from its front porch for no apparent reason, had not been carried off by its predator—I had a right to panic. Just in front of it were two men, obsessed over documenting the event, and inside my tent was an old woman who had warned us that something wanted us to die.

I didn't want to stay. I didn't want to enter the tent either.

What if Linda was wide awake, staring at the doorway with those vacant eyes, channeling DIE DIE DIE again? Empty of soul and filled with another's energy. In the distance, I heard the thrashing of water and knew that the alligators were arguing, fighting over what morsels of food they had found. Though they continued to stay away, I knew gators were curious creatures and would eventually want to see what we were up to.

We had to leave in the morning. I'd do whatever I could to convince them. I knew chances were slim, because I had little evidence of anything wrong, except for the raccoon and my *feelings*, but I couldn't explain my fear.

My people had been right. Had been for years. Villegas House was not to be messed with. As though the island wanted to prove my point for me, a cool breeze blew through, rattling the tents, winds of sweet, heavy rain. Overhead, vast dark clouds rumbled. Big Cypress was about to catch a summer storm, and the crew of *Haunted Southland* would finally get a taste of a real thunderstorm. The choices were to stick to our tents, airboat back to the village under a deluge to threaten all technical equipment, or seek shelter inside Villegas House itself.

I would've taken any of those options, except the last.

ELEVEN

The sky opened, as shards of rain pelted us like bullets. Everglades thunderstorms were no joke, and this crew was about to learn the hard way that their tents were no match. Camp broke into a panic, as everyone scattered to collect things.

Sharon shot out of her tent in unbuttoned shorts and tank top.

Linda and BJ shuffled out of their tents, as we all rushed to gather bags, equipment, pillows, blankets, anything we could carry. "You take this! I'll take that bag!" Linda shouted.

Detached, I watched the crew scamper.

"Bring it all into the house!" Kane shouted through the deluge.

While I'd been caught in many *Kahayatle* thunderstorms during airboat tours, this one was special. I hadn't seen it moving in. I was usually adept at telling when it was about to pour, but the raccoon death had distracted me. The ghosts in the woods had distracted me. I wasn't myself, and that alone put me at unease.

Overhead, the sky boomed, raindrops splashed my sweaty skin and soaked my hair. A mixture of acrid and sweet scents rose from the earth, as rain hit peat moss, activating bacteria, living things from under the earth, even the stench of the dead raccoon through the garbage bag. Everything sprung to life. All I could do was stand there and watch. I loved the panic, felt like I'd seen this scene before in another lifetime long ago.

"Avila!" Linda shouted through the curtain of rain. "Avila, come on!"

Rooted to the spot. Like watching a dream unfold in my head through a different dimension than my own. I heard my name being called, but I couldn't respond nor spring into action.

Like déja-vu.

One by one, the crew disappeared into Villegas House.

I wouldn't join them.

Seeking shelter was the last thing on my mind, especially there. The storm infused me with an energy I couldn't place. Closing my eyes, I heard them—the voices I'd heard earlier. Voices plotting in hushed tones. It frustrated me to know so many things, but not who was talking. The unmistakable sound of an airboat grew in the distance then whizzed by. I couldn't believe that anyone would be out here boating at this time of night.

"Someone is here," I said to no one.

I stared straight through the cypress trees to the riverbank.

My God, I felt like I was going crazy, but yes, that had definitely been the sound of an airboat. Were gladesmen out for a nightly hunt? Heading toward the shore where we'd left our airboat tethered, I heard the shouts of the crew behind me trying to coax me to come back. I picked up speed through the needles of rain headed for the riverbank. Several times now I'd been drawn to an area for no apparent reason.

When spongy land slowly gave way to water and my feet became soaked, I spotted our boat tied to a tangle of mangrove roots and squinted to make sure the sound wasn't our own boat being stolen. I was sure I would hear the motor again, but there were no ripples or wake in the river, or any sign that anyone had been here. Less than twenty-four hours later, and already I was hearing things.

I wanted to be near the investigation—it was why I'd come—but I hadn't asked for this.

For a sixth sense, a third eye, psychic vision, whatever you wanted to call it, but maybe this was what my mother meant by inviting it in. *En maheem, Avila,* I could hear her now. *You asked for it.* Opening myself up was a bad thing. Fine. But how could I make it stop now that I was here?

Take the boat, a voice said.

I could do that easily, but no—God—I wouldn't. There was no way I could leave these people here stranded on this island to their own devices with a day's worth of food and no means of getting back. They'd die, not the kind of thing I needed on my conscience.

Without my knowledge of these lands, these people would perish.

"Avila!" The distant shouts snapped me out of my trance.

I was soaked from head to toe through my clothes. It felt damn good. Like awaking from a long cyclical dream out of which I could not escape, a hamster wheel of the neverendingness that was my life. The sounds of airboats dissipated like an echo in a canyon but something new replaced it. There, in the pouring rain surrounded by darkness, the humid woods, and a whole island abuzz with invisible energy came laughter.

My skin erupted into goose bumps. Chills ran through me.

Men's laughter.

They spoke to each other, the types of things men said when they were in on a joke and you were their female target. The types of things white gladesmen said when you walked into the Winn-Dixie on the edge of town wearing your patchwork skirt down to the floor instead of the shorts and T-shirts their little blond barefoot children wore.

Hey, dirty girl, your mama make you that? Come here.

I shook my head. The rain created a curtain of white noise all around. I shouldn't have been able to hear the men. I closed my eyes, not wanting to see them. I could run to the house where everybody was hiding from the rainstorm and calling for me, the house I wasn't supposed to visit, but now it was too late. I could stay out here with the trees that sheltered ghosts of the past wishing to taunt me.

I can give you some real clothes. They're in my van…

I didn't have to open my eyes to see them. They lived forever in my mind, as fresh as the day I'd run into them while my mother was cashing a check at the grocery store customer service. Most people were nice, but every now and then, *they* came out of the woodwork—hateful sons of bitches with no respect for other cultures, as if their nicotine-stained teeth and stringy hair hidden underneath Florida Marlins baseball caps were the finest examples of their kind.

Come on, come to my van. I put in a mattress just yesterday. It'll be fun…

"Go away," I gritted my teeth at them. "Go the hell away."

I hated the fathers. And the children, too, even though they didn't taunt me. I hated them because one day they would. The hate would be passed on like disease. Why did they have to be rude? I'd never felt hatred for anyone until that day. I'd done a pretty good job of putting the memories away. You had to, or else you couldn't function. There was no use going around worried what people from other cultures thought of you.

"Leave me alone. Can't you ever leave me alone?" I muttered.

"Who are you talking to, love?" I felt cold hands gripping my arm and turned to see Linda standing next to me getting soaked. "Come on inside, Avila. Don't listen to them."

She understood.

For that, I was grateful. Anyone else would've told me I was crazy for talking to thin air, whether from my own mind or another realm. "Yes…okay…" I mumbled, letting Linda lead me away back through the trees toward the clearing where the camp had been but now was mostly empty except for a few plastic bags and Rubbermaid containers.

Still, I looked back twice to make sure the men and their children were gone.

The house gaped at me out of the darkness, and every cell of my soul fought going towards it. I stopped short of the crumbling structure about ten feet, while Kane and others stood at the door beckoning me to come inside. They were alive and drier than I was, but at what expense?

I had to put aside my kid fears and just walk in already, tell myself it was like any other house, and maybe it would become true. If we lied to ourselves enough, eventually we'd make our own reality.

"Come on, Avila, honey. It's okay." Linda tugged at my arm. I felt bad that her pretty red hair was now a plastered mop of dark auburn punctuated by light gray roots on top of her head. Her age showed through.

I nodded, staring up at the house.

The rain imbued the energies, didn't it?

A murder had taken place here. All for what? Over a house? For a spot of land which amounted to an invisible speck on a map? What was it with people fighting for land so damn much? Land didn't belong to us anyway. We borrowed it, along with time, rented it from Mother Earth.

"God, why is this so hard?" I heard myself say.

"I know, honey. But come on. It may not want us here, but it's not going to hurt us." She said that just to get me inside and out of the rain, but I knew it wasn't true. The thing that came for me in the dark when I was little…that thing wanted to hurt me. I'd spent my life hiding from it.

"Oh, for hell's sake, just leave her out there if she doesn't want to come in."

The voice belonged to Sharon speaking just out of range near the open doorway. She must've thought I couldn't hear her, though I watched the accompanying hand flail to her words like I was a used rag to be forgotten about.

"Catching a cold for trying to help that woman is the last thing

Linda needs. Come on, Linda!" Sharon bellowed.

Linda tugged on my arm, and finally, after a series of three quick bolts of nearby lightning in a row, I moved. Not because of the lightning, but because I didn't want to get the poor woman in trouble, make her look like a fool for helping me out.

"There you go, honey. Come on…" She ushered me up the porch steps and through the front door into the darkest house I'd ever been in my life.

Inside were pine wood walls rotting away underneath a sagging ceiling that leaked with rain in multiple spots. The inside space felt warm, humid, and body-scented from the sweating pores of five individuals. In the middle was a staircase leading up into even darker recesses. To my right was a living room mostly empty except for a wooden cupboard inside which sat cracked old porcelain plates.

A wooden spindled chair sat lonely in the corner. To my other side was another empty room except for another two chairs that matched the one in what I suspected was a dining room. Everyone was scattered across both rooms, running their hands through their hair or fanning themselves with random objects—baseball hats, stapled papers from their belongings, or expired airline tickets. Rain leaked through the ceiling in the corners.

"We shouldn't be here," I said.

Everyone looked at me like I was an idiot. Being inside was the very reason they'd come, the whole purpose for the trip.

"We won't be here for long, Avila," Kane said. He knew I was afraid of this house. I'd only told him a hundred times the day I met him.

BJ walked up to me and handed me a mostly wet green towel with a few dry spots on it. "Here, for whatever that's worth," he said. It occurred to me that I hadn't heard the tone of his voice before this.

"Thanks." I took the towel and handed it to Linda, who'd begun coughing, instead so she could dry herself off. I couldn't shake the feeling of dread inside me, but I told myself it would be over soon.

"Alright." Kane turned on a flashlight-lantern combo and stood it upright in the middle of the floor before standing and addressing everyone with a big exhale. "Listen up, people. Things are not going well, obviously, and time is money. Looking at the radar is tough because cell service is spotty at best. I don't think this storm will last long—"

"It won't," Quinn interrupted. "Everglades storms are flashes in the pan then they're over."

I loved how Quinn had suddenly become the Everglades expert.

"Well, this don't look like it's going to be over anytime soon," Sharon mumbled under her breath. "In fact, it's getting worse and all our equipment's gonna go to shit."

"Our equipment is fine. We came prepared. Watertight cases, plenty of plastic lining. Let's not jump to conclusions," Kane said to placate the hostess who had long ago gotten on my nerves.

For her lack of manners? For her brusqueness, I wasn't sure. All I knew was that she kept giving me dirty looks not unlike the ones I'd been reminded of outside with those old memories.

"We knew this could happen before we came, remember? We talked about the rainstorms and how they could put a damper on things, no pun intended."

Eve, wanting everyone to agree with her husband, as always, sat on the floor looking up at him, nodding, checking the crew's faces for understanding. "We did. We talked about it." When her line of view caught mine, she smiled.

I looked away, not used to people being as nice. When I first met her, I thought Eve's likeability was fake, but now I realized she was real. And she was some kids' mom, too, which made me like her even more.

"Right. So, my suggestion is we wait here in the house for the rain to stop. Once it does, we film all we can. Alright, Sharon?"

"Assuming the damn cameras work," Sharon said.

"Obviously," Kane replied. "Catch whatever we can on tape, get the hell out of here. If it's a loss, it's a loss. This was risky from the beginning, best laid plans, and all that. Now—"

"So, you're saying we came out all this way for nothing?" Sharon crossed her arms. "Because I don't think I'm ready to go."

Nobody said anything. It seemed that nobody would dare. Only Kane, because he was in charge. Or was Sharon in charge?

"It happens, hon," Kane told her, flipping his palms up.

"Don't 'hon' me, Kane."

"Okay, what do you want me to do?" Kane bit back.

Sharon scoffed. "Don't you think we should stop at nothing to get what we want, especially since we've already been through so much? I mean, shit. First, the flights were delayed, then we had to pay triple for the damn airboat because nobody was a licensed operator when we rented it. Then Linda here tells us we're going to DIE, then a stupid raccoon up and flips over. Then, the rainstorm from Hell nearly ruins all our equipment. I mean, we're here, damn it, let's just do this."

From across the room, Quinn nodded. He of the gun agreed they should stop at nothing. That didn't make me feel any better. Everyone else seemed to have mixed thoughts, from the way they avoided Sharon's gazes.

"Like I said, we're going to give it a go," Kane said as calmly as a man in his position could. "Once it stops raining. But like I said, some gigs are a loss, Sharon. You need to accept that."

"I don't need to accept shit, Kane. I came here to find the truth."

The truth?

I looked at Linda, but she played with a ragged thread hanging from the hem of her shirt. Was it me, or was everyone starting to get on each other's nerves now that we were inside the house? What was this about the truth? Some cases were a lost cause and Villegas House was one of them.

Kane sucked in a breath, looked at me, then back at her, as though this was not one conversation I was privy to. "I know this episode was your idea, Sharon, but you're asking me to bypass circumstances. We'll do what we can, but some houses don't want to speak with us, and I'm not going to stick around while wild animals get killed and the elements bear down on us just so you can find your answers."

I agreed wholeheartedly with Kane, though I wanted to know what answers it was that Sharon wanted. "Why the interest in this house?" I asked out of the blue.

Again, all eyes fell on me.

"I mean, most people have never even heard of it, but you talk like it's meaningful to you. Why?"

"Doesn't matter, Cypress. Just let it be."

"Tell me."

"I told you, let it be!" Blue eyes narrowed and warned me.

I looked at Linda who widened hers at me, as if urging me to do just that—let it go. Did Sharon have a connection to this house? If she did, I wanted to know about it. Hell, I deserved to know about it, considering my grandfather had been killed here. "What do you know about Villegas House?" I asked again.

Sharon whipped her head around at me. "Alright, you know what? The problem isn't what I know, it's what I *don't* know. So, since it seems we're going to be losing our time and money here,

Kane darling, why don't we hurry things up then and do what we always do when we're pressed for time and the spirits won't cooperate?"

"No," Eve said, shaking her head. "Absolutely not."

"Why not?" Sharon asked her. "You know it's the easiest way when the ghosts don't want to speak. Let's do this already."

"Do what? What is she talking about?" I leaned toward Linda.

"A séance." She closed her eyes and inhaled deeply. "She wants me to conduct a séance."

TWELVE

In all the episodes I'd watched, I hadn't seen them do a single séance, which was perfectly fine with me. The idea of having one always freaked the heck out of me. A bunch of people sitting around a table, holding hands, inviting the spirits to speak and possibly take over your body? No, thank you.

Not even would I participate in a séance to talk to my own brother.

What was dead was dead.

Let the spirits rest.

But the only thought skating through my mind at the moment was Uncle Bob and my mom at dinner two weeks ago telling me that, by telling ghost stories on my airboat, I'd be inviting in dark spirits. I didn't believe it at the time, didn't buy the connection they were trying to make, and yet here I was two weeks later, sitting crossed legged on the floor of Villegas House listening to Sharon Roswell suggest they hold a séance.

Why was I scared by the thought of one if I hadn't believed my mother?

The crew looked at Linda and waited for her input. Kane, Eve, Quinn, and BJ all seemed to be in favor of holding the séance if it meant possibly getting out of here faster, and Sharon was, of course, waiting on pins and needles. I thought for sure Linda would object. After all, she knew all about the negative energy associated with this house, so imagine my surprise when she shrugged and shook her head in defeat.

"This is the last time I'll do this, people."

"Linda, you don't have to do this," I whispered.

She ignored me. "I already told you the spirits don't want you or anybody in this house. It upsets them, shows them what they can no longer have—a life. But let's do this and get this over with. Maybe we can be done with it and leave by morning."

"Sounds like a plan." Kane clapped in that way he loved to do to get himself motivated.

I couldn't believe this.

It was almost five in the morning, we hadn't slept, and now we were about to invite the spirits to speak through a fragile woman. I wouldn't participate. I couldn't. When judgment day came for me and my camp asked if I had led this group of non-Indians to our most reviled, feared location, I would admit to taking them here and endure their disappointment, but I could not participate in these rituals.

I would sit nearby and observe from a safe distance, if there were such a thing.

Linda held out her hand to me, so I would help her up. I guided her to the side of the house that seemed driest, all the while I couldn't believe this was happening. Having a séance, a communication circle of the dead, in a murder house during a thunderstorm. Good God.

Linda sensed my trepidation. "The faster we do this, the faster we go home, right?" She patted my hand. "I'm so sorry we brought you into this, Avila."

"It's fine," I said though it wasn't. Why did I always insist things were fine when they weren't? Evil was going to come pouring into this house faster than a waterfall of shit.

Kane gave orders to the crew who quickly set up their cameras and voice recorders and other tech stuff. I heard BJ telling Kane that the one camera which had malfunctioned earlier was still acting wonky though better than before. "Lock off the cam," Kane told him. "We'll need to open the aperture wide and boost two-stops. Drop some cans against the wall with some low red splash."

Quinn pulled a plastic film out of a bag, unfolded, and proceeded to place it on top of the camera, which he set up on a tripod. About ten minutes later, they were ready for their circle of death, and I wanted to scream, *This is not a good idea! Maybe in a peaceful home with a mischievous spirit whose name you wanted to know, but not here. Not at Villegas House.*

What if we called the murderer through?

I had zero say. I sat as far back from the circle as I could blending into the gray pall of the house. I didn't even so much as want my skin touching the walls if I could help it, so I lingered on the fringe. Clutching my gator tooth necklace, head atop my knees, I watched in silence. Maybe Linda was right and this was best. It would satisfy the crew's curiosity, give Sharon whatever the heck she was looking for, and be easy to produce into an episode. They could take footage of the séance and edit it into an easy, hour-long show later on without having to stay another full day.

We could leave by morning.

Linda rummaged through the bag Eve had handed her and began taking out what appeared to be a sage smudge wand, an abalone shell, little figurines of various saints, a white pillar candle, and a lighter. Once she lit the candle and gave Kane a nod, he turned off his flashlight and everyone fell into a circle with Linda. Taking the smudge wand and dipping it into the flame, Linda blew out the end and the wand smoked beautifully. Droplets of rain played at the edges of the candle.

"Smoke of air, fire of earth, cleanse and bless this home and hearth…" She chanted off a simple prayer that had me feeling like it wouldn't be enough to conquer the dark entities I was feeling here. "Drive away all harm and fear…only good may enter here."

She called to Archangel Michael for protection and summoned the help of Archangel Gabriel for clear communication, as the smudge stick got passed around and everyone had a hand in sage-ing themselves and the circle as it made its way back to Linda. Around me, I felt a lightness of being, like that of someone kind and gentle, but it could've been psychological or the spirit of my little brother again.

"Billie, if you're here, please go," I whispered. "I don't want you here."

Nothing came to me, and a moment later, the safe feeling was gone, replaced by a heaviness filled with sadness and guilt. So much for sage. I held onto my charm for protection. *Grandfather, please, keep me safe.*

"In the name of the Father, and of the Son, and of the Holy Spirit," Linda said, opening up her towel and pulling out a small cross. She held it up to the ceiling. I closed my eyes. I was Christian—many of us were from years of private schooling—and the prayer felt protective.

Around me, the atmosphere grew heavier, darker. To the naked eye, nothing had changed, but I felt unseen presences flowing through the room like floodwaters reaching every corner. I swore on my life, on my brother's life that when I got back home, I would never mess with the supernatural again. The core of my body trembled as though I were caught stuck in a meat locker. With eyes closed, I felt more sensitive to the energies, so I reopened them.

The camera's red light blinked steadily.

"We ask for protection and implore that any spirits in this home, please come forth and tell us your name." Linda put down the cross and joined hands with Kane to her left and Sharon to her right, as everyone else held hands to form a circle.

For a whole minute, nobody spoke or moved.

The candle flickered gently, though outside was still pouring and rogue drafts blew randomly through the house. The smoke from the sage wand billowed gently, creating a haze in the air above their heads.

"If you can hear me," Linda said, "please come forward and tell us your name."

We waited. I knew where it was. Right in middle of the room. Though I couldn't see it, I felt its hatred. Overwhelming, angry, and now…ticked off that we were summoning it.

"*You…*"

From thin air, a voice spoke in a low, dull thrum. It felt male and old.

I wanted to DIE just like the spirit had asked of us.

The crew all looked at each other making sure none of them had spoken. *Please, God, no, God no, God no…* This couldn't have been happening. There couldn't be an actual male voice belonging to none of us channeling through Linda's lips. I was living a nightmare. Watching Linda, I saw her lips move in time with the voice that was not hers, not anybody's.

"*Get out. Don't you know when you're not wanted? GET OUT!*"

The voice coming from Linda Hutchinson's lips didn't sound human. I covered my ears, shook my head. *God, please make it stop…* They weren't faking this.

"Why do you want us to get out? If we do that, how will we ever help you?" Sharon wanted to know.

"It doesn't want our help. It wants us *dead*," I muttered, gripping the gator tooth charm.

"Keep rolling," Kane mumbled, one eye on DJ. "You gettin' this?"

BJ nodded, his mouth agape, as he stared forward.

Every single one of the crew members startled and adjusted their seating, clearly uncomfortable. DJ's forehead had broken out into huge beads of sweat, Quinn shook his head angrily, and Kane and Eve exchanged confused glances across Linda's body.

Sharon cleared her throat. "Who are you? Why do you want us to leave?"

No response.

We all watched as Linda's head hung back, her chin tilted into the air, as a line of saliva slowly dripped from her mouth. Slowly, she began to tremble until she was shaking, convulsing, yet nobody would help her. I wanted to leap forward and assist her but did not want to enter their sacred circle.

"Maybe we should end this," I suggested. "She's not well. This isn't right," I said louder. It didn't look right to have an older woman shaking that way with her neck loose, nor to have these people abusing her abilities and kindness this way. "Hello? Anybody hear me?"

Only Eve looked my way, but her expression was one of helplessness. She seemed to agree with me, sympathized but didn't make the decisions, and everyone else was hell-bent on going through with this. I would rather go back outside in the rain. I would rather deal with my own personal demons haunting the woods than this.

"You are not safe here," another voice spoke from Linda's mouth. This one had an English accent, and I immediately knew it could only be that of Gregory Rutherford who'd been murdered here.

"In the name of the Father, and of the Son, and of the Holy Spirit…" Eve murmured, and I crossed myself. "Hail Mary, full of grace, the Lord is with you…" All her catechism came pouring out of her, as she randomly rambled prayers out loud. I was grateful for them.

"Cursed woman…" the first voice continued in its raspy tone. "Leave now."

"We will leave when you tell us what happened here," Sharon said, holding tightly onto Kane and Quinn's hands.

"Cursed woman. It was *you*…"

"Who are you talking about, spirit? Or are you a demon?" Sharon asked.

Spirit, demon—did it matter? There was no body, no face, no eyes, but I felt like he—IT—was talking about me.

"You must go. It's not safe," Rutherford pled with us from beyond.

I felt something surround me, a cold breeze followed by a dark shadow that crossed in front of me and swirled into the middle of the circle forming a vortex that spun faster with every second. The darkness reminded me of the energy I had seen as a child. It was here—it wanted me.

Sharon ignored the environmentalist spirit's request. "Were you murdered? Or were you the murderer? Tell us then we'll leave." Sharon spoke for Linda who was no longer in control, her soul having been overtaken by someone…something. Grabbing the pencil on the table, she again gripped it like a four-year-old might and again scribbled on the bare floor of the house like she had on her crossword puzzle.

"What does it say?" Eve asked, tears in her eyes.

Vulnerable in my corner of the room, I moved closer to the circle, peeking to see what Linda was writing. Sharon shot me a look. I didn't care if my presence was disturbing the energies or disrupting the séance, I needed to see what she wrote.

DIE DIE DIE… Linda scribbled without looking at her words, her body continuing to convulse harder and harder.

CYPRESS

CYPRESS

CYPRESS.

What? No.

"I think we should stop," Kane said, looking at me. His hands still held onto Linda's arm and Sharon's hand.

"Not until he answers us!" Sharon shouted.

Who was the boss here—Kane or Sharon? What the hell was this woman thinking, and why was Linda writing my name? I couldn't hold it anymore and let out tears of frustration that welled up and spilled over.

"Tell us what happened here, spirit, and we will leave! Who are you?"

"I'm out of here." I stood and stepped to the front door. Who would know my name in this place except my grandfather? Could my grandfather be trying to contact me, and this demon wasn't letting it?

"Don't move!" Sharon shouted at me. "It's trying to scare you."

I nearly went back and slapped her. She was nobody to tell me what to do, especially not now when I didn't feel safe, when I feared for my life. "Yeah, well, it's doing a great job."

"I have forgotten my name," the spirit uttered then shouted, "I won't tell you again!" Nameless spirit opened Linda's mouth wide and from where I stood, a dark cloud of energy emerged from her cracked, dry lips tinged with pink old-lady lipstick. It rose into the air and slammed into the ceiling, knocking a loose beam onto the ground, inches from DJ.

Our screams echoed off the walls, as we scattered. We covered our heads, dispersing and breaking the circle. Enough was enough, and I hated Sharon for forcing the issue when it became clear that we shouldn't have been meddling to begin with.

"Damn…" Kane breathed into his hands, looked away, then breathed nervously into them again. He crouched to the ground and placed his hand on Linda's back, checking her breathing. She had slumped forward, her face pushed into the cracked wooden floor of the house. He pulled her up by the shoulders, checked her breathing.

Limp, motionless.

My stomach gripped around a knot in my core.

Kane's fingers pressed against her pulse points on her neck. No reaction. He pinched the bridge of his nose. "I think she's dead."

THIRTEEN

Yes, she was.

I knew, because I saw it—the familiar soft light rising out of the old woman's body into the ceiling, same as I'd seen the night when my little brother had passed. She was gone—Linda was gone, and we were all to blame.

Especially me.

I hadn't argued with them enough, hadn't warned them enough, not that they would've listened. I'd tried but they blew me off.

"Dead?" Sharon lay her down flat on her back. The woman's body fell limp. "What do you mean?"

"I mean *dead*, Sharon! What the hell else do you think I mean?" Kane shouted, then began pacing in a circle to calm himself down before crouching beside Linda's body again. "Jesus Christ."

Eve threw her arm around her husband's shoulders. "Babe, don't. Let's think about this for a second."

Kane nodded in quick succession.

"Check her breathing, Sharon," Quinn said.

"I already checked it," Kane told her. "CPR…who knows CPR?"

"Nobody. Jesus…" BJ turned his back to us and rocked back and forth.

Sharon tilted back Linda's head, opened her airways and prepared to administer CPR while Quinn attempted chest compressions. There was no point to any of this, because I'd seen her spirit leave. I crossed my fingers anyway, hoping I was wrong and had seen a trick of the light.

They did everything they could do, while Kane and I attempted over and over to get a signal on our phones to call emergency services, but the storm was too heavy and service had been shitty out here to begin with.

Damn. We shouldn't have come out. All signs pointed to staying away, to warning us it was a bad idea, but this was what happened when six stubborn people got together and tempted fate.

Quinn stopped with the compressions, as Sharon stopped with trying to reactivate Linda's lungs. "Lord have mercy," she said, sitting back on her heels. For the first time, she was quiet and resigned. "In the good Lord Jesus's name, Amen." She gestured the sign of the cross over Linda's body. "I can't believe this…"

"What do we do now?" Eve pressed back tears with the palms of her hands.

"That's it. We're done," Kane said. "Let's pack it up, get Linda back to the Indian village or Miami. From there, we'll call an ambulance. Game over, y'all."

"In this storm?" Quinn asked. The man of few words said exactly what I was thinking. It's be better to pack it up and wait, *then* leave.

"What else are we going to do?" Kane asked, his agitation rising once again.

"He's right, though," I said. "We can't go back until the rain is over. Airboats are light. They can't handle conditions like this."

Eve knotted her sweaty locks into a tight bun on top of her head. "Then we have to cover her, keep her comfortable until the rain stops. Let's pack it up while we're waiting for the storm to blow over. When it does, we leave."

Besides the glaring error that Linda would no longer have a need for comfort, Eve was right. All we could do for now was pack this party up. I watched as Eve held Linda's limp hand and shed tears for the woman.

"Exactly," I said, sorry that it took the death of a lovely woman to realize this. We all looked at Linda's body—a dead body right there in the middle of the floor. A woman we all knew, who'd been breathing and talking moments before, now lying lifeless. It was surreal and nobody would mention the elephant in the room.

Why had she collapsed? What had caused it?

"It was nobody's fault," Kane assured us. "Got it? The situation was stressful. Her heart naturally gave out. We all know she had a heart condition."

She'd a heart condition. *Disease…* Yet they'd allowed her to come on this investigation? Wasn't that selfish and irresponsible, even if she *had* insisted on helping them?

Only Eve and Sharon nodded in agreement. Quinn seemed to think otherwise from his grim thin-lipped stance, but kept it quiet, and BJ was busy rocking himself in the corner, like a mental patient at Briarcliff Manor. "The spirit killed her…" he mumbled.

"BJ, you got something to say, buddy?" Kane asked, hands on his hips.

"I said the spirit killed her," the man said louder, still rocking back and forth. "She warned us to stay away but we kept going and going, then it warned us that someone would die, and someone did!" He was shouting by the end.

"No, bro, that's not what happened. You know damn well the spirits can't hurt us," Kane said.

"If they can't hurt us, then why do we burn sage?" BJ asked through tear-stained face. "Why is there footage and photos of us with scratches on our arms and backs? Savannah Garden House, anyone?" He'd turned around now and was eyeing the group with anger in his red-rimmed bright eyes. I couldn't remember what had happened on the Savannah Garden House episode. "You say they can't hurt us, yet they do. And now look what happened."

"No, BJ," Eve continued with the theory she and Kane were selling. "She was old, and her heart gave out."

But there was truth in BJ's words. The spirit did warn us that someone would die.

Shit. Shit, shit.

I felt his pain as though it were my own, or maybe I felt exactly as he did, like getting the hell of this island and feeling trapped. There was nothing we could do at the moment, however, and standing around arguing wasn't helping. I stood and charged to the nearest pile of tech gear, lifting random things off the ground and stuffing them in bags.

"What are you doing?" Quinn asked.

"Packing."

"That's not where that goes," he said.

"Then put it where it goes," I stammered, shooting him a severe look. "We need to pack while it's raining so the moment it stops, we can get out of here. If you're not ready by the time the sun is up and the rains have stopped, I'm leaving without you all."

I threw down a boom I was holding and stormed off to find my own things somewhere in this evil house, make sure they were ready to go. I packed Linda's things as well, finding her crossword puzzle and stopped cold. In the corner of the page, she'd created a beautiful sketch of a young woman. Hair floating in the wind, gauzy dress billowing behind her.

The woman from the woods.

In the opposite corner of the page, connected with tendrils of smoke to the woman in the dress was another woman who looked a lot like me—long, straight black hair loose over my shoulders, medium build, stocky, not very romantic by comparison but just as proud. Hanging around my neck was my necklace with little lines coming out of it as though it emitted power of its own.

I placed the crossword book inside my own backpack to further examine later.

Nobody spoke though everyone had begun moving, slowly collecting things while in shock.

From the beginning, I'd known this was a bad idea, but I couldn't even blame them because I'd gone along with it. I only blamed myself, though I also felt Kane's guilt like a slow fog spreading from his aura to mine. But I didn't want to hear his excuses or pep talk. We had one job and one job only at the moment—to get Linda Hutchinson's body to the nearest hospital, so I could go crawling back to my village to confess the stupid things I'd done. I didn't want payment for my time. It'd be blood money anyway.

Whoever the evil spirit was who'd spoken to us, he still hung oppressively in the room, bearing down his hefty influence, because every single one of us, from the sounds of grunts and sighs and the charging around angrily, acted like we would kill each other if anyone spoke a single word.

I took Linda's sleeping blanket and laid it over her body.

Eve came over and exposed her face in the hopes she might come back to life and breathe suddenly, but I looked at Eve somberly and covered Linda's face again.

I could forgive curiosity in coming here. I could even forgive letting the old woman come along if she'd been part of the team for a long time, so much that they all overlooked her ailment, especially if she'd insisted. What I couldn't forgive was Sharon's insistence that the séance continue, even as Linda showed signs of physical distress. We should've stopped it while we still could. But we didn't. Because Sharon was selfish and needed what she damn well needed.

The house could take the bitch alive at this point for all I cared.

FOURTEEN

By sunrise, the rain had slowed considerably enough to step out of the house. Quinn and Kane walked over to the airboat to assess the situation. Also to scoop out rainwater using red Solo cups so we could load the boat up and get the hell out of here. BJ, Sharon, and I dragged all the boxes and bags we could out of Villegas House and set up a triage area.

Inside Villegas House, Linda was dead.

A lifeless body covered with an open sleeping bag.

We didn't dare move her. Everyone seemed too nervous to be near her, except for Eve, who wouldn't leave her side and continued to hold the old woman's hand sticking out under the cover.

Had this happened in our camp to one of our family members, we would've cooked for four days as mourning, and part of me wanted to do the same for Linda, but I was not with people of my own tradition, and we'd be leaving soon anyway.

I lingered outside the door watching her still body while Sharon tried getting a signal on her phone.

BJ stood near a tree, talking to himself.

Two hours ago, a sweet woman had been breathing, and now she was gone.

What would we tell her family? Did she have a husband or kids? It made me sad just how little I knew about her. Fifty or so years ago, death had come to my grandfather and others in this same spot. It made sense that the energy of this house wanted more of the same to feed it. This was why my tribe had told me to stay away.

Some houses wanted to be miserable.

Twenty minutes later, Kane and Quinn returned, told us the

airboat was ready and that gators had crawled onto the land and piled into a hissing heap.

It was the dead body within olfactory range. We needed to get a move on.

The men all carried the heavy boxes loaded with tech equipment while Sharon, Eve, and I carried the backpacks and lighter items. I heard Kane tell BJ that he'd need to board the airboat first to center his weight so we could load the rest of the items around him. BJ, in massive shock over Linda's death, more so than any of us, lumbered on without a word.

I watched him.

Head down, mumbling to himself. I wondered if BJ had ever dealt with a death before, if this incident might've provoked painful memories of some sort. I could empathize, having witnessed my brother's death twenty-one ago, but BJ hadn't spoken or interacted with anybody in hours.

Watching the boat rock back and forth, we waited until BJ centered himself in the middle of the vessel before piling boxes and bags around him. All that was left was one backpack and Linda's body. Kane wiped sweat from his brow using the hem of his tank top. "Be right back," he said, and we followed him, slapping mosquitos and flinging away sweat.

I hated the idea of driving the boat along the waterways with a dead body onboard. Traveling in the wild with a body in the beginning stages of decomposition didn't seem like a good idea. We didn't need medical help to confirm she was dead, but I knew we had to bring her to a hospital. Her family would want her body recovered.

Tears had welled up in my eyes thinking about it.

For the last time, I walked to Villegas House, hating myself for having come here and inciting trouble. Once again, I'd survived what someone else had failed to live through. Sharon and I didn't speak to each other, because if she even tried, I would snap at her for being a wench and that would not be good mojo for the ride back. Her life was in my hands since I was the one who'd be driving her selfish ass back to civilization. She needed to be nice to me.

Eve and I stood by while the men entered the house to lift Linda by her shoulders and feet and pull her out of the rotting house. Once they did, they set her on the ground and made room for one or two more of us to help carry her.

"Babe, can you take the last two bags?" Kane asked Eve. I supposed that meant Sharon and I would help him carry Linda.

We each took an opposite side of her torso. It felt incredibly odd to carry a dead woman. Her skin felt cold through her shirt, and it seemed that rigor mortis was already starting to set in despite the intensely humid air.

Taking a last look at Villegas House, I closed my eyes. "Hope you find your peace," I told the house in a whisper. Too much had happened here. Too many lives taken. Too many buried on the property. Now that I'd seen the place with my own eyes, I would never return. Good riddance.

We had taken three steps in the direction back to the airboat when we heard it—the sound of the airboat's engine.

"What the hell is that?" Sharon asked.

"Is that our boat?" I said. Or had someone passing through decided to stop and help us, having seen our boat off the island?

"Put her down, put her down!" Kane barked, and as we set down poor Linda's body, he and Quinn ran off in the direction of our boat. A sinking feeling dropped through my torso. It couldn't have been. He wouldn't have.

Sharon, Eve, and I ran after the men, tripping over our own feet in an effort to reach the boat before being stranded on this patch of cypress for the foreseeable future. When we reached the point where sloughing was necessary, Quinn and Kane, ahead of us by thirty feet, began yelling.

"Hey!" Kane shouted, wading into the water then stepping back out once he spotted the gators. "BJ!"

Unbelievable. He'd done it. BJ had taken off with the airboat, the skiff leaving a heavy wake trail all the way back to the gators making a beeline for our shore. If there was ever a good time to sic alligators on a fellow human, this would be it.

"He left." Eve vocalized what most of us could only begin to process. "He left us."

Quinn pulled forward his shotgun and began shooting in the direction of the airboat, not close enough to hurt BJ but what I'd hoped was an attempt to scare him into coming back. After four rounds, he cocked it back and shot again before it was out. For the first time, I wondered if he had more shells on him. We would need more if stranded here.

"Get your ass back here!" Kane kept yelling. "Not cool, man!"

"Is this happening?" I mumbled. "This is happening."

"Idiot. I knew he shouldn't have come," Sharon said, pacing back and forth, picking up sticks and flinging them high into the trees. "I always knew he'd do something like this one day, weakling piece of crap."

"How did you know?" Eve faced her angrily. "Huh? How, Sharon? Nobody could ever know. Jesus Christ, now we're stuck here." She pulled out her phone but again, the storm created a weak signal, and she slammed the phone onto the ground and stamped her feet. "Damn it! We have no chargers. Babe! We need to call for help."

"Sure thing, honey," Kane said over his shoulder. I could feel a darkness growing in him that wasn't there yesterday or even two hours ago. "Let me just pull out my dead cell phone and charge it using the generator that was on that freakin' airboat, and everything will be great!"

I tried my cell phone too, as Quinn stopped shooting and put the gun back over his shoulder. "I told my family I was going fishing," I talked to myself. "How are they going to find me? They're never going to find me."

"FUUUUUUUCKKKKK!" Kane yelled again, his voice an echo through the trees. He kicked a cypress root with his sneaker then scrambled back onto land, squatting with his hands over his head.

Eve flew to her husband's side, even though he'd given her major shade a minute ago. "He took off. He took off, babe. What do we do now?"

"Where's the nearest place to swim to?" Quinn asked me.

"There might be a gladesmen outpost somewhere, but they move around," I told him. "They wander and hunt. Could be anywhere. Besides, we can't swim here."

"When we arrived, you said we could."

"Six feet maybe. But not far enough to find help. The gators…"

"Then one of us needs to wait here until another airboat passes by, flag them down," Quinn said.

I hated to say it, but unless someone had brought a flare, that was our only option. Waiting for another boat to pass us could take days, a week even. This was how news was made, when teams of soccer players got stuck in cave systems and television production crews got stuck on abandoned cypress islands surrounded by flesh-eating reptiles.

"Unless there's a flare inside one of those two bags?" I asked.

Kane and Quinn exchanged glances like maybe they should've thought of that. They shook their heads.

This was pretty far off the beaten path, but we could always take turns yelling for help and hope that someone airboating could hear us. "You could keep shooting every so often and hope that someone hears us," I said, pointing to Quinn's back. "Did you bring more rounds?"

"I brought a box," he said.

"Was it on the boat with BJ?" I asked. "'Cause only one backpack got left behind with us."

"Was it the one with the ponchos?"

"I think so. It's over by Linda," Kane said. "I'll check."

Quinn sat by the mangroves. "I'll keep watch over there."

"We'll stay with you. It's not like we're going back to the house," Sharon said.

Eve looked at Quinn from her cross-legged position next to Kane. "Actually, the moment the sun starts beating down on us and the monsoon comes back, we may need to get inside that house again. My God, this is a nightmare. I have to call the kids. I have to call them…" Eve broke down crying.

Behind us, Kane held up the box of shotgun rounds while holding the last backpack, and I had to say, I was surprised by how relieved I felt. He came back and plopped down next to Eve to hold her.

Damn Eve, she was right. Until someone rescued us out here, Villegas House would be our only shelter from the storms and beating sun. Between the lack of sleep, stress, and incredible guilt I was feeling, I suddenly felt light-headed and wanted to break down. Eve did, against Kane's shoulder.

Kane hugged her, holding her tight.

Avila…

No.

Avila.

Leave me alone. Unless…

Grandfather?

God, I hoped it was Grandfather and not whatever demonic spirit had taken possession of Linda. I didn't want the same to happen to me as happened to the old woman. If death was her reward for connecting with the spirits, I wanted nothing to do with this "gift," yet the last twenty-four hours had served no purpose except to develop and accelerate it.

Suddenly, it dawned on me—I was the medium of this operation now.

I shook my head until it hurt. "Stop."

"Headache?" Sharon asked.

Avila…

If the dark entity knew I could hear and feel its presence too, would it do the same to me as it had to Linda? It had asked for me. Linda had written my name over and over again during the séance. It wanted me. I was a cursed woman.

"Please stop." I was losing it and knew there wasn't anything I could do about it. In fact, as conditions deteriorated and options waned, I knew it would only get worse inside my head. Feeling overwrought with guilt didn't help either.

Kill them.

"What? No."

"Are you okay?" Sharon touched me, but I shook her off.

"Don't touch me," I growled.

"Jesus, fine."

Around me, it seemed that everyone was starting to lose their shit in different ways. Kane sat on the floor, arms over his head, rocking back and forth the way BJ had done. Eve sobbed, her face pressed against her husband's back, and Quinn paced along the edge of the land just before it dunked into swampy marsh.

"I can't…I can't…" he kept saying. "Can't die here…can't."

"Oh, shut up, Quinn. None of us can die out here. Like you're so goddamned special." Sharon turned and marched back toward the woods. "I'm going to go find a tree to pee on. Screw this."

"We'll have to walk," Quinn said, taking out his gun again and pointing it in the direction BJ had gone with our one and only airboat full of supplies. "I don't want to die out here."

"Nobody's going to die," I said. "Please put that down."

"And you know this because?" He aimed a beady glare my way that sent a chill up my arms.

I had no answer for him. Yes, we may very well die out here with no food, no cell service, no boat to get back to the village, and an army of hissing gators slowly approaching the dead body. One hope was that BJ would use his good conscience to, at the very least, alert authorities that we needed help once he got back to Miami, or…that he'd come back for us himself.

I kept thinking about my mother. She'd be so worried.

"You're dead when I get my hands on you. Hear me, ASSHOLE?!" Quinn screamed after BJ. "DEAD!" He fired off a couple of rounds into the marshlands. Kane jumped up suddenly and wrestled the shotgun out of Quinn's hands.

"You don't need this right now." He slung the weapon over his shoulder then took off back to the house.

I followed him. We needed to stick together to figure out what to do. If only so we didn't lose our minds. Though with the way I was feeling, for me it may have been too late.

FIFTEEN

A woman was dead, and our only transport off this island was gone.

BJ lost his shit. If he wanted to leave, fine, but why wouldn't he have waited for us? It wasn't like we all wanted to stay and he was the only one who wanted to vacate. I imagined BJ getting to the access road where we'd left our cars and struggling to get off the boat. I didn't care if he slipped and fell into the water, feeding gators, turtles, and fish for days to come. The man had left us in a serious predicament.

Stress piled on us by the minute, tearing at our ability to think rationally.

Kane walked in circles, hands behind his head. The heat was starting to evaporate the rain that had fallen overnight, and clouds of steam rose into the air creating curtains of fog that swirled every time he let his arms drop by his sides.

"I have about eight percent battery left on my phone," Sharon said, tapping her cell and holding it high in the air.

Searching for a signal was pointless this far from a cell tower but she could keep trying for all I cared. Restless, I needed to move and find a solution. I couldn't stay by this house with the gunmetal gray aura, near a dead body starting to decompose. Soon, the corpse would give off a smell, as the day gave rise to temperatures near a hundred. There had to be a way out that didn't involve waterways. It might've involved lots of sloughing through shallow water but we would do whatever we had to survive.

I took off in the direction of the woods behind the house. Maybe I could find an old beaten path for walking the thirty miles home or a discarded old boat.

"Wandering off again?" Sharon asked.

I didn't answer. I didn't feel like part of this team. Maybe I never had, but especially not after the way things were going. I blamed them for our predicament just as much as I blamed myself. I'd let my ambition get the best of me, something my grandmother had often warned me about. Instead of being grateful and staying humble, I had to go looking for excitement, finding death and abandonment instead.

If that wasn't karma for greed, I didn't know what was.

"Avila!" Kane called. "We don't need another dead body on our hands."

I walked on. As I headed for the woods, I glanced over my shoulder to find Kane, Eve, and Sharon all standing next to each other, watching me walk away. I wasn't this callous, but this whole island had changed my temperament.

Kane shrugged before flipping a hand my way, like forget her.

Yes, forget me. And if I found a path back to civilization, I wouldn't share it with anybody. I'd just walk and wade in brackish waters until I made it back. But I knew I couldn't do that, knew I'd end up doing the right thing and telling the others.

I'd never felt so pissed toward anyone before. In fact, it was overwhelming. Something made me want to hurt them, pummel that Sharon to a pulp for what she'd done, tackle Kane for still talking to her like she'd done nothing out of the ordinary. Knowing someone's terrible attitude and doing nothing about it made one implicit in their actions. I held Kane and Eve equally responsible for Linda's death as Sharon.

I wandered through the woods hoping an answer would pop up. Any indication of a gladesman outpost, maybe. A marked trail back home—anything. But the trees grew denser and me without a machete, I had to stop and try a different direction. I thought of the ghostly woman who'd appeared here, the one with red hair who I'd thought was Linda before finding her still alive. The one Linda had sketched in her crossword puzzle. Was she one of the dead buried here?

The soil was soaked and in spots, my boots sank deep into waterlogged holes. The air smelled awful, what with all the rotting leaves, rotting wood of the house, and now a rotting woman just outside of it, the stench of decomposition carried on the wind.

I heard a laugh.

I stopped and looked. Nothing but trees and tangled roots. I checked behind me. Another low laughter rumbled through the trees. I had to be going crazy, one vision at a time. If I wasn't careful, I'd end up a statistic of the Everglades dead. Somehow, I had to get off this land, back home to try and resume a normal life.

"Who's there?" I asked. My voice filled the space and sounded alien.

It had to be ghostly. Nobody walked these woods with me, not in real time anyway. I was the only person for yards in one direction and miles in another.

Another laugh fluttered through the woods, only this time accompanied by another voice, talking to the first, telling him to be quiet, or they'd be discovered. My heart stopped. Blood ran cold. I kept my eyes pried open. I was scared to close them, scared my earlier visions would reappear to haunt me.

Billie, the ginger-haired woman, and the men from the grocery store.

Ghosts everywhere. A slow-moving river full of them.

I'd always known this land was haunted. There was no way people could try to live on this giant waterlogged sponge and not encounter tragedy. Tragedy always occurred where there was water, where man did not rule, where limestone beds absorbed fallen airplanes, disintegrating them, swallowing pirate ships whole that were meant to sail the ocean.

Out here, there were no rules.

And somewhere out there, men were plotting. I heard them, nearly saw them as wisps of energy laying dead animals around the property in an attempt to scare away Rutherford, his wife, and two assistants. The Nesbitt brothers. I had come out here to distance myself from the noise and connect with nature only to find more spirits.

Why me? I was the last person capable of handling visions.

I didn't want to be an antennae for the dead. I only wanted to see Villegas House then come home again. Stupid for thinking it'd be so simple. Now I couldn't walk ten feet without encountering voices from the past.

I stared straight ahead and saw them, fully formed this time—two white men in long pants and undershirts plucking dead raccoons, Snail Kites, and other small animals off their belts and tossing them in the direction of the house. I felt like they wanted to infuriate Rutherford, animal-lover and rescuer that he was, to try and get him to leave. They would stop at nothing until he'd left.

I stepped backwards, a branch snapping underneath my feet.

The brothers paused, looked in my direction. Could these men with shotguns slung over their shoulders see me? But I existed here, now, in another time fifty years into the future.

"Did you hear that?" one asked, slowly taking steps in my direction.

My belly filled with the deep cold terror that comes when you know your luck has run out, and you're about to be discovered. Slowly, I backed away, as one of the Nesbitts took slow steps toward me, sliding his shotgun off his back and moving it into position. My heart pounded against my ribs. I'd felt a less elevated type of fear around white people before, before a racial confrontation, but now it was all too real. He was the hunter, I was the prey. His eyes, bright blue, sparkled with amusement, the thrill of the kill, as he inched toward me.

I lifted my hands in surrender.

Had I slipped into the soul of an endangered animal, or was this exactly as it seemed—man stalking woman? My back hit a tree, one of its spiny branches jabbing deep into my skin. I bit my lip to keep from screaming in the event there was still a chance I could avoid this by keeping quiet.

The man stopped, sniffed the air.

He could tell I was here. In another dimension.

Would that bullet travel through time?

A shot rang out and I squeezed my eyes shut, braced for impact as time slowed. I doubled over, gripping my stomach. He'd shot me. This man had really been able to see me and shot me, but when I looked down at my hands, there was no blood. No pain. Though I heard a scream. Turning, I saw another form, taller than mine, darker skin. A woman stepped around the tree, a thin small brown woman with a gunshot to her stomach, bleeding profusely. She cried out once before falling to the ground, just as the man who'd shot her looked back at his buddy and laughed.

Sick. Bastard.

A moment later, another woman came running through the woods from the direction of Villegas House. Her white nightgown flowed out behind her. "Brigitte? Brigitte?" she called. Upon seeing Brigitte on the floor of the woods, she covered her ears and let out a bloodcurdling scream.

"Gregory!"

He hadn't seen me after all. I wasn't here.

This was Elena Rutherford, and holy shit, I'd just seen a Nesbitt brother shooting one of Rutherford's assistants. It could only mean that he'd shot the entire clan too. I'd just been given a glimpse into time. The man retreated into the woods, silent as a ghost so Elena wouldn't see him.

But I saw him.

And now I knew what happened—he'd murdered that woman right beside me, the iron-tinged scent of her blood still lingering in my nostrils.

SIXTEEN

I tripped over my feet, scraped my knees on the gritty ground before running back to the house because at least other living people were there, and as much as they were on my shit list right now, at least they were real and not trying to kill me. I stumbled onto the porch and heaved.

Sharon, Kane, and Eve surrounded me. I caught the cadaverous scent of Linda's body flaring up in the heat. "What happened? We heard a scream," Sharon asked.

"I heard…I saw…" I began but couldn't finish.

"What? What did you see? Is someone out there?" Kane asked.

I shook my head, felt the lie burn in my chest. "Nobody real. I think I can see…I don't know…" I trailed off. Why should I tell any of them that I could see ghosts? It wouldn't help our situation. A bunch of dead people replaying significant scenes of their lives. None of it would help us get off this island. "Nothing, don't worry about it."

"You can see them, can't you?" Sharon gripped my shoulder. Funny how she only seemed to care when there was something in it for her. "You can see them, just like Linda could."

I shrugged her off. "What does it matter?"

"It matters because there's little written about this house, Avila, and I don't know when we'll ever get the chance to come back here again. You're the only one of us who can tell me what truly happened here."

If I told her about the woman in the woods, the gladesmen shooting Brigitte, my own personal demons out by the water, she would only use me like she'd used Linda. As it was, she had already used me to get here.

"People got killed, Sharon. That's all that matters," I grunted.

"Wrong. It matters who did the killing," she said.

Her voice grated against my eardrum. Why was she so damn insistent? What interest did she have in this whole affair? "The Nesbitt man did. I saw him do it. Just now, out in the woods. There, are you happy?"

"Which Nesbitt brother?"

"I don't know."

"But did he kill everyone? Is that what you saw? Because I don't think he did."

"Back off, Sharon." Kane stepped up to me, setting a reassuring hand on my back. As much as I didn't want anyone touching me, not even Kane, I appreciated his telling her to stop.

"Seriously. Enough already," Eve scoffed.

A wave of undeniable hate rose in my chest. I wanted to reach out and strangle this woman, even though I'd never wanted to strangle anyone in my life, not even the men at the supermarket. "Don't you know when to stop? That's why Linda is dead."

She recoiled like a wounded snake. "Don't you blame me for Linda. Everyone here knew that she was already sick!" Sharon shouted.

"Then, she shouldn't have come," I insisted.

Sharon scoffed. "She *wanted* to help. She came of her own accord. Ask Kane and Eve since you don't trust me."

"It's true," Kane said. "Linda was happiest when she felt needed and wanted."

"None of this is helping." I growled, holding the temples of my forehead.

"Neither is the pointing of fingers," Sharon hissed.

It didn't matter. Linda was dead and nothing would bring her back. We were here because something about these murders was of interest to Sharon. Did she have family in Florida at the time of the murders? Any other day, I would've been intrigued to know, but right now I only wanted away from this house.

"We shouldn't be focused on the house anymore," I said. "We should be focused on getting home. Has anyone been able to get a signal?"

"Both mine and Eve's phones are dead, Sharon can't get a signal, so that leaves you. You were taking video early this morning when the raccoons broke into our tent. Do you still have battery? Let me see your phone." Kane held out his hand.

I pulled my phone out of my pocket and saw it had 11% battery left on it before handing it over. "I don't get a signal either. We could try walking east as far as we can to see if we can get on the fringe of Miami's closest cell phone tower," I said. "West toward Naples is out of the question—we'd have to swim through the river."

"And those gators are getting closer," Kane said. "I went out there to check on Quinn. They're creeping in."

"They smell Linda's body," I explained. They were braving the evil of the house just for a snack. We had to figure this out. Walking east as far as we could until we hit the edge of cell phone service might've been our best bet, but that was assuming the haunted woods would let us through. I hadn't come back by choice.

"We're going to have to give them the dead raccoon and any other dead animals we find," Kane said, looking at Eve whose eyes were filled with exhaustion and tears. In just a little over a day, Eve had gone from looking like a rich Housewife of Atlanta to a corpse bride, not that I or anyone could blame her.

"What'll happen otherwise?" she asked.

"They'll make their way inland if they're hungry enough," I explained. "Gators have been known to walk into people's homes, swim in their pools, sleep on patios just to find food. They've stayed away all this time—I think they're afraid of the house—but now they're building up courage."

"Because of the body," Sharon muttered, arms crossed and looking out toward the riverbank. "We have to warn Quinn."

"It's easy to outrun an alligator," I told them.

"Run in a zig-zag pattern," Kane spouted off the myth most everyone knew.

"No, just run," I said. "You can outrun one easily, and the best way to do that is in a straight line, because it's the fastest way to get away. Speed outweighs strategy in this case. Let's bring Quinn in. He's been close to the water long enough."

Suddenly, we heard shouts and all turned in the direction of Quinn by the water's edge. Kane took off jogging in his direction. My heart rate kicked up in the hopes he'd come across boaters or hunters in the woods.

"Quinn?" Kane called. "You alright, man?"

The shouting continued, repetitive, as though he were trying to get someone's attention. We found him deep in the woods past the spot where I'd seen my vision earlier this morning. He crouched near the ground looking like a kid who'd found a hidden ant pile under a rock. "Check this out, guys."

Carefully, we made our way through the dense brush to where Quinn crouched in front of a bush. When we arrived and surrounded him, he pointed and we saw what he had found. A small litter of kittens. Panther kittens.

"Cute, aren't they?" He reached out to stroke the soft spotted belly of one kitten. "I heard meowing, almost like chirping, when I was walking this way looking for anything dead I could feed those gators and found this." He petted the kitten again.

"Don't do that," I said, kicking his hand away.

He looked at me with fire in his eyes. "I'll touch it if I goddamn want."

"Sure, put your human scent all over it, so when Mama comes back, she'll know exactly whose ass to kick," I said.

"She has a point, Quinn. Leave them alone," Kane said, backing away. "In fact, we shouldn't even be here. Now we'll attract gators *and* wildcats. Come on. You and me need to go for a walk to try and find cell service."

Stepping over rocks and fallen branches, I made my way out of the woods only to realize we weren't the only ones who'd sensed the kittens in the brush. Two six-foot alligators, bellies on the ground, hissed up at me, exposed pink mouths showing off perfect rows of teeth.

"Okay…nice boy. It's okay…" I stayed calm and talked smoothly like I usually did, but these weren't village alligators who were used to being around humans. These were wild and judging from the way they'd made it inland this far, curious and looking for a snack. "Guys, don't move."

"What is it?" Eve asked.

"Gators. And it's breeding season. Let's try and move slowly in the other direction."

"Are you serious?" Eve whined.

"Those assholes have been encroaching on our territory all morning," Quinn said from behind me.

"This is their territory, I hate to tell you," I said, keeping my eyes on the reptiles who slowly were accompanied by two more aggressive pals. Now there were four, and more ornery than I'd ever seen any gators. "When I tell you to move, move in the *opposite* direction. They can't navigate through the trees too well."

"Avila? I don't like this…" Eve was crying. "What do we do if one bites?"

"You bite back." I mumbled under my breath, keeping my gaze on the reptiles. "The real answer is gouging it in the eye but with this many to gang up on us, there's a good chance we won't survive, even with excellent eye-gouging skills. So, start walking slowly away. I'll stand here until you're gone."

"What about you?" Kane asked.

"Just go." As the only native Floridian here, as someone who shared territory with gators in the wild and as the most guilt-burdened person among us, I should sacrifice myself.

Just then, one of the gators tired of warning with hisses charged at me. I broke into a run back to the woods, as the others dispersed in different directions, Eve screaming like a child, Kane pulling out the shotgun, aiming it at the reptiles. He fired one shot that stilled one of the gators, just not the one chasing me.

"Run!" I yelled at him, searching for the highest ground possible. There was no point in wasting several shells on animals that would soon encounter trees to slow them down.

But then, Quinn began throwing something at the reptiles and it took me a moment to realize what he was doing. The second I saw the gators pile on top of each other frantically fighting and thrashing, I realized the horror of what he had done.

"No!" I screamed and climbed several feet up a cypress tree, as another panther kitten flew through the air on its way to becoming gator meal.

"You rather they eat *you,* Cypress?" He reached for the last kitten, holding it high. As he aimed for leverage, the man seemed to take pleasure in his actions. I wished I could say it was pride in his strategy for defending us. After all, the gators were now preoccupied with tearing apart the defenseless kittens, but it wasn't.

It was pleasure in killing.

Quinn didn't look like himself at all. His normally unreadable face took on a more rugged, ferocious appearance. Someone primal, careless, and heartless had taken over him. One of the Nesbitts, down to the jeans and white undershirts, appeared as a transparent overlay on top of Quinn.

I blinked and the double vision dissipated, leaving only Quinn.

Then, I saw her.

She moved out of the corner of my eye.

Leaping from the woods, shiny tan coat without markings, long slinky body rippling with muscle, fierce golden eyes. Ready to kill. She paused, assessing. No roar—Florida panthers couldn't, and that was a shame for Quinn—but make no mistake, she was intensely pissed. In all my years living in the Everglades, I'd only seen the elusive creature once, hit by a car on US-41. This was the first time I'd seen the endangered cat up close in her natural habitat, and I never knew rage until seeing her now.

She watched angrily, as the human murderer of her babies held her last cub high in the air, about to fling it. The cat hissed, teeth bared, nostrils flaring. She crouched on her hind quarters, preparing to spring forth on the unsuspecting interloper. My body pulsed with energy.

I did nothing to warn him.

SEVENTEEN

In the split second it took Quinn to toss that last kitten toward the heap of gators, the cat had pinned him onto his back and torn into his face. Using the force of her massive paws, her claws ripped into his cheeks, goring out his eyes. They hung from their sockets, from the optic nerve, dangling on his cheekbones. His arms and legs thrashed, fighting against the creature, as blood spilled all around him.

I watched, horrified and eerily satisfied.

Screams echoed from the woods, then came frantic debate on whether or not to shoot the cat and risk killing Quinn, but from my vantage point, the damage had already been done. Quinn had stopped moving. The cat had torn an enormous hole into his chest, and his lungs hissed as they leaked air. From my low branch, I clung to the trunk perfectly still, in case the grieving mother thought I had anything to do with this. She paused to glare at me with golden eyes. She didn't come for me.

I felt her pain.

I'd seen it before—in different eyes—the day my brother died.

Even the gators had stopped fighting over their food, paused mid-wrangle, watching the cat, listening to her chirps that belied what should've been furious roars. The panther tore into Quinn's neck, the screams from the woods continued, and finally, a shot rang out, as the mother cat fell onto her side.

I screamed, keenly aware of how odd my cry must've sounded.

How could I explain that while yes, I cared for my fellow human, at the moment, he'd been a murderer of innocent lives? That I felt he deserved his death for callously discarding infants of a majestic endangered Florida cat? A mother watching her children die was still a mother watching her children die, regardless of species.

I looked at Kane, tears blurring my eyes, but then I saw Sharon holding the shotgun. She pushed the butt of the gun into the peat and shot me a glare. The gators dispersed to the edge of the water.

"Don't give me that look. I had to do it."

Florida panthers were shy and wouldn't hang around to torment us. Her reasons for doing so were now gone. I said nothing to Sharon, only watched through an excruciating headache, as Kane and Eve crept closer to survey the carnage. Eve covered her face, unable to bring herself any closer. She stepped into a small clearing and vomited.

I hopped out of the tree, doubling over for breath.

"What do we do now?" Sharon slung the shotgun over her shoulder. I didn't feel any safer with her wielding it than I had with Quinn.

"Like I have a plan? This is a nightmare." Kane coughed into his fist.

"Well, we can't just leave Quinn here," Sharon said. "The gators will get him."

"We can't bring him into the house either."

"Why not?"

"Sure, let's start a body pile, Sharon. Why not?" Kane scoffed. "Great idea. I love the smell of rotting flesh in the morning. Doubling the scent will draw them in faster. Hell to that. We have no choice but to move on. Our kids expect us to come home. I have to get my wife back. Do you see her? Look at her." He pointed to a distraught Eve, sobbing and losing control of her breathing.

"We all have to go home, Kane. We all have lives, but what do we tell Amy when she asks where her husband's body went?"

"We tell her the truth—that we had to leave him behind. There's only so much we can do. End of story. Help me cover them, at least." Kane had begun picking up underbrush, dead leaves, and foliage and carried them over to cover Quinn's feet and legs. One of his shoes had come off, blood seeping out the ankle of his pants.

I staggered over to help Kane, my headache blinding me. I crouched, picked up armfuls of dried leaves and dumped them on top of Quinn's torso, which was partially crushed by the weight of the large animal. About twenty yards away, the remaining gators basked in the sun after the warm meal.

"What about you, Cypress?" Sharon watched us. "What do you guys do when stuff like this happens?"

By *you guys,* she meant my tribe, my people, and her assumption that Miccosukee folks often had to dispose of people expired in the wild due to their idiotic choices was unacceptable. I wouldn't give her the pleasure of a response. All my life, I'd heard questions like these, designed to provoke. Most of the time, I stood against them, but today, I wasn't as strong.

"We dance around the body and pray to the panther gods," I said without a hitch.

"Do you, really?"

"Idiot," I muttered under my breath.

I thought of my mother and grandmother. Even Uncle Bob, as annoying as he could be, wasn't the kind to fight back with words, but if Sharon kept this up, this attitude of supremacy, linked with the stress devastating us at the moment, it wouldn't be long before I had no choice but to kick her ass.

"Very funny," Sharon said, taking off toward the house. "Come on, Eve. Let's find you some water."

This. This was the dark spirit's influence. All of it. This quarreling. It wanted us to argue and turn against each other. It wanted us to fail. What it didn't realize was that we wanted to get the hell out of here just as much as it wanted us out, but now our chances of doing that were even slimmer than before.

Once Kane and I covered up the bodies, he headed to the house while I stayed outside, unwilling to go inside. I'd have to eventually—the afternoon rains were on their way again—but for now, I would only sit outside and ground myself. If I got too close to Sharon, I'd turn into someone I wasn't. And with weird energies affecting us, possibly even causing the tragic events of the day, I didn't trust myself. When Sharon had fired that shotgun, I'd wanted to rip her throat out, and nobody wanted that.

Least of all Sharon.

My headache hammered, a combination of stress and dehydration. For an hour I'd been hearing Eve sobbing inside the house, her husband consoling her, and Sharon arguing with Kane about whether or not he should leave to go find help. I heard them in a detached fog of head pain, like listening from behind a wall from another realm.

I couldn't believe what a massive fail this expedition had been. How it had deteriorated from bad to worse. Couldn't believe I hadn't listened to my own intuition.

All my life, my instincts had kept me safe, even at the expense of others. If that weren't true, my brother would still be alive today. Why hadn't I listened now? The disappointment that awaited me at home would be unbearable and possibly insurmountable.

I wouldn't be surprised if my family asked me to leave.

To make things worse, I couldn't stop the invisible energies from surrounding me. Facing the house, I could see the aura Linda had talked about, the gunmetal gray atmosphere that surrounded it like a straitjacket. I felt a deep pain between my eyes like my forehead ripping open. In my soul, I knew it was more than a headache—it was gut instinct coming back to taunt me like I hadn't had enough already.

A full-blown attack on my psyche ensued, and I could do nothing to stop it.

I heard crying and arguing, only this time it wasn't Sharon and Kane. It was two other people, and I saw them clearly. An older gentleman on the steps of the house, wearing white pants and a white shirt to deflect the heat. He sported a thick, dark mustache and held a cigar clenched between his teeth. A woman collapsed against the steps in a long light-colored skirt stained with deep red. She cried into her knees, dark hair spilling onto the steps.

I wanted to look away but found myself riveted.

"He shot her," she said. "Just…shot her. For no reason, *amor*. Oh, Gregory. I couldn't do anything to help her."

"Why didn't you stop him?" the man demanded, nervously chewing on his cigar.

"How would you expect me to stop him? You mean to suggest I could have prevented this?" Her voice sounded irrational and wild, the voice of a woman who'd seen too much and could never be whole again.

"Darling, if this ever happens again, you take the rifle and meet them outside with it. Or better yet, alert me to the problem and I'll do it!" He shouted at her. "Now we have to find help. Come and assist. We have to get her to a hospital before she bleeds to death."

The woman bawled, blubbering about everything being so easy for her husband, because clearly, he had all the answers. She sobbed against the porch railing, while the man kicked a column and disappeared inside the house to fetch his things.

I blinked and tried to shake the vision. I was dealing with enough in present day. But when I reopened my eyes, the ghosts were still there, and there was Villegas House in its earlier days—pretty and cleaned up. Its inhabitants were in a world of hurt. A field of negative energy hovered over them, influenced them, ran unwanted thoughts through their minds. Curiously, the house's aura was gray even back then.

It hadn't turned dark because of the events taken place here.

It'd always been dark.

Something about this island, about this spot, made it that way.

The man I assumed was Rutherford ran out of the house with a bag over his shoulder, preparing to tell his wife something about Brigitte who I saw was lying inside on a bed. That was when another man appeared from the water's edge, along with a little boy of about ten years old. The man was dressed in my tribe's traditional colors, his long hair tied into a long ponytail. The child beside him looked familiar.

Billie. But that was impossible.

He greeted Rutherford and Elena and asked to know what was going on. He'd heard rumors in the camp that continued arguments existed between two families out here and wanted to know how he could help. As a tribal leader of the Miccosukee, ending conflict was his main concern.

My heart pounded inside my chest.

"Grandfather?" Night after night, I'd seen him in my photos. I'd spoken to him and told him about my woes, and now here he was, real enough to almost reach out and touch him.

Rutherford explained that his assistant had been injured and was lying inside the house. His wife had witnessed the senseless attempt at murder, committed by one of the warring brothers, though he wasn't sure which, and he was about to take her back to the city.

"You should not have come here," Rutherford said with a grimace.

"I came because a mediator was needed," Grandfather replied.

"You did so at your own peril. This island is good for no one." Rutherford rushed into the house. From the moment they'd arrived two years before, terrible things had happened, he explained. Arguments with his wife when they had always enjoyed a peaceful marriage. Animals left dead on their doorstep and around the property as a warning to get out. The gladesmen brothers were possessive of the home their father built, a home without a deed, one he had abandoned of his own free will.

The house was fair game, he said. It'd been empty, abandoned.

My grandfather explained how Roscoe Nesbitt had meant to raise his family there, but they hadn't been able to live here long. The house had been cursed. It was understandable that the Nesbitt sons would feel possessive of the home.

"Well, he was right," Rutherford said. "Because cursed is how I feel."

Then he asked a favor. Would my grandfather be able to stay and take care of his wife and the other biologist, Peter, while he traveled with the injured Brigitte?

"I can do that," my grandfather replied.

The little boy tugged at his arm, as if to argue against staying, but I sensed that my grandfather had brought him as a buffer, hoping his presence would force the two parties to act respectfully and peacefully.

Things moved quickly after that.

At times, it was like watching a movie playing out in front of my eyes, step by step. My grandfather's gaze, at one point, seemed to burn right through me, as though I had caused the problems here. I felt so ashamed, I had to look away. At other times, the blurry visions shifted quickly, like film on fast-forward, and one moment later, Brigitte had been loaded onto my grandfather's dugout canoe while Rutherford pushed off, on his way.

The ghosts moved about at will. At times, they hovered in front of my face, their eyes dark and faces gaunt.

Rutherford's words as the boat drifted down the river: "Keep a wary eye out, old man," he called out. "This island changes you."

My grandfather watched him leave, entered the house, and a moment later, the video in my mind's eye fast-forwarded again then flew backwards. And back. And back in time again. Suddenly, the front yard was covered in still, bleeding bodies. Dozens of them. Some wore traditional Seminole colors, others wore U.S. uniforms of the old days.

They'd been killed in battle, because they'd refused to leave their land and relocate west to Oklahoma. They'd resisted force, resisted bullies. As a result, death had come to these lands. They'd been promised safe haven but the Seminoles knew it was a lie to get them to vacate. In the end, they knew their way of life would never be the same again as long as these foreigners were here to stay.

When I blinked, they were all gone, only a handful of dead lay scattered across the peat moss. One of them was my grandfather. Three other men lay sprawled in poses of sudden death, two I recognized from the woods. They were buried here, all of them. The energy here was intense because they had not rested in peace.

Standing, I shook my head and squeezed the visions from my mind.

When would it ever end? I was ill-equipped. The wrong person to be shown visions of the past. Never had I wanted to be home so much, living my ordinary life instead of this.

Off to the side was a dead body, dark eyes wide open, face and neck bloated and puffy. From the reddish hair, I knew it was Linda, though she'd been decomposing a long time. Her skin was gray, black, and mottled. Slowly, she sat up and looked at me with expressionless eyes, as spidery cracks spread all over her rotting face. She spoke straight to my soul.

Stop fearing your visions, Avila. Listen to them.

Her putrid body collapsed back onto the ground, her head snapped off, and my scream echoed through my mind before my world turned black.

EIGHTEEN

Rotted planks of wood, grains of sand and dirt, and deep grooves covered the wooden floor. It was raining again. And screw my life, I was inside the house again, the house that wanted to kill us. Water dripped in through the ceiling, as someone twisted my face and poured a small capful of fresh rain into my mouth.

"You fainted." Eve's face came into view. "Also, you're dehydrated."

My tongue and throat felt dry, and my forehead felt like it had seized up. Suddenly, I remembered the visions. The battleground, the Seminole, the dead bodies from 1967. I'd suffered another psychic attack, only this one had been mammoth. For what felt like hours, I'd traveled through time in this very spot. Floating above it, not really there but witnessing it just the same.

I had smelled the burning scents of dry land, the sulfuric smoke of warfare.

I'd seen my grandfather, the little boy that could've been Billie in modern times but was impossible since he hadn't been alive back then. I tried sitting up but my head exploded into a field of stars.

Eve held me down gently. "Don't try to get up. You hit your head out there. See?" She swiped my temple and showed me half-dried blood on her fingertip.

The house smelled like shit. It had to be Linda's body. We couldn't keep her here much longer or her decomposition would take an ugly turn with all this heat and humidity. At this point, there was no guarantee we could bring her back either and may have to cover her with dry grass just like we had Quinn.

Two were dead.

Hard to believe since just yesterday, we'd arrived bright and early and tried to make a day out of this production. Less than twenty-four hours later, it had all taken a turn for the worse. It made me wonder which of us would be next and if we'd ever make it out of here. Shock wore off, replaced by anger, exhaustion, hunger. I thought of BJ. If I ever saw that asshole again, I would surely kill him with my own hands.

My nostrils flared from the rage running through me. I had to look up at Eve's feminine features to remember that not everyone in the group had turned out to be a jerk. Not everyone thought only of themselves. Though Eve could sometimes drown in a glass of water, at least she had a nurturing side to her.

"Shh…it's okay, Avila. Keep sleeping. We're figuring out a plan to get out of here."

I couldn't sleep. And that plan better present itself quick.

Because behind her, hovering from the ceiling came a dark mass that swirled but wouldn't take shape. The core, the entity that had spoken through Linda was making its way toward us. Right now, it watched us, observed, attempted to intimidate us, made me feel that rage, even as the others were oblivious to its presence.

I closed my eyes against it. Somehow I had to fight its power over me. Kane and Sharon were arguing again at the far end of the room, a pissing match to drive anyone crazy.

"The moment the rain stops, I'm out of here," Kane lashed out. "I don't care how far I have to walk, but I have to find a cell signal."

"Your phone is dead, Kane."

"I'll take Avila's. It has 5% left. For all we know, the edge of cell service might only be a mile away, and we're here all worried for no reason. I have to at least try."

"So, you're just going to leave three women alone in this house."

"No, you can all come with me."

"It's not safe, babe," Eve said, eyes brimming with tears. For a woman who cried a lot, she held on pretty strongly. Maybe that was the secret. "There could be gators or other panthers. Snakes, wild hogs…" She slapped at her leg. "Mosquitos, rain, lightning…"

"Baby, what do you want me to do? Sit here and pray and hope to be found? That might never happen. By the time any one of our families realizes we've been missing and calls authorities, we could be dead. I can't let that happen."

The dark shape hovering near the ceiling still watched us. Listened. Then, it floated down and swirled near Sharon and Kane. Sharon slammed her hand against the wall, vibrating the weak integrity of the inner wall. "Damn it. There's no way out of this. We're not thinking!"

"Like hell we're not thinking, Sharon!" Kane shouted in her face. "If you think you can do better, then by all means, suggest something. But I haven't seen you come up with a single solution to this situation but you sure as hell are full of criticism!"

"Stop! Can't you guys stop arguing for one minute?" Eve's tears squeezed out of her lids and landed on my face. She continued feeding me small sips of water, as though the action itself were keeping her sane.

Kane rushed over and squatted next to his wife. He drew her face into his hands and kissed her hard and full of determination on the lips. "I'm sorry, but what kind of man would I be if I stayed and did nothing? I *have* to go find help and I *have* to do it while I still have energy."

"Then I'm coming with you."

Kane took his wife's hand. "Right now, we can't go anywhere. But the minute this rain stops, we leave. I'm going to try and doze while I can to save up energy."

The thought of staying with Sharon, just me and bitch-face alone in this house while the Parkers went on a mission to find civilization was not doing my headache any favors. I was too weak to speak my mind, mentally and physical exhausted, emotionally drained and channeling a storm of anger. I hated the thought that now I was one more problem for these people to have to handle.

One way or another, I had to figure this shit out.

For generations, we'd lived in the Everglades and survived. But we had the tools, we had implements, we had each other to solve problems. Here, we had an evil house, rainwater, a shotgun, a bowie knife, and a backpack containing random things.

I wanted to sit up and think my way out of this, but my head continued to pound.

I dozed in and out without meaning or wanting to. I hadn't slept the night before, so sleep came intermittently. After a while, I lost sense of time and had the distinct impression that either Eve or Sharon were dozing off as well, since the steady sound of rainfall and thunderstorms were lulling us all into a stupor.

The dark cloud in the corner of the room was no longer there. I exhaled a sigh. Lying on my side, my right hand splayed out against the wood of the floor. It was a deep dark wood, so vastly different from other areas of the house that were lighter. Whoever had built the house had used whatever timber they could find, a mixture of different trees, but this wood had a different energy to it.

Yes, energy.

When we first arrived, Linda had pointed it out and even placed a piece in my hand to feel. I'd felt a jolt of power flow through me, which was how she learned I possessed psychic gifts. I'd heard of the ability before, being able to gather information from somewhere else or the past just by touching an object. It was called psychometry.

Between the steady rhythm of the rain, the soft snoring in the room, and the rolling thunder getting farther and farther away, my hand vibrated gently. Before I knew it, my whole arm vibrated, as though it were alive with its own beating heart. This vibration wasn't visible to anyone else, only to me. It reminded me of times when I was young, right before dawn when the energy of the sun would immerse my bedroom and I'd feel like I was floating out of my body.

Something about those still, early morning hours.

Don't move…

The voice was my own subconscious talking. I couldn't move if I wanted to. I was in a trance-like state, my hand pulsating with crackling sensation. After a few minutes, the floor came alive. Moved right underneath my hand, swayed, rocked gently back and forth, the feeling of being on a boat. I was dizzy from exhaustion.

I saw my grandfather's shoes walking along the dirty floor, heard his conversation with Rutherford's wife, as she fought tears while describing what had happened to their assistant. Brigitte had gone out to bring in the traps they'd set up for studying the snail kite, when the Nesbitt brothers appeared, like they often did, only this time they were determined to make them leave.

Depositing dead animals around the property hadn't worked, running their airboat back and forth late at night hadn't worked. Finally, it seemed they'd gotten fed up with their being at the house and shot the first person they saw.

Brigitte had been a warning.

It could've been any of them, Elena said.

Grandfather gave her the bad news that she'd died at the hospital. How did he know, Elena asked. He just knew.

My grandfather had the gift before me, the gift of knowing. Did that mean he'd been susceptible to the energies here, like I'd been? We were more alike than I'd ever imagined. It saddened me that I hadn't gotten to know him in person.

The conversation lingered in my mind. Evil acts had taken place here, sure. These were no-man's lands. Most people knew terrible things occurred in the Everglades and nobody would know any better. It was a well-known fact that bodies were dumped here for good reason, because the earth and water had a habit of swallowing people up, and if the glades didn't get them, the reptiles would.

Murder was an unfortunate byproduct of these lands.

No, what stood out in my mind was the wood my hand still touched, the rocking motion that persisted, and the notion of water and boats and humans who mastered both.

Open yourself, Avila, I heard Linda telling me in a washed-out dream.

The visions served as clues. I'd been here once, long ago, and I'd be here again and again. Our souls recycled. The water, the boats, were a part of my higher self. My grandfather had arrived here that day to help, not on an airboat, but the way all my people had traveled these waterways in the old days—by dugout canoe.

And if we wanted to get off this island…

…all we had to do was make one.

NINETEEN

"What happened?" Kane mumbled himself awake.

"We build a boat. A dugout canoe. That's how my ancestors got around. I can't believe I didn't think of it before."

"And how are we supposed to do that?" Sharon asked, disdain in her tone like she'd already decided it wouldn't work.

I actually understood the process from hearing it explained in the village so many times to tourists. "We need a dried cypress log. There's tons of fallen ones outside. Add fire to burn the cutout, rope…granted, we need a hatchet or machete to carve the shape, so it won't be exactly like a real one, but—"

The words flew out of me. I visualized it in my mind like I did everything else. It'd be something like a dugout, not perfect maybe, but it'd work.

"Where are we going to get a hatchet?" Sharon smirked.

Kane brushed Eve's hair out of her face as she slept. "True, we're fresh out of hatchets and ropes."

"We need to explore the house. We haven't since all this began and maybe we'll find items. At the very least, we can build something to float out of here—a raft or whatever. All we need is to get far enough 'til someone sees us. We have the wood to start. Look at this place—it's falling apart."

"It's true, babe." Eve stretched. "We can pull the rotting wood coming off anyway and maybe float the hell out of here."

"Or the doors. Pull them off, tie dry brush to the undersides, use palm fronds to affix them to the wood," I said, feeling hope for the first time in a while. "We won't know until we take a good look at all we have. What about our backpack?"

I already knew it contained a box of rounds.

Kane got up and headed to the one backpack still sitting by the front door. He opened it and dumped the contents on the floor. The box of shells tumbled out. "There's that. BBQ lighter. One…two…three ponchos. Mosquito repellant. Aaannddd….a bunch of cables."

Orange, rubbery coils spilled out.

I grabbed a cable, pulling it taut. "That's our rope. We can always split it open and use the individual threads if we need it to be lighter. Kane, you have your bowie knife for that. The ponchos can line the bottom of the rafts, help keep water from seeping through." The idea illuminated my brain, the positive thought counteracting the negative vibes prevailing in the house.

"But can a raft hold five people?" Eve looked at Linda's dead body. "One of them lying down?"

I hated to tell her that I didn't think Linda's body would be making it off this island. "Depends on how we make it. Maybe we build individual ones, depending on what we find, and we each float on our own. Our biggest problem right now is the amount of rain and finding dry wood."

"This is crazy, you know that?" Of course, Sharon had to have an opinion, even though I was willing to bet she'd never contributed a single useful idea in her life. "This isn't freakin' Gilligan's Island."

"You have a better idea?" My heartbeat kicked up a notch. If Sharon could just not speak the rest of our time here, that'd be great. "How about from now on, unless you have a solution to the problem, you don't knock anyone else's idea? Good? Great."

Yes, I was being sassy with *the* Sharon Roswell from *Haunted Southland*, but who cared at this point? She'd shown her true colors, and I was done. My whole life I'd learned that if something weighed you down, you cut it from your life. I was not beyond putting her in her place if I had to.

"I never knocked the idea, Cypress. I only said it was crazy."

My hands shook with anger. Something primal inside of me wanted to rush at her and grab her by the neck. "It's the crazy ideas that end up working and making news, aren't they? It's not like we're trapped somewhere we can't get out. The only thing separating us from home…"

"Is the water. She's right. An airboat's basically a raft with a motor on it." Kane sounded enthused. I couldn't wait to start working with him on getting this done. Finally, a ray of hope in this dismal situation. "How long will it take?"

I shrugged. That was another problem. "Could take days, weeks."

"Weeks? Without food, only water?" Sharon scoffed.

"We can survive without food, Sharon," I blurted. "And we have tons of water, because…" I gestured to the outside world. "I present to you…Florida's rainy season. The problem is finding *dry* wood, we need *fire*, which we can start but it might get put out thanks to the storms."

"And there's no way in hell we're building one inside this bundle of sticks," Kane said about the house.

I stood by the front door and watched the torrential rain come down in sheets. Whatever we built, it'd need to withstand the elements, and it'd need to keep us away from gators. I couldn't imagine a raft that fell apart as we rode along, leaving us impervious to the gnashing of teeth.

A dugout canoe took months to make. The wood had to be carved then dried and baked out in the sun over several weeks. It was simple in design but we were lacking supplies and time. A makeshift raft, however, would work better but could get it get us down the River of Grass thirty or so miles?

"Whatever." Sharon got up and moved throughout the house in her restlessness. "You guys do whatever you want. I think we should hang tight. Someone *will* find us, just like they found those kids in the Thai mountains."

"They found those kids in the Thai mountains because they spotted their bicycles outside the cave system," I said. "We don't have anything to show that we're here. Did any of you tell your friends and family where you'd be this weekend?"

"I did, but nobody knows where Villegas House is. That's why we hired you." Sharon kicked an empty can of beans the wind had rolled into the room and sent it flying.

And when my family realized I was missing, they would ask Kellie for my whereabouts, and Kellie did not know where I was this weekend, because I only told her about the production team hiring me for a tour around the Everglades. I didn't mention Villegas House.

"By the way." Kane held up my phone. "Your battery just died."

"Of course it did," I sighed.

All the more reason to get started.

It was late evening when the rains finally slowed, and Kane

wasn't about to go walking in pure darkness.

We'd spent the time scouring the house looking for items we could use to build our raft. In the upstairs rooms, we'd found a dresser full of clothes, old hairbrushes, and hangers. I took the wire hangers, figuring we could bend them into shapes to help tie the wood planks together, but without any tools to chop the planks or wire cutters, the idea would prove difficult.

Another room contained an old wooden table with drawers filled with papers mottled with heavy mold. Sharon spent most of her time here, reading through them, blowing mold around. She discovered them to be Rutherford's research papers on birds, flora, and fauna. She was obsessed with finding a journal, or something that would clue her in as to what happened her, but I was done caring about the past.

All the past had ever done for me was make me fearful.

We'd begun building a foundation inside the house using planks, palmetto fronds, and cables. The house reeked something awful, but we did our best to stay away from Linda's corpse. At random moments, I kept expecting her to sit up and speak to me, so I'd go around exploring cabinets and closets, anything to keep away from Linda.

Sharon would read out loud from Rutherford's observations, as if we cared. I swear, if I heard one more entry about birds and animal eating habits, I was going to roll the papers into a tube and shove them down her throat.

The body's stench got worse throughout the heat of the day and filtered into the upstairs rooms. If nobody brought it up first, I was going to be the one to suggest we move it outside. Whatever happened to it happened to it. In my culture, we didn't make a big deal about memorializing people. We moved on and eventually, people were forgotten. We didn't construct monuments or statues. She'd return to the land, same way she'd come in, though I knew these people's ways were different.

They hung onto everything. Put their people in ornate boxes in the ground. Didn't they realize, as investigators of the paranormal, that Linda's true essence was no longer physical? Her soul had moved on. Left was an empty vessel. I would never say it to their faces, but the body rotting downstairs was garbage and not serving us one bit.

We explored every inch of the house as much as we could until the sun began sinking and the absence of light put an end to our work. I wasn't sure how long we'd been at Villegas House, but I believed we were going on Day 3.

The darker the sky got, the more I feared what would come. Would I see visions again? Would the gloomy cloud permeating the home hover over us again? I felt like it was studying us, watching our every movement, trying to figure out how to make us leave.

Out of the corner of my eye, I kept seeing shifts of light moving in the darkness, orbs flitting back and forth. Some felt harmless, while others felt cold and oppressive. The moment I'd address them with straight eye contact was the moment they'd disappear. Ghosts. They may not have been haunting us every moment of the day, but they were definitely making life harder for us, telling us what to do, as in the case of my grandfather reminding me we came from river-navigating people.

I was using the remaining ambient light from sundown to hunt for tools when a foul smell overrode Linda's and a little boy stood in the doorway to the upstairs hall, blocking my path.

"He's here," Billie said, his dark hair covering eyes that stared out of the two dark shadows of his eye sockets. He stood perfectly still, not looking at me, but past me.

"Who is?" I asked the moment I could breathe again after he scared the shit out of me. He wouldn't respond. "Billie?" My little brother's presence continued to baffle me, since he had nothing to do with this house.

"I don't want to stay. I'm scared, Avila."

"Why are you here?" I asked him. "You never lived here. Why don't you go home?" I felt silly for suggesting he find his usual place to live.

"I follow you," he said then looked over his shoulder and sank into the shadows.

"What do you mean you follow me?"

"I'm always with you, Avila. I love you."

"And I love you." My chest filled with a pain I couldn't process. My little brother had left this life for a better one and the best he could do was hang around the sister that had betrayed him? I wished I could go back in time and treat him better, do it all over again, be the big sister I should've been. Instead I'd treated him like an annoying pest. "Are you my spirit guide?"

He nodded but wasn't paying attention.

I took the chance and asked him more questions. It wasn't every day my little brother materialized in full body right in front of me. As used to his visits as I was becoming, what if I never saw him again after tonight? What if, once I got off this stupid island, the house's effect would wear off?

"Why were you in my vision today?" I asked. "With Grandfather. You were here at the house. I saw you."

"I am not with Grandfather."

"Then, who was it?" I asked, my own answer coming to me in another moment of clarity.

"Uncle Bob," he said.

Uncle Bob.

My grandfather had brought his son with him to Villegas House, to show him how to make peace with others. A lesson in diplomacy. Uncle Bob had somehow survived the murders and came home to tell what happened. My uncle had seen it all. It would explain why he wanted me—all of us—to have nothing to do with this place, why he wanted nothing to do with spirits and ghostly tales at all.

"Your gator tooth is Grandfather's." Billie pointed at the charm around my neck hanging from a leather string. I'd always known it belonged to my grandfather, but I never knew how I'd come into possession of it. "Uncle Bob brought it home."

I touched the charm around my neck.

It was imbued with energy.

My grandfather's energy.

This house's energy.

Which meant the darkness had always been with me.

I'd always worn it, assuming it was a token of the grandfather I never knew, but it was more than that. It connected me to this place. No wonder I often felt immense sadness when my fingers grazed it. Today, I felt the sorrow again, but also resentment that I'd been carrying around pain all my life in one form or another.

Would I ever be free of it?

"Avila?"

"Yes, Billie." I couldn't see my brother anymore. His spirit form had receded into the background, though I could still hear his disembodied voice, I couldn't see his ethereal shape. But I knew he was there, crouching.

"I'm scared."

"Don't be," I told him, though I empathized. I was scared too, but even now, I had to be his big sister. "Scared of what?"

"The angry man," Billie said. "He's right behind you."

TWENTY

I turned slowly.

The "angry man" was the shadow energy shape I'd seen moving throughout the house, only now his form was human. Without a face or discernible features, I couldn't see what he looked like clearly and got the sense that I never would. The spirit felt older, more ancient, like he'd lost his identity over the years.

I held my breath and hoped it would pass right over me.

But the shape floated toward me from the center of the room. I wanted to run but couldn't move. Frozen, all I could do was stand and watch, my lungs seizing breath, my feet rooted to the floor.

"What do you want? Why won't you leave us alone?" I asked.

I could ask you the same.

"You're not living anymore," I tried reasoning, watching the cloud creep closer. The hairs on my arms stood up, as its chilly gale blew over me. "You don't need a home. You can go. Go anywhere you want."

Who decides this? You? He laughed a cackling sound that would haunt me for the rest of my life. It resonated through the house, shaking the walls and my inner core. *A house built with remnants of my own. No one asked permission. They took what didn't belong.*

"Because you *died.* The things you leave behind are no longer yours."

Like the talisman around your neck.

I fingered the tooth charm, nearly yanked it off my neck as I finally backed away from the form. Was this activating the unwanted spirit activity all along? I nearly ripped it off me, if it meant not having to see or hear these ghosts anymore.

No, stop, Avila.

Linda's spirit was nearby, talking to me.

It serves you.

It didn't serve me! Nothing about the spirit world had ever served me! And the one time I thought it would was this time I followed a production crew out to Villegas House, and now I was stuck here with them. Stuck in my house of nightmares.

One slow step at a time, I backed into the hallway, the fuming black cloud cornering me. If I tried to run, I knew it would attack me and last thing I wanted was to become the third death of the day. "This used to be my grandfather's but he's no longer here," I told the spirit. "Just like this house should be someone else's. You are the one who needs to leave."

I will not. My home was fractured, hacked, repurposed.

"I'm sorry that happened to you, but you're free to move wherever you want."

I do not nor can I.

"You can if you want to. Accept, forgive, and love. Didn't you love anyone? You can go find them." I tried. I tried words and phrases to reason with this spirit, but I felt its pain and anguish, and it wasn't easy to digest.

My only love was the sea, and I cannot reach her. I am cursed.

He spoke without a voice. To any of the others, I was upstairs talking to myself, yet I heard him clearly in my mind, no English words, just universal language, meaning, thought. And here he was, telling me he'd loved the sea. Well, that made sense for a spirit trapped on a peninsula surrounded by ocean. But whoever he was, he was in pain. He'd done terrible things in life and being stuck in this house was his punishment. He'd paid that price many, many times over and over again through the years.

I wanted to help him. I really did but I wasn't a medium, a healer, or anyone who could guide him. I had my own life to worry about. Besides, this primordial entity didn't want to be helped. He was a demon, a beast now, a spirit out of touch with his original humanity.

"What's your name?" I asked, stumbling backwards further down the hallway.

The entity hovered closer, bearing down on me. It'd pushed me up against the hallway wall, a few feet from the stairwell. I turned my face when I felt it approach, felt the sour breath of rot and decay and salt coming from the misty being, or it could've been the corpse's stench emanating all the way up the stairs. My little brother had disappeared. It hurt me that he had to exist on the same plane as this thing, whoever he'd been in life.

I am no one.

"If you're no one, then you don't need to live here."

I live here because it is no place. No man's land.

No one and no place belong together. We are both forsaken.

"Tell me your name," I demanded. If only I could wield its name, I might be able to guide it out of this dimension. Linda kept telling me not to be afraid, but how could I not when a massive oppressive spirit slowly, menacingly, kept aiming its focus on me?

I am he who rules all who live here—the huntsman, the bird man, your diplomat grandfather—all who dare call themselves captain. There is only room for one *aboard this ship.* Extensions of mist ejected from the sides of the shape and now began encircling me.

Ship? "This is a house, not a ship."

Planks from my wreckage serve as the foundation for this place. A captain must never abandon his ship. Therefore I must stay. There is only room for one. Leave or serve me.

I watched in horror as this shape continued to bear down on me. I felt the choking waters of the salty sea suffocate my lungs, the acrid smoke of his last battle burning my eyes, tasted the blood of those he'd eradicated on the same beams of wood supporting what was left of this structure.

This had once been a ship—a pirate ship.

And the suffering soul was a captain I'd talked about countless times—Bellamy.

For so long, I'd assumed the tale of the pirate ship doomed to roam the Everglades was just a tale, a ghost story to recount around a campfire or an airboat full of tourists at dusk. But legends are born from truth and truths are born from facts. It'd never occurred to me to research and see if Bellamy and the *Vanquish* had been a factual vessel that had sailed.

"Captain Bellamy of the Vanquish," I called on him. "That's who you are."

Blasphemer! Where did you hear that name?

The angry spirit whirled around me, lifting my hair in a harsh tug, raising my feet off the ground. I was rising, being taken, rather, higher up the wall until my head smacked against the ceiling. My skull banged against the wood, and I felt a surge of pain bolt through my spine. One more hard shove, and my neck would split in half.

He was pissed because I knew him.

Undo this curse, wench!

"I can't. I don't know how," I said, gasping for breath. Did he think I was the woman who cursed him to begin with? My vision and lungs choked with smoke and stench. I felt like I'd been dropped in the middle of an ocean battle between ships, and I was being forced to walk the plank while breathing sulfuric acid. But how? Like my other visions, it had happened centuries ago, not today.

I had power over *him*, because I was real and corporeal. He existed no longer and couldn't do this to me unless I allowed it. "You cannot hurt me, Bellamy," I insisted.

Undo this curse, I say!

"Put me down…or…I won't help you!" I sputtered. Suddenly, my body dropped and fell to the floor. The force of my fall ripped open a rotten hole, and my leg sank through the gaping hole down to my knee. In pain, I yanked it out, got to my feet, and stumbled to the stairs. I began hobbling down, desperate to get outside. Where had everyone been while I'd practically choked to death?

I hit a solid real body at the foot of the steps—Sharon.

"Move," I grunted, shoving her. She cursed, stumbled to her knees, then stood again, following me outside. Even the rain felt good, as I tilted up my chin to the sky and felt the very real water pelting my face. Kane had been outside, ripping wood off a weak section of wall and Eve was doing her best to help him.

"What is your problem, Cypress?" Sharon asked.

I faced her. Why the hell hadn't the captain's spirit pestered her instead of me? Clearly, she was the one who thought herself the leader, the captain of this group, so why me?

He thinks you're the Red Witch, Billie said. He was still here. My little brother still lingered, though I couldn't see him.

"Who the hell is the Red Witch?" I asked.

The one in your story—the one who cursed him.

That was ridiculous. How could I be Maria Pilar Carmona, the wife of the Spanish captain who created the curse? I lived three hundred years later and looked nothing like her.

Sharon winced. "Red Witch? What the hell are you talking about?"

"I wasn't talking to you. And my problem is that you have not once tried to be a team player. Instead of asking me what's wrong, you ask my problem. Instead of saying what a great idea making the raft is, you tell us we're out of our minds. It's like you can't stand not being in control."

"This show was my conception, Cypress, or did you not know that? I hired Kane to produce it, but this and every investigation we've ever been on was *my* idea—my stupid crusade to find answers. So, yeah, I *am* in control."

"Well, then you suck at it significantly. People in charge make decisions for the good of everybody. Whereas every decision you've made so far has been for yourself."

Sharon cracked her neck and took deliberate slow toward me. I stood my ground and refused to be moved aside again as the ghost upstairs had done, but the black cloud of energy had widened and spread until I felt like he enveloped the whole house.

"This whole trip was for me, Avila. Kane works for me, Linda works for me…"

"*Worked* for you. Not anymore, you killed her. How many people are you going to sacrifice until you get your answers? What are you looking for anyway?"

"That's between me and the house, sister."

"Then talk to the house, not me…sister."

"You *are* my link to the house," Sharon said. "I can't talk to the spirits like you can."

Two people had died, one had abandoned ship, and she still wanted to talk to spirits. She still wanted to bring the unnatural world into this.

"There's four of us here, Sharon, and three of us want to get off this island. Meanwhile you want to commune with ghosts." I laughed. Of course the host of the ghost show still wanted to commune with ghosts. Just like every ghost host I'd ever seen on TV, they rested at nothing until they got that golden nugget—the holy grail—the full body apparition.

Sharon's nose moved inches from mine. I looked into her steel blue eyes, eyes that would've been beautiful, reflective of a summer sky had there been less anger in her heart. "What did the entity tell you? I heard you talking to it."

"Nothing to do with you."

"*Everything* to do with me!" she screamed, lines around her eyes deepening as her temper grew. She chuckled, caught herself, calmed down. "I need to know what happened here."

"If I knew, I would tell you," I said, doing my best to get away from this crazy woman. I slipped out the door into the refreshing darkness of the outer part of the house to find Kane. I needed to know where the shotgun was without asking him in front of Sharon, but she'd followed me around the side of the house. I needed to feel safe. "Leave me alone."

"Sure I'll leave you alone."

Sharon stopped in her tracks, as though Kane, Eve, and I had grown an electric force field over the last few seconds. She looked past me. I checked behind me to see what she was looking at. It was too dark to see anything. Shaking her head, Sharon took two steps back then headed inside.

"Holy Jesus," I said to Kane whose shirt was tied around his head. He stopped, wiped sweat from his face, grimacing. "I heard shouting. What's up?"

"What's going on with that woman?" I pointed in the direction of the house. He knew who I was talking about because there was only one highly exasperating woman in Villegas House. "I know she came here on a mission, but the history of this place is now the last thing we need to worry about. Why are you out here at night, by the way? It's pure darkness."

The moment I spotted the good pile of planks on the ground, I understood why.

"It's easier to do this out of the sun." He reached for more siding, wrapping his fingers around the flat pieces of wood and tugging. "Sharon's obsessed. Thought you'd have noticed that by now."

"We're all obsessed about something. That doesn't make it right to harass people when you haven't gotten your way."

"Yeah, I get it," Kane said. "But I also know where she's coming from. She's adopted. Wants to find her birth mother. She's been on a mission ever since someone posted info about Villegas House on that one website—*Deadly Florida*."

The one John got in trouble for talking about on a message board. One little paragraph of information about this house had led her here?

"Wait, what?"

"Sorry, thought you knew. She chose this locale for our next investigation because of personal connections she has with the house."

"Years ago, Linda told her her father was killed here," Eve added, throwing down a plank of wood. I felt bad for Eve's nails that she was having to do this kind of physical work, but I had to admit it was nice to see her helping. "She went to her for answers, and since then, she's kept Linda close to her everywhere she went."

"Her own personal medium," Kane added.

"Who she used and abused until she got what she wanted." I scoffed, deciding to join in and start pulling wood off the walls. "How much do we need?"

"I'm pulling enough to make a big pile. In the morning, we can assess how many rafts it'll make. Some of this is too rotten to use, I think. We may need to pry off the doors," Kane said. "Anyway, she grew up in Georgia mountains. When she was a kid, she learned she was adopted after she kept having dreams about a woman running out of a house wearing a white dress. A house like this one."

Oh, man.

"Her parents took her to a psychologist who suggested they tell her the truth about her adoption. Ever since they did, she's been trying to find her birth mother," Kane explained.

"Which I can understand," Eve said.

"Sure, I can too, but why would that lead her here?" I asked. "Lots of houses look like this one."

Kane and Eve exchanged looks. "Linda also told her that a woman by your name in South Florida would be able to help her."

"Me?" I remembered hearing this a few days ago, but how would I know anything about Sharon's birth mother? So Linda was to blame for sending Sharon my way.

"Yes, and through her research, she thinks one of the Nesbitt brothers might've been her biological father. Were either married?" Kane asked.

"I have no clue," I told them.

Kane panted, out of breath. "Years ago, she found a photo of this house online and swore it matched the one in her dreams. She's been wanting to find it for the longest time but could never find any info on it."

"Until the *Deadly Florida* website," I guessed.

"Right," Eve said. "And you were the one to take us there."

I shook my head in dismay. "I brought you here and look at all that's happened."

"Not your fault, Avila," Kane said, wiping more sweat. He doubled over to catch his breath. "Not your fault at all. In fact, we were just talking about this. We're sorry for putting you in this position. As producers of the show, we should've told her that this one would be impossible."

"She wouldn't have taken no for an answer," I said.

"So you have figured her out by now." Kane smirked.

I appreciated the apology but couldn't shake the feeling that it was still my fault. If I could get rid of something forever, something that had plagued me my whole life, it would be the irrational fear that I was responsible for everyone's misery including my own.

Had I insisted that Villegas House was off-limits, that there was no way in hell anyone from my tribe would escort them there, we wouldn't be in this position right now.

Some frontiers are better left unexplored.

Sharon appeared around the side of the house like a meek spirit harassed by stronger ones. "I'm sorry for the way I spoke earlier," she said, looking at me. "That wasn't fair of me."

I glanced at Kane and Eve who said nothing, then back at her. Something was up. "No problem," I replied, but I wasn't a hundred percent convinced.

"Could you come with me a minute? I want to show you something."

I stopped mid-pull on a particularly difficult plank that would've been so much easier to remove with the proper tools. Our hands would be shredded by the morning. I gave her side-eye. "I can't right now. I'm busy solving a problem."

It was sassy but I wouldn't follow *that* woman into *that* house again, even if they coughed up a million dollars.

"It's about your grandfather."

TWENTY-ONE

He died two entire decades before I was born.

In fact, my mother was born the same year he was killed and didn't know him either. Uncle Bob had only been a kid, and it was because of him that we had stories about him. They were diffused through the lens of a child, but they were our only connection to him. Him, my grandmother, and others who knew him.

And the necklace around my neck. Every time I touched it, I thought of him, of this house, and the mystery surrounding it. If Sharon had found something related to me through all her rummaging of papers and random items, I wanted to know what it was.

But the gators were encroaching.

In the dark, I watched them creeping toward the house, lured by the prospect of a meal. I wasn't sure how we would sleep at this point, how we would fight them off, how we would even get a raft finished under their watchful reptilian eyes. A vision of us feeding them Linda's corpse struck a chord—if we had to do it to keep them away from us, we had to entertain the option.

Sharon led me into the house, and as usual, I tried not to look at Linda's body but I caught a glimpse of the poncho someone had put over her to help protect her from the rain. Not sure doing so was a good idea, as the plastic material would help trap the heat and gases emanating from the corpse. I was also on the lookout for the "angry man," for the ominous energy cloud now identified as Captain Bellamy. I had nothing to prove it, except that the information had come to me the more my third eye opened to the portal that was this house in the middle of nowhere.

Sharon led me to an area behind the room used as a kitchen,

judging from the crude gas stove rusting away in the corner. From the inside of the house, it looked like a closet but just beyond it, it sank a few steps into a secret room. A small window near the top let in just a small amount of light. This house had been built in the mid 50s, early 60s. It would make sense if it were a bomb shelter. Americans in those times feared the threat of nuclear war more than its own systemic racism.

A small desk lay on its side, its carvings intricate and indicative of a civilized person having once occupied this home. One drawer was open, papers spilled everywhere. Sharon bent to pick one up and handed it to me. "More research papers."

"Okay, and?"

"Rutherford wrote tons about daily life. Somewhere here there has to be evidence of my father passing through." She picked up a piece of hurricane lamp glass that had shattered beside the desk. Standing, she placed it in my hand. "Hold this."

"Why?" I pulled my hand away.

"Tell me what you see when you feel it."

"Sharon, no. I'm not Linda. I don't have a handle on this yet."

"Please just do it."

"I'm not a performing monkey, Sharon. Just because you snap your fingers doesn't mean—"

"Just do it!" Sharon shouted then bit her bottom lip in a failed effort to calm herself. "I saw you holding that wood that Linda gave you. I saw the way you reacted. I watched your hands spread all over the floor right before you woke up to tell us about carving a boat, and I know you keep that gator tooth around your neck to remember your grandfather."

"You don't know shit about me."

"That's where you're wrong. Linda told us so much about you before we even met you."

"Why? How would she even know me?"

"She didn't. It wasn't her job to know anything, just to relay information. To tell us what she sees, what she feels, what she knows…" Sharon still held out the broken hurricane lamp. What did this have to do with my grandfather? Nothing. She had lured me in. This woman was not to be trusted.

"I can't stay here." I turned to leave, but she reached out and grabbed my arm.

"You and Linda both could see things attached to objects. Just hold this and I'll be done, Avila. I swear to God. Just do it. Please."

I stared at her eyes in the darkness, a light within them, imploring me. Like Kane had said, she was a woman on a mission. Adopted. Haunted. More than the homes she investigated. I guess if I had one chance to find answers related to my birth mother, I might act a little crazy too.

"I can't see visions in everything I touch. Look, I know you came here with a goal in mind, but that goal has changed and every minute is of essence. We need your help out there, and all you're doing is exploring this house."

"It's changed for you, Avila, but not for me!" She shoved the glass into my hand. "Hold it. Please." Her bright, pained eyes demanded, and something inside of me told me I needed to comply.

Sharon was not right in the head.

My eyes bounced around, searching for the shotgun, knowing I'd feel a hundred times better if I knew it wasn't anywhere near her. When I didn't move fast enough, she pressed the glass into my hand, drawing blood. "I said, do it."

"Bitch. You cut me," I growled, yanking the curved piece away and slamming my elbow into her chin.

Sharon gripped her chin and gave me a demented smile tinged with blood. "I'm going to forget you did that, because I need you. *Concentrate* and tell me what you see."

"Shut up," I said through clenched teeth. "This is the last parlor trick I do for you. After this, I'll be getting the hell out of here."

She said nothing but I caught the ire in her eyes, the determination to make her time here worth every minute, even at the cost of others. Sharon Roswell, doing what she did best—using others.

I breathed in deep and let it out slowly to ground myself. I let any thought run through my mind, whatever it may be, and out of a jumbled mass of worry and fear, I imagined this room as it'd been fifty or more years ago. This office, bomb shelter, or whatever. Fifty years ago, that small window facing east had been open. The morning sun shone through it, though it wasn't as hot as it is today. A cool breeze wended its way into the subterranean room.

A set of slim fingers curled around the edge of this desk.

A woman gripped the edge, lurched forward, then lurched again.

Her arms rigid, her face like the surface of the river on a clear morning. Young, beautiful with dark hair falling over her cheeks, as her hair moved in agitated waves. She held on tightly, a swatch of fabric tied over her mouth and knotted behind her head, as a man stood behind her, wide hands gripped over her hips. She'd been instructed not to make a sound, and even now as she looked at me, or appeared to, she couldn't ask for help. Even though her life depended on it. The knife blade against her neck promised her that.

Over and over the desk lurched forward, an inch at a time.

My lungs felt constricted, my pulse quickened, and I thought I might be having a heart attack. I released the glass and it fell, shattering into even smaller pieces on the wooden floor. Shards disappeared into the rotted holes of the wooden flooring. "Get that thing away from me."

"You idiot. I can't believe you broke it. What did you see?" Sharon yanked my hand down toward the floor, placing it on the desk. "Tell me. The faster we get this over with, the faster I'll help you outside."

"You mean you won't help until you've gotten what you wanted?" I fought her grip on my arm. I never expected a woman like her to have this much strength. Glaring at her, I said, "You might never know. You may as well *get used to the idea*."

"I *will* know, one way or another."

"You won't if I don't help you," I said. "And with those gators headed this way, you'll be the next one dead. Once you cross over into the spirit world, you'll have all your answers." It hadn't meant to come out as a laugh, but it did.

The next thing I knew, Sharon Roswell, host of the TV show *Haunted Southland*, had slapped my face with the back of her hand. "Cheeky little shit," she hissed.

My cheek stung. A fire flared inside of me.

Hold it together, Avila, I thought. *This woman is not well.*

It was better to give her what she wanted and quietly slink away than to fight. If I struck her now, we might never get off this island. Kane and Eve would be dealing with two more dead bodies.

"Just tell me what you saw."

"A woman," I spat and hesitated on how much to tell her. Something told me this was her mother. But this was it—this was what she wanted. Better to get it done and out of the way. "She was raped in this room. I think it was one of the assistant biologists," I lied.

What if telling her the truth angered her, made her worse?

"Who was raping her?"

"I don't know." Another lie. It was one of the Nesbitt brothers, possibly her father. I hadn't seen his face, not that I would've recognized him, but I didn't have to. I knew he was a Nesbitt from his camouflaged pants and dirty undershirts, the shotgun strapped to his back, same way the brothers had appeared out in the woods where they were buried.

"You're lying to me. Tell me who it was."

"It's like you want to hear that it was your father. Is that what you want me to tell you?" I yanked my hand away from her and stumbled to my feet. "It was one of the brothers, I don't know which."

She stared at me then shook her head. "Do you know why we're here, Avila?"

"Because you dreamed about this house. Kane told me."

She smiled. "That's right. Because I dreamed about this house every night during my childhood. All my life I've been searching for photos of it in books, on the internet, even articles on microfiche, never finding it. You don't even know what microfiche is, do you?"

I watched her laugh for a whole thirty seconds. I didn't know what was so goddamn funny.

"You fucking millennials. You wouldn't survive without mommy and daddy to do shit for you. My search has led me to hundreds of houses, hundreds of locations for our shows. But never this one—never the one I actually needed to find. Then, finally, last year I find *one* photo of it."

"On the *Deadly Florida* website," I said.

"That's right. So now I'm here, after a lifetime of searching, fifty-one years old, Avila, and you want me to just give it up, accept it, move on?" Sharon grabbed my wrist and twisted it, slapping the piece of glass back into my hand. "I'm not going to *get used to the idea.* Try again. Who is the man committing rape?"

As someone who knew exactly where I'd come from, the history of my people given to me every day by my elders, stories orally crafted and lovingly delivered, I felt for Sharon Roswell—I really did. I felt sorry for anyone who didn't know their origins and I was grateful to know mine. This woman had been searching for her parents, and my touching this stupid piece of glass could give her the missing piece she'd always needed.

So, why did my body warn me with every fiber of my soul?

I closed my eyes.

Again, I saw the woman, her face clearer this time. Crystal blue eyes shone from a pale face, as she realized someone was in the hallway, someone who could help her if only they could hear her all the way over here in the bomb shelter. Her assailant paused, pulled away, and stood on his toes to see out the window. She cried out through the gag, prompting her rapist to slap her, press his blade to her ear.

"What did I tell you? No noises."

Seeing him clearly now, he was definitely one of the two men out in the woods who'd shot the assistant, one of the two brothers fighting to get this house back. The knife he used to threaten her had etch marks on the side—W.N.

"William. It's William Nesbitt," I croaked.

"Bill," Sharon whispered.

But it wasn't so much the rapist who stood out to me, it was the victim. Bill Nesbitt hadn't raped the assistant biologist—this was Elena Villegas with the pleading eyes and the rag stuck in her mouth. I'd seen her in the other vision crying on the front steps when my grandfather arrived to help.

"What are you doing here?" Bill paused, fixing the waist of his pants and coming around the table the moment he saw me. I dropped the glass and moved away, sure as hell that this ghost from the past had noticed me watching him committing a crime.

He was coming for me.

"Get away," I said.

"There's nobody here, Avila," Sharon said.

But he was—he was coming for me.

I ran from the room, positive that Bill Nesbitt had seen me watching him—witnessing his crime. Running down the hallway, I looked for a way out, felt Bellamy following me, laughing. I was supposed to be watching her, keeping her safe while her husband was away, only her husband was back now—just outside—and his wife was here with this man.

What was happening?

I looked down at the shotgun in my hands. Hands that were darker, wider, and more wrinkled. Hands that were not mine. How had this appeared?

This was crazy. When had this shotgun appeared in my hands? Who was I, and why could I only think about the rage I felt? The pure anger coursing through my veins, the resentment of having been tricked by a wicked woman, condemned to the sea of grass forever. I wasn't Captain Bellamy, and yet Captain Bellamy lived inside of me.

I tried shaking the images from my mind to no avail.

My thoughts weren't my own; they were someone else's. I was

trapped inside the mind of someone else entirely—and now I knew who. My fingers clutched the gator tooth necklace around my neck. My grandfather's. I was supposed to be keeping Elena Villegas safe, but instead, I'd been outside with my boy, and as a result, this animal had sneaked in and assaulted her.

I lifted the barrel of the shotgun, even though I'd never shot a man before, and aimed it at him. At the offender. Fury flowed through me at both him and his brother. Wrath at myself for not doing my job, the one job I had promised Rutherford. The other Nesbitt brother stepped into the house at just that moment, met in a hallway and both of them looked at me, pleading to give back the gun.

Rutherford announced his arrival, demanding to know what was going on. I felt the fury within even at him for having moved into this house, for not having left the premises when trouble first started. Because of him, a woman had died at the hospital, a family wanted their home back, and a spirit possessed this home, even me.

Now they would all DIE…

"Mr. Cypress, sir. Don't do this," Bill Nesbitt pleaded, hands up. "You don't want to do—"

I pulled the trigger, heard the screams.

Multiple shots.

In every direction.

Watched them fall—both brothers—slumped to the floor. A pool of blood spread throughout the rooms and hallway. I shot again. All of them, every last one of them—Rutherford, the male assistant, Peter, who'd come out of his room to see what was going on. All their faults. I wouldn't even be here if it weren't for them. The biologist's wife watched in horror as I murdered the entire outfit—both warring parties. I could not shoot her, as she'd been my charge to protect, and the boy I would spare, because he was my own flesh and blood. But I had to end this reign of terror before I caused more harm.

I turned the gun on myself.

What had I done?

Oh, God, what had I done?

TWENTY-TWO

"Avila!" Sharon shook me so hard, I held onto the handrail to keep from tumbling back into the small room. Bomb shelter. Wherever the hell I was. "What the hell?"

Kane and Eve rushed into the kitchen and found us at the steps leading down.

I panted, gasped for air, reality, and all the sanity I could find. I pulled at my hair and sobbed full sized tears. I wasn't Robert Cypress, my grandfather. I was me and it wasn't 1967. What the hell had just happened?

"My grandfather…"

"You were screaming." Eve caressed my hair.

"My grandfather…"

I couldn't say much else. The words felt stuck in my throat. The blood—my God, the blood was everywhere.

He committed the murders. But that was impossible. My grandfather had been a peaceful man, a diplomat, a tribe council leader, for the love of God. He'd come here to mediate, to make peace between the feuding families. He hadn't come here to kill anyone.

I needed space, to sort this out, and so I stumbled through Kane and Eve, through the kitchen, on a heat-seeking mission to find air and space. I felt claustrophobic. It was impossible. Impossible.

"No, it's not. It's not…" I rambled incoherently. Exhaustion and emotion welled up inside of me. I didn't know what was up or down anymore. Without sanity, I would never get out of here. I was already halfway gone.

"Avila, tell us what you saw." Sharon reached me, sidling up to me and grabbing me by the arm, whirling me to face her.

I shoved her off and her back hit the wall. "Tired of your demands. Leave me alone."

"No, listen," she insisted. "If my father didn't commit the murders, then I need to know who did."

I couldn't help sneer at her. "You need to know, you need to know. Your need to know everything has ruined our lives. He didn't commit the murders," I growled. "Now, leave me alone."

"Who did then? You saw who did it, didn't you? I heard you saying, 'What have I done?' Who did it, Avila? God damn it, stop walking away from me!" Her fingernails dug into my arm.

Ripping my arm and cocking it back, my fist came pummeling forward with a mind of its own and cracked into the side of Sharon's face. If I made it out of here alive, I would deserve an award for dealing with this woman, the house, and the psychic attacks I never asked for.

"My grandfather."

Sharon stood, shocked, hand to face, staring at me.

I stopped in the hallway and gaped around the living room.

At Linda's dead body.

At the rotting, festering walls dripping with rainwater.

At the black cloud of hatred and cursed death seeping through the walls.

At the pools and pools of dark liquid spilling from innocent veins.

I couldn't shake them off, the images.

Grandfather Robert Cypress had walked into Villegas House—cursed, haunted Villegas House—after taking a slow walk with his son, my Uncle Bob, and found Elena Villegas getting assaulted. The guilt had consumed him at first, and then a wave of rage had risen over him. Because the crime he was witnessing had been his fault, to some extent, for not watching over her, sure.

But none of that had been the real reason he'd snapped—the real reason he'd snapped was because his spirit had been taken over by the oldest entity here. Same reason why Roscoe Nesbitt had vacated the house ten years before. Same reason why nobody had been able to live here in fifty years. Because Bellamy had been a cursed soul, first in life, then in afterlife, condemned to ruin the lives of everyone he came across until his curse was lifted.

He possessed the body of whoever was in charge, and for some reason, he thought that was me.

"Your grandfather killed everyone?" Sharon's mouth was agape.

"Not everyone." I spoke into the wall as more visions came to me. They were everywhere. I couldn't escape them. The only way they would let me go was for me to leave their influence. Until I could do that, I would never be free again. "He spared my uncle who was a child then. And Rutherford's wife."

I looked at Sharon.

Same heart-shaped face, same eyes as the woman who'd been raped.

"Your mother."

"No," she said slowly. Blue eyes pierced mine. "No, Avila. My mother was a Florida gladesman's wife, Bill Nesbitt's wife who's still alive and living somewhere in Big Cypress. Linda told me Nesbitt was my father, but first I had to find out which Nesbitt brother…"

"No, Sharon."

"Yes. It's just a matter of narrowing it down, and besides, she couldn't bear to raise a child alone without her husband, so she gave me up for adoption. See what I mean?"

My head shook slowly.

I stared at her.

She had it wrong. "I'm telling you. Your mother was Elena Villegas of this house, wife of the English avian researcher, Gregory Rutherford. It's why you're drawn here, why you've dreamed of this home so much, because of the trauma imprinted in your soul the day you were conceived."

The words flew out of my mouth, the information coming to me through a portal that had opened up inside my higher self. Streams and streams of information, all by touching these walls, this necklace around my neck, by looking into the mind of this woman.

I wanted nothing more than to get off this island and close this portal forever.

She stared at me with blank, disbelieving eyes. "So I'm looking for the wrong woman."

"Yes."

"Then where is she?" Sharon asked. "Where is Elena Villegas then? Wasn't she murdered here too?"

"Your father raped and impregnated her. My grandfather shot him when he realized what he had allowed to happen, then went crazy and killed everyone else, including himself, out of guilt. He spared your mother. She left the house, bringing my uncle back home with her. Nine months later, she gave birth to you."

"Where is she?" Sharon was losing patience. Every moment of

the last fifty-one years of her life was hinged on this one.

I breathed out slowly. There was no other way to tell her. "She committed suicide the same day as your birth. I'm sorry, Sharon."

Sharon absorbed my words like a fish out of water desperate to breathe again. Her gaze would not move from mine.

I bent over and breathed to avoid heaving.

I felt sick with guilt, with knowledge I wish I had never received.

All my life, Uncle Bob and the tribe had been telling us to avoid Villegas House, telling us it was evil. Uncle Bob had remembered his father as a martyr, but he never told me he'd been there the day of the murders. He'd been there. And he'd *seen.* He'd witnessed what his father had done with Nesbitt's shotgun. He'd even taken my grandfather's gator tooth necklace back home with him as a memento. Why had he given it to me?

All these years, Uncle Bob had lied about what he'd witnessed.

Lied about the truth of Villegas House, but why?

To keep our honor as a people, otherwise, what would others think? What would officials think? What would government think? Fear, so we wouldn't lose our benefits. Fear, so we wouldn't be relocated. Fear that we would lose respect for our council leader, for a man with an immaculate moral record. To preserve his reputation.

Only it'd been a lie. ALL OF IT.

My grandfather hadn't been an honorable man who'd been caught in the crossfire, killed by gladesmen out for revenge, like everyone had rumored. My grandfather had been possessed by the evil spirit of this house, had murdered people in cold blood. Maybe that made him a victim himself, but the facts were still the facts.

A murderer lived in my past.

And I wore his charm around me like a talisman.

"I need air." I stumbled toward the front of the house, past the rotting, decomposed body of Linda Hutchinson. Outside, a group of gators stood hissing in the rain, asking for handouts. I screamed at them, wild angry animal to wild hungry animals, mouth wide emitting all the rage I felt.

They continued to gape, mouths open, minus the hissing.

"Avila," Sharon called from the front door.

I turned and faced her. "What now?"

Just looking at her, I saw through her soul.

Elena Villegas Rutherford had escaped the horror along with my uncle, taken him down the river back to the village before disappearing. Where she had the baby, I didn't know, but Sharon had been adopted by a nice family and raised near Atlanta. A life of wanting to understand her roots had led her here. Whether I'd learned all this through psychometry or through Linda Hutchinson who had somehow passed her knowledge onto me before she died, I didn't know.

I didn't want to know.

"All my life, I was scared that my father had been a murderer. But now you're telling me he didn't commit the crimes. Your grandfather did."

"He committed *a* crime, Sharon. Rape is a serious crime, in case you didn't know. Because of that, Elena gave birth to you. Because of rape, she couldn't handle life and checked out. These are the impressions I'm getting thanks to you making me touch objects I didn't want to touch."

"Aren't you glad you know the truth?"

"Not especially. You?"

"I'm alive because of your grandfather. But Nesbitt didn't kill anyone—your grandfather did, and that takes a burden off my back."

"And places it on mine. Thanks for the reminder. That's what I needed right now," I said.

"You know what this means?"

"What?"

"You're the one we should watch out for." She pulled up the shotgun and cocked it. "All this time I thought it was me, thought a curse lived in my veins. But it's you we need to be careful of. You we need to get rid of."

I slowly stepped away. "You're crazy, you know that? I'm not a killer."

"You're not? You have all the makings of one. You're wracked with guilt, you live in the Everglades where it's easy to dispose of bodies, murder runs in your family…"

I backed into a gator who snapped at my ankle, setting off hisses from the other gators. I kicked the lunging creature in the eye. The gators all stumbled into each other, forming a heap, as I jumped to avoid their teeth.

There was no denying that Sharon had lost her damn mind, but part of me wondered if she was right. With all the rage I'd been feeling, I could snap at any moment, and the first one I'd come for was her.

"Come back here, Avila."

"Enough of this." Kane tried wresting the gun out of her hands, but she shoved him down the steps and he tumbled onto his back.

Sharon took aim and fired off one shot that grazed my shoulder. I dove for cover, ending up in a thicket of trees near the bodies of Quinn and the golden panther. The smell reached my nostrils. Around me, two snakes slithered off in protest.

Eve shrieked and cried from the corner of the room, and Kane, back onto his feet, slowly made his way up the steps toward Sharon. "Listen to yourself. There's no proof that a curse passes on through generations."

"She walked in her grandfather's footsteps, Kane," Sharon said. "I watched her. I heard her talking through her grandfather's spirit. Don't we see this all the time? You want to wait and find out after she snaps? You want to die? Because it's Avila causing these deaths. Open your eyes."

"You are out of your goddamned mind," Kane said. "Maybe her grandfather was already angry before he did this, maybe the entities here didn't help. Maybe the builder of this house was already angry, too. You can't just go and blame Avila because she's related to him anymore than we should've blamed you for being the daughter of a murderer."

"But he wasn't a murderer. You heard her."

Kane took slow steps toward her. "He shot a woman, Sharon. A woman who died later on. Put the gun down," he ordered, moving closer. "None of Avila's visions are facts anyway. The past won't matter to a jury when you're in jail. Put. The damn. Gun. Down."

But Sharon continued to aim out the front door in my direction, as gators debated between rushing at Kane and getting too close to the house they reviled. She'd lost it. The biological mother she'd sought all her life was dead. Had been since the day she was born.

She would not be meeting her on this trip.

Also, because of the deaths of two of her crew, because of being trapped here, because of the endless rain, because of the revelations, because her tormented life had led her to this moment, because of the ghosts… The reasons didn't matter anymore, only the facts. Sharon was our enemy.

Sharon's finger was on the trigger, and that was reality. I'd felt the temper within me too, but I hadn't pointed a gun at anyone.

I closed my eyes and imagined Kane swiping the shotgun from Sharon's hands.

A moment later, I heard the struggle unfold. As Eve screamed and covered her ears, Sharon and Kane grappled for control of the shotgun. Had I caused it? She kicked him in the groin but he fought through the pain, crumpling, knees buckling but still fighting for the gun. Both his hands twisted and pried the shotgun from her hands, and as they both fell to the ground, kicking and fighting.

Eve reached into the melée and yanked the shotgun from Sharon's hands. I watched it all—this house of madness.

"You're making a mistake," Sharon yelled after her. "She'll take it from you. I've kept my eye on her since she arrived. She's been wanting that gun, Eve, honey."

I stepped out from the shadows, hissed at an approaching alligator. Grabbing a stick off the floor, I jammed it into its snout, as I walked by. The reptile retreated back to the group. It would take more than alligators to scare me today.

"I never wanted the gun. I wanted it away from her," I clarified. "For this exact reason. So crazy bitches like you couldn't touch them."

It took all my power not to kick her face in as I approached. She'd been cut on her forehead from scuffling with Kane who gasped for breath and had broken out into waterfalls of sweat all over his body. Eve backed into a corner holding the shotgun. "Give it to me. I'll put it somewhere safe," I said, holding my hand out.

"Don't give it to her," Kane ordered his wife and shot me a glance.

"Are you kidding me? I'm not the one to mistrust here."

"I don't know that," he said. "None of us can be trusted at this point."

That was true. None of us were in our right minds, especially not Sharon who stood, helped Kane up with an outstretched hand then promptly punched him square in the face. "Asshole," she mumbled.

Kane reached out to grab Sharon, but she'd moved away, stumbled toward the stairs, and rose into the shadows, straight into the overhanging cloud of darkness that awaited her.

TWENTY-THREE

Not only had the gators arrived at our doorstep, but so had turkey vultures. They'd been circling above the cypress trees since earlier today, and now they'd landed in search of their treasures. Without a front door, they'd soon walk into the house and find themselves a meal.

I walked into the house as though floating through a dream.

Bellamy's oppressive mist had grown, now taking up most of the house. I felt the darkness the moment I stepped inside. We were all under his influences—me, Kane, Sharon, even Eve. As long as Sharon didn't take possession of the shotgun, the situation was still manageable. Though Eve held the gun, and Kane had his bowie knife, I had zero ways to defend myself.

Just as I was about to climb up the stairs, I heard movement to my right. I paused, one hand on the railing and looked over. Linda was sitting up, the sleeping bag and poncho fallen over to one side. Her exposed upper half was gray and black, her eyes bulged out and her tongue pushed out of her mouth.

My heart literally stopped beating.

From her corner of the room, her head twisted toward me.

She's up there. Waiting for you.

"Who?" I asked, my voice shredded by fear. Sharon? Yes, that was why I was going up there. One way or another, Kane, Eve, and I had to handle this situation.

The witch, she said using no voice whatsoever, but I heard her clearly. I was horrified by the sight of the old woman, rotting away undead. *The Red Witch.*

My feet stumbled on the first steps, as I slowly backed away from Linda who continued to stare at me, stench emanating from her. Yes, she'd been a nice lady in life but I didn't want her staring at me, sitting up, or looking like she wanted to walk the way she did right now. This house and everything within was doing this. Torturing me.

I tore my gaze away and slowly ascended, following the sounds of Kane and Sharon arguing, checking back frequently to make sure Linda wasn't following. They were upstairs in one of the front rooms where a chair lay on its side and a pile of dirty rags sat in a corner. The sun was starting to dawn over the darkest night of our lives, but it was only the beginning.

Eve stood in the corner holding the shotgun, as Sharon encroached on her slowly. "Sharon, listen to me," Kane said from the door to the room. I stood at the other door to the same space, keeping my eye on Sharon. Four of us stood in four corners. "I get it. We've been through a lot, and we're all going a little cuckoo for Cocoa Puffs."

"Understatement of the month, Parker," Sharon mumbled.

"But we need to hang in there. We can't get at each other's throats. We can't lose our shit. That is what the house wants. Do you hear me? It's what it wants. We cannot lose our composure," Kane said. "We have to focus on getting out of here. So, let's all cool down and take a step back."

"If she gives me the gun, everything will be alright, Kane. Tell your wife not to be an idiot. I've always known she was useless to the production team, but now she's taking it to a new level."

Kane feigned a scruffy laugh. "Sharon, I ought to drag this knife straight through your back for that. But I won't. Because I know you're talking from a place of stress. Baby, don't give her the gun. Do not...give her the gun."

Eve had taken to crying again. "I can't take this anymore. I don't know what's happening to us. Kane?"

"Baby?" Kane approached slowly like four live bombs were about to go off. "Like I said...we're losing our minds, but you've gotta hang in there. Whatever you do, don't give it to her. In fact, hand the gun to me, baby. Hand the gun to me."

But Sharon had walked Eve into a corner, and the poor woman shook like a shivering, wet mouse. "Stop. Get away from me, Sharon. I swear I'll shoot you."

"Let me do it, honey," Sharon said, holding out her hand. "Let me save you the trouble and do it for you, for all of us. It's the best thing we could possibly ask for right now."

Eve's tears ran down her cheeks. With eyes swollen and shut, she shook her head, holding the shotgun like a teddy bear, arms crossed over the barrel. God, I wanted to jump in and grab it from her then run the hell out of the house away from all these people. "This is all so pointless."

"What is, baby?" Kane asked.

"All of this. We're going to die out here anyway. It was a mistake to come here. I told you but you wouldn't listen," Eve cried, turning her cheek into the wall, smearing her tears into it. "You wouldn't listen."

"This isn't the time to be pointing fingers, Eve," Kane said, keeping his distance. From Sharon's peripheral vision, he mimed the action of shooting at the ceiling to Eve. Eve did as he asked and fired off a round right into the ceiling. Wood chunks spattered in all directions. In fact, I'd never seen a time when Eve didn't do as Kane asked, and she cocked the gun and warned Sharon with another round. "Stay away from me."

If Sharon had reloaded the gun, that meant there were three, maybe four, left inside.

"Give me the gun, Eve. Or better yet, turn it on yourself."

"Shut the hell up, bitch. Are you even listening to yourself?" Kane said.

"She's lost it completely," I told him, as I stepped closer to Sharon from her left side.

Sharon swiveled her neck to give me a look. "Says the girl on the brink of killing us all. The girl who learned the truth about her grandfather. The girl who walks in his shoes." She lunged at me, ripped off the gator tooth necklace and tossed it across the room, laughing when another blast rang out.

Eve had shot the ceiling a third time. Pieces of wood splintered and rained to the ground, as dust exploded everywhere.

"That's enough," Kane told his shaking wife.

Sharon covered her head but still reached out a hand toward Eve.

"We're going to die anyway," Eve blubbered. "Let her finish us."

"No, Eve!" Kane yelled. "That's not you talking. That's the house, the demon within these walls! You said nothing of the sort when we were outside working on the raft."

"I know, but I can't…I can't take this anymore." Eve sobbed. "It hurts too much. Please let her end this pain."

"Smartest thing I've heard all day," Sharon said. "Let me do it so we can all die quick."

"No." Kane rushed at Sharon who rushed at Eve. He shoved her aside, pushing the flat edge of his bowie knife against her neck, pressing its point into her jugular. "Don't freakin' move. Babe, give me the gun." He pried the shotgun from his wife's trembling hands and aimed it into Sharon's laughing neck.

"Look at us. And not a single camera rolling." Sharon's eyes squeezed shut as she laughed over and over again. "We finally have a scrap of real drama worth putting on TV and nothing."

Just then, we heard it—a voice.

A woman's singing.

We turned toward the source of the sound but found the hallway empty. Shadows covered the walls and floor and ceiling, and I felt Bellamy's ire with every breath I let into my lungs. I hated these people. Hated them with a passion for being self-serving, for not listening to me in the first place, for insisting we come here and letting it get to this.

I wished I had Kane's level-headedness to recognize that it was the madness inside of me doing the thinking, wishing we'd all be dead, so this could end. But I felt the pain with every cell of my body, even as I knew I was under the influence. Felt Bellamy's years of isolation, humiliation, and penitence for the wrong deeds he'd committed. Felt Roscoe Nesbitt wishing his wife and two teen boys would be dead. Felt Rutherford slowly losing his mind in the isolation of studying the *Kahayatle.*

"Who is that?" Sharon twisted to look.

The woman's voice came from deep within the walls, from the ceiling, from the ether. I knew her voice as though I'd heard it in my dreams, and maybe I had. Maybe I'd heard it a thousand times as I'd told the tales, maybe I'd even invited her into my life and now she was here. The woman Linda said was upstairs waiting. The same woman I'd seen out in the woods and on Linda's crossword puzzle sketch.

The woman with the fair skin and red hair.

A long green dress curled through the walls before I could even decipher where she was coming from. Her hands were tied behind her back and she sang a Spanish lullaby as though nothing were wrong, as though she weren't walking to her death. Because she was. To the edge of the ship, ablaze with fire and heat. A crimson tangle of smoky tendrils she was, with her orange hair kicking dust into the air like a fiery Medusa.

She looked at the wall, or at Eve, a sad, resigned smile, like we would soon understand her fate. The angry man bellowed through the house. I knew we all heard him, because everyone, even Kane and Sharon, especially Eve, cowered upon hearing his booming voice. He shouted, *And ye be the last to die, wench!*

No, she laughed under her breath. *For all you've done, for your sins, you will roam the glades forever, trapped in a sea of grass. I'll have the last laugh, captain. Aye-aye.*

And she floated through the room.

We watched her in awe.

Each of us, all of us, witnessing the specter's full glory, full-body apparition, the holy grail of ghost hunters right here in wicked glowing splendor without a camera to capture it. She was beautiful to watch, horrific because this would only end one way, and because I knew her pain. He'd killed my husband, my one and only love. And for that, he would pay. An eternity would not be enough for his sins.

I felt her pain.

I knew her pain.

I *was* her pain, because I'd known her long ago.

She danced to her own rhythm in this room frozen in time. Where we each were, I couldn't say, since I floated and swerved in a darkened room tinged with sunrise in time to the woman's singing. Transfixed we were on the ball of orange light moving through the room, singing a Spanish lullaby.

Duermete mi niño, duermete mi amor…

We were satellites orbiting around her. The wife of the Spanish captain, the witch who'd cursed Bellamy forever. Her soul had moved on, but now she was back for one last appearance on her way to walk the plank, or perhaps she did this every morning, replaying out her fate for the empty glades to see. What a lonely existence.

Transfixed in her presence, we froze while she made her way to the window.

Duermete pedazo de mi corazón…

Dream sweet piece of my heart.

I had brought the woman home.

Through centuries of rebirth, the Red Witch was me.

The gunmetal aura of the house deepened, so much that it was hard to see anything else except the scene playing in front of us. Taking invisible steps to the window, the angel of death turned and pointed her gaze right at me, silky, torn, green threads billowing behind her as though moving underwater. I saw the space where her ear should have been, where it had been cut off and fed to the reptiles. Her dress was soaked with blood dripping from the side of her head.

I felt the pain on my own skin, the searing burn of cut flesh.

This ship is diseased with wrath and greed.

But you will break the curse, Avila.

How?

How can I break the curse?

Of course, she wouldn't tell me—she wanted Bellamy to rot in hell forever. But I felt it now. Yes. I had come to Villegas House to undo the curse and release the souls within it. It had taken death, it had taken fear and my grandfather's tragedy to finally bring me out here. The necklace around my neck had been made from the animal that had refused to extinguish the Red Witch's life—a crocodile, not a gator. The crocs too frightened to come near her. Imbued with her energy from the waters of her drowning, it had allowed the continuation of her soul into everyone who had ever found it on these sacred lands.

On the shores of Florida Bay, someone had found it and relocated it to the Everglades. My grandfather had worn it before me and several others before him, including an unwilling soldier on the battlefield of the Second Seminole War near this spot. They were all inside me. I was the ongoing result of many lives.

I was Miccosukee, I was American, I was Spanish.

We were all connected.

Calmly resigned to her fate, the Red Witch walked through Eve, seemed to bring her along. Her naked feet stepped over the edge of the precipice, and then she was gone.

In my suspension, I floated to the window to look out and see where the captain's wife had disappeared to and found her falling slowly, timelessly down toward the alligators waiting below. The stench of death mixed with salty seas and the ferrous scent of spilled blood filled my nostrils, as the house ebbed and flowed back and forth, rocking over invisible waters.

Bellamy shouted, his voice shaking through the ship.

He'd lost his fortune, lost his chance at appeasing the king, lost half his crew in the fruitless chase. And now, because of this damned woman (everyone knew that women were bad luck aboard a ship), he was forced to leave this house. Screams filled the home, of anger and rage that seemed to last forever, ancient fury that would never see completion. This ship—this house—was an endless trap of grief and would always be unless we burned it to the ground.

Burned it to the ground.

That was what I needed to do—burn the infernal thing down.

The Red Witch knew but hadn't told me.

But I knew anyway.

Because the Red Witch had *been* me—long ago.

The entity moved through the room, charged out through the ceiling, blasting a corner of the roof open, and the darkness lifted slowly. We found ourselves back in the present, wondering what the hell had happened. Sharon's back was pressed against the wall out of utter fear, Kane's mouth hung open wide, soundlessly, his breath lost on the last of Bellamy's curling, pervasive shouts.

I'd traveled through a dream back in time.

Eve, though—was gone.

"Babe!" Kane's shouts echoed through the empty house. Had she slipped out while the ghost woman in red had captivated us? "Babe! Where are you?" Kane ducked into the hallway to search for his wife, but my gaze remained transfixed on the window.

This house made of pirate ship wood made you feel its pain, forced you to walk its footsteps, feel the throbbing agony of all its fallen, slain, and cursed.

I knew where Eve was.

TWENTY-FOUR

My hope was to confirm what I already knew and to get to Eve before her husband saw her. I ran to the window and there she was twelve feet below, broken body on the ground below, torn by alligators. They wrestled over the meatiest pieces at the meal that had dropped from the sky. As we'd watched the woman in red, transfixed, it'd been Eve who'd stepped to the window, Eve who'd cast her last words, Eve who hadn't been able to handle the stress.

"Shit." I closed my eyes.

"Babe!" Kane continued to call for her.

"Kane…"

I didn't know how to tell him. This moment, caught between normality, if we could call this moment normal, and the instant where your life changed forever, this moment charged with electricity.

"What? What is it?" His eyes filled with understanding and he flew to the window, pushing me aside by taking up space. His gaze fell on what I'd seen, and the wave of terror and unspeakable dread I felt emanating off his soul crushed me.

"Kane…"

"Oh, no. God, no. No, no, babe……no." Kane sank to his knees, the gun slipping to the ground and resting beside him.

I tried, like any fellow human, to console him, but what do you tell someone who's literally watched their wife get torn apart at the seams by animals of the earth doing nothing other than being animals?

"I don't know what happened. We saw the ghost…the ghost came in the room…" I tried putting together coherent thoughts, but there was nothing to say. No explanation that would bring her back.

Words mattered as much as running down to save Eve.

"She wanted to die," he cried into my shoulder. "I felt it."

"I did too."

She did. She'd been losing her ability to cope faster than the rest of us. I had seen it in everything she said and did. What little emotional strength she had, she had because of Kane keeping her together, but Eve, from the beginning, had not been fit for this excursion.

"What happened?" Sharon asked from her spot, back still pressed against the wall. Still in shock from the ghostly encounter, she looked at us with the energy of a dying vine.

I shook my head at her and held Kane's shoulders as he sobbed. The man's energy leaked from his pores. He was dying as I held him, maybe not a physical death, but a spiritual one. There was nothing left to live for, try for. Everything he ever did, he did it for Eve. He wailed like a wounded animal, a sound I never cared to hear ever again. If I ever made it out of here alive, that was.

As his broken spirit disintegrated in my arms, I thought about where we'd go from here, how we'd ever find the energy to finish building that raft now that he almost certainly wouldn't want to anymore, and then something slipped from between us, creating a pocket of air alerting us to its displacement.

The shotgun had moved, slid along the floor, and was now back in the hands of Sharon Roswell, its barrel pointed straight at us. "Sharon…" I pleaded, holding up my palms in surrender. "Haven't we been through enough?"

Her eyes were filled with resignation. "We have. Every moment of my life has led me here, to this house, and this is how it ends."

Ends?

"No. Listen, this is the only the beginning," I told her. Wasn't sure what I meant for her exactly, but she needed to hear positive words, something that would inspire her, remind her that we were all connected. Surely the words should mean something to her personal story. "Sharon…"

Slowly, she got to her feet, still aiming the shotgun at us, hands trembling. For the first time in days, she looked human. I almost agreed she should kill us out of mercy.

Almost.

With every step closer, she pointed it more at Kane. I wracked my brain trying to figure out a way to swipe it away, to jump at her like the panther had jumped on Quinn, to move faster than the speed of light and knock the gun from her hands, but we were at her mercy. And being at the mercy of a woman going mad was to die a painful death.

"It's better this way," she said. "Right, Kane?"

To my shock, Kane nodded, his cheek brushing against my shoulder. He'd lost his will to live. In my arms, I held a dead man.

"No," I told him, hoping my shake would snap him out of it. "Sharon, no. We'll move on from this. It's traumatic, but we'll find a way. Life goes on, finds new meaning. Sharon, don't…" I thought of my mother sitting at her table in the village, talking to tourists on a Sunday, not realizing I wasn't home yet. Or realizing it and worried to death. It was Sunday, wasn't it? Unaware that her daughter was caught in a house of hell miles away. I thought of my grandmother, my uncle, my little brother, of the life I'd led.

It'd been a good one.

Even with all I'd complained about and all the guilt I'd carried, it'd been a good one. My grandfather's had been too. The American soldier. Maria Pilar Carmona's had been too.

But I wouldn't die today.

The shotgun blasted, the force sending Kane backwards in my arms. I looked at the bleeding hole in the middle of his stomach, at the life force leaking out of his gaze, and my lungs filled with fury again.

So, we were doing this today after all. This bitch and I would be fighting to the death, because screw this woman if I was going to let her take me down in her whim of miscalculated insanity. She would not have the upper hand, not if I could help it. From the beginning, she'd thought she'd been the head of this whole expedition to hell, but I had news for her—this was *my* territory.

With one last pulse of energy left in him, Kane whispered, "Get her."

I charged at her with full force, knocking her against the wall, pushing the length of the shotgun up under her chin, choking her with it. In my mind's eye, Sharon's eyes bulged and her tongue pushed out and she died right here, at my hands, but her knee jumped and caught me in the groin.

Motherfu—

We swapped places at the wall and then I was the one with the weapon under my chin. Our strengths felt about the same, a surprise considering she was older. But she was also more fit than I was and it showed. Her pressure on the rifle against my chest was excruciating, the tension in our tangled arms faltering. We could break at any moment, but I wouldn't.

I kicked her hard in the knee, and as she cried out, I stumbled out of her grasp and headed for the backpack in the corner of the room. A can of mosquito spray. If I could reach it, I could blind her. She shot at me and I ducked, bulldozing into her midsection, head down, as she shot again.

At this point there had to be zero shells left in the damn thing.

Taking hold of the shotgun, I wrestled it out of her hand and threw it against the wall, watching it bounce off and land near Kane's limp hand. His body was still twitching in agonizing death. Chest heaving, gasping for breath, Sharon charged at me.

"You could've shot me," she said, slamming me, knocking me down. "Why didn't you?" A punch slammed into my face.

"I'm not a killer." Running out of strength, I reached and flailed, catching my fingernails on her face and tearing off little strips of skin.

She screamed as she hit me again, ramming her fists into my face over and over. I began blacking out and knew it would be a matter of time before I couldn't see anymore. From somewhere behind me, or maybe above me, or within, I heard laughter—the captain's laughter, the "angry man." Bellamy loved this, lived for this.

As my eyes swelled shut, I spotted my little brother in the middle of the room, disappointed that his big sister was a lame fighter who couldn't end things in a big wicked witch way. He wanted to help any way that he could, and then—he did.

The backpack slid across the room. Reality felt warped, time slowed down, and Sharon and I rolled on the floor, fighting for the upper hand. At one point, I was the one above Sharon, glaring down at her, focused on the bruises forming all over her face. Our shoulders had tapped Kane's, and she had reached out and snatched his bowie knife from his belt. A second later, I felt searing pain in my shoulder, as the blade sliced through, jagged edges ripping away at muscle. It burned, and I blacked out for a moment, falling onto my side, gripping my shoulder.

Any moment now, I'd feel the knife again, this time in my chest.

I waited for it, expected it, even cocked my knee back, ready to kick forth if I had to fend her off. My hand rested lightly on the backpack, but I'd already forgotten what was inside. I could focus on nothing. All that was clear to me was a violently angry woman poised to kill me, the mad laughter of a scorned pirate echoing through the house, and my little brother trying to shout through dimensions that silenced him.

Get it, Avila.

Billie, I'm sorry. I'm so sorry you were taken.

So sorry I couldn't save you.

It should've been me.

It should've been me in the front seat.

My grandfather stood in the room too, watching me lose this fight to the woman who'd used me to get here. Taken from me, taken from Linda, taken from everyone, and for what? Truth? Had that truth given her peace? Truth had only given her permission. Permission to act like the animal she always was, only now she had a legitimate reason.

The only way to win this would be to kill her, and I could never do that.

I wasn't my grandfather, and I wouldn't let Captain Bellamy win over me.

That only left death—my own.

The bowie knife whooshed down, straight for my chest, but I blocked Sharon's hand with my arm, heard bone crack. Whether hers or mine, I wasn't sure, though I felt blinding pain spread through me again. I was made of pain at this point. In my hand was the can of mosquito spray. I'd pressed down on the nozzle and was shooting her face with the mist.

She stepped back, tripped over herself and fell to the hole-riddled floor.

"Damn it. Why? Why would you do that?"

"Sorry, not sorry," I said.

Using what little strength I had left, I dragged the backpack closer to me and fished my hand around for the barbecue lighter. The minute Sharon rushed at me again, I was on my feet, gaining my second wind. I slapped her hand hard, knocking the knife out. It slid along the floor, whirling like a fidget spinner.

Pressing down on the trigger, I turned on the lighter.

"Don't come closer," I told Sharon whose hands were pressed over her eyes. She stumbled to a stop. "Fair warning, there's a lighter in my hand and a can of mosquito repellant in the other. If you come closer, I'm torching your ass."

If I did it, I'd be no better than my grandfather, the man who murdered a slew of people in this house in 1967. I'd become a victim of the curse, and I'd only prove Sharon right.

Walking backwards, I found the bowie knife again, jammed it

into the can and watched the flammable liquid spray violently into the air. I covered the walls, the doors, entered the hallway and covered the handrails of the stairs. Covering everything I could until the can ran out, I stood there with the lighter in my hand, its flame flickering and ready to set this house on fire.

Sharon managed to open her eyes to a squint. "Go ahead, Cypress. Burn the house with me in it. You'll end up in the news as the Indian woman gone mad, responsible for multiple deaths out in the Everglades."

I laughed hard. And couldn't stop.

I would.

And it would be worth it.

TWENTY-FIVE

"Nah."

The voice was not mine, nor Sharon's, nor any ghost's from what I could gather.

Our attention was brought to the man on the ground, coughing up blood.

"It'll be the Black man who finally got tired of all this shit." Kane's fingers curled around the cold metal of the shotgun and a moment later, a shell ripped open Sharon Roswell's forehead. She dropped to the floor into a puddle of her own life force.

It was done.

I rushed to Kane's side, guilty for not having tended to him sooner. Always with the guilt. I would live with it my entire life, wear it like a badge of honor. "I thought you were dead."

"Go. Burn this motherfucker to the ground."

I pulled up his shoulders. "Let's get you out of here first."

He groaned through intense pain. "I'm done." His breath was laced with finality.

"You're not done. Let's go." Me pulling and tugging at two hundred pounds of solid muscle did not go well, and Kane's head lolled to the side. I lifted his face and tapped his cheeks. "Hey…hey. No, you don't. Kane…"

There was no reply.

I did it all. I pumped at his chest, took off my blouse and pressed it into the bleeding wound of his torso, happy patchwork colors compressing death. I pumped his chest again and blew air into his trachea. Nothing.

I was surprised to find myself resting my forehead against his chest and sobbing pitifully, as though I'd known him personally. I hadn't. But what it had taken most people to learn about another in a whole lifetime, I'd learned about Kane in two days. If I ever got off this island, I would remember this man as my friend.

I cried for what could've been.

I could have been friends with Kane and Eve. I could've moved to Atlanta and started a new life. I could've gotten to know their adult kids. I might've worked in production, and they could've taught me things about myself that I never knew. But it wouldn't happen now. And their kids would never see their parents again.

Holding him against my chest, I raised my face and screamed into the newly risen sunlight. How dare the sun dawn on this mess, revealing the carnage and chaos we'd fought so hard to avoid through the night? It came anyway. It came because some forces were not to be messed with, and Villegas House was one of them.

The warnings had all been true.

I breathed in deep and touched Kane's face. If Eve were here, I'd touch hers too. I'd link her fingers entwined with her husband's and back away slowly, leaving them to rest together, saying my goodbyes and offering pitiful excuses of regret. I was sorry, sorry for having accepted their offer. Sorry for having brought them here. Sorry for believing that things might go better than expected, that good might prevail over evil.

I'd been naïve.

Five people were dead.

Grabbing the backpack, I gave the dead one last look, offered a silent prayer, even for Sharon, who I could forgive—she had not been in her right mind—and backed away. I lit the walls on fire, the door, the handrail before descending the stairs, heard the booming shouts of Captain Bellamy, telling me not to go in his wordless language of hatred. His job was not done, not until we were all dead, and as much as I felt the pull to stay and let myself burn in this house along with the rest of the team, out of guilt, out of fate—I wouldn't.

Linda wouldn't want me to.

Kane and Eve wouldn't want me to either.

I would finish what we started, one way or another.

While the house slowly burned from the dry inside out toward the water-soaked exterior, I worked on the raft, pulled together pieces and tied them with electrical cable. I sliced the outer plastic coating with Kane's knife and used the thinner wiring to make the frame lighter. Every now and then, I'd look up and watch the plumes of smoke climb into the air, flesh and bone and souls rising up with it. My only hope was that the smoke would alert local gladesmen or tribe members or researchers working out in the *Kahayatle.*

Anyone who otherwise might not think to come this way.

If I got out of here alive, then Kane and Eve's efforts would not have been in vain.

It took two days for the bulk of the soaking wet house to burn, the same number of days it took me to finish building the raft. I tore planks of wood off the burning house with bare hands, tied more planks together with cables and dry palmetto leaves, drank rainwater, slept with one eye open, braided dry cypress fronds for more rope, and tied plastic ponchos to the underside to create an extra layer of protection against water seepage. I found several good sticks for wading through the grass and sucked blood from my shredded hands.

On the third day, the house burned to the ground.

Charred black remains smoldered in the heat.

When police would ask why I'd burned the house down, I wouldn't be able to say it was my strategy for breaking a curse so I'd tell them it was my only defense against wildlife. Because of the fire, the stench of rotting flesh had shifted to cooked flesh, and the gators had moved back into the water in search of cooler temperatures. This was the only way I was able to drag the raft into the river.

A girl had to do what a girl had to do.

Kneeling on the raft, holding onto the wading stick, I watched the last of the house burn down. Two center walls finally collapsed in what had been the living room, and the orange, scorched pieces erupted into columns of ashes and smoke.

Goodbye, Kane.

Goodbye, Eve.

Goodbye, Linda and Quinn.

Later, Sharon.

Quinn had long been digested, and BJ—God only knew where that POS coward had gone. Watching the house burn, I drifted away slowly, knowing there would be peace on this land from now on. With no one to disturb it, no crazy humans to set curses or go mad in solitary confinement, nature would soon reclaim her. Tranquility would once again reign supreme.

The blackened remains drifted out of sight, and the ghosts of all who'd walked this land waded with me. The production crew, the avian expert, Rutherford, his wife, Elena, the man who'd raped her and fathered Sharon, the assistants, my grandfather, even my Uncle

Bob as a child.

They followed me down the river.

Past the fields of sawgrass.

Past the mangrove tunnels and rows of anhingas stretching their wings to dry in the morning sun.

We passed the upturned wreckage of the airboat. Of course it would spill. BJ didn't know how to maneuver the skiff, and he'd had the balls to take off and maroon us during a rainstorm, no less. Of course karma got him. Gators did too. There was no way for an inexperienced man like him to survive this. I stopped and tried to recover items, but the boat was upturned, and heavy tech equipment boxes were of no use to me on my lightweight raft anyway.

I had zero energy. I had to lie down.

The sun beat down on my shirtless body. Floating through the morning brightness and heat in just my bra, I heard my little brother's airy voice telling me to hang on just a little while longer—I was almost there and shouldn't give up now. In fact, he'd already alerted Uncle Bob in a dream. He and other tribe members had been notified of a non-brushfire blaze and were on their way up the river.

Okay, Billie. I love you.

I felt a deep sense of peace but also sadness. What messes we humans made.

I thought of Captain Bellamy, of the Spanish witch who wouldn't go down without a fight who'd cursed him to this very last day. Me, in another life, I was certain. We were all connected in a cycle of life and death. I wondered if the captain was with me now, too. After all, a captain never abandons his ship, and this raft had been fashioned partly from his own vessel, the *Vanquish*.

They say that on dark nights when the moon is only a sliver, you can see still see the doomed pirate ship sailing along, searching for a way out, its ghostly crew trapped in a prison of watery grass… I looked up and saw the waning quarter moon. I laughed at the irony.

History repeated itself.

Only Bellamy wasn't the captain now.

I was.

A HAUNTED FLORIDA NOVEL
CITY OF
SPELLS
GABY TRIANA
From bestselling author of ISLAND OF BONES

ONE

1921
Prohibition

Julia Harding stared at the bay, waiting for a man who was not her husband. She cradled her small belly, thankful that the housekeeper had not yet begun asking questions.

The Siren was late, and her nerves were shot.

Her husband, Peter Wallace Harding, New York City millionaire, had been hired by railroad tycoon, Henry Flagler, to oversee construction of a new hotel—the Palm Oasis—in West Palm Beach. Problem was, he'd been there the last year and a half. His last trip home had been two months ago and only for one day. When he'd next arrive—*if* he'd arrive at all, for his activities had grown more and more lawless as of late—he would come by Flagler's new train.

Originally, Mr. Harding wasn't supposed to supervise construction of the Palm Oasis in West Palm Beach. He'd been hired to oversee the Flamingo Hotel in Miami Beach, a much-shorter twenty miles from their newly-built home. Else Julia never would have agreed to settle here. But Mr. Harding had insisted all these new hotels would make even more money for them, and so she'd agreed.

Now, she regretted doing so, for Julia felt forsaken. Discarded like a cancelled stamp. Left to live out lonely days by the sea with no one other than her Bahamian housekeeper to talk to, and Mimi could be so…*insightful*, it scared Julia.

Whenever Mimi would stroll into the room carrying fresh linens, she'd catch Julia standing at the lavatory, pressing a towel to her flushed face. Every morning, Julia would rush upstairs and empty the contents of her stomach into the water closet in a futile attempt to keep breakfast down.

She knows, Julia thought.

Still, it could be her husband's.

No one would know until June the following year. And then, the moment of truth would come. For her husband had been home the same week as Roger Gibson's delivery, and Roger Gibson, like Mimi, possessed dark and lovely Bahamian features.

It should've been a charmed existence, living in this mansion by Cayo de Biscainhos, a gleaming azure body of water dazzling with diamonds in the sunlight. Her husband had convinced her that moving to freeze-proof Miami, a world away from frigid New York, would be a magnificent opportunity. He could take advantage of the booming land development business. He could take advantage of Mr. Flagler's superior wages.

Best of all, he could take advantage of the lack of law enforcement in South Florida. For this reason, many men had migrated south. It was harder to be arrested in No Man's Land, easier to deal with smugglers, and the proximity to the Caribbean islands where rum was produced at a frantic rate made Miami's coastline a bootlegger's dream come true.

Except that Julia had been left to fend for herself, and she knew her onions. She knew what her husband kept hidden in the subterranean cellar behind the false façade and 300-lb vault door, surrounded by walls of limestone and crushed shells. Four hundred cases, maybe more, of illegal spirits.

How could Mr. Harding leave her to protect such a thing without so much as a single weapon?

And so every day, she watched the vessels in the bay, hoping one would be Roger in *The Siren* come to visit and deliver more cases. She allowed herself to fantasize that one day, Roger might take her away from this lackluster life, love her, give her what her heart had always wanted—attention. Roger was the only man who kept her sane, the only one who cared about Julia, but unfortunately, he was also the man with whom she could never be.

With a repressed sob, she turned back to the house and found Mimi coming up the walk.

"Mrs. Harding," Mimi said, out of breath. "A man called on the telephone. He said to tell you that your husband would be home soon."

"What do we call soon today?"

"A month's time."

"A month?" Julia exclaimed.

She would be showing by then, if her body survived it, and sometimes she wondered if it would be better to lose the child. God only knew the consequences that might befall her if he or she did not resemble her husband come June?

God also knew how much she had always wanted a child to keep her busy during these long days and nights. But she had never expected to be dumped in this forsaken tropical hell, as beautiful as it was. She had never expected to feel so lonely, to stray like another man's Sheba. But it was her husband's custom to always dump her somewhere. In New York, it was at the Ladies' Empire Club, or the Tea Room, as long as it allowed him to conduct his business without interference.

Her life meant nothing to him.

"Sure, tell it to Sweeney," Julia said with a sigh. A month would become three, or four, or never. "Please get supper started. The men are not coming today."

The sun was already setting, and if deliveries were to be made, she would have spied them on the horizon by now. Julia turned her back to the bay and headed to the house, Mimi following close behind, when the faint sound of a motor reached Julia's ears.

She turned.

Her heart lifted, but only for a moment.

From the vessel's silhouettes, it was not Roger nor one of his rum runners stopping by to check on her. Lead plummeted into her stomach.

"Go inside, please," Julia told Mimi.

"Yes, ma'am."

She turned and waited for the Coast Guard to come closer, so she could assess its intentions. It did not appear to be passing through—it was stopping. Julia braced herself. Moments like these made her resent Mr. Harding the most.

When the boat finally docked, out stepped the captain, a handsome, older man. "Good evening, missus. Is your husband home?" he asked, lighting a cigar.

"No, he's a land developer doing business in West Palm. Is everything to order?"

"Not exactly. We're intercepting boats from Bimini and Gun Cay along the Rum Line. Some have been seen headed for these coasts. You wouldn't happen to have seen any stopping here, would you?"

Julia swallowed her dread as quietly as she could. "Of course not. Why are they being intercepted?" she asked, hoping she sounded innocent.

The captain looked at Julia through eyes that had seen too much. "Nothing to concern yourself with, missus, but if you'll excuse me, I'll need to inspect your property."

"For?"

Nerves jittered inside her stomach. Had she sounded too brusque just then?

The Coast Guard had stopped once before to ask questions but never to inspect the house. Mr. Harding shouldn't have gotten involved with the trade. She'd never voiced her concern, though, as it had not been her place.

"Again, matters you needn't worry yourself with. Won't you show me in?" He tipped his hat politely.

Julia felt trapped. "Yes, of course."

She had no choice. If she appeared the least bit resistant, it would mark her as guilty, or suspicious at the very least. Like her husband had coached her before he left: *Anyone shows up, show them around, be pleasant, offer coffee or tea.* She never thought they would actually stop in—after all, this was the beauty of living close to the islands—but news around town was that law enforcement was beginning to catch on.

The captain, along with two other men, stepped out of the boat and followed her down the unlit path to the house. Julia eyed the banyan tree in her garden and wondered if she would ever sit beneath it again.

Their cellar was filled to the brim with illegal spirits, but if she was lucky, it'd be difficult to find. They would have to stay a while, probe, raid the home.

Julia showed the men into her house. "May I offer you some coffee, tea, perhaps some fresh water?"

"You sure those are all the choices?" The captain chuckled under his breath. He strolled the house, tapping on walls, peeking behind framed art.

Julia did not reply.

Normally, she would turn on her charming self, but as of late, she was not feeling much like a hostess. It could've been her delicate state, or the fact that Roger had not visited this week, or perhaps it was the enormous lie that was her entire life weighing heavily on her.

"Water would be fine," the man replied.

Julia glanced at Mimi who nodded and set to serving the Coast Guard captain a glass of water. She wondered if there existed some way to inquire about the captured speedboat without incriminating herself.

"The, uh…speedboats you intercepted. Were they Bahamian vessels?"

The captain raised an eyebrow, as Mimi brought the glass of water then disappeared down the hall. "Why the interest in Bahamian vessels, missus?" the captain asked.

Julia touched her collarbone. "Why, I'm simply wondering where the rum is coming from. Making small talk." She forced a smile.

"It comes from all over the region, Mrs…"

"Harding."

"Mrs. Harding. And not just rum but whiskey, wine, all sorts of booze. The ship we intercepted this morning was from Nassau."

"Nassau?"

Roger was from Nassau. Julia tried to keep a steady expression.

Mimi emerged from the hallway leading to the door underneath the carpet, the one that dropped into the cellar. She gave Julia a knowing look, and Julia knew she had gone like a good girl to double check on the latches.

The men lingered near the hallway.

Seeing the housekeeper emerge from there, one officer slowly stepped down the hallway, checking behind the large Egyptian tapestry Mr. Harding had purchased from John Rockefeller in Manhattan.

The captain kept one eye on his men and another on Julia. "The details are apt to frighten a young woman such as yourself, Mrs. Harding. I'd rather not say."

"Oh, you'd be surprised, Captain. Not much goes on around here. I'd be grateful to hear a tale or two." Yes, that sounded sincere.

"Very well, then." He took a long chug of his drink before wiping his mouth with the back of his hand. Roger did the same whenever he'd come in from spending days at sea.

"Captain McCoy is out there. And he's a smart one, you see. Brings spirits from all over the Caribbean to just outside that three-mile international line. Then, he lets smaller boats take over, face the danger of getting intercepted. We've caught onto his strategy."

"I see." Julia tried to seem interested, but inside, her chest imploded with anguish.

"These boats, some of them fitted with plane engines from the Great War, are faster than we are, Mrs. Harding. And the captains of these boats, some of them make several hundred-thousand dollars a year. I make *six* thousand for abiding the law. Do you think that's fair, Mrs. Harding?"

"Oh, definitely not."

"Definitely not." He puffed on his cigar.

Roger's boat was one of the ones fitted with a plane engine. He had talked incessantly about it last time he'd visited, he'd been so proud.

The captain stepped closer. Deep blue eyes burned with something unreadable.

"So, when we see these boats creeping up to homes like yours behind their smoke screens in the middle of the night, Mrs. Harding, I get a feeling deep inside my gut. You understand, don't you?"

Julia did not answer. He wanted her to incriminate herself, to say something—anything—but she would not.

If she had just *one* thing to live for, it was seeing Roger Gibson again. If these men discovered the contents of their secret room, and if the rum runners captured this morning included Roger, her life would be over.

The captain laughed then handed her back the empty glass. "Thank you. For the water." He winked at her.

He knew.

Through her moment of silence, she'd told him everything he needed to know.

Suddenly, one of his men walked into the house from the dock, waving a cracked bottle of rum in the air. "Captain, found this under the dock along with a few others."

Damn it, she and Mimi had cleaned the shore as best as they could, but these bottles washed up all the time.

The captain gave Julia a burning glare. "Raid the house," he ordered.

"No," Julia said. "Please."

He ignored her and headed straight for the secret door, as men bustled all around her.

Mimi's terrified stare met hers.

"Run," Julia told her. "Go out the front door and run as fast as you can. Do not look back."

"Yes, ma'am." The young woman dropped her apron and ran from the house away from the hubbub while Julia thought of what to do for herself.

Minutes blurred together, as she helplessly watched the raid on her home. Men ran everywhere, bullets sounded from deep inside the house, and she could imagine the vault door getting torn apart. Door by door, tapestry by tapestry, floorboard by floorboard, they ripped apart her home.

But it had never really been home, had it?

Julia stood by, too panicked to move.

"Oh, and Mrs. Harding?" The captain calmly puffed on his cigar. He paused at the top of the cellar stairs. "*The Siren's* captain opened fire on us this morning. We had no choice but to shoot him. You can tell your husband his rum runner is dead."

He disappeared into the cellar, taking Julia's heart with him.

No, it can't be.

Julia backed out of the house, as chaos erupted all around her. Men yelled to each other, brought out cases, cracked them open, confirmed the smuggled goods. Yelps of victory signaled her demise.

He'll never stop to see me again.

He'll never take me away from this life.

Or see his child.

As in a slow-moving dream, Julia floated toward her garden and stood perfectly still, staring up at the great banyan tree. It had given her hours of comfort during her year and a half of solitude. Cradling her belly, she thought of Roger, of the life they would never have, the one she'd dared to dream could ever be reality.

Dreams that had kept her sane.

Kept her alive.

Now with Roger gone, so had all hope.

Removing her shoes, she climbed the tree as she'd done many times before. Soon, Mr. Harding would be arrested. Their mansion would be sold, and new residents would eventually move in. Slipping one of the hundreds of hanging vines around her neck, tying it tightly, Julia muttered a curse.

As long as this house stood, facing the bay like a woman awaiting her lover's return, she could not allow another to experience the happiness that should have rightfully been hers. No love, no children, no family.

Closing her eyes, Julia dropped from the banyan's great branch, freeing herself from misery forever.

TWO

Present Day

The lucky knot bracelet around my wrist felt tighter than usual. I loosened it, remembering the day I got it. It was last year when Samuel and I visited the Buddhist temple in Miami Beach. The monk who'd put it on me had recited several mantras, infusing the bracelet with positive energy. He'd told me that when it was time, I should pass it onto someone else. Passing good energy was good karma.

It would bring me a world of luck in no time.

Good, because I need luck, I remembered thinking.

As a general rule, I tried not to think of things I *needed.* The more we put desires up on a pedestal, the more unattainable they seemed. Instead, I tried thinking of my desires as things I already *had* or were on their way. Like stuff I'd ordered on Amazon Prime, *God-Universe Edition.*

Well, my luck hadn't arrived in two days after that temple visit like Prime Shipping. But a year later, here I was inside my brand new shop—my dream come true.

It might've been the bracelet.

Or the Universe having heard my prayer.

But most likely, it'd been my own hard work.

Nestled on a side street off a main shopping plaza in Coconut Grove, *Goddess Moon* was now officially open for business. My little new age shop was filled with beautiful spiritual items, everything from crystals to incense, to religious statues, to yoga clothes, books on every metaphysical topic, but more importantly—wonderful people.

I'd assembled a team of three talented women and one sweet, non-binary lovely, Rain, who stood by ready to offer awesome services, such as aura photography, tarot readings, yoga classes, reiki energy healing, past-life hypnotherapy, and much more.

But only Bibi, Maggie, and I were on the schedule for today. Lorena, my reiki master, and Rain, my aura photographer, would be in tomorrow.

At twenty, Bibi was already a talented intuitive. She'd told me things about myself nobody could possibly know. She'd been doing so since the days when I used to babysit her. Maggie, older than me at forty, was an amazing hypnotherapist. According to her cards, I'd been a politician, a gravedigger, and a hippie in another life. The hippie I could see, but a gravedigger?

Really?

I'd hoped she'd tell me I'd been a psychic, a healing woman, a shaman, or some other kind of *bruja*. All my life, I'd identified as a witchy woman, minus the talent. This was why I'd hired such amazing people for my shop.

Because I envied them.

I didn't go around admitting this to my psychic friends, but I wasn't one of them. As much as I tried, I couldn't see ghosts, couldn't speak with spirit guides, couldn't see colorful auras, no matter how much I stared at people against a white background.

I meditated every day, sometimes twice. I tried tips and tricks from every religion to reach that prized alpha state, but I hated to say it—I was just…normal. My worries about bills, thoughts about whether my husband was happy, whether or not we'd ever be blessed with children, what I should make for dinner that evening always ruined my sessions. Never did I receive messages from my higher self.

Spirit guides did not visit me. Portals to the universe did not open up in my third eye. Candles did not flicker around me when the presence of a spirit was near.

Zero.

Nada.

As my Cuban parents would say, No arrugue que no hay quien planche. In other words, Stop making waves, Queylin, you're just like everybody else.

Still, with or without the world's encouragement, I would keep trying.

My spiritual journey began three years ago when Samuel and I went to Sedona for our honeymoon. I didn't know it at the time, but something about the vortexes there (not vortices) awakened a pursuit inside of me.

We came home, and this thirty-year-old Catholic girl launched on a mission for answers. I studied it all—Hinduism, Buddhism, Judaism, Santería, Haitian Vodou, pagan witchcraft, you name it. Miami was perfect for this, because its millions of residents cast their wishes into the Universe a million different ways.

A city of spells.

Maybe *Goddess Moon* was my way of being special, of showing commitment. If I hung around psychics long enough, I was bound to become one, right?

In the meantime, I tried not giving the sad, sympathetic looks from my psychic friends who knew I was born a "Muggle" any energy. I tried to ignore their gripes about how having been born with a sixth sense was *soo* annoying. After all, here I was wishing I could have one.

So, this bracelet gave me hope. If my dream store finally opened, maybe that elusive third eye would blast right open too.

I'd just finished lighting my seventh Nag Champa incense stick of the day and was rearranging the essential oils Bibi had put in alphabetical order (I preferred to have them grouped by desire the oil would attract—love, money, sex…) when the store bell rang ten minutes before closing.

"Welcome to *Goddess Moon*," I chirped.

"Hello!" Bibi added by her spot by the Tibetan singing bowls.

Only a handful of customers had come through today, one to buy a tumbled quartz crystal, one to buy a Tree of Life pendant, and a woman who couldn't decide on anything, so I was happy to wait on more. So far, the store hadn't begun turning a profit.

I turned to see an older gentleman with white hair and a sun-weathered face. He was fit for an older man and wore an almond *guayabera* with the requisite cigar in the pocket, the standard uniform of my grandparents' generation.

"*Buenas*," he said in Cuban Spanish.

"*Buenas*," I replied.

My Spanish was okay. I was a second generation American. My parents had come to Miami from Cuba in the 1970s. They spoke perfect English by the time they had me, so I was raised speaking both languages in the home. My mother called it "kitchen Spanish," the kind used in casual conversations. It was the best I could do.

"Can I help you find something?" Bibi asked.

Bibi was young and pretty, and this man, coming from a different time, place, and sense of *machismo*, stared at her body unabashedly as he walked past. Bibi breathed in deeply and returned to a sketch she was working on in a Moleskine journal. I didn't need to be psychic to feel her annoyance halfway across the room.

Ripping his gaze away from Bibi, he touched the table displaying crystal spheres to balance himself. He seemed exhausted, mentally or physically, I wasn't sure. Removing his glasses, wiping them on a tissue he pulled from his pocket, he spoke with soft command.

"I need someone adept in the spiritual arts," the gentleman said in his heavy accent.

"By spiritual arts, you mean…" I walked toward him with a smile.

He placed his glasses back on his nose, the tissue back in his pocket, and he looked at me. "Someone who can speak with ghosts."

"Ah."

I immediately thought of Lorena. But also Maggie. And Rain. Hell, Bibi could probably qualify as well, but I knew she didn't like doing house calls, and it seemed this man wanted just that.

"You don't have someone who can speak with ghosts?" he asked after my moment of silence.

"I do. We do, actually. But what, specifically, do you need?" I asked.

"I need someone to come to my home. To rid the house of unwanted…pests." He placed the unlit cigar between his teeth then plucked it out between two fingers and waved it around. "You know, like a…*cómo se dice*…ghostbuster." He chuckled at his joke.

"Right," I said. "So you need someone who will cleanse the house, try and convince the spirit to leave?"

"I don't know what you do or how you do it," he said with a handsome smile. "I just know that my wife and I are at our wit's end. We would like peace and quiet, and we would like it to begin tonight."

Bibi and I exchanged looks. Behind him, away from his stare, she shook her head, a silent message that she didn't want to do it.

But the man was a customer, and he needed a service, a service I had not yet provided to anyone but always knew would one day come. Presuming his house cleansing didn't involve demonic possession. For that, he could contact the Archdiocese of Miami, as only those who believed in the Devil could fight the Devil.

I wasn't sure I did and hadn't for ten years now.

"Is the presence haunting your home a dark one?" I asked just to be sure.

"Dark?"

"You know, a negative energy? Is it causing anguish, arguments between you and your wife? Are bad things happening? Any bad smells?" I tried clarifying.

The man smiled again in his charming way. "I'm sorry, what is your name?" He stepped closer to me.

"Queylin," I said. It sounded no different than Kaylin. Why my mother decided to spell my name this way and curse my school years, I would never know.

"Quey*lín*," he pronounced it with an accent on the last syllable to my annoyance and extended his hand. "My name is Dr. Alberto Rivera. *Mucho gusto*."

"*Encantada*," I replied.

I caught the scent of aftershave. His shoes were Italian leather. His jawline sported a closely-cropped white beard. He was handsome in an old world way, and I could see him strolling the cracked, colorful tiles of an old home in Havana.

But when his hand slipped into mine, it felt cold. "I need someone, and I need them tonight."

"I understand," I said, pulling my hand away, "but to find you the right person will take time. I need to call around."

"What about yourself?" he asked.

"Me? I…"

Don't have that skill? Present myself as having spiritual gifts through clothes, tattoos, and personal narrative when the truth is I'd never seen a single spirit?

"*Señorita*, I have a lot of money to pay, provided the person is qualified to do the job. I live at the Harding Estate in Palmetto Bay. Surely you can find someone quickly, no?"

The Harding Estate? Most spiritualists would give anything to investigate this famous home that had sat abandoned for several years when I was a teen. I remember trespassing the property just to climb their big banyan tree.

"Oh. I had no idea the house was now occupied. How wonderful for you!" I smiled.

What a lucky son of a bitch.

Dr. Rivera's deep brown eyes were the kind that could see right through you. "Except for the ghosts, *está bien*, I suppose." He shrugged then looked over at Bibi.

He caught her off-guard, as she stood staring at him with her port-wine stain in full view, which was why she'd turned her left cheek a moment later.

"What about you, *niña*?" Dr. Rivera asked.

"Me?" Bibi gripped her clear quartz pendant shyly. "I only do consultations in the store."

"Very well, then," Dr. Rivera said, tipping his chin and turning for the door. "I'm sorry to have bothered you. I will find someone else to help me, unless you can recommend someone?"

"Wait..."

This was what I'd always wanted, a chance to prove myself, and at a beautiful historic Miami home, no less. There was no harm in checking it out. I would call Samuel and let him know I'd be home a little late.

"I'll go," I told the man. "As soon as I close up shop, I'll stop by and do a quick assessment before deciding. You said you had a wife?"

He must've found my suggestion amusing, because he suppressed a quiet laugh. "Yes. You needn't worry about me, Quey*lín*. But by all means, bring someone along if it makes you feel better."

He looked at Bibi again, gave her face a moment of extra attention the way most people did when they first saw her birthmark.

"We will see you soon?" the old man asked.

"Yes. But Dr. Rivera?"

He turned to look at me.

"If I can't speak to your ghosts," I said, as doubt crept in. "If the job requires a more qualified individual, I'll refer you to someone else tomorrow. You can pay me for the hour of my time. Does that sound fair?"

"More than fair. Do you need the address?"

"I know where it is. Thank you."

Everyone knew where the Harding Estate was. It had a reputation for being haunted. In fact, it was probably the famous *Dama de Blanco* making her presence known—the infamous woman in white. The thought of possibly meeting this ghost excited me beyond reason.

Still, I shouldn't have accepted.

I should've referred him to one of my more qualified staff members, or give him the number to any of Miami's paranormal societies. But I couldn't. I was stubborn and needed to do this. For myself.

I was eager to prove my worth. I was also crazy. Either way, I'd be visiting the famous Harding Estate tonight at the owner's request to get rid of unwanted spirits. Baptism by fire.

And that made me a *bruja* of sorts.

A lucky one at that.

THREE

I sat in my car at the Taco Bell on US-1, scarfing down a dollar burrito. I'd read articles suggesting that a vegan diet helped open psychic intuition and had been doing all I could to develop that, but I needed food.

Beef burrito it was.

Also, my bank account had less than a hundred bucks in it. Even though tomorrow was Sam's payday, he'd need most of that for his trip to Chicago tomorrow for the dental conference.

"Hey, babe." He answered my call with that low rumbly laugh I loved. "So, now you're a ghostbuster?"

I'd texted him the minute Dr. Rivera had left, telling him about the strange visit.

I laughed, too. "Tell me if you've heard this one before…an old man walks into a new age shop…"

"Was he a hot old man?"

"He looked like my grandfather."

"Okay, good. So, the Harding Estate, huh? I didn't know anyone lived there. Thought an historic society ran it."

"Shows how much we know."

"Do you need me to come with you?"

"I'll be fine. You need to pack tonight. I bet your suitcase is still empty."

"Uh…of course not. Whatever do you mean? It's full of clothes and toiletries for the next five days. Yeah, that's it."

I laughed. "Babe, you leave at 5 AM. You need to get packing already."

"Throw in a few shirts, five underwear, one pair of shoes. I mean, come on, Quey," he said. "No big deal. Seriously, I'd rather you not go alone."

I sipped from my water bottle. "He has a wife. Besides, I'm not staying long. I told him if I didn't feel I was the right person for the job, I'd refer him to someone else tomorrow."

My husband fell quiet. I knew he was questioning my craziness. "Babe…"

"Yeah."

"Why are you doing this? You could ask Rain or Maggie, any of your staff who've done this sort of thing before."

"I don't know. A personal challenge, I guess."

"Who cares if you can see ghosts or not? I love you either way."

"I know, Sam, but I've always wanted to do this."

"Queylin, it doesn't make you any more special than you already are. You know that, right?"

"I get it, Sam."

"You're already perfect to me."

"Thank you, baby."

Samuel wanted me to drop this personal challenge, my obsession with the "other side." But I'd always been on a quest for evidence. Millions of people could not be lying about their psychic experiences. Sure, a few were charlatans, but most could not be faking it.

There *was* life on the other side.

And I wanted proof.

If I never faced real ghostly activity, I'd never know if I had the gift or not. The house I'd lived in all my life—my parents'—was not haunted in any way, and if it was, I'd never been aware. Our apartment in Coconut Grove was as unremarkable as black ants. Or white sheep.

"It'll be good for me," I added.

"Okay."

"Seriously, it will."

"Okay. But if I'm asleep when you get home, wake me up. If you want to tell me about it, that is."

"I will."

"And if you want anything else, too. Heh, heh."

I smirked. "As if there's any waking you once you're asleep."

"If it means getting some before I leave for five days, I'll wake up. Trust me."

"We'll see. Love you, babe. Wish me luck."

"Good luck. But you won't need it. You make your own luck every single time."

And this was why I loved my husband. He got me, weirdness and all. He was right, though—I'd always had a way of making things work out for me. Rain told me once it was because I was a latent witch. They said I'd been manifesting my dreams all my life like a boss without realizing it. I thought maybe I was just persistent and hardworking, but maybe it was both.

I spent my last few minutes before the appointment searching videos on YouTube about the Harding Estate. I found videos of paranormal investigators checking the place out when it used to be owned by the historical society for twenty years.

In one, several orbs were seen floating through rooms. In another, someone pointed out a dark shape hovering in the corner. One woman investigator said she felt a female presence tap her on the shoulder, but there were no full-body apparitions or appearances from *La Dama de Blanco.*

I wanted to sit and watch them all before going to the house. But I had to get cranking, so I wolfed down the rest of the burrito, turned the engine of my Kia Soul, and headed down Old Cutler under the cover of banyan tree darkness.

Miami didn't have many remote areas left, but Palmetto Bay boasted a few good ones. The road to the Harding Estate was twisty and winding, and I had to check my map app a few times to make sure I was going the right way. Finally, I arrived at tall double iron gates.

One was open.

Slowly, I drove through, tires crunching onto gravel. I was off the beaten path now and opened up the car windows to take in the beautiful tunnel of trees leading to the main house.

After a while of driving underneath a unified canopy of countless trees, it emerged from the murkiness—the Harding Estate—named after the land developer who'd built it in 1919. In those days, there'd been nothing out here but this mansion and a mangrove jungle. Even now, a hundred years later, there was little out here but trees.

What was it about this land that had kept so pristine? When gorgeous, out-of-control Miami mansions had been constructed for miles around, this one still sat solitary facing the bay like some lonely ghost.

I pulled all the way up to the house, rolling around the circular driveway before cutting the engine and stepping out. The air smelled like ocean, and royal palms on either side of the house swayed in the salty breeze. The French colony gas lanterns on either side of the front entrance were lit, which made me smile. I'd trespassed here with friends back when the house was unoccupied and always marveled at how beautiful they were. Dark and abandoned, but beautiful.

At the front door, I took a deep breath.

Here we go.

I allowed myself to imagine that I was a well-known psychic healer called to this home after the owners had heard of my talents, rather than the truth—they'd randomly walked into my shop, desperate for the first idiot they could find.

A shadow passed over me. I looked up the rock exterior to find a feminine shape skirting past a second-story window. It closed the wood shutters and turned off the room light.

The Lady in White.

Doubt it. The wife, most likely.

I rang the doorbell.

In the quietude of the front porch, I listened to the trees rustling in the wind and wondered if any of Dr. Rivera's restless spirits watched me now. My skin prickled with goose bumps at the thought of what I was about to do, and for a moment, I considered leaving a note saying I couldn't go through with it.

You're not a medium, Queylin.

Stop pretending.

But everything I'd ever read said that *everyone* could be born with psychic abilities. You only had to cultivate them. I could do this. I just had to believe in myself.

On the other side of the iron door, footsteps shuffled closer. I heard a latch slide. The large door opened, and there stood Dr. Rivera, cigar clenched between his teeth, only this time, it was lit.

"There she is! Won't you come in?" He stepped aside, holding the door open.

I stepped into the house, and my jaw dropped. "Oh, my."

"You like it?"

"It's beautiful."

Sweet baby Jesus in Heaven, the place was a 1950's Havana dream resurrected from the past. The floor was made of checkered green and cream Mediterranean tiles instead of Dade pine like so many old South Florida homes. Potted *areca* plants were in every corner, colorful paintings of Cuban landscapes and *rumba* dancers graced the lemon walls, and soft sounds of a *son cubano* played in the background as if coming from an old record player.

"I never imagined it would look like this on the inside."

"My wife, she's an artist. Used to sell her paintings at art fairs years ago. You could say she made this place her own." Dr. Rivera closed the door and led me deeper into the house.

"Kudos to her," I said. "All the online photos show the house falling apart."

"Well, I'm a retired therapist, you see. I saved quite a lot to purchase this place one day."

"And you did an amazing job."

"I'm so glad you like it. *¿Quieres refresco o café?"* He offered soda or coffee like any good Cuban host or hostess.

"No, thank you. I just ate. Where's Mrs. Rivera?" I asked.

"She'll be down in a minute. We don't have many guests. I think she's nervous about meeting you."

"Me?"

"Well, she's nervous about discussing the issue. Barbara doesn't like to talk about the…happenings, shall we say?" His smiling eyes disappeared into little crinkles.

"You mean spirits?" I cocked my head. "Why not call them what they are?"

He nodded, cigar bobbing between his teeth. "You will find we are very old school, as you kids say. Millennials, they talk about anything. But us, you know…we are Catholic."

Ah, understood. Talking about spiritual matters was considered taboo in some families if it didn't jive with *la Biblia.*

"But Catholics believe in the Holy Spirit."

"You say that like you are not Catholic?" He raised a bushy gray eyebrow.

"Me? Well, I…was raised Catholic, but I don't practice anymore."

"What *do* you practice then?"

I bristled.

Wasn't sure why.

After all, it was a fair question for someone hired to deal with the spiritual world, but it felt too personal. I hadn't explained my conversion from good ol' Catholic girl to experimental spiritualist to many people. It was hard enough looking my parents and grandparents in the eye, two generations who'd fought hard for the chance to preserve their established ways in a new country, that I didn't entirely walk their path.

I couldn't tell him that, more than anything, I studied manifestation of personal goals. Prayer without the God quotient. I spoke to the Universe and made it do my bidding.

Fine, I practiced witchcraft.

But the good kind. Herbs and candles and oils and setting intentions through meditation. But people like Dr. Rivera heard "witchcraft" and wrongly assumed I was in a Satanic cult. Problem was, you had to believe in Satan to be in a Satanic cult.

"I'm finding my way right now," I said.

He studied me a long time. What the doctor was thinking was a mystery, but it probably fell along the lines of Latino family judgment—a thing in my life.

"I never said we were *practicing* Catholics," he said in a low voice, staring at me. We all go our own ways, *sí?*"

I nodded. Whatever that meant.

When I didn't reply, he pulled his gaze away, leading me down a narrow hallway. I felt out of place. I tried getting the conversation back on track by clearing my throat.

"Believe it or not, the spirit world is a normal part of everyday life, Dr. Rivera." I said it more to calm my nerves than to convince him of anything.

"The spirit world," he replied, pointing a finger in the air, "is nothing but an overactive brain, *señorita*."

FOUR

I wouldn't argue with the patriarchy today.

Thirty years surrounded by Cuban men of all ages—my father, uncles, brothers, and grandfathers—taught you that sometimes, it was best to stay quiet. No matter what you tried to make them see, they were always right. In their minds. Especially Dr. Rivera, a psychiatrist, who'd made it his life mission to study the brain.

The music grew louder, as we came into a Great Room with tall ceilings filled with more paintings and brightly colored ceramic frogs, lizards, and a gorgeous mosaic coffee table. There on a large, classic *mueble* of dark wood like my grandparents used to have was an old 1940s-looking radio.

"You have one of those?" I ran my fingertips along the old credenza. "Is it your family's?"

"It came with the house, along with that short wave radio." He pointed to another old wooden box. "We brought nothing from Cuba but the clothes on our backs. You should know this."

Heyyy.

"Of course, I do," I said. Every Cuban descendant knew the exiles—many of them doctors, lawyers, teachers, professionals of all kinds—had come to the States with nothing after leaving it all behind. They'd had to re-earn their degrees and start all over from scratch, re-proving their worth a second time.

It was any wonder they were still sane and thriving sixty years after Castro's revolution tore their world apart. Me, I'd only done four years of college and felt drained.

"So, how do you plan to address our problem, *señorita*?" He sat on one end of a long tufted sofa and gestured for me to sit on the other.

Not wanting to encourage a longer visit than necessary, I perched myself on the edge only. "Well, first I'm going to take a look around. What can you tell me about the haunting?"

"The haunting," he repeated.

"Yes, the manifestations. Your *ghosts*," I said just to bother him.

"*Bueno, vamos a ver.* My wife wakes up screaming in the night. She suffers psychological disorders brought on by childhood separation."

"Oh, I'm sorry."

"She's had it since she arrived in Miami as an eight-year-old in 1961. Part of the Pedro Pan Operation. You should know that, too."

"I know what Pedro Pan is," I said, trying not to sound indignant. He was judging me again. The old ones always had to make sure the new generation knew their Cuban-American history. So it would never repeat itself.

"Good, I was just testing you, *niña.*" He smiled. "Your generation calls it PTSD. Post-traumatic stress dis—"

"I know what PTSD is, too," I interrupted with a short laugh. "Sorry. So where does the spirit activity come in?"

"Her screams prompt other screams."

"I beg your pardon?"

He planted both feet on the floor and leaned toward me. "When she wakes up screaming, it triggers something else to scream in the house. Sometimes, there's crying. Sometimes, things move."

"Move?"

"Yes. Objects fall to the floor. Of course, this could very well be the ideomotor effect, or mass hysteria."

My eyes felt like they would pop. "Oh, wow. Does this happen often?"

"More often than I would like."

"Which part of the house should I concentrate on most?"

"I would prefer not to answer any more questions. I would rather you give me your own impression of the house, if you don't mind." He puffed on his cigar again.

He was testing. Withholding information so that I, the talented psychic—after all, I ran a new-age-medium-mystical-arts shop—could tell him where the activity was located.

He didn't trust me.

But I wouldn't let him intimidate me. I would focus my energies, explore the house, and get a sense of where the trouble areas were. Based on gut instinct, I supposed. It was all I had.

"Do you mind if I get started then?" I asked. "I only have an hour."

"You have a husband?"

I looked at him.

If he didn't want to provide me with any info, why should I give him any? *Yes,* I wanted to tell him. I had a big strong man, one that would arrive at a moment's notice if he tried anything funny. One that would kick his old man ass in a heartbeat if the need should arise.

"Yes, I do."

"Why isn't he here with you?" he asked, insinuating that a proper husband should always accompany his frail wife to the home of weird old men.

"He had to pack." The moment I said it, I regretted it. Dr. Rivera didn't need to know anything personal about me or Samuel, especially that he was leaving town.

"Ah, a traveling businessman."

"You could say that."

Telling him that my husband was a dental hygienist would be a mistake. He'd only shame us and say the occupation was a woman's job. That Samuel should be a dentist or a maxillofacial surgeon instead. I knew his kind.

I stood and moved through the house, aware that his eyes were following me, glad I hadn't worn anything that might've been misconstrued as sexy or overly feminine. Not that it should matter, but men like him would take that as permission to stare even more.

The home had no open kitchen. Old homes like these had hidden kitchens with service pantries, areas where staff would cook and prepare without being seen from the dining room.

I entered the dining room and took note of the slow-twirling ceiling fans with blades in the shapes of palm fronds, as well as the bright blue curtains. The table was formally set for three, including dinner fork, salad fork, shrimp fork, every other fork you could think of, plus wine glass, water glass, and maybe even a glass for me to cry my tears into, they were so damn rich.

It made me feel I would never live in a house like this, not in a million years. Not even with all the opportunities I'd been handed.

Dr. Rivera's voice startled me. "We were hoping you would join us for dinner."

"Oh." How had he moved into the room without making a single noise that way? I pressed a palm to my heart. "Thank you, but I can't. *Muy amable.*"

He shrugged, opened a cabinet in the hallway to move a liquor decanter a millimeter to the left, then closed it again.

Once my heartbeat settled, I resumed my walk around the house. Where was his wife? It occurred to me that perhaps he'd lied and here I was alone with a strange man in a house far removed from civilization. Considering Dr. Rivera had asked where my husband was, the thought made me pause.

Quickly scanning to see if he was following me, I found him lingering just outside the room, so I opened a random door and stepped inside.

Once my eyes adjusted to the darkness, I found myself standing in a ballroom that hadn't been decorated like the rest of the house. Stacks of chairs were covered in fabric, round tables leaned on their sides against the walls, and an eerie mustiness filled the room.

The Harding Estate's ballroom.

For a moment, I imagined this space full of people in the 1920s enjoying a cocktail party, waltzing on these parquet floors. I saw them perfectly in my mind's eye, and then I saw the emptiness.

A certain stillness that belied the relative activity going on in the rest of the house.

Were there ghosts here?

I unfocused my vision and tried to see through the atmosphere. Maybe this would be the one time I finally saw them. But nothing materialized except a sense of self-pity, and before I could start feeling sorry for myself, I slipped out a service door and ended up outside.

I was on the veranda, the back porch where multiple rocking chairs were lined up in a row, and the outer walls looked like they were made of coquina, a hard-but-porous, crushed-shell material harvested from the shores of Florida beaches.

I'd only explored one corner of the home and already I felt disoriented, flushed, and overwhelmed. The Harding Estate was expansive and confusing, and I would definitely need more than one night to peruse its corridors.

The cellar, a rogue thought hit me.

Yes, this house had a cellar. I'd read about it in articles and heard the ghost investigators mention its existence in their videos I'd watched earlier. In the old days of Prohibition, it'd been used to store illegal spirits.

A French patio door opened, and Dr. Rivera stepped through onto the veranda. So much for exploring the home by myself. "Finding anything so far?"

"I'm just getting a feel. Does this house have a cellar? I thought it did," I asked.

"A cellar…" He looked out into the night. Just beyond the reaches of the patio lights was Biscayne Bay, its soft waves whispering across the wide lawn. "It used to, but it was flooded during Hurricane Andrew."

"So, there's no cellar now," I clarified.

He turned to me, as if he'd forgotten I was here. "Correct. Not since 1992. The historic society had it filled and sealed." He stared at my face, his eyes roving over my features, then he inspected me from head to toe.

Ick.

"Nice. Well, am I, uh…going to meet your wife?" I asked. Because if he didn't produce a woman soon, I'd probably be going without concluding my investigation.

Dr. Rivera seemed a nice enough man, just old-school in a way that made me uncomfortable.

"Yes, she's eager to meet you," he said, snapping out of it and stepping into the house again. "Go ahead and explore. See the garden. There's a statue there you might find interesting. I'll go find my wife, okay?" He blew out a puff of the sweet-smelling smoke and closed the patio door.

I blew out a long breath. Why was I here? Ah, yes, because Queylin Sanchez-Gold could often be a hard-headed woman.

This would be a good time to do a simple cleansing, ask my spirit guides and angels for protection, and burn some sage. I set down my purse and began to pull out some goodies I'd packed.

Something in the distance caught my attention. At first, it was a light—a burnt, yellowy light glowing through what seemed like aged, dirty glass. Then I saw the shape behind it. A pale human contour standing perfectly still on the lawn.

Ice spread through my veins.

I stared at it, my eyes adjusting to the darkness, gazing on with unfocused vision until I realized it wasn't a spirit standing there checking me out but some sort of solid statue.

Picking my bag up, I walked toward it. As much as the house reeked of impeccability on the inside, on the outside, the lawn was overgrown, and my sandaled feet itched as I walked through the tall, unkempt grass.

The closer I moved to the strange humanoid shape, the clearer it became. The statue was of a beautiful winged angel holding a lantern. It was neither male nor female and smiled with cherubic innocence. I thought of Rain and knew they would love it.

The angel's face looked troubled or serene, depending on where I stood.

My senses took in the surroundings—the lovely night, the crickets, the faraway sounds of tree frogs, the soft swishing of the water's edge a mere hundred feet away. This was quintessential Miami charm—mysterious gardens and angel statues, moonless ocean and strange houses, discussions of religion held in old houses while slow Cuban rhythms lulled you, European cultures clashed with Caribbean ones, blending with tropical beauty and Tequesta lands that never should have been tamed to begin with.

It was all here, and the angel knew it with their secretive smile. Staring at the statue, studying their genderless beauty, I felt sadness.

Longing.

Uncertainty that he would ever come home.

But who? Samuel? Of course he would come home. He always came home. Where was this doubt coming from?

I had studied enough paranormal investigations to recognize what could be happening. I might've been channeling something else, someone else's emotions. In fact, I was certain that if I closed my eyes and focused hard enough, drove away all distractions, that I would open them to find a disembodied spirit standing right in front of me.

"I ask Archangel Michael for protection, Archangel Gabriel to help me communicate," I muttered as a quick charm.

Around me, the air tingled with something I couldn't describe. Some kind of energy. I felt like I stood on the edge of a cliff about to jump to jagged edges below. Someone was nearby. *Or it could be the ideomotor effect, mass hysteria, or carbon dioxide poisoning,* I could hear the doctor man-splaining in my head.

"Who are you?" I asked.

I waited for a reply.

With baited breath, I waited, a thousand percent certain that I would find a person standing there watching me when I opened my eyes. My hands shook, my breath hung suspended inside my throat.

I opened my eyes.

But there was no one.

I sighed. Any pride I'd experienced left my chest like a deflated balloon. I was no one to believe I held special powers. Powers to reach them. Talk to them. See them. I was a regular person, and my husband was right, I didn't need to see them to be special. I was already special to *him.*

Wasn't that enough?

No, it wasn't. I wanted this. But I couldn't make myself turn into someone I wasn't. Time to pack my stuff and call it a night. I was not a spirit medium, no matter how much I wanted to be, and felt like an ass for believing I could help these people.

Just then, however, a chilly breeze coiled around me. Something made me stop. And look up. It was the lantern's dim light growing brighter.

FIVE

It grew then dimmed a bit, then glowed again—pulsating in the gloom of the disheveled garden. This happened three times then stopped.

Part of me told me to get the hell out of there, this wasn't normal. Another told me to stop. *Just stop with your imagination, Queylin.*

Faulty wiring was the cause, more than likely.

It was an old house. The salty air probably didn't help the outdoor electrical circuits either. Mesmerized, I stood still, watching the light, realizing I never burned sage, sprinkled salt, or got around to doing any of my rituals before the statue distracted me.

The night felt balmy. Rain clouds began moving in. Not unusual for a November night in Miami. From somewhere on the other side of the house, the air conditioning unit turned off, amplifying the silence even more. The fluty sounds of the *son cubano* echoed from deep inside the house.

Behind the statue, the canopy of the massive banyan tree of my youth rustled in the wind. Banyans always looked like prisoners to me, serpentine roots reaching for the earth like heavy chains. I couldn't shake the loneliness while staring at it.

"Someone here?" I whispered.

Only sounds of nature shuffling in the night replied.

Walking past the statue, I moved into further darkness toward the tree. My whole life, I'd loved strolling through trees at night, in gardens, parks, and cemeteries. As a teen here with friends, we'd trespassed on these grounds, climbed this exact banyan. There was something timeless and serene about it. The Harding Estate's grounds were exceptionally wild and beautiful.

I stopped at the banyan and stared at it, studying its complicated network of roots. I couldn't explain why I felt isolated, forgotten even, and wondered if something about the tree was bringing out these feelings in me. I had no reason to feel this way.

I'd been married three years now to a wonderful man, one who knew how to make me happy. Still, I couldn't shake the feeling that he'd left me here to fend for myself, but that didn't make sense, since he'd asked if I needed him to come along.

Ripping my gaze away, I walked around the yard, my senses on full alert. Even the sweet smell of humidity felt magnified. Besides the huge banyan, smaller banyans surrounding it, and the angel statue, there wasn't much in the yard except a couple of stone benches and lots of overgrown vegetation, but every so often, I'd run into wild orchids hanging from random braches and bushes.

I headed back to the statue, examining it from behind now. The angel's wings pointed up, its drapery filled with dirt, moss, maybe even mold. There was a crack from one shoulder to where it connected under its armpit. As I came around to gaze into their beautiful face once again, something stopped me.

A word.

You.

Before I could analyze where it'd come from or what it meant, something flew toward me. A rush of air preceded it—whatever it was—and my hair blasted back away from my face. Something invisible and angry slammed into me, knocking the wind right out of my lungs. I hit the ground backwards and cried out, my fingers gripping tall blades of grass in an effort to gather my bearings.

What the hell?

There'd been nothing there!

My breasts felt sore from the impact, and my whole torso ached with a blunt tenderness I'd only felt during my period. Holding onto the statue's pedestal, I scrambled to my feet, chest heaving, lungs gasping for air. I was shaken to my core.

Immediately, I scanned the grounds to see who—or what—might've attacked me. I'd heard of owls and bats living in primitive areas of Miami but being a city girl, I'd never seen one. But did owls or bats go around smacking people in their chests? There was enough ambient light to see what would've caused it, yet I'd seen nothing.

Nothing at all.

I stood up and caught my breath, grasping for any explanation. Had I imagined it? No, of course not. I'd been shoved by someone.

Yes, *someone.* As exciting as the prospect of coming here to investigate the Harding Estate might've sounded a few hours ago, now I reconsidered.

I'd felt hands—actual hands—pushing me.

Shit. I should've come with someone more experienced. Things like this happened when I insisted I could handle them, when I actually wasn't prepared for them. I picked up my bag and slung it over my shoulder, getting ready to head back to the house when I stopped cold in my tracks.

"Jesus Christ." I pressed a palm to my chest. The silhouettes of a man and a woman in a wheelchair stood against the flood lights of the house. "I didn't see you there."

The woman, obscured by shadows created by backlighting and a wide-brimmed sun hat, wore a long skirt and a ruffled top, but I couldn't see her face very well. I didn't need to see her face to realize she was very sick. I moved toward the couple until the light shone on the doctor's very ordinary, non-ghostly features.

I breathed out a sigh of relief.

"Sorry to startle you," Dr. Rivera said. "I wanted to introduce you to my wife. Barbara, this is Quey*lín*? Sanchez?" He cocked his head at me.

"Yes. Queylin Sanchez-Gold. Hello," I said, wiping my hands on my jeans to get rid of the dirt from the fall. I extended my hand toward the woman. "Nice to meet you."

The woman made no attempt to shake my hand, and I felt silly trying to engage someone so severely disconnected. I suddenly felt very sorry for Dr. Rivera that he had a wife with special needs.

"She cannot speak," he explained, touching her shoulder, gently fixing the angle of her hat.

"Oh. I'm sorry," I replied, unsure if that was the proper etiquette when meeting someone incapacitated as Mrs. Rivera was.

When he adjusted the brim of the hat, the lower half of her face appeared in the light, and I saw a fair amount of makeup to enhance pretty lips and apple cheekbones. But she was clearly disabled, though I was happy to see that she at least smiled. Her arms and legs, hidden by long sleeves and skirts and frozen in her chair, seemed thin. In younger years, she must've been beautiful. Even now, she was pretty in her own way.

Dr. Rivera smiled sadly.

"This is why we moved here," the doctor said. "For fresh air, a little distance. It's also why she paints. And sculpts, and creates." Dr.

Rivera looked at his wife so lovingly, I saw him in a new light. "She's an extremely talented artist."

"I've noticed." I smiled. "The art all over the house is absolutely stunning." I wondered if Mrs. Rivera could hear anything I said, if she could appreciate my compliment, or if she was completely disconnected to the world outside her mind.

"Are you alright? I thought I heard a noise as we were coming out," Dr. Rivera asked.

"As a matter of fact, no. Well, yes, I'm fine," I stuttered. "But something hit me."

"Hit you?" His eyebrows showed genuine concern.

"Yes, I was standing here admiring your garden statue when out of the blue, something pushed me backwards and I fell." Saying it out loud felt validating, but now I was keenly aware of how crazy it sounded.

"Oh? Any idea what it might have been?"

"I don't know, doctor, but considering why you called me here, I have a few theories."

He pressed his lips together in the first sign of sympathy I'd gotten from him all night. "This doesn't surprise me. May I ask where you were before it happened?"

"Right here." I walked over to the spot next to the angel statue. "I was standing right here looking at the angel. Its light glowed in a strange way, like pulsating brighter then dimmer. Does that happen often?"

Dr. Rivera looked at his wife, who simply looked forward. "It's happened a few times," he said. "Would you like to come in for a glass of water? Some wine to help calm you down?"

"Oh, no," I said, checking the time on my phone. "Thank you, but I really do need to get going. My husband's waiting for me, and besides, I think I'm not the right person for this. I'll see who else can come and help you." I backed away, signaling it was time for me to go.

It was hard to admit I was way in over my head, but maybe it was for the best.

"Oh, but you're doing fine, *señorita.* You seem to have made more contact with her than most people."

"With whom?" I asked, baffled. Made contact?

"*La Dama de Blanco.* The Lady in White."

"The Lady in White," I repeated, staring at him. "You think that was The Lady in White?"

He nodded. "We're pretty certain it's she who haunts this home, along with a few other spirits we don't know who they are. In fact, this angel…"

"The Lady in White," I said again. "She's the one who hit me?"

He stepped through the grass over to the statue and laid his hand on the angel's hip. "*Probablemente*," he said. "After all, this is her grave marker, ordered installed by her widower from prison after her death in 1921."

My eyes widened. I must have looked insane to him.

"You didn't know?" he asked.

"No, I didn't. I haven't been here in fifteen years," I replied.

I supposed anyone could know that piece of history by digging online. After all, much was written about this famous home built by a New York City millionaire and bootlegger in the early 20th century, but I hadn't exactly had time to research anything before coming over.

I'd watched YouTube videos and eaten a burrito, though.

I narrowed my eyes at him. "Dr. Rivera, I thought you didn't believe in ghosts. The brain overreacting and such."

"Quey*lín*, I believe most experiences can be explained through science. But every so often, something comes along that baffles researchers to no degree, and The Lady in White, for me, is one of those phenomena."

"Have you ever invited other mediums here to try and speak to her?" I asked.

"Yes, several."

"And?"

"Had they been successful, I wouldn't have wandered into your shop, would I?" He smiled that handsome older gentleman smile, but I noticed his teeth were stained with nicotine.

"Fair enough."

"You're the first person besides us she's actually interacted with while I've lived here, and I've lived here fifteen years now. I need you to stay the night, Quey*lín*. So you can experience our experiences for yourself."

"Sir, I'm feeling a little scattered right now after what happened. But I'll come back better prepared. I promise."

"Bring your friend with you."

"Which friend?"

"The one from the store. With the *manchita* on her face. She looked insightful to me."

I wondered how Dr. Rivera could get the sense that Bibi had been insightful from four seconds of interacting with her, but he was right. Bibi was eerily connected with the spirit world. The problem would be getting her to come.

"I'll see what I can do," I said. "I have to go now." *Or lose my mind.*

"Wait a minute. I'll go inside and write you a check for your time."

"It's okay. Next time I see you."

I could have used that check right now, but I needed to put some distance between this house and my brain.

"*Pierde cuidado.*" He said "no worries" in that special way my grandmother used to when she wanted me to feel guilty for turning her down. "Thank you for coming."

Ugh.

Turning, I exited the property through the archway of a stone wall stretching from the house through the garden and into the darkness. I didn't stop until I'd reached my car. Getting in quickly, I cranked the engine and paused to look at the silhouettes of the doctor and his debilitated wife again.

She seemed to watch me through the darkness with eyes hidden beneath her hat, but how aware could she be, really? I drove off the circular driveway, through the tunnel of trees, and passed the front gate.

Only once I'd reached the end of the road, when the streetlights of US-1 finally came into view, reminding me that I wasn't in the middle of nowhere but in a bustling cityscape, did I let go of the massive breath I'd been holding.

SIX

I lay in bed like I always did, husband asleep to my left, soft meditation music playing on my nightstand—when the ghost walked out of the closet.

She wore jeans and a dark-colored top. Her hair was long and blond, and she almost looked like a younger version of myself.

My body froze.

At first, she stalked through the darkness of my room unaware that I could see her, but the moment she felt me tense up (she sensed my fear like a dog), she turned her face and stared right at me.

To my horror, half her face was missing. Or rather, half the skin of her face, her skull exposed with pieces of flesh still attached. But it wasn't until she shifted her whole body and started walking toward me that I screamed.

Hiding my face under the covers, I felt her weight pressing down on me. I struggled to be free, screaming and pushing with everything I had, but she had me pinned to the bed. When she spoke, her voice sounded watery and distant, and toward the tail end of whatever she was saying (I couldn't tell), she sounded like Samuel.

"Babe. Babe, wake up."

My husband hovered over me in the darkness, and it was him I was fighting, as my screams turned to whimpers. I held onto his arms and breathed in the normal, familiar scent of his skin.

"Oh, my God…"

"You okay? What were you dreaming?"

"There was…a woman. Coming at me."

"A woman?"

"A ghost. Her face…it was…forget it."

There was no point explaining the nightmare, because there wasn't anything particularly terrifying about it. Yes, the woman was missing half her face, but my terror was more about seeing a ghost in my room than anything else. Besides, he'd only lecture me that I was taking things too far.

The sleep paralysis didn't help either.

I felt stupid for waking him up.

"I've never heard you scream in your sleep before, Quey. Go back to sleep. Everything's alright. Everything's okay, baby." Strong hands rubbed my arms and pressed against my forehead.

The loving tone in Samuel's voice slowly brought my heart rate down. He curled up next to me, and though I gave the ghost woman another thought or two, my baby's arms and warm breathing finally lulled me back to sleep.

In the morning, my phone alarm went off. I felt the bed space next to me. Samuel was gone. On the bed was a folded sheet of paper. I opened it—

Babe, here's a little guy to fight the monsters. Sorry about your bad dream. I'll call you when I land.

<3

At the bottom, he'd drawn one of his funny cats doing yoga, holding a crystal between his paws. I smiled and pressed the note to my heart.

Holy shit, the dream last night.

I remembered it now. I didn't normally have nightmares, and if I did, I usually recognized when I was having one and woke myself up. But this time, I'd screamed my head off, something that had never happened before. I must've scared the crap out of Samuel.

The Harding Estate was affecting me. I knew it was. When I'd gotten home last night, I'd found Samuel asleep, all packed for his trip, so I hadn't gotten the chance to tell him. Talking to my husband about my day always helped me release negative energy, but this time I'd gone to bed with it all to myself.

I hadn't told anybody about what happened in the garden. As my brain slowly woke to the realization, though, the details of it came crashing to my mind.

I'd been knocked over by a ghost.

Something invisible had come right through that statue and smacked into my body. I knew it'd been real, because my body ached.

Arms, stomach, whole torso, especially my chest hurt from the impact.

I got out of bed, showered, and meditated to set good intentions for the day. Then, I dressed for work, dotted Samuel's note with a drop of rose essential oil for love and happiness and put it in my jeans' pocket for the rest of the day.

Goddess Moon buzzed with busyness. What was it about Friday mornings that made *all* the yoga moms show up for class? Because most would be cheating on their diets and having wine this weekend? Then I realized it was a teacher's planning day, and a few had brought their little ones.

I helped a customer pick out her first pendulum (she couldn't choose between an amethyst and a pretty copper one), while her little girl, clinging to mom's legging-clad thighs, couldn't stop staring at me. All my life I'd had an affinity for attracting babies' and little ones' attention, but this child kept gawking at me like I had a rooster on my head.

"Hi." I smiled.

She drew behind her mom's legs.

"Say hi, Mellie," the woman cooed in a high-pitched voice. "She's just tired."

"It's okay," I said.

"I'll take the copper one. You said it's good for divination?"

"Either one. The quartz will give you clearer answers, the copper will have strong magnetic energy."

"Copper then."

"Great." I helped the woman at the register and noticed Maggie, Rain, and Lorena all conferring in the corner, trying not to look right at me, though it was super obvious they were talking about me.

Once the woman left, the store was empty, and I snaked up to my staff. "What's going on?" I asked.

Rain cocked their head. "We know you went to the Harding Estate last night. How was it?"

I looked at Bibi, working on a sketch at the checkout counter.

I hadn't told my staff anything, but Bibi knew, because she'd been here when Dr. Rivera came in. It wasn't that I didn't want them to know, but I felt curiously possessive about the case and didn't want to get bombarded by their advice.

"I didn't say anything," Bibi assured me.

"Sure."

"It wasn't her." Maggie held up her phone to show me what was on the screen—a text from my husband. "Sam asked us to take care of you while he's in Chicago."

"Ugh." I shook my head. No wonder he'd been texting me all day asking when I'd be going back to the Harding Estate and who I'd be taking with me.

No one.

Rain crossed their arms and looked at me with those big blue *gringo* eyes I envied. "Don't be mad, Quey," they said. "He's just worried about you. Said you didn't sleep well last night. What happened? Was it the house?"

I sighed and took a seat on the stool behind the counter. I told them all about the Harding Estate, how Dr. Rivera had strolled into the shop needing assistance and how I'd taken it upon myself to help him.

"I'm shocked that you went." Lorena said, her Day of the Dead skeleton earrings jiggling from shaking her head. "But proud of you."

Lorena knew I wasn't particularly witchy on the inside but always wanted to be. She'd been the one to teach me about meditation when I used to get tarot readings from her a different store. Still, she seemed a little envious, if my Spidey senses were working properly.

I side-eyed her. "Hey, you're the one who told me we all had it inside of us."

"It's true—we do," she said with a little flair of her hand. "But you shouldn't have gone alone. Just like with the living, the dead can carry bad energy. You need to be protected next time."

"I cleared my space, burned sage, all that," I said. Actually, I never got around to doing so.

"Yeah, but…" Maggie swapped dark looks with Lorena. "Girl, just tell us next time, so we can send you off to battle the right way." Her overarched eyebrow hinted that I should think deeper.

"What does that mean?" I asked.

The door chimed. A customer walked in. Maggie and Lorena left to their respective spots without answering my question.

"You know what it means," Rain whispered then turned to the customer. "Hi, welcome to *Goddess Moon*!"

Bibi gave me a knowing look.

Okay, maybe I did know.

Lorena and Maggie, besides excelling at hypnotherapy and reiki, were also practitioners of an underground Miami secret—*Santería.*

They didn't go around advertising it, especially since followers of the Afro-Cuban religion worshipped in secret—also because judgmental people loved to give followers shit over it—but they were Santeras.

Meaning, they danced, chanted, kept religious sheds in the backyard containing statues and offerings, spoke a secret African language, worked spells, and yeah, I hated to say this…sacrificed chickens when necessary.

And *they* knew that *I* knew that *they* knew.

I didn't agree with all aspects of the religion, but there was something to be said for their skills at manifestation. If someone wanted more spice in their marriage, they had a love spell for that. If someone needed to keep an ex away, they had a binding spell for that. If a home filled with negative energy needed a *despojo*, they had a cleansing spell for that.

Somehow, Maggie and Lorena made things happen. Call it witchcraft, the power of prayer, or coincidence if your religion was Science—but they did.

Maybe that was why I hadn't called on them for Dr. Rivera's house. Because I wanted to feel, for once, like a case was *mine* to handle. For once, someone had walked into our shop and not asked for the **wink-wink** voodoo queens.

But when I thought about the invisible spirit that had attacked me, I realized it could've been much worse. I had to take someone with me for the next investigation. Not only for my protection but for Sam's peace of mind as well.

I sidled up to Bibi who was rearranging the essential oils in alphabetical order again. "Will you come with me tonight?"

"Where?"

"The Harding Estate."

"Uh, no, Queylin, please don't make me. I didn't like that guy."

"Me neither, but listen, I met his wife. They're just a basic old couple. I don't want to go alone. Please? Besides, he asked for you." I wasn't telling the whole truth about them being a basic couple. There was nothing basic about a woman in a wheelchair whose whole face I couldn't see.

"Even creepier."

"All we have to do is clear the energy, talk to the spirits if we can, ask them to leave, that's it." I moved the rose and yling-ylang oils together.

"That's it? What happens when the ghosts don't want to leave?"

"Why wouldn't they?"

"Queylin, some spirits don't want to go. They become part of the house. Like a light fixture. Or a bookcase." She moved the oil bottles back.

"Look, it's not just for Dr. Rivera," I said, arranging the eucalyptus and tea tree oils together, because hello, healing properties. "I want to do this for me, too."

She smirked at me. "I knew it."

"What?"

"You're on a personal mission."

"How do you know these things?"

"Samuel said you were."

"Damn it." So much for psychic awareness. My husband would give out my social security number to strangers if I let him. "Please, just one night? We get paid for it, we do our best, and we're done."

"We have to sleep there?" She scoffed.

"Yes. That's when the magic happens. Literally. That's when their ghosts go bump in the night, he said."

She thought about it, but Bibi was not having it. "I don't like doing house calls."

"I don't either, yet I babysat you every week when your parents used to go out. So you have to do this for me."

"You did that for my parents, not me. Fine," she snapped. "Only because there's money involved, and I need money. But if we go, we take Maggie and Lorena's kits with us."

"Kits? No, no. We don't have time for kits." Maggie and Lorena often put together ingredients for their "special" clients—mojo bags with herbs like *Rompe Saraguey* for banishing evil spirits, or a traveling Elegua statuette. Spells in a do-it-yourself kit.

"Too late. They already made them for you. Pick me up at seven."

SEVEN

I couldn't wait for Bibi to see the house. She wasn't old enough to have ever trespassed on the grounds like I did during the home's vacancy, but I was sure she'd appreciate Mrs. Rivera's artwork, being an artist herself.

We arrived in time for dinner. This time, a housekeeper wearing a black dress and white apron let us in. I didn't remember seeing her last time. The woman was all of maybe five feet tall, scents of Haitian cooking wafting off her aura, deep set dark eyes that told of secrets.

"Hi. We're here to see Dr. Rivera? I'm Queylin. This is Bibi."

The woman opened the door wide, letting us in, but she didn't speak. Her gaze fell downward in respect or shyness, I wasn't sure. As during my last visit, the home felt alive with a quiet energy that might've emitted from Mrs. Rivera's oil paintings and colorful mosaics. The old-time Cuban music played in the background again.

"Pretty house, huh?" I asked Bibi.

She nodded, wide hazel eyes taking in her surroundings, but she didn't seem convinced.

The wordless housekeeper showed us through the warmly lit home into the formal dining room, the one I had peeked into during my first visit. Dr. Rivera was seated at the table, reading from an actual newspaper, and rose from his seat when he saw us.

"*Buenas, niñas, buenas,*" he said, teeth clenched around another cigar. He wore a white *guayabera* this time and slacks just short enough to show off brown dress socks. "Ah, you brought your friend. How nice."

"This is Bibi," I said. "From the store."

"Yes, I remember," Dr. Rivera said, extending his hand. Behind him, his wife sat in her wheelchair, facing a window, staring out into nothingness.

Bibi gave the doctor her hand but didn't shake long before pulling her fingers away. She seemed to hold her breath uncomfortably, as Dr. Rivera studied her cheek again in the most unabashed way. For eighty percent of his personality, the doctor seemed nice enough, if a little old-school, but every so often, he did something, like give us lingering stares, to make himself seem creepy.

Bibi turned her face and took in the details of the ornate room. I could almost feel her holding her breath. The Riveras' wealth could easily have come across as off-putting to some. Even Mrs. Rivera, in her black off-the-shoulder dress with purple shawl and another wide-brimmed hat, was dressed more for the opera tonight than a simple dinner at home.

"*Amor*, our guests are here. Won't you say hello?" the doctor glanced her way, but Mrs. Rivera continued to stare out the window.

It saddened me that Dr. Rivera continued to expect normal social interaction from his wife, but maybe that was part of her therapy—to speak to her as though all was normal—to keep her involved.

He raised his eyebrows at us and sighed. "Please excuse my wife. We do what we can."

"No, of course," I said. "No worries at all."

"Please, have a seat. We were just about to eat." Dr. Rivera gestured to his dining table, clearly proud to be hosting.

"Thank you so much." I eyed the housekeeper who'd come to stand by Mrs. Rivera's wheelchair. She stood next to it protectively, one hand on the disabled woman's shoulder. "What are we having?"

Dr. Rivera snapped with two fingers, and the woman broke out of her reverie, giving me and Bibi a cursory look before disappearing through a door into the kitchen.

Bibi and I looked at each other. The patriarchy was in full effect.

Dr. Rivera waved his cigar around. "*Diri ak djon djon*," he replied, carefully pronouncing his Creole. "It's black mushroom rice with shrimp. Have you had it before?"

"No, I haven't. Sounds delicious," I said.

"You'll love it. Well, you're a Miami girl."

By that, he meant I should be familiar with the cuisines of various Caribbean nations, which I was. Even though I'd never had this particular dish before, now I realized the housekeeper must've hailed from Haiti.

"Sounds great, doesn't it?" I asked Bibi, trying to engage her. But Bibi sat politely with hands folded in her lap. Seemed like she, the housekeeper, and Mrs. Rivera were all competing for most tongue-tied tonight, leaving me and the doctor to face off on small talk.

"We appreciate you retuning to our home and bringing assistance with you," Dr. Rivera said, dropping a cloth napkin onto his lap. "Where, may I ask, will you be concentrating your efforts this time?"

As he reached for his water, I thought about how to answer the question. "Well, I thought we'd do a simple cleansing tonight, and—"

"Yes, about that," he interrupted. "When you say cleansing, what exactly are you referring to?"

"There's many ways to do it, but usually it involves burning any number of substances traditionally known to clear negative energy."

"I see. And this works?"

"Yes. It absolutely does."

"How do you know if you've never seen it?"

"Who says I've never seen it?" I retorted.

I didn't mean to sound snarky, but he knew nothing about me. For all he knew, I was incredibly psychic and could see dark energy lifting right off people's bodies like black mist rising into the skies. I found his assumption off-putting.

Dr. Rivera may not have liked this cheeky young woman challenging his idea on the inside, but on the outside, he seemed visibly amused. "I don't know. I suppose I am testing you." He smiled.

Calm down, Queylin. I had to remember that he was a paying customer only testing out my qualifications. Still, he could've been nicer about it.

I looked at stony-faced Bibi then let out a sigh. "To be fair, I haven't actually seen it, but I've felt it. A space feels different after you've cleared it."

"How do you know it's not a psychological effect? You perform a ritual, your brain wants to believe it has followed through…and there you go."

"I don't," I replied. "But if believing is half the battle, then who's to say it serves no purpose?"

The doctor nodded, listening.

So I went on. "Prayer, belief in any god, any religion…it all works the same way. It's about intention, the power of thought."

He tilted his glass at me. "The power of thought. And there, we will agree. What about you, miss?" He turned his attention to Bibi. "Do you believe that 'cleansing' a space will clear us of our pesky ghost problem?" The doctor chuckled.

Bibi cleared her throat. "I think it's a place to start."

"And if it doesn't work?" he asked.

"Then, we'll go from there," Bibi replied.

"Fair enough." The doctor stood from his position at the head of the table and stepped over to his wife. He placed her napkin on her lap, gently kissed the top of her head, whispering something to her, then returned to his seat.

It was melancholy to watch. It made me wonder if Samuel or I would ever reach that point of having to take care of each other in this way. When you first get married, you never think of things like this, but we'd promised to love and cherish through thick and thin, and Dr. Rivera, annoying as he could be, had followed through on that promise. For that, part of me praised him.

The housekeeper (or servant, or nurse) brought out the dishes and set them in front of us. Steaming coils of delicious scents rose from the dark rice. I wasn't much into seafood but would eat this plate containing shrimp, not only to be polite, but because it smelled amazing.

"*Muchas gracias,* Lovely," Dr. Rivera said, waiting until we all had our plates before digging in. "*Bon appétit!*"

"Thank you…Lovely?" I asked the woman, unsure.

"Yes, popular Haitian nickname." The doctor winked at me before she could reply. Did he always have this habit of answering for others?

She bowed her head and backed into the kitchen, closing the door after her. I couldn't imagine being in her position of inferiority. Then again, I was making assumptions. For all I knew, Lovely might've been happy to have a job taking care of a disabled woman and cooking meals she loved.

I had to remember that the world did not only exist through Queylin-colored glasses.

"Mmm," the doctor murmured, taking a bite of the *diri ak djon djon.* "This dish is one of my favorites, and Lovely has been making it for me for fifteen years. Since…" His comment trailed off, almost as though he realized he wasn't alone.

Since his wife had fallen ill, I took it to mean. With a sigh, the doctor resumed eating.

"So, Bibi, is it?"

"Yes." Bibi looked up and took a bite of her food, mentally preparing to be interviewed, or so it seemed.

"I am guessing that is a family nickname, or am I wrong?" he asked.

She nodded. "My brother named me that when I was born. He was only two at the time and couldn't say 'baby.' My actual name is Carina."

"Ah, well, Carina," Dr. Rivera said, even though Bibi never gave him permission to call her as such. "Tell me about the *mancha* on your face…the stain. Is that a burn or…?"

I felt Bibi cringe next to me. God only knew how many times she'd been asked this question. I wouldn't blame her if she wanted to hit the "pass" button and go to the next question instead.

Her sigh was barely audible. "It's a birthmark," she replied flatly. "Port-wine stain. I was born with it, hence…the word, birthmark."

I almost choked on my *diri ak djon djon.*

Instead, I gave Bibi a coy smile. "I'm sure you get asked that a lot," I said in an attempt to soften Dr. Rivera's forwardness.

"I do, yeah. All the time. I guess it's natural for people to be curious, but it makes me uncomfortable."

I gave her a sympathetic smile.

"Have you ever thought of having it removed?" the doctor asked, as though he hadn't just heard the part where Bibi expressed her discomfort regarding the topic.

Her sigh was heavier this time. "No. It's a part of me, just like my eyes, my hair, or your silver hair and spare tire."

"¿*Cómo*?" Dr. Rivera cocked his head like a dog who'd just heard a high-pitched whine.

Some phrases did not translate well between languages, and this was one better left un-translated.

"What she means is that she likes her birthmark." I smiled at her. *Spare tire?* I looked at her, holding down a laugh. "I like it, too. It suits her."

"Thanks, Quey," she whispered.

"Well, it's all in what we believe, isn't it?" the doctor said.

I leaned into Bibi. "Just one night and we're out of here," I whispered.

"I hate you."

"I know, I'm sorry."

Dr. Rivera broke a piece of bread and gave half to Lovely, so she could pass it onto his wife. Lovely stepped out of the shadows to take the bread and give it to Mrs. Rivera who had no interest in food at the moment. Lovely shrugged then stood awkwardly next to the wheelchair, holding the bread in her hands.

I couldn't tell who looked saddest, the housekeeper, the wife, or the good doctor.

After dinner, Lovely (or Lovelie, or Loveli) showed Bibi and me upstairs. We lugged our bags up the old wooden staircase, through a landing boasting an old mahogany bench in front of a curious painting of a semi-nude woman, and up another set of stairs. In fact, most of this hallway contained similar paintings, and some were more explicit than others, hence their more hidden locations.

"Thank you," I said, as she opened the door to the guest bedroom for us, pointed to two sets of white, fluffy towels, then closed the door quietly.

"Thanks," Bibi said.

Once alone in the room, we let out huge breaths. I dropped my bag into a chair and sat on the edge of the bed. "Well, this has been an interesting night."

"You owe me huge," Bibi sighed.

"Dude, I swear he wasn't this creepy the first night."

"He was this creepy at the store, Quey. But for some reason you didn't see it."

"Nah, he's just old," I said, walking around the room, admiring the weird and tacky furniture art. "Loves to hear himself talk. I know the kind. You know the kind."

"Doesn't excuse him."

"Yes, I see that now. But I also wanted to see this house really bad. Aren't you glad you can now say you've seen the Harding Estate on the inside?"

"Yes. So wonderful to see this private home on the water so far removed from civilization, owned by a rude man who doesn't allow women to talk."

"Hey, it's not his wife's fault she doesn't speak. She's sick. He said something about PTSD."

"She's got more than PTSD, my friend," Bibi said, falling quiet for a minute. "It's like she's not allowed to speak."

As we walked around the room, examining the strange furniture, I thought Bibi was being a little judgmental. After all, we'd both witnessed the doctor treat his wife with sweet affection. A man oppressing his woman would not have done that. But she'd done me a favor by coming, so I kept quiet about it.

"There, now we've seen the house. Can we go now?" She scoffed.

"And miss the amazing chance to stay in the gaudy bedazzled bedroom from hell?" I glanced around. "I mean, look at this place!"

Whereas the rest of the house told of Hollywood golden days blended with Caribbean flair, the guest bedroom looked like someone had vomited their fashion jewelry drawer onto every square inch of surface area. The lamps had been stamped with old earrings, the edges of the 1980s furniture were hot-glued with necklace charms—silver cats, gold snowflakes, fake crystals—every style discarded bauble and trinket you could think of.

I mean, major points for repurposing old shit, I suppose. But it made for a very…*eclectic* style.

The curtains were made from denim scraps, but I had to admit those were pretty cool. There were even pockets in some of them, which made me remember my own jeans pocket where I'd placed the love note from Samuel this morning.

Taking the folded paper out, I pressed it to my nose, inhaled the scent of rose oil, and set it on my nightstand—a little something to keep me company through the night.

"Should we get started?" Bibi checked her phone then threw it onto the quilted bedspread made from different patterned fabrics. "This whole room could use a massive smudging."

"Yes. Listen, thank you for coming. I know you didn't want to. And I know I was excited to be here, but now that I am, I don't think I would've taken well to sleeping in this room alone."

"But it sparkles. It glitters."

"Nothing can save it. Not even sparkles."

We laughed and went through our bags, preparing to sage the heck out of the room. Releasing the tension felt nice, if forced. Bibi lit the end of a smudge stick and placed it in her abalone shell. Together, we stood facing east toward the bedroom door.

"You do the honors, little witch," she said.

I smiled. Whereas Bibi was highly intuitive, I, at least, knew something about ritual. If I couldn't bring natural talent to the table, I at least knew procedure.

Closing my eyes, I lifted my palms to the ceiling. "Guardians of the East watchtower, keepers of air, we welcome you into this sacred space. Lend us your intuition and lightness of being."

It was something I had learned to say from the countless books I'd read over the years, and if my Catholic parents ever heard me, they'd disown me. But this was why I'd surrounded myself with like-minded individuals—Bibi, Lorena, Rain, and Maggie—my coven, one might say.

Bibi drew a pentacle in the air with the white sage smoke and waited as I turned south before following suit. "Guardians of the South watchtower, keepers of fire, we welcome you into this sacred space. Please lend us your passion, your drive, and your spirit."

We asked the elements of water and earth to join us, ending with Spirit, the most important one of them all, after which I drew a circle of protection around us using an athamé and imagined us in a bubble of light. Once the circle was cast and the quarters summoned, I asked for anyone whose interest it was to protect us to join us. Angels, spirit guides, ancestors. To protect this room, this home, from any entities that wished to harm us, harm this family. Let them know it was time to move on, time to let this family live in peace.

Bibi and I cleared the room, meditated, and said a prayer together. Once it seemed like we could resume the evening in peace, we closed the spell circle, took turns showering in the adjoining art deco bathroom, and got to bed early.

Tomorrow, we would clear the whole house. We would use Lorena and Maggie's magickal kits and ingredients to wash floors and smudge corners. We would use everything in our arsenal to cleanse this home, and if nothing helped the Riveras, well then we'd pass the torch to someone else.

"I don't like this house," Bibi said with the quilt up to her chin. "There's something here."

"Even after we cleared?"

"Yes. They're keeping their distance," she said, her words sending goose bumps up my arms. "They're not leaving. They're not ready."

How she knew that both freaked me out and fascinated me.

"Then, let's get some sleep," I said. "Maybe we'll have better luck tomorrow."

Bibi was quiet.

I sent Samuel a round of goodnight texts. It was earlier in Illinois. I'd spoken to him on the drive to the Harding Estate, but now that we were here, I didn't want anything of my own interfering with the home's energy, so I refrained from calling him.

I hadn't turned off the light for more than a minute when Bibi sighed in the darkness.

"You okay?" I stared at the ceiling fan that twirled slowly high above us.

"Sure." She rolled away from me. "If you don't count that woman standing in the corner."

EIGHT

"Woman?"

"Yes, by the door."

Slowly, I turned my head.

It wasn't that I was scared of seeing a woman standing in the corner of the room, but—I was scared of seeing a woman standing in the corner of the room. I'd never done this before. I'd never seen a ghost. Now that the opportunity was here, I wasn't so sure I welcomed it anymore.

As my heart rate kicked up, I tried focusing my fuzzy night vision near the door. A woman. If I relaxed and let my third eye take over, I'd see what Bibi saw, too. However, all I saw was an old bedazzled mirror, a chair holding clothes, and a rack with an umbrella hanging from it.

"I don't see her."

"She's leaving."

As much as I tried to see the shape of a woman moving through the room, I couldn't. My life's frustrations. "Is it Julia Harding?" I asked.

"Don't think so. She's wearing jeans. Julia lived in the twenties, didn't she?" Bibi asked.

"I think so."

"Anyway, she's gone now. Go to sleep, Quey. Sorry to scare you." Bibi settled into bed with another sigh. I could tell this was old hat to her, but to me, my hopes were still lit like St. Elmo's Fire.

"It's fine. I'm more jealous you can see them than anything," I muttered, rolling over and closing my eyes. As if I could sleep tonight.

A woman.
A woman in the room.

It took a long time, but eventually I fell asleep with the covers over my head and body turned toward Bibi. It was times like these that I wondered what my fascination with seeing spirits was all about, and I knew what drove it—fear.

Once something stopped being scary or fascinating, I no longer obsessed over it. But this was one obsession that, no pun intended, had haunted me my whole life.

For hours, I dreamed about the Harding Estate and the cleansing we'd be performing in the morning. I dreamed of going through the motions, getting everything just right. I dreamed about Mrs. Rivera's lips being sewn shut, and about Lovely's tongue being cut from her mouth.

Why didn't these women speak?

In another part of the dream, I saw the two speaking to each other, carrying on a conversation. So they had things to say after all. Why couldn't I hear them? And what were they saying?

I was in the middle of dreaming that an unidentified woman in jeans stalked our room in the middle of the night when I felt a presence near me in bed. I opened my eyes—at least I did in the dream—and found I wasn't wrong. There was someone. I could feel it in the air displacement.

A woman.

A woman in the room. Similar scenario to the nightmare I'd had last night when Samuel had to talk me back to Earth, only this time the ghost hovered over me.

Eye sockets hollow.

Cheekbones protruded, as the rest of her skin drew against her face bones. She wasn't evil, but she scared me anyway.

In her thin hands, she held trinkets and baubles collected over the years. She showed them to me with urgency, as though I should look deeper, find meaning in the items. I wanted to scream—I didn't like having anyone surprise me while I slept, especially a gaunt, desperate ghost. I'd always said I wouldn't mind seeing one as long as it didn't hover over me bedside, but here my fears were coming true.

"Bi…bi…"

I might have spoken aloud, or it might've been in my dream.

"Bibi?"

The woman continued to stare at me with missing eyes, stringy dark hair hanging on either side of her face. Those thin fingers holding that tangled mass of jewelry…

"What do you want?" I asked the dream spirit—at least I thought it was a dream—forcing myself to be brave.

She wouldn't reply.

Couldn't reply, I realized.

Her mouth had been sewn shut, too, just like Mrs. Rivera in my dream and the housekeeper who'd been silenced another way.

Paralysis gripped me. As much as I wanted to run from the skinny woman presenting baubles to me in my sleep, I couldn't move. As much as I wanted to believe these ideas about the women in the house, my rational brain knew they weren't true. Mrs. Rivera had post traumatic stress disorder or some other degenerative disease. And Lovely might have been a woman rescued from the harsh realities of Haiti, had witnessed the hell of earthquakes and famine, and had nothing left to say. Dr. Rivera was kind to them, nothing more or less.

Change your viewpoint, Queylin.

I curled into a ball and rocked as hard as I could until I ripped awake in real life and found myself sitting up in bed. No ghost anywhere in sight. Something outside scraped against the window pane. Branches. Branches in the bay breeze.

"What? What is it?" Bibi startled awake by my jerky movement.

"I saw her."

"Who?"

"The woman in the room."

I reached over to the nightstand and switched on the lamp, scared to see her lurking there, but she was gone. Or invisible now that I wasn't dreaming. I'd sleep with the light on for the rest of the night if I had to, but I was not going back to darkness. I wasn't even sure that she'd been real. Like Dr. Rivera believed, it could've been my brain.

But then, Bibi confirmed it.

"She's still here," she said, staring into the corner of the room. "But leaving now."

"Where? What does she want?" I asked, feeling panicky. What gift did Bibi possess that I didn't, and why? If ghosts were real, why couldn't they show themselves to everyone? One, great mystery of life would be solved, just like that.

"She's trying to tell us something."

"Was this her room at one time?" I panted. "Does she want us to leave?"

"I don't think so. It's more like she's warning us."

"About what?"

"I don't know, Quey. I don't have all the answers," Bibi said, throwing her legs over the side of the bed and pushing her face into her hands.

"Sorry." It was 4 AM and here I was, making demands of a friend who didn't want to be here to begin with. I rubbed my eyes and felt sick suddenly, same as I had after yesterday's nightmare. These new experiences were getting to me.

Scrambling to my feet, I ran to the bathroom, leaned over the toilet, and heaved. Nothing came out but the warm saliva that had filled my mouth a moment ago. If Samuel were here, he'd insist I go home and forget this nonsense right this second.

Bibi stood in the doorway. "You okay?"

"Just give me a minute."

I heaved again, but the feeling passed. Lifting my chin, I breathed in and out deeply to catch my breath. Bibi touched my shoulder.

"Quey, I think we should leave in the morning. I don't like the vibes I'm picking up from this place."

"Which is why they need our help."

Bibi was one of those people who, though blessed with this gift, did not like having it, so it made sense that she'd want to go, but I wasn't ready. Though a ghost had knocked me onto my ass and two others had shown me things in my sleep, I wanted to know what they wanted.

I wanted to help this couple.

All thirty years of my life so far, I never saw spirits. Then, since yesterday, when one of them had slammed into me in the garden, something had changed. Maybe the house's energy was waking up my intuition, or maybe Julia Harding herself had unblocked my third eye chakra, because suddenly, things felt different.

I felt closer to hearing them.

To seeing them.

I stood and washed my face in the sink, rubbing the sleep out of my eyes and spiking cold water from the 1920s faucets over my face. Even the mirror frame had old baubles and buttons glued to it. When I looked into the reflection to gauge how shitty I must've looked…

I saw her.

Sunken cheekbones, long brown hair hanging over her face, cracked lips, and eyes—I couldn't see them but I knew they were there, recessed into the hollowed spaces. Luminous blue-violet, her eyes had been bright at one point.

I couldn't move.

She wrapped her hands around my mid-torso as if to feel how solid I was. As though she missed being real and made of flesh. I pushed her away, feeling solid body, and screamed.

But it was only Bibi standing there, perplexed at what was going on with me. "Quey? What is it?"

"She was…I thought…you were…" I couldn't complete one thought to save my life. All I knew was that my pounding heart would crack a rib any moment now. "Damn it."

"She's with you," Bibi said, her voice sounding distant and trance-like. Her hollow voice startled me, dislodging another shriek from my throat.

I ran from the bathroom and sat on the edge of the bed, rocking myself. I couldn't be afraid. I'd come to this house to perform a service. I'd asked for this. How stupid would it be if the medium they'd hired was too terrified to do her job.

Get your shit together, Queylin.

"Okay…" I said, mustering up courage. "Let's do this. Right now. Let's talk to her."

"I agree. Let's do this, so we can go soon. Stand up," Bibi ordered. "Hold my hands."

I stood and slipped my cold fingers into Bibi's warm ones. In the feeble light of the room, I watched her close her eyes. I closed mine, too.

"God and Goddess, we create this circle to strengthen our energy. Lend us your light and your love…" I'd only heard Bibi summon deities once before when she'd read my tarot cards. Her voice soothed me immediately.

"So mote it be," I said.

"So mote it be. And we ask that the spirit in this room tell us her name if it will serve our higher good and help this family."

We waited a few moments.

Then Bibi said, "Thank you, I understand. We wish you no harm. Is there something you want to tell us before you turn and move into the light?"

Another moment of pause. I tried to hear the conversation going on in another dimension, and for a moment, I thought I heard her voice clear as a bell.

Not ready…

"You have unfinished business?" Bibi asked, and again, we waited. "What are they? Are they yours?"

I knew Bibi was asking about the baubles in the ghost's hands. About the trinkets all throughout the room.

"I see. Thank you for telling us. You can leave now. There's a light. Walk towards it and go in peace."

"What did she say her name was?" I whispered.

"She said she can't remember."

How awful. How incredibly sad that a spirit couldn't remember who she was or why she was here. Only that she wasn't ready. Oddly enough, I felt her pain, the urgency for us to know why she wasn't ready. She'd been done harm.

And the harm had been done in this house.

The woman's hollow, pecked-out eyes appeared in my vision. I dropped Bibi's hands and stepped back clumsily. "What was that?" I demanded.

"You can't just break the circle, Quey," Bibi chastised. "Give me your hands."

"I'm sorry. I just…I saw her. I heard her say something," I stammered. "About this house."

"About this room? Jewelry that belonged to her? And others?" Bibi asked.

I shook my head. "No. About women who'd lived in this house. The stuff glued to the furniture used to be theirs." Where had this information come from? I had no idea. It was as if it'd been passed straight into my consciousness from those hollow eyes themselves.

"So this 'art' was made from jewelry of the deceased?" Bibi asked.

"I think so."

"Ugh, that's not creepy at all," Bibi said. "Let us close this circle. Go in peace, so mote it be."

So mote it be. Blessed be. I couldn't vocalize. I'd been so utterly shaken tonight. Here we were, surrounded by items of the dead. No wonder I couldn't sleep. The emotions of the deceased were imprinted on these belongings all around us, and the main impression I got was sadness and anger.

"She's gone," Bibi said.

"Are you sure?"

"Yes."

"Who was she?" I asked.

"I'm guessing she lived in the house at one point, but I don't know the history of the place. I can't tell you who."

"We should look into it tomorrow."

"Doesn't matter who she was, honestly." Bibi stepped into the bathroom and reached for a towel. "What matters is that she move on and find peace, but something tells me she can't do that."

"Why?"

"Quey, you need to accept the fact that sometimes, there's nothing that will help. Some houses, especially these old ones, come with their ghosts. It's a package deal. And anyone who agrees to live there needs to accept that."

I felt what she was saying, but at the same time, I couldn't accept it. I wanted to help. I'd come this far on my spiritual journey for a reason. My impressions of the ghosts so far were that Julia carried sadness, and this other female spirit was desperate to communicate. Both needed guidance so they could move on. But who was I here to help—the living or the dead?

NINE

Despite being awake half the night with me, Bibi woke up early. I got the point—get up, do our thing, then leave. She didn't say much, and I could tell she was upset.

"You okay?" I asked.

"Fine." She pulled up the comforter, drew it over the pillows. "But I'm out of here, Quey."

I smirked. I saw this one coming a mile away. "You're not going to stay and help me cleanse the house?"

"I want to, but I can't shake this feeling. It's like the house doesn't want us here or want anyone to be happy, so I'm not sure a spiritual cleanse will help. You can stay if you want to, just don't stay another night."

I was disappointed, but I couldn't be upset with her. First of all, I'd asked her to come as a favor and she'd already followed through when we performed the basic clearing. Also, last night was stressful for us both. Finally, her shift at the store started at noon anyway, so I understood her wanting to get a move on.

"I don't blame you," I said, watching her gather up her bag and stuff from the bathroom. "You want me to drive you back?"

"I'll take Lyft. But listen…" She faced me and took my hands. "You know what to do, Queylin. You've been training for this your whole life."

I laughed. "You make me sound like an Olympic swimmer."

"This is harder than swimming. Do the cleanse then come home. Okay? But don't linger here anymore than is necessary. Remember what I said: sometimes you just can't help. Plus…"

"Plus?"

"I didn't want to tell you this before, but…"

"But?"

She sighed, shook my hands. Her big hazel eyes implored me. "Your inexperience makes you more susceptible. You know how I can't explain what I feel sometimes? You're going to feel a lot of that. Vulnerability. Don't let the house drag you in."

"Okay," I said. "I won't."

I wanted to feel indignant for her leaving me all alone, especially if she felt I was more vulnerable than usual, but I couldn't. She was well within her right to leave. On another hand, she was right—I could do this. If anyone was ready, it was me. I'd studied the metaphysical arts more than anyone on my team, *because* I hadn't been born with natural talent. I was a veritable *Wicca*-pedia of information.

We followed the musical sounds of silverware clinking against plates to find Dr. Rivera in the dining room having breakfast. Behind him, just outside the window on the back veranda, Mrs. Rivera sat in her wheelchair silently contemplating the bay.

The old man stood and gestured to the extra place settings. "Won't you please join us? We didn't want to wake you."

"I will, but Bibi is leaving. She has work to do," I explained. Bibi's nervous eyes glanced around the room to avoid direct contact with the doctor.

"Oh." Dr. Rivera seemed genuinely disappointed. "I'm sorry to hear that. Did something happen last night? We thought we heard a scream. But that is also a common occurrence around here." He chuckled.

Bibi touched the dining table with her fingertips and looked at me to handle the question.

"As a matter of fact, yes," I said. "We both encountered…a ghost in our room last night. The spirit of a young woman. Do you know who she might be?" I asked Dr. Rivera.

The doctor used his nail to pry something from his teeth. He looked at Lovely who'd come in to refill the doctor's cup and fill ours. "I have no idea, as I have never seen them myself. Did she speak to you?"

Bibi adjusted the bag on her shoulder uncomfortably. "She showed us jewelry," she said, "fashion jewelry. You know, the fake stuff. I think she was trying to tell us something about the room we were in, since, well…there's a lot of jewelry in there."

"Yes." Dr. Rivera nodded slowly. "One day, my wife dumped all her drawers on the bed, and she and Lovely began making art with the stuff she no longer used. Clever of them, *verdad*?"

"Uh, yes." Clever was one way of describing the artistic style. Mrs. Rivera must've been hoarding a *lot* of crappy old fashion jewelry to cover that much furniture.

"So, why do you think the spirit would've shown that to us?" I asked Dr. Rivera. "Is there something special about it?"

"Not that I know of. Like I said, it was old stuff. Rather than throwing it away, she repurposed it. What did she look like? The spirit?"

"I only saw her for a moment, but—"

"She was modern," Bibi finally spoke up and stared at the doctor. "Jeans, T-shirt…not from any other era. She was a white woman, brunette, pretty."

"*Bueno*, you just described every woman in Miami," the doctor said with a chuckle.

Bibi did not laugh. She stared at Dr. Rivera, and I thought I sensed some tension between them.

"Her eyes were bright," I added. It was the only thing I truly remembered from my dream. Even through sunken eye sockets, I remember them staring at me. "A peculiar shade of blue."

The doctor stared at me, narrowing his eyes. "Is that so?"

"I think so. It's hard for me to tell sometimes," I said, nearly adding that I was still new to this, though Dr. Rivera knew nothing about it.

After a minute of gazing at me, he finally tore his stare away. "Anyway, stay and eat, Queylin, while I accompany Bibi to the door."

"Thank you, but I can find my way out." Bibi gave me a final nod, before turning and heading toward the hallway. "I ordered a car."

"Nonsense, I'll see you safely and also have something for your time." He pulled a folded bill from his pocket and handed it to her.

Hesitantly, she looked at the money. Knowing Bibi, she was wondering if she should take it, if it contained bad energy or not. "Thank you," she said after a moment, taking the bill and putting it in her bag. "See you later, Quey. Call me."

"I will."

As Dr. Rivera followed her to the door, I sat at the table while Lovely appeared to place bagels and spreads in front of me. "Thank you so much," I said, giving her a smile. For a moment, my brain remembered Lovely with her tongue cut out, bleeding from the mouth, as my dream had shown me, but now, in person, it was clear she was just a shy, quiet woman, and my imagination was on overdrive.

I cleared my throat. "The, um, guest room is really interesting," I told her. "That must've taken you and Mrs. Rivera a long time to bedazzle all the furniture like that."

Lovely just stood in the corner of the room, unsure if she should reply, smiling softly at the bagels. Maybe she didn't know English, but I didn't speak Creole either, so small talk was a problem.

"Did all that jewelry really belong to Mrs. Rivera? Or did you guys raid Goodwill?" I laughed, reaching for a bagel and smearing cream cheese onto it. Silly question, but it was better than silence with a stranger.

As I ate my breakfast, I thought about the mystery surrounding the Harding Estate. I thought about Bibi's impressions and why she felt the need to leave early. I thought about Mrs. Rivera out on the veranda getting fresh air and taking in the lovely view.

What would she say if she could speak? Were her memories of coming to America that traumatic, or was she on the brink of Alzheimer's and her husband just didn't want to admit it? Was Dr. Rivera controlling like he seemed, or was he sweet like he'd demonstrated on multiple occasions?

Who knew where the truth lay, really, and in any case, it was none of my business. I had to remember that I was here to do a cleansing and not get wrapped up in this family's problems.

Speaking of which, it was time to get to work, and Dr. Rivera was taking a long time to get back to the table. In fact, about fifteen minutes of silence had passed in the dining room with Lovely tending to my breakfast needs.

"Excuse me," I told her, as I stood. "I'm going to see if my friend is okay."

Lovely's perpetually happy daze seemed to dissipate, as her dark eyes filled with blankness. I slipped out of the dining room, through the house, to the front door. Opening it and walking to the front circular driveway, I glanced around at the emptiness.

Bibi had left, and Dr. Rivera might have gone to the restroom or to check on something. I sent Bibi a text: *Thanks for coming with me. LMK how the store is doing later.*

After a minute, she replied: *I will.*

Smiling, I turned and started heading back into the house when something stopped me. Pausing to listen, I heard a sound coming from the side of the house. I closed the door and stepped around the bushes and large windows, following the source of the noise.

For a moment, I could've sworn it was Bibi, but she'd just replied to my text. Was someone crying?

I was met with the large iron gate leading into the side of the house, where the garden stretched for acres across the property. As much as I felt drawn to whatever was behind the gate, I didn't want to get smacked in the chest by Julia's ghost again. Then again, interaction with ghosts was why I'd come. If I didn't face them head-on, I may as well call it a day.

Trying the latch, I found it open, same as last time. I slipped in and closed the gate behind me. The crying sounds seemed to get closer, but it was difficult to tell where they originated. At times, they seemed to be coming from the yard. Other times, from inside the house, through an open window. But it also could've been the wind cooing through a screen.

I stepped over broken flagstones and walked into the dense overgrown vegetation taking up most of the yard. The rogue purple, white, and tangerine orchids sprouting from the trees provided a touch of color and elegance to the otherwise creepy garden.

The angel statue seemed to watch me approach, as if happy to have a visitor again. I imagined living in this house and fixing up this area to make it inviting for guests. I could make an incredible meditation garden out here with a stone bench and a trickling water fountain. Maybe then the angel wouldn't look so melancholy.

Was the angel the one crying?

Pausing in front of the statue, I looked up and watched, waiting for the sobs to resume their chorus in minor key. For a long minute, it felt as though the angel would move this time. After a few minutes of studying the angel and absorbing the silence, I heard it again. Heavy weeping. I closed my eyes and allowed my heart to feel every drop of anguish as though it were my own. Only then would I know who it belonged to. Trust my instincts.

Will he ever return?

Will I raise this baby all alone?

My eyes popped open.

Baby?

Suddenly, the same feeling I'd gotten when the spirit had pushed me over yesterday returned—soreness all around, especially around my chest and mid-torso. I'd been expecting my period all this week, but now I couldn't tell if I was having cramps of my own, or this sensation was a psychic impression I'd picked up from someone else.

Julia Harding. Maybe she'd been pregnant when she took her own life. I hadn't read that anywhere. I hadn't researched too deeply, but that would make sense given the way I'd been feeling. I'd even experienced nausea on several occasions, but who was this person she was waiting for?

"Julia?" I whispered. "Are you okay?"

Unsettling silence spread over the grounds. I could hear every cricket, every worm, every blade of grass rising and settling under the sun's movements.

"Mrs. Harding?"

I could almost hear her answer, *not* of my imagination. I heard her in the breeze, in the distant boat horns, in the lapping of waves against the mangroves. No, she was not okay. She was trapped without options. I felt this in a way I couldn't explain. I felt it deep inside my soul.

The angel's downward gaze seemed to focus on me just then, heavy-lidded eyes snapping to my face, and then…the lantern blinked on.

I gasped, stepping back, wrapping my fingers around a narrow fruit tree. I shouldn't have been out here without my tools, without having performed a cleansing yet. I probably should've gotten on with the job, but this house had a way of sucking me in, catching me off guard.

I remembered Bibi's warning: *don't let the house keep you.* Get my work done and get out. I did not want a repeat of yesterday's psychic attack.

The lantern's light pulsated same as yesterday, brighter then lower, then brighter again. My instincts were to flee the yard, get inside in the house, but I stopped myself.

Stop it. This is what you wanted, Queylin.

The crying intensified.

I followed the sound as best as I could, stepping over rocks, wading through tall grass. The weeping led me deeper into the garden and straight for the banyan tree. The tree I'd always loved. Maybe it was the banyan crying. I stared up at the massive thing, imagining it in this same place a long time ago. This tree had witnessed more changes in the last hundred years than any of us had.

It knew things about the families who'd lived here. About the house that had stood for a century. About the Tequesta who'd lived here long before any of us settlers came along. This tree, and the angel, both told me things about Julia Harding that nobody could have known.

She'd been pregnant.

The information slid into my mind. How did I know? I didn't. I felt it to be true.

And the father…

Jesus…

It all overcame me so powerfully—the emotional pain of separation, the uncertainty, the hopelessness—I doubled over and threw up right on the ground. My hands and knees shook from the sickness, and my stomach trembled. I battled overwhelming thoughts I couldn't differentiate from my own.

When I gathered enough energy to look up, I saw the dirty pair of feet. Then the bright red blood dribbling in a thin line down the inside of her leg, seeping between her toes, dripping into the earth.

Her head tilted to one side, neck broken.

It was Julia, swinging peacefully in the ocean breeze.

TEN

My breakfast rose again, but I tamped it down with gulps of fresh air. I couldn't scream. I was too shocked by the sight. As horrible as Julia looked up there hanging from that great branch, I was too petrified to move.

It took a long time before I could rip my eyes away from the vision, and my limbs felt like Jell-O that'd been left outside after a summer picnic. Why had I always wanted to see something this horrible? I couldn't remember what had seemed so exciting about it. Now I just wanted to run from here.

It was time to do what I'd come to do, then go.

The vision dissipated before my eyes. I backed out of the garden, eyes glued to the spot, making sure she wasn't going to climb down from that branch and follow me home. A stupid idea, I knew, but right now, I felt like anything could happen.

At this point, I was 99% convinced that whatever Julia's ghost did to me yesterday when it slammed into me, it worked. She must've dislodged the calcification over my pineal gland, the gland purportedly responsible for psychic vision. Because here I was—seeing things.

Those ghosts I felt so jealous for never seeing?

There they were.

I reached the house and rushed inside to catch my breath. There was no one around from what I could see, though Dr. Rivera could've been watching from any hidden corner, and I felt like he was. Like I was live on a reality TV show, and audiences were getting a kick out of watching me coil away in terror.

Rushing upstairs to grab my things, I felt like a hundred pairs of eyes were following me. In the middle of the staircase, one particular cold spot blocked my way. It could've been a draft, but I felt like it was a person standing there. Out of the corner of my eye, I thought I'd see them, but they'd only turn out to be a banister, or an open door casting shadows on walls, or paintings of 50s-era women in rumba dresses.

All eyes watching me.

"Not scary, not scary…" I whispered.

I couldn't let anything distract me from my task. And yet I felt like everything in the house wanted my attention.

I reached the guest bedroom and found the bed made and my things neatly stacked on top of the dresser. I attributed this to Lovely tidying things up, and while I didn't think she'd tampered with anything, it still felt weird to know someone had touched my things.

I opened my ritual bag, checked to make sure everything was still inside, and changed into white pants and white shirt. Not that I practiced Santería, but if I was going to incorporate a few of the religion's traditions, then I may as well do it the right way. White represented purity, and that was my goal. Purity of heart, purity of light, positive energy.

With my stuff, I hurried downstairs eager to get away from the guest bedroom and the ghost who lingered there when I stopped cold. Lovely stood by the entrance to the service kitchen staring at me.

"Oh, hello, there," I said.

She didn't reply, just looked at my bag and the clothes I was wearing.

"Do you have a bucket? And a mop?" I asked. I knew that sounded strange, but the first ritual I'd be doing involved literally sweeping ghosts out of the house.

I shouldn't have been surprised when she simply nodded and disappeared down a hall. A moment later, she returned with a red bucket and damp mop inside. So she understood English after all.

"Thank you." I watched her slip back into the service hall, curious wide eyes watching me remove all sorts of bottles the ladies had put together for me on top of a coffee table. I felt a little strange having someone watch me, but I also thought that maybe she was familiar with it all.

Eventually, she slipped out of sight.

I sighed and entered a half bathroom to fill the bucket with cold water then returned to the living room and poured all the bottles into the bucket. Herb blends like *Quita Maldición* (curse remover), *Yo Puedo*

Mas Que Tú (for empowerment), *Rompe Saraguey* (negative spirit remover), and other stuff from the *botanica lucumí*.

To begin, I pulled out a piece of charcoal and lit it inside of an abalone shell, along with a sage smudge stick. I knew I was blending all sorts of witchcraft from different cultures, but hell, this house needed all the help it could get.

Time for the *limpieza*, or cleansing.

I pulled out the piece of paper Lorena had included with the kit containing phrases in Yoruba, the West African language of Lucumí or Santería. Taking a deep breath, I began with regular words of my own.

"I ask the Universe to cleanse and bless this home, fill it with light and love, remove all negative energy that is not welcome here."

Spreading the sage, I wandered through the house, paying particular attention to the corners where negative energy was said to build up. Then I came back to my starting point and glanced at Maggie's instructions.

Perform when not on your period and while smoking a cigar.

Well, I wasn't on my period, that much I knew. And a cigar? Shit, I hadn't smoked one of those since I was fifteen at my *quince* birthday party, when Abuelo made me try one for his own amusement. Looking through the bag, I noticed they hadn't included one.

Ugh, fail.

As weird as it seemed, this was an important part of the ritual to those who practiced, and I didn't feel right skipping it. But I knew, if I walked around the house, I was sure to find one, as Dr. Rivera, like most elderly Cuban men, kept a stash of cigars somewhere in the house. I was sure he wouldn't miss one if I borrowed it.

"Where are you suckers?" I walked through the living room, opening and closing random trinket boxes. If I was a random cigar, where would I be? The lid of one trinket box was upholstered in leather and smelled sweetly of tobacco. Opening it, I found it contained an assortment of cigars.

"BINGO."

Finding a cigar in a home decked out in Cuban décor had proved easy. Next, I checked to make sure nobody was watching me steal, nobody alive anyway. I swiped a box of matches from inside the box and a cigar from the bottom of the stack before returning to my spot.

"Alright, I'm ready now," I said to myself, lighting the cigar and puffing on the end until it glowed orange. I coughed, feeling a burn in my throat, coughed again. My eyes stung with smoke. "Amateur," I muttered.

As I'd done with Wiccan spells over the years, I tried to take it seriously and focus on my intention to rid the house of spirits. The magic wasn't in the items themselves—it was in the practitioner who believed they could manifest change.

Opening the back French doors as well as the front, I returned to the mop and bucket and, as quickly as possible, began mopping the tile floors while repeating the words on the piece of paper.

"Elegua, abreme camino, librame de mal," I said in Spanish then switched to the Yoruba on my paper. "Eshu Elegua, oga gbogbo na mirin ita algbana baba mi mulo na buruku nitosi le chocncho kuelu kuikuo oki cosi ofo, cosi eyo…"

I had no idea what I was saying, but I tried to infuse the same feeling I'd used with the English phrases. Intention, intention, intention. What did I want to achieve? I envisioned myself achieving a clean house, spirits moving away, peace being restored. I mopped the floors, the idea being to usher the negative spirits toward the door, to "sweep them out."

When I was done, I returned to my bag, pulled out a white candle, set it on a small plate, and lit it in the middle of the coffee table.

"Ashes to ashes, dust to dust," I said after a long exhale, "may the wind blow all wandering spirits, clear the world of the living, turn you to where you belong, and—"

Something fell.

I startled, touched my chest.

My eyes flicked around. Through the cigar smoke, I spotted something lying on the floor. A photo frame. Slowly, I walked over to pick it up. The photo was a faded color image of Dr. Rivera next to—now this part was a challenge—either Mrs. Rivera in her younger, healthier years (but that would've made her much, much younger than Dr. Rivera) or…they had a daughter. Either way, I could see the familial resemblance. Whoever the gorgeous woman was, she smiled joyfully and cradled a baby bump.

I put the frame back.

The room felt chilly, though the doors were open and warm South Florida air wafted through the house. Someone was here with me—someone from the spirit world.

They didn't want to go, just like Bibi had said.

But I wouldn't back down.

I had to make them leave.

"Eshu Elegua, oga gbogbo na mirin ita algbana baba mi mulo na buruku nitosi le chocncho kuelu kuikuo oki cosi ofo, cosi eyo…"

I read from the paper, repeating the chant, picking up the smudge stick and dipping it into the white candle flame again. Spreading the sweet sage smoke through the air, I envisioned the spirits leaving out the front door, even the one who hadn't liked the framed photo and knocked it over.

But my confidence waned. If a ghost was sticking around, then I wasn't doing a good job. And if I didn't believe in my powers, my powers wouldn't work.

"Please leave," I ordered the lingering spirit. "There's nothing left here for you. It's time to move on."

Suddenly, the living room walls reverberated with the sound of pounding. Whoever was here in spirit had not liked what I had to say. I gasped, clutching my wrist and lucky bracelet.

"You'll be happier if you go," I insisted, heart pounding. "Trust me…let it go."

Another shadow slipped in my peripheral vision, but when I faced it head-on, nothing was there. I closed the doors, grabbed the bucket containing spell water, and headed for the stairs, desperate to get the hell out of this creepy-ass room.

At the base of the stairs, I paused.

It was that music again.

The old-style 1950s music that sounded like it was playing on a vintage record player. It might've been coming from the dining room. Putting down the bucket and bag, I tip-toed down the hallway into the dining hall only to find it empty, yet the music felt discernibly louder.

Where was it coming from? Like the phantom cries in the garden, the notes were difficult to pinpoint.

More importantly, I felt obsessed with it. Slipping out the same door I'd found on my first visit, I found myself inside that empty ballroom, the one that, in my mind's eye, could've hosted dignitaries and millionaires from all over the country in Julia Harding's time.

I walked all along the perimeter of its walls, trying to see if there was another door to another room only to find myself on the opposite side of the house in a long, dark hallway that turned like a hairpin at the end.

I swallowed a lump in my throat.

Good Lord, I couldn't go down that path. It felt musty in here, disconnected from the home's main A/C, like an annexed, unused area—a ramp descending into Hell. I had no idea where it led and wasn't sure I wanted to know. But the music was louder here, and I felt like I was onto something.

Opportunities like this didn't present themselves often, and the gothic girl in me couldn't resist. And so I walked. Slowly. Down the hallway. Following the music like a guest in a mad scientist's castle out of some old Hollywood monster movie.

I touched the walls on both sides as I went, feeling off-balance before realizing that the hallway was leading down. It was hard to tell because the corridor was so long, and the descent was gradual but when I reached the end and slowly turned the corner of the wall to see where the hairpin turn led, I noticed another hallway descending the rest of the way.

The music grew louder.

This was the cellar—it had to be.

But Dr. Rivera had said it'd been closed years ago after Hurricane Andrew. I picked up speed and let gravity and momentum carry me down the ramp until I reached the bottom where a pocket of cold air greeted me.

But no door was there. I'd reached a dead-end. I ran my fingertips along the walls, trying to feel inconsistencies in the murkiness and did come across a different texture. A rough patch-up job. New drywall, new-smelling materials. New addition. The cellar had been sealed after all.

But the music came from inside.

At least, it seemed to.

I turned back the way I came before someone might find me down here when suddenly, I stopped frozen still in the ramped hallway. A figure stood in my path—a woman in a pale blue dress, gaunt, with thin hair pulled into a messy ponytail, bleeding from the chest and a large chunk of skin missing from her collarbone. Her knees knocked together, and she popped her chin up and stared at me.

Imploring, angry eyes.

How can you not help me, she said without a word. How can you stand there and do nothing? Especially in your condition?

This time, I screamed my head off.

ELEVEN

I wedged my way past her, squeezing my eyes shut, pretending she wasn't there. I pushed my body against the wall. As if she were real and needed space in the hall. As if she were made of flesh and bone. Screams echoed in my ear—her screams. She was one pissed-off woman. But she couldn't be real. There was no way a person looking so dead could possibly be so alive.

"Okay, I'm sorry, I'm sorry..." I reasoned with the woman, trying to get past.

The chill in the hall intensified, as I blasted past the ghost and up the ramp with blinders on, my hands shielding the sides of my face, as if doing so would make her disappear.

How can you go?

How can you let me die?

"I didn't. I'm not," I assured her.

I rushed around the hairpin turn and up the long hallway toward the entrance into the main house. Her bloody features would be imprinted in my memory as long as I lived. I could hear her moaning behind me, groaning about how nobody would help her.

"Get out, get out, get out..." I chanted to myself, still ridiculously using my hands as blinders. All I had to do was reach the lit doorway and I'd be free from this hellish hall way. Why? Why did I have to come this way? Why did I have to "investigate?" I was a glutton for punishment, that's why. I'd led such a boring life so far that I needed drama.

Needed bloody, screaming ghosts in order to feel alive. The scary thing was, it wasn't too far from the truth.

But then, because Life decided it was time for me to learn my lesson the full-immersion way, my body smacked right into another solid body smelling of cigar and old man cologne.

"Oh, my God! I'm so sorry," I panted.

"*¿Qué haces aquí, muchacha?"* the old man asked with a stern look in his eye. "You're not supposed to be here."

"I did? No, I didn't. I mean…who…who is that woman down there?" I pointed down the shadowy hallway.

"What are you looking for?" He ignored my question.

"I heard music and…followed… I thought maybe…the cellar…who was…?"

God, I sounded like a bumbling idiot, and Dr. Rivera took full advantage to glare at me like one. Then, he glanced at my white pants' pocket and cocked his head.

"*¿Qué'eso?*" He forcefully stepped toward me, wanting to know what was in my pocket.

Instinctively, I backed away. After the ghost woman in the hall, I couldn't be sure that he wasn't after me, too. But he only grabbed my arm and pulled me toward him, so he could fish into my pocket. "Where did you get this?" He raised the cigar I'd borrowed from his box.

Oh. That.

"I was going to put that back. I needed a cigar for the *limpieza* and forgot one at home. I'm so sorry, I—"

Was an idiot.

"So, you thought…" The old man's eyes took on a menacing look mixed with disbelieving amusement, as he held up the cigar. "That you'd borrow my Montecristo, No. 2, of all the cigars you could have chosen in that box…for…let me get this straight…a *despojo*?"

He scoffed.

"I didn't know—"

"Let me guess, you'd like some of my best rum to go with that, too? Come, I'll show you where my most expensive flask is."

"No, sir. I didn't know that was one of your best cigars. I'm so sorry. I'm going to go now. Clearly, I haven't been the best person for this job."

What had I been thinking? I couldn't have botched this up any worse, and who was I kidding? I couldn't deal with that ghost in the pale blue dress and bent knees either. I was unequivocally, undeniably unqualified.

"I can't believe this," Dr. Rivera laughed. That was an improvement. At least he had a sense of humor, assuming it was a real laugh and not one of those mad-scientist maniacal ones that comes right before a person loses their shit on you. "Do you know why I went to your store, Quey*lín*?"

"Because you needed help."

"Because I needed someone *reliable*, someone intelligent. Someone who had studied religions and the metaphysical relationships between them. Real religion, not esoteric pseudo *mierda*. For Santería, I would've gone to Calle Ocho or Hialeah."

Damn. Don't hold back, old man.

"So, I'm guessing you don't believe it works?"

"It's voodoo," he snapped, shaking the cigar for emphasis. "I thought you were finer than that. I never imagined a store owner from Coconut Grove would smoke a cigar and wash my floors with Rompe Saraguey. *Qué verguenza*." He shook his head of perfect white hair disappointedly.

"And yet, you know what Rompe Saraguey is," I said, my voice full of tone. You know the one. The one that made patriarchs arch their eyebrows at you.

I shouldn't have. Not now, not after I'd stolen his best cigar and lit it to do what he considered to be an uneducated country bumpkin's religion.

"Of course, I do. Anybody who has studied does."

"Okay, then," I said, out of breath. So far, this day had taken a lot out of me. "I'm sorry I took your cigar. And I'm sorry I tried to help you without getting the full scope of your religious views first. My mistake."

I headed back to the hallway to get my things. I didn't need this shit. I'd only tried to help the man and sure, make a few bucks, too. Oh, yes, and gain myself some paranormal experience. Well, I definitely got that.

"Quey*lín*," he said softly.

I paused to look at him.

"I'm sorry. I didn't mean to offend you. I don't have anything against Santería, if that's what you believe. I just…I don't believe. I thought you'd be working with God."

"Why not call an exorcist, Dr. Rivera? If God is what you believe in, and the Devil is what you fear?"

He didn't answer.

We stood looking at each other. I'd disappointed him, but to be fair, he never asked exactly how I'd be performing my task, and besides, Santería wasn't the only form of spellcraft I used today. I'd also talked to the Universe, called upon the elements, and spoke directly with the spirits.

If my shop, if my own beliefs were anything, they were eclectic.

"There's no cellar," he simply said. "I told you that already. You can go anywhere in the house. Use whatever method you think is best. I apologize. Just, please…stay away from here."

He brushed past me, clearing his throat.

I headed toward the foot of the stairs to grab the bucket and my things. Even though he seemed fine with me staying, I wasn't sure I wanted to anymore. Yes, the money would be nice, but I didn't need shame stamped onto my forehead. I didn't need to upset this man with my methods either, and I sure as hell didn't need the old-fashioned guilt.

At the door to the dining room, he looked at me again. "Careful what you look for, *niña.* You just might find it."

By the bay, I sat on the cement dock, knees drawn to my chest. I was still shaking, even an hour later. If I smoked, this would the moment I'd light a cigarette to calm my nerves. Maybe take a hit of weed. But I'd never indulged in either, so all I could do was meditate.

I focused on the water, on the sparkling surface of the beautiful blue ocean. On the warm breezes and the swaying palm trees. As peaceful as these grounds were, I couldn't escape everything that had just happened inside that house.

For thirty years, I'd managed to never see a single ghost, and now in one day, I'd seen several moving shadows, a photo frame fall off a shelf by itself, and two full-bodied apparitions, both of them ghastly as hell.

It was confirmed—the Harding Estate was haunted. Also of notable assessment? I was ineffective as a medium.

I sighed.

I closed my eyes, breathing in and out, doing my best to calm my nerves. "Spirit guides, tell me what I should do," I spoke quietly into the air.

I'd never actually seen my spirit guides, so why did I continue to talk to them? Why couldn't I do the same with God before I'd decided to explore other spiritual options?

"Do I leave or stay until I've finished?" I asked the silence.

I still had the upstairs to clean and then I'd hoped to do a final spell on the whole house from the outside, but what would be the point? Other than getting paid?

So many questions burned at me. Like, where had that ethereal music come from? Had it been real or from another realm? Who was the woman in the pale blue dress? Why had she been missing a chunk of skin? Was she really talking to me or someone else?

Explanations flowed through my mind like binary code on a computer screen, not a single one helpful for getting the job done. Maybe the female ghost had been hit by a car and died nearby. Maybe she'd died in a boating accident off the shore. Maybe she'd died in the house.

Who knew? It wasn't important for me to figure out who the ghosts were. Doing so could take forever, and Dr. and Mrs. Rivera only wanted them gone. I understood why Bibi left this morning.

It was too much for anyone.

I pulled my phone from my bag to check in with her and noticed several missed calls and texts from Samuel and Maggie, both asking if I was okay.

I replied to Sam first, telling him that yes, while everything was okay, I was rattled at the moment, though dealing with it. At that moment, a call came in from the store.

"Hello." My voice sounded distant and haggard.

"Queylin, it's Maggie. How are you, hon? How's it going?"

"Not that well."

"Why, what's going on?"

"I'll tell you about it when I leave, but basically, I have a lot to learn."

"It was too much for you then?"

"You could say that. How's Bibi? She didn't look too good when she left here. She seemed eager to get back to *Goddess Moon*."

"What do you mean? Bibi hasn't come in. I thought she was with you."

I sat up straight. "She's not. She left early and said she'd be at the store by noon." Alarm bells went off in my head, as I tried to remember everything Bibi had told me this morning, though she hadn't spoken much. I was fairly certain she said she'd be going back to work, though.

I needed to contact her right away. "Hey, let me call you back."

"Yep. Let me know if you find her."

"I will."

"And Queylin?"

"Yup."

"Be careful, hon. I don't know why, but I'm getting past life vibes from inside the house. I don't think you were ever Julia Harding in the past, but you're very connected to her for some reason. I just read that she killed herself."

"I got that impression, too."

"Okay. So if you feel at all like you're in danger, get out. Got it?"

"I will. Thanks, Maggie." I hung up and immediately called Bibi, but the call went to voicemail. I texted her instead.

Hey, you OK?

The text was delivered, but no reply. A million scenarios blew through my mind, not a single one being rational. Maybe she'd been in a car crash. Maybe she'd fallen ill and headed straight for the doctor. Maybe she took the long way and wandered into another creepy house at the behest of her former babysitter turned employer.

I couldn't contain my worry, though I knew it was irrational. Finally, after a minute of staring at my phone and listening to seagulls soothe my mind, the bubbles of imminent reply showed up on the screen.

I'm OK, she said. Felt sick. Went home to rest.

Didn't know. Maggie was waiting for you, I replied.

Sorry. I should've called her. Headache. Bye.

I sent her a Bitmoji of myself doing yoga, hoping to cheer her up, but no stickers came back.

Still, it was a huge load off my mind knowing she was fine, though I'd hoped to tell her what happened to me then ask her for advice. But Bibi wanted nothing more to do with this house, so it wouldn't be right to bother her anymore.

I was about to call Maggie and ask what she thought I should do—stay or go—when I thought I saw something. Someone standing far away directly in front of the back patio. I had to squint to make sure I wasn't seeing things.

Long period dress. Hair pinned into a loose chignon at the top of her head, hands cradled around her belly. Watching me.

Wearing *white.*

The more I stared at the female figure, the more I realized she wasn't looking at me at all, but watching the horizon, waiting nervously, full of anguish, for someone to arrive. I followed her line of sight toward the water, as though I could see what she stared at.

A boat.

Yes, she was waiting for someone to arrive.

Then I got that odd thought again. The one where I felt like the love of my life would never return. It wasn't a fear about my own husband, I now realized. It was about another man. A man Julia waited for, day in, day out. It wasn't my own thought at all, but belonging to the woman I was staring at.

If I closed my eyes and focused hard enough, I could almost hear the man's name, the man on her mind. But one thing was for sure—it wasn't her husband. It wasn't the same man who'd put her in this house and forgotten about her. It was the man she'd hoped would steal her away.

A man who would never come.

The man she'd hung herself out by that tree for, knowing it was the only way she'd ever be reunited with him. The father of her unborn child.

TWELVE

I wiped my eyes.

How did I know all that? Where was this information coming from? Yes, I'd always felt connected to that tree in the garden, but being near it was doing something to me. I wasn't sure how to react. I only knew that Dr. Rivera was right—I should be careful what I looked for, I just might find it.

Walking up the broken flagstones toward the house, I stared at the banyan. The roots dropping from the branches made it look as though the tree were melting. Memories of Julia hanging from the tree still freaked me out. She'd used one of the hanging roots as rope. It'd been so easy—too easy—to tie one into a noose and…

I shook off the vision.

Heading up the path to the spot where I'd seen Julia a moment ago, I was determined to try and do good. To communicate. She had appeared to me for a reason, and I'd finally seen a spirit. I had to try and help. When I reached the gravel walkway a few feet in front of the back patio, however, I stopped and tried to find her. I searched the grounds.

I waited, taking in the silence.

The unsettling silence.

She did not materialize again.

"Julia, I'm sorry for whatever happened to you," I said, my whispers carrying on the ocean breeze. Birds' chirping and bugs' buzzing filled in the stillness. "I saw you waiting for a loved one. Whoever he was, he must've been special."

No voices, no words.

Only the rustling of palm fronds.

"But you should probably leave now. You'll be happier if you do. He's not here. In fact, I'm willing to bet he's waiting for you on the other side."

My body tensed, as I braced for another attack, just in case she didn't like what I had to say and wanted to run me over again. My arms crossed over my breasts which still felt sore when I stopped to think about it. After a few minutes of trying to feel her energy, I gave up and went inside.

I had to finish what I started, get my check, and say goodbye to Dr. Rivera. This whole experience had been…eye-opening, to say the least. Grabbing the bucket and my bag, I headed for the stairs, determined to complete the *limpieza* when the bucket fell from my hands.

Or rather, was *knocked* from my hands.

It toppled over and the water spilled all over the veranda.

"Shit."

I didn't have more of the enchanted herb solution, so I'd have to finish with nothing but intention. A good witch could make anything happen, even without "ingredients." The items were only there to guide your thoughts toward your intention.

Reaching the top of the stairs, I asked for guidance, love and light from the universe, and then I filled the halls with the sweet scent of burned white sage while asking for protection. The protection part was especially important after what I'd seen in the hallway leading to the site of the former cellar.

Dr. Rivera might've insisted that no cellar existed, but I wasn't so sure. It was there, and though that hallway had led to a sealed wall, I knew I'd heard music playing on the other side. The pale dress ghost guarding the sealed wall knew it, too.

As I mopped the floors with what little was left of the special herb blend and read aloud the African incantation, I focused on the woman in the pale blue dress. She had asked for help, wanted to know why no one would assist her, and I would do my best to address her specifically.

"Universe, please help Julia, the woman from my dream last night, and the woman in the downstairs hallway," I said, calling them to the forefront of my memory. "Please help them find peace from this realm. Please help them find closure."

And then I realized.

They were probably here for that reason—because they hadn't found closure to their pain. No amount of inexperienced Santería, prayer, or pleading on my part would change that, or they would've left already. Anything I was hoping to accomplish was for simple hauntings, for ghosts who couldn't find their way. But this house required aggressive action, forcing them to leave.

I mopped the guest bedroom with the mop which was getting dry now, keeping an eye out for the woman holding the jewelry. I also mopped a mostly empty room containing a large display case filled with bath towels and linens, and two other bedrooms containing dated furniture, simple shelves, and no artwork. As I finished up in the hallway, though, I caught a scent.

Something cooking.

It could've been soup, chicken, stew, or any number of dishes, but I couldn't pinpoint exactly which. Then again, if Lovely did most of the cooking in this house, I wasn't familiar with many Haitian meals to recognize which. I had to say, though, it wasn't a very appetizing scent.

In fact, it countered every pleasant scent I had mopped onto the floors, undoing the positive energy I was working so hard to lay down.

As I entered the guest bedroom to change out of my sweaty clothes, I heard a soft sound coming down the hallway. Terrified of seeing the woman in the blue dress again, or the woman from my dream, I returned to the hall cautiously, focusing on the floor in case an apparition awaited me. Slowly, I looked up. Nobody was there. I timidly checked the opposite end and didn't see anyone there either. But I still heard the sound.

Crying.

Someone was sniffling again, quietly sobbing in private. A woman's cries. It could've been Lovely or Barbara Rivera, but if it was Lovely, then someone else had to be cooking. Only I realized then that I couldn't smell the food anymore. Either I'd gotten used to it quickly or the scent had dissipated.

Or…

The smell had never been here to begin with. Not today anyway. A phantom smell from another time.

Sneaking quietly, I followed the sound of crying to the end of the hall, to the room with the closed door. I'd avoided this room earlier figuring it was the master bedroom. Though it probably needed a good clearing more than any other space in the house, I hadn't wanted to intrude on anyone's privacy. Now, I noticed the door was slightly ajar.

The crying grew louder, as I got closer.

It was definitely coming from inside.

The hairs on my arms stood on end.

"Hello?" I called softly.

At the door, I leaned my ear. Someone was definitely inside the room sobbing their heart out. I shouldn't have been eavesdropping. I should've respected their space and walked away, except I needed to know if they were okay. Given the fact that the women in this house had not uttered a word in my presence, I needed to know if they were in need of help.

"Please, are you okay? I want to help."

The crying stopped.

Ever so slightly, I pushed the door open an inch at a time, analyzing each item that came into view in order of appearance—an ornate dresser, a wicker laundry basket in the corner, more gorgeous art of nude women, the edge of the bed draped by a white macramé coverlet. When I caught sight of metal and rubber, I stopped.

Mrs. Rivera's wheelchair.

Here was this woman who hadn't spoken a word to me since I'd arrived, who the doctor had insisted had degenerated, yet she cried as though her pain were fresh. I felt so incredibly sad for her and wanted to offer sympathy, if I could.

"Mrs. Rivera?" I took one step into the room, just far enough so I could look past the wall leading into the master bedroom, so she could see me as well.

Her chair was parked in front of a large floor-to-ceiling window covered in gauzy white curtains. The sunlight filtered through them, casting soft shadows throughout the elegant room. The old woman stared outside, gripping her armrests like she always did. Her large yellow sunhat belied the lack of energy she displayed.

"I'm sorry for interrupting," I said quietly. "I just wanted to make sure you were okay. I heard you crying."

I stood there a minute, hoping for a response. Now that she was alone, maybe she'd feel safe enough to open up to me, tell me more about what was going on. So far, I'd gotten her husband's point of view, but I was sure there was more to hers, if only she would speak to me.

But Mrs. Rivera wouldn't acknowledge me. I'd caught her in a private moment, and now I felt ashamed.

"I'm sorry, I'll go—"

From the other side of the wall, a shadowy silhouette came at me, placing itself between my view of Mrs. Rivera and the sunlit curtains, creating a dark shape, scaring the shit out of me in the process. My heart nearly stopped until I realized it was Lovely, the housekeeper, ushering me out of the room with aggressive haste.

Her hands waved me away, her eyes pleaded with terror for me to leave. As if she feared what might happen if the old man of the house were to find out I had stepped into this room or attempted to speak to his wife outside of his presence. As though my being here had triggered a momentary lapse in security.

"I'm sorry." I backed out of the room, as Lovely pushed me out. Her fingers jabbed at me to go, go, go. "I was only checking on Mrs. Rivera. Is she alright?"

But catching sight of Lovely's face in the brightness of the hallway made me wonder if I'd been wrong about so many things. Her eyes were tinged with redness, two glistening patches of skin underneath them. I wish I could say her tear-filled eyes were the most prominent thing about her face in full daylight, but they weren't.

Her mouth was.

Seeing Lovely up-close for the first time, I was able to notice that her lips wouldn't part. They seemed almost fused together, as though the line that divided most lips wasn't even there. It was probably a trick of the light, but considering I'd never heard her speak either, something inside me crushed the air out of my lungs.

"Was that you?" I asked, stepping back, my eyes riveted on her mouth. "Was that you crying? Do you need help? Should I bring the police here?" I whispered the last words. This was my one chance to help her if I could. Soon, I'd be gone and back to my world.

Why I felt like she needed assistance was beyond me, but I was grasping at straws, trying to guess what her heart needed but her lips couldn't tell me.

Lovely's dark eyes widened with dread.

No, she seemed to say. Whatever you do, please don't do that.

Suddenly, she opened a hallway closet filled with knickknacks and boxes and pulled something out of the corner. It was long and tall, a dark pole, like those African rain sticks my elementary school music teachers used to pass around and let us play with, only longer.

Her face took on a determined expression just then, so deep, I thought maybe she was going to hit me with the stick, but she grabbed it with both hands, and with fierce determination, struck the wooden floor.

I couldn't help but notice that she actually marked the old wood, and I didn't know how Dr. Rivera would feel about that, but if this was my house, I would've scolded her for marking the floor.

Apparently, she didn't care and struck the floor again. And again.

All the while, her eyes grew wilder and focused on me. Her breathing intensified through her nose, as her nostrils flared, a result of not being able to open her mouth. But this didn't impede her from humming, and she droned out a tune, something like an old folk song, something that sounded vaguely familiar.

Last night.

I'd heard it last night as I was trying to fall asleep with Bibi.

Lovely struck the floor again, closed her eyes, and raised her free hand to the ceiling. Her sandaled feet shuffled in tune to her song, and I felt caught up in a dream. I watched with fascination as one hand clutched the handrail.

It wasn't strange to see a Haitian woman engaged in what seemed to be a ritualistic dance of some kind. Many people in my city hailed from Caribbean islands, from cultures derived from slavery, from West African nations before that. Their religions morphed into Santería in Cuba and Puerto Rico and *Vodou* in Haiti. Plus, I got the sense that, having seen me mop the floors earlier while smoking a cigar, Lovely felt comfortable showing me that she, too, followed a secret religion.

None of that was strange.

What was strange was the mist that appeared in the middle of the bedroom opposite the master. A gray haze that took form into the shape of a man. The particles swirled and coalesced, as my legs weakened, and my knees touched the floor, and I couldn't believe what I was seeing, because only two days ago, I hadn't had this ability.

All I could do was watch in awe.

The well-built, dark-skinned man stood in the middle of the room before my eyes, and I knew that Lovely had summoned *un muerto*—a dead person, a spirit—and something told me, from the way he stood comfortably, to the sun-faded pants he wore, to the amber stains on his shirt and the yellowed captain's hat, that this was someone who had appeared in this bedroom quite often.

His hands reached out, implored me. His mouth opened. He spoke, but I couldn't hear him. It was as if we lived on different radio frequencies, but I felt his desperation, knew he wanted me to give someone a message. That he loved her. That he'd been on his way back before he'd been intercepted, shot at sea.

Tell her, please.

Tell her Roger is waiting.

THIRTEEN

Julia's man.

The lover she cried over while wandering the grounds of her stately home, the man she waited for by the ocean. The father of her unborn child.

Roger.

No wonder Julia Harding had hung herself. Not only was she pregnant by a man not her husband based on the visions I'd had, but they'd been a biracial couple in the 20s in a country rife with racism.

Roger appeared as a gray mist that gave off a cold energy, freezing my body from the outside in, until my core was shaking. One second, his outline and features were clear—tall, muscular, handsome. The next, he swirled with the mist and appeared as a cloud. It felt like a dream, and I knew I would question what I'd seen later on.

"I'll tell her," I muttered, as my midsection ached with soreness. I winced and wrapped my cold arms full of goose bumps around myself. "You can go. You're free."

Just leave, I told him without words.

But I wasn't sure Roger could hear me, even though I could "hear" him, though no words were spoken aloud. I heard his message as a "knowing." I didn't like a feeling I got from his presence, though, as if he hadn't gone peacefully from this world. As if he'd been tortured or drowned.

Roger wasn't one of the resident ghosts at the Harding Estate, though. If he were, Lovely wouldn't have had to summon him with her *muerto* stick. His spirit had traveled through time and space to get here. His was a soul that had moved on without regrets, called back to Earth as an ancestor. His message had been for Julia to join him.

The cramps that interrupted the visit just then felt so real, so corporeal, I couldn't tell if they were mine or Julia's. My face lowered to the floor, touching the mopped, wooden floorboards to ease the pain. I couldn't see Roger from this position anymore, yet I knew he had gone. A veil of energy lifted off the hallway, just as an obscure tunnel closed in around my vision.

Make it stop, make it stop…

I closed my eyes and was gone.

I'd been hit by a bus.

Attacked by linebackers.

Squished in a human panini press.

That was how I felt—ample soreness, dull aches, and sharp pains all over my body. My collarbone and breasts hurt more than they had yesterday after Julia's ghost had slammed into me. Opening my eyes a little at a time, I saw I was lying in bed, but couldn't tell what time of day it was.

Or where I was.

Someone touched my arm, waking me from a prolonged alpha state. I saw the housekeeper, or nurse, medicine woman, or whoever Lovely really was, setting down a glass of water on the nightstand. She gave me a worried glance and felt my forehead for fever. I was grateful for the attention and thought of my mother somewhere in the city, assuming her daughter was fine. Little did she know what I was up to.

I blinked and tried to smile at Lovely, but then I saw through her body, laid over her body, connected to her same aura was the woman who'd haunted this room last night. A clear overlay of the dead on top of the living.

God, no.

Too many ghosts.

I'd heard of people who suddenly became psychic after traumatic events, such as the death of a loved one, or a car accident. But I'd never heard of anyone becoming psychic after getting hit by an angry spirit, though. Or from spending time in a haunted home. I'd spent plenty of time at haunted hotels in my life, hoping to catch a glimpse of the supernatural, but nothing like this had ever happened.

It made sense, though.

But it might've been a dream.

Dreams and reality blended at Harding Estate.

When I opened my eyes, the mystery woman was still there, only now she'd moved out of Lovely and sat in the corner of the room, dirty knees drawn to her chest, nervously chewing on her fingertips. Lovely had gone from the room, and now it was just me and this woman.

I sat up to make sure the vision was real and not a lucid dream.

Aside from being a ghost, there was nothing terrifying about the woman. Not like the lady in the pale blue dress with her screams and bleeding wounds. No, this lady projected sadness. She desperately wanted to say something but couldn't. As if she'd long forgotten what she felt sorrow for.

When I blinked, she was gone from the corner. Then something shuffled above me. I looked up and saw she had moved. Now, she sat, cross-legged, upside-down on the ceiling staring down at me like Charlotte dangling from her web. I didn't care if she was harmless, I'd reached my ghostly vision quota for the day and bolted from the room.

Barefoot and confused, the smell of cooked meat returned to my consciousness. Burning flesh. Now, the scents coming from downstairs were infinitely better, provoking my empty stomach. Herbs, and vegetables, and foods meant for consumption. I glanced nervously into the guest room again to see if she was still watching me.

Empty.

Heading downstairs, I followed the light sounds of silverware to the dining room where Dr. Rivera was seated alone, drinking soup with a glass of wine.

"Ah, there she is." He said this using a grand gesture with his hand and another charming smile to welcome me.

I wasn't having his formalities anymore. More than charm, I needed to know what was going on. "What happened?"

"You fainted."

"How do you know I fainted?" I asked. "You weren't there."

"Lovely told me."

"Lovely doesn't speak," I said.

The doctor sighed and set down his spoon to rest against the inside of the bowl. "She came to find me, Quey*lín*. She speaks, just not with words. We lifted and carried you to the bed. *¿Te sientes mejor?* You slept quite a bit. Here, sit, so you can eat."

I had, in fact, slept quite a bit. In fact, the sun was low in the sky, judging from the darkness in the house.

As much as I wanted to decline the meal or any other courtesies the good doctor might've extended, I was starving for something to eat. Dehydrated, too. Apparently, all this sudden psychic ability had made my throat parched.

I sat on the edge of a dining chair without committing to full posture, poured myself a glass of water from a glass decanter, and chugged the whole thing down in one, long chug.

"God, I feel so sick," I mumbled.

"Yes, you don't look too well. Maybe you have *fiebre*."

He might've been right—I did feel feverish.

"Where's Mrs. Rivera?" I asked, looking in the usual places—the windows, the veranda outside. "Haven't seen her around much."

"She wasn't feeling well either."

"Why is that?"

"What do you mean?"

"Why doesn't she talk? Your wife. Or move?"

I know I sounded curt, but I wasn't in the most polite of moods, especially after the way he'd spoken to me earlier after I'd discovered the ramp leading down into the non-cellar.

Dr. Rivera studied me a moment before resuming his soup. "I told you, she suffers from many mental disorders. But I'm glad you bring this up, Quey*lín*. Since you are so curious about my wife, about the *cellar* that doesn't exist anymore, and other things on the property, I thought I might tell you a few facts about the things that walk here at night."

"Not just at night," I added. "They're everywhere. At all times of the day."

"So you have seen them."

"I have."

"Did you ask them to leave with your *brujería*?" He chuckled.

"I did."

I watched as he took two more spoonfuls of soup then wiped his mouth with a cloth napkin and set it down across his lap again.

"I'm sure you've seen Julia. She's the one who haunts the outside of the house, the one most psychics see. Though my wife has seen her inside the house from time to time, always confused and searching for someone."

Probably her lover, I thought.

"Yes, I've seen her." Julia Harding's ghost seemed to have a one-track mind, being reunited with Roger and little else. Then again, it was my understanding that most earthbound ghosts were obsessed with something, else they'd move on.

"Well, she died in 1921 near the beginning of Prohibition, and it's believed she was pregnant when she passed."

"She was," I blurted. "At least that's the impression I've gotten from her."

He stared at me, and a slow smile unfurled on his face. "Yes, that makes sense."

"What does?" I raised an eyebrow.

"Psychics over the years have all reported an angry woman in white, *La Dama de Blanco*, as you already know. But for a while, they didn't know she was pregnant. It was interesting how they figured it out."

"How?"

The king looked around at his castle. "This house has an unfortunate history with pregnancy. Any child born here dies shortly after. Other pregnancies have ended as stillborn or miscarriages. It seems Julia is curious of pregnant women. Envious, too. A couple of the mediums over the years were expecting, and she gave them the hardest of times. That's why no family has occupied this home for very long."

"You're saying she cursed the house from ever having kids live in it?"

"Well, I don't know if I believe in curses," he said. "But I do in coincidences. And the screams we hear in the night, I believe those are screams of childbirth from another time. Of loss and pain. I believe ghosts are past traumas, energies imprinted in a home."

And I believed ghosts were the souls of people who endured those traumas. Either way, the atmosphere in these spots was tainted.

Like the horrible cramps and soreness I'd had all day, especially after I fainted. If I was picking up Julia's emotions, it made sense that I was also picking up her physical sensations as well. Ghosts, energies, imprints. All residue of past lives.

"That's horrible," I said. "This house has a sad, negative energy about it. I never noticed it as a teen when I trespassed here. Then again, I never came inside. But now…"

"Now it's different."

"Why?" I asked.

"You are different than when you were a teen, Quey*lín*. Didn't you have experiences last night and today? I do recall you running up the ramp terrified."

"Well, yes. But what about you? You don't consider yourself psychic, yet you called me here because you claim to hear ghosts at night."

"My wife hears and sees them," he clarified. "I don't see them."

"Not even a little? You don't feel them?"

"No. I am doing this for her. Why does she hear them and not me?" he asked.

I searched my mind for an explanation. "Everyone has different sensitivities. When your brain is at rest, like when you're sleeping, you're more likely to tune into that frequency than you are during the day. Which is why many people report seeing ghosts in the middle of the night."

"Or, they could be dreaming." He smiled facetiously. "The brain is powerful, Quey*lín*."

If he wasn't sure that ghosts prowled his house at night, then why had he invited me here? You wouldn't expect the person who hired the medium to be the skeptic. There was more to my being here.

But I wouldn't argue anymore. People like Dr. Rivera, living as recluses, craved conversation. He was engaging me in a discussion just to have someone to talk to. I knew ghosts were real and not a manifestation of our own imaginations or overactive brains. Granted, they *could* be hallucinations, but not always. Why would my mind conjure up four different spirits all in the same day inside the same reputably haunted house?

"There's something else I should tell you," Dr. Rivera said, reaching for his glass of wine. He took another sip then set it down again. "My wife lost our child fifteen years ago. When we first moved into this house."

"Oh, I'm sorry." I hadn't expected this to be his confession. Now I understood the connection, why he thought there might be a curse.

I imagined Mrs. Rivera in her catatonic state, reliving her loss fifteen years ago. I could see how losing something so meaningful could ruin your mental wellbeing for life, how it could age you significantly, too. But wasn't Dr. Rivera too old to be a new father? Suddenly, I thought of the photo in the living room, the one that had been knocked down during the cleansing. I'd thought the woman had been his daughter.

Was Mrs. Rivera a much younger wife?

He picked up his napkin to dab his eyes. "She went into early labor at twenty-six weeks. The fetus was too weak to survive. Help did not arrive on time. The baby died here. In this house."

"Oh."

"I'm sure now you're thinking this place is beyond help," he laughed, taking another sip of his wine. He wiped his lips and folded his hands in his lap, thick fingers interlaced. "That's what the other mediums believed. But I tell you all this, to be fair."

"To be fair?"

"Yes. I didn't know this when I invited you here, but…well…you're pregnant, too."

FOURTEEN

"I'm sorry…what?"

I stared at the old man. Why would he say something like that? How would even *know* unless he was psychic himself?

"Well, you are, aren't you?"

"Are you asking me, or telling me? I don't know. I…" I stammered. I mean, I hadn't really thought about it. Samuel and I weren't exactly being careful, but we weren't actively planning a child either.

"*Ay, Diós.*" He pinched the bridge of his nose. "I didn't mean to upset you. I thought you knew. I was only letting you know that I knew."

"But how would you know if I don't?" I stood, pressed a shaking hand to my forehead.

"That's true. It appears you're still early." His gaze slipped to my mid-section.

Instinctively, I crossed my arms over my belly. "How do you know this? I mean, why do you think this?" I stammered.

There was always the possibility that Dr. Rivera was utterly shitting me for some reason. The power of suggestion, like many magicians used. A mental trick to get people to divulge information themselves. It hadn't occurred to me until now but maybe he was mentally ill himself.

All I knew was that I had the sudden urge to go find out. To leave this house and drive to the nearest CVS and buy a pregnancy kit. Was he psychic all this time and just fucking with me?

"The angel statue," he said, all of a sudden.

"What about it?"

"The lantern glows bright whenever a pregnant woman is near." He seemed proud of himself when he said this, like he was imparting Harding Estate trivia during a ghost tour. "You were standing next to it last night, remember? When Barbara and I went outside to meet you, you had just been touched by Julia, you said."

"Attacked is more like it."

"Okay, attacked. *Lo que sea*. Anyway, *ten cuidado* is all I'm saying. Be careful with Julia. If she knows you're pregnant, you may suffer."

I sat up straight and pushed my silverware from me in final gesture. "I don't need to be careful with her anymore, Dr. Rivera, because I'm done in this house. I'm going home. The only reason I'm sitting with you now is because I fainted and woke up starving, or else I would've left already. Don't take that personally, but I've done all I can. It's time for me to go."

And pee on a stick—STAT.

He nodded. "*Sí,* I understand. Do you prefer cash, or is a check okay?"

"Cash if you have it," I replied.

Was I really pregnant? A million thoughts swirled through my mind—of telling Samuel, of telling my parents, all my friends, of wanting to move to a new house, make a proper start for the baby. It would make sense after how I'd been feeling since yesterday—the soreness, the boobs hurting, the nausea. It would also make sense that I'd connect with Julia Harding's spirit if she'd been pregnant after all.

Maybe the ghosts, like Dr. Rivera, had been trying to warn me. What did the pale blue dress lady say, among other things? *Especially in your condition?*

While Dr. Rivera left the room to go fetch my payment, I snuck into the ballroom, exited through the service door, and went outside for fresh air after a stifling thirty minutes in the dining room. I had to see the angel statue for myself, see if the doctor had been right and wasn't just a batty old dude pulling my leg.

Though it was getting dark, I strode into the garden and found the angel statue looking as melancholy as I had last seen it. Staring at the angel's face, I waited to see if the light would come on.

"Well?" I asked after a minute of nothing happening. Maybe I'd just been lied to. Maybe it had been the power of suggestion after all, to make me spill a truth. But why would he care if I was pregnant or not?

The nightly ocean air felt warm though cooler than yesterday, and my whole body chilled. I hugged myself in the breeze. "Julia, are you here? Am I really pregnant?"

I couldn't believe I was talking to a tombstone angel statue to find out what should've and could've easily been verified via Science at the nearest convenience store. This was absurd, and I had to go. But suddenly, something dropped from the roof and landed by my foot.

A pebble.

I picked it up. Just an ordinary tiny stone falling off the roof. Loose debris getting blown by the breeze. I glanced up anyway and nearly lost my breath when I spotted the silhouette of Mrs. Rivera staring out her bedroom window, as still as a statue herself, backlit by a soft glow.

In the darkened window of the room next to her, a curtain fluttered slightly, like an air conditioner or fan blowing the drapes, except it stopped after a moment. At this point, I had to question my exhaustion and fragile state of mind. Wasn't that what Bibi had said? That I could become vulnerable here?

Still, I couldn't remember where that room with the billowing curtain was in the house. My mind went over the upstairs floor plan and all the rooms I had cleaned while doing the *despojo*. I didn't remember seeing that room with the curtain nor could I even figure out how to access it from the upstairs hallway. This would require another look inside the house.

Turning back to the angel, I half-expected Julia to be standing there or see her hanging from a tree or any of the other horrible sights I'd seen today. But the garden stood empty, tall grasses swaying in the draft.

"Julia," I said. Somehow, I had to make peace with this spirit. If I really was pregnant, I hate to go home with a vengeful ghost following me. "I'm sorry for everything that happened to you. I'm sorry if you really were pregnant when you passed. But here's something that might make you feel better—I have a message. From Roger."

I waited. For a split second, I thought I noticed the angel blink at me.

"He says he's waiting for you on the other side. He wants you to leave this plane and go be with him, Julia. He loves you. We all do. You'll feel better if you go. You don't need to suffer anymore."

It occurred to me then, having grown up Catholic and hearing about the souls of those who'd committed suicide, that maybe she couldn't move on. Maybe she was stuck here, condemned to all eternity because she'd taken her life. Banned from the Kingdom of Heaven.

"I don't think it's true, Julia," I said. "You're allowed on the other side. You can join Roger in the Light."

And then, it happened again.

The dim light of the angel's lantern grew brighter and brighter, too bright for such an old lamp, until I had to shield my eyes. A light this bright could probably be seen from sea. After a few moments, it died down.

Julia could hear me.

I wouldn't stick around to test if the lantern-pregnant theory was right by asking a bunch of questions. My visit was getting creepier by the second. As per my habit whenever I was nervous, I plucked at my lucky Buddhist bracelet on my wrist and realized it had gotten even tighter overnight. Water retention much?

I headed back to the house.

Dr. Rivera was waiting for me in the living room. "Are you sure you want to leave? My wife, she has a beautiful private collection of art she created to mourn the loss of our baby."

"I'm sure it's gorgeous, but I really do have to go. My husband will want me home soon."

"Oh? He's back from his trip?"

It unnerved me how much he knew what he shouldn't have known, but that was my own damn fault for talking too much.

"Yes, and he'll be very upset if I'm not home soon." I tried appealing to his machismo sensibilities—the little woman getting in trouble with her husband if she wasn't home soon. Surely, this was one item on which we could agree.

"Ah, *bueno*." He threw up his hands in defeat, as though he'd tried his best. I felt sorry for him. He might've just wanted company.

I went upstairs into the gaudy jewelry bedroom and collected my things, shoving them into my bags haphazardly—the bottles of herb blends, candles, hairbrushes, dirty shirt…

I could fix it all when I got home. The thought of going back to the apartment and sleeping there all alone made me equally as nervous as staying in this creepy house. Samuel wouldn't be home for another two days. At least here, I wasn't alone.

Rushing downstairs before any more ghosts could manifest for my attention, I found Dr. Rivera waiting for me in the living room. He cocked his head and held out his hand for a handshake.

"Miss Quey*lín*, it was a pleasure to meet you. I'm sorry you won't be seeing my wife's private collection. She doesn't show it to too many people and was hoping to get your reaction." I wondered how he knew what his wife wanted and was thinking when the poor woman couldn't even speak or move.

The brain is a powerful thing indeed, Dr. Rivera.

The doctor handed me cash. Considerably more than he'd offered. A thousand, to be exact.

"This is unexpected," I said.

"I've given you a hard time, *niña*."

Out of the corner of my eye, I saw Lovely lingering by a wall near the staircase. She wrung her hands, watching me interact with Dr. Rivera. I gave her a little smile as if to say it was nice meeting her, and thank you so much for introducing me to the dead man upstairs.

"Thank you." I held up the bills. "Are you sure this is the right amount?"

"Yes. I know I'm a cranky old man and you didn't deserve my interrogations or for me to *regañarte*."

To punish me or give me a hard time. No, I didn't deserve it, especially when I was doing him the favor.

"Especially when you were the only person out of seven who I went to who would come out," he added.

"I'm sorry?"

"I asked seven people. Psychics, ghost hunters…whatever you want to call them. They don't like coming out here. Surely you knew this house had a reputation."

"For being haunted, yes, I did. But lots of people love exploring haunted houses."

"Not this one. Not in the fifteen years I've lived here."

So the psychics who'd visited had all come before Dr. Rivera's occupancy?

Something in the doctor's smile chilled my skin and made me feel like I'd walked right into a trap. Like the last two days had been nothing but an illusion of me thinking I was free to move around when really I was a rat in a large cage. I shook it off. If that was true, he wouldn't be saying goodbye to me now, paying me for my time.

Walking to the front driveway felt liberating.

I threw my things into the car, slipped in, and pushed the key into the ignition. I should've have been surprised when my car wouldn't start. *No, come on. Come on, you piece of crap.* I smacked the bottom of the steering wheel gently while Dr. Rivera watched from the doorway. Like all good Cuban folks, they waited while you drove away and only disappeared into the house once you drove out of sight.

Dr. Rivera lingered. Now I would have to suffer the humiliation of my car not starting while he looked on.

"Everything okay?" He stepped over to the car. "Want me to take a look? I used to be pretty good at fixing my own. Here, step out and I'll see."

I hated the thought of needing this man to get inside my personal space to solve my problem and wondered why I never took that basic "car trouble" course my college offered back when I took classes.

"Thanks, it's weird. I just bought this car." Granted, it was two years old, but still. Why did it have to fail tonight of all nights?

"Yes, but that's what cars and most technology does best. Test our patience." He slipped behind the wheel and tried starting it. Then, he popped the hood, scrambled out, and stood in front of my car, staring into it.

As he worked the problem, I hugged myself in the chilly night and wondered what to do in case my car wouldn't start. I'd have to call a Lyft to come get me or see if Bibi or Maggie could come pick me up. I couldn't tell my family, because that would require having to explain my crazy mission.

Standing there wishing this night would end, I caught a glimpse of something in the driveway. Shiny and embedded between the brick pavers. I walked over to it and squatted. A long piece of cut quartz without its chain.

Glancing at Dr. Rivera to make sure he was too busy to notice me, I picked it up and turned my back to him to examine the stone in the light. It was a familiar stone, Bibi's quartz, the one she always kept on a chain around her neck. I searched for the chain and found it near the spot where the quartz had been.

A piece of the chain anyway.

Why would there be a *half* a chain and not a whole one? If my necklace were to fall off, I'd think it'd break in one spot, causing the thing to slip off my neck. It wouldn't be broken into multiple pieces.

There'd been a struggle.

"*Hija*, I think it's your battery but it could also be your alternator. Do you want to wait inside while I go find some jumper cables?" Dr. Rivera took out a handkerchief from his *guayabera* pocket and wiped his hands and forehead.

My heartbeat kicked into high gear.

I didn't like finding Bibi's charm on the ground where she'd probably stood waiting for her ride, and I didn't like that she hadn't shown up at work, and a little while ago, a pebble had fallen from above, from a window. A curtain had moved from an unknown room.

I didn't like that either.

But I didn't want to clue the doctor in on the trepidation and fear I was feeling either, so I smiled, which might've been a dead giveaway considering I hadn't smiled all day.

"Sure, I'll wait inside."

"*Bien*. Give me a minute. I'll go find the cables."

I faked heading in, while he disappeared around the other end of the house between the south porch and a free-standing shed or separate garage.

The cables. Was he really going to go find the cables? Or something to hit me over the head with? I should leave, but if Bibi was here, I had to find her. I couldn't leave her alone. Shit—I had to stay.

And that upstairs room was my first priority.

When an old Cadillac drove up, and the doctor stepped out toting actual cables, my chest released a sigh of relief. He wasn't going to kill me. Not now anyway. I felt a surge of guilt that I'd thought of him in a negative light, but I couldn't be too careful. Not until I located Bibi.

The doctor opened his hood and connected the cables between his battery and mine and smiled at as if to say, see? I'm being cavalier and helping.

Maybe I was overreacting. It'd been a long two days, and if I really was pregnant, then the hormones plus exhaustion wasn't doing me any favors.

I glanced at the upstairs windows of the house. From here, I couldn't see the two rooms I'd watched from the garden. What if Bibi was up there right now, unable to speak, lips fused together, trying to get my attention? I texted her right there on my phone and waited for a reply.

Nothing came.

When the doctor couldn't get my car started, I wasn't at all surprised.

"You know," I said, carefully exploring all my options, of which there weren't many. "I think it'd be fine if I stayed another night. Your wife's art collection does seem like something I'd find interesting, after all, and tomorrow I could call someone to come get me. Would that be okay?"

My ulterior motive wasn't to sleep over again. Not in a million years. It was to buy time. Get upstairs. Wait until everyone was asleep, then search the house for Bibi. Leave unnoticed after that, regardless of whether or not I found her.

"Sure, no problem." Dr. Rivera smacked his hands together to shake off the dirt. "But won't your husband think it's strange? I mean, since he's back home from his trip and everything?"

The doctor smiled.

FIFTEEN

"He'll be fine with it." My fake smile belied my hesitation. "He's asleep with jet lag anyway." As if there was much jet lag between Chicago and Miami. My lie was completely see-through, I knew that, but I pretended to be absorbed by my phone screen, just so our eyes wouldn't meet.

"Jet lag, eh. Well, as long as you're both okay with it." Dr. Rivera shrugged, closing up the hoods of both cars and handing me back my keys. When his hand lingered in mine, I looked up at him. He stared amusedly into my eyes. "I'll have Lovely prepare your bed again."

"Great, thanks." I tried to ignore the feeling of dread creeping up my back, like I was about to enter a burning building without a smoke shield.

The old man ambled into the house first, while I waited a beat out on the driveway to see if I could find anything else of Bibi's. More signs of struggle, more fallen objects from her purse, anything.

"You coming?" he asked.

"Yep." I casually followed him like nothing was wrong, stepped into the house, my eyes roving the living room, the wall connected to the staircase. If God forbid, Dr. Rivera really had abducted Bibi, he probably wouldn't have taken her through the front door where I'd been performing the spiritual cleansing. He would've dragged her around the side, put her in that outside garage, maybe driven her somewhere else.

But I visually examined everything I could while making my way to the stairs. *Please, universe, let clues jump out at me, if there are any.* Seeing nothing special about the gorgeous interior of Dr. Rivera's old tropical home, I headed to the stairs. Once I felt it was safe and nobody's prying eyes were on me, I'd try and find the room I'd missed while cleaning, the one I'd seen from the garden.

I couldn't get over how surreal it was that I even had to do this. My life had shifted from white to gray in the course of one day. I headed upstairs, locked myself in the bathroom to catch my breath, and saw my own reflection.

I looked tired. Was that woman looking back at me really pregnant? I'd always wanted to be a mother. Samuel and I had talked about it many times, but I never wanted to find out from a creepy, old man who argued religion and the supernatural with me.

Sitting on the toilet lid in the privacy of the bathroom, I did the first thing that came to mind, and not what one would think while sitting on the toilet. I called Bibi. Her phone went to voicemail, which wasn't at all strange. She was twenty-one and preferred texts like everyone else of her generation, except she didn't answer them this time.

I took a photo of her quartz crystal and was about to send it to her, asking if she was missing it when it occurred to me not to give details away. She would *know* if she was missing it.

Hey, hon. I know you left in a hurry, but did you lose anything important? I texted.

And waited. No reply. In fact, my last text went from blue to green, indicating she'd either turned off her phone, or it'd gone dead.

Before unnecessarily alarming Bibi's family, I tried something else—I held the crystal in my hand and closed my eyes, clearing my mind of as much distraction as I could, given the situation. If I had even a fraction of Rain's talents, I might be able to see what happened to Bibi the moment she lost her necklace in my mind. But I wasn't that talented, and I must've tapped out any new abilities over the last two days, because I couldn't pick up a single thing.

All I could see was Bibi lying unconscious in a room, but I knew that was fear, not reality. My fears *always* hijacked my brain. Fear of not having enough money, fear of losing my husband, fear of alienating my family through my new beliefs.

Fear—always the freaking fear.

Outside the bathroom, feet shuffled inside the guest bedroom. I could see quiet shadows moving underneath the door. Lovely was probably preparing the bed for me. Even though it wasn't necessary, having another human nearby was comforting. I waited until the footsteps left my room before calling Samuel.

I needed to hear his voice at this moment more than anything. "There's my gorgeous girl. Been busy, huh? I've been sending you pics all day about the conference and nothing."

"Babe, the weirdest things have been going on." My voice sounded tired and shaky. If I were him, I'd be concerned about me right about now.

"What is it? Tell me." His voice shifted from jovial to worried.

"You know how I'm always wondering when or if I'll ever see a ghost like half the people I know?"

"You saw one," he guessed.

"I've seen like four, babe. *Four.* Not only that, but I was finally leaving this house tonight when I came across Bibi's charm lying in the driveway."

"The pendant she wears?"

"Yes, the one she *never* takes off. The one she'd go on a worldwide crystal-hunt for if she were ever to lose it. Why hasn't she come back for it, or called me to find it for her, or text to ask if I've seen it? This thing means everything to her."

"Maybe she hasn't noticed it's gone?"

"Babe."

"I don't know, Quey. Maybe she's too scared of that house to go back? Why, what do you think?"

Sucking in a deep breath, I glanced up at the ceiling and pinched the bridge of my nose. "I don't know. I might be overthinking this, but what if she never left the house?"

"What are you saying?"

"Sam, she hasn't returned my calls, only texted back once when she first left. Said she had a headache. That was before her phone died, but what if it wasn't her sending those texts? What if…ugh."

"Say it."

"What if someone has taken her phone?"

I couldn't believe I was actually suggesting this. It sounded absurd but entirely plausible all at once.

"Queylin, you need to leave that house now."

"I can't. I need to see if she's here."

"Leave the house and call the police. Do it, now."

"Babe, listen…"

I'd unnerved him—understandably. I couldn't make him come home from the most important convention of the year, one that might possibly advance his career, all because I was a little nervous.

"It's fine. I'm going to take a cursory look around the house once everyone's asleep. Hopefully, it's nothing, and this is a case of 'better-safe-than-sorry.' But if I see anything suspicious, I *promise* I'll call the cops and get the hell out of here."

"*Run* the hell out, Quey. Don't wait for anything, not even a cab. Shit, I knew I shouldn't have let you go alone. I had a bad feeling about it, and I didn't tell you."

"Yeah, you only told everyone at the store."

Pause. Silence.

"I only did that because I was concerned."

"Because you didn't trust me, you mean."

"Are you serious right now? So, you're seriously mad at me, because I worried for my wife?"

I couldn't get into a fight with him now of all times. But that was exactly why he'd contacted the employees at the store—because he'd thought I needed backup. He'd thought I couldn't handle it.

"Look, I'm telling you I'm fine. I just want peace of mind that Bibi's okay, not locked up in a room somewhere, hoping someone will find her. Trust me."

Unless that's too hard for you…

"I do trust you. Whatever you need, call me. I can step out of any presentation. I can get on the next plane home."

A knock came at the bathroom door. I stared at it.

"You heard me?" Sam asked.

I covered my mouth over the microphone. "Yes. I'll call you back in a few. Somebody's knocking on the bathroom."

"I'd rather stay on the line until you know who it is."

"Yes?" I called out. "Someone's in here."

No reply.

If it was Lovely, which it probably was, letting me know there was a fresh towel for me or a glass of water at my bedside, she wouldn't be able to talk. Having Sam on the phone helped calm me, as I made my way to the door and slowly popped it open.

Nobody there.

If it had, in fact, been Lovely, then she probably took off after I took too long to answer. Either that, or the guest bedroom ghost was back.

"I gotta go," I told Samuel. "I'll keep in touch."

"Babe?"

"Yeah?"

"Be careful. Use your instincts. They've worked for you in the past. You don't need superpowers. You're smart already. You know what to do."

I smiled. "Thank you."

"I love you."

"Love you more."

Hanging up, I sighed and waited in the bathroom for a minute. Then, I strode into the room, mentally preparing to see the ghosts I'd come to expect. They were a part of this space, I'd learned, so I should never at any point assume I was alone.

Taking out my charger, I plugged in my phone by the nightstand, so it wouldn't die like Bibi's had. So I could call the police in a matter of seconds if I had to.

I lay down on the bed and stared up at the ceiling, scared of seeing the woman hanging upside-down like a spider, but even she couldn't hurt me. That was the thing with these ghosts—they could freak you out, they could startle the hell out of you, but they couldn't really do anything to you except mess with your mind.

The ghosts were merely distractions. It was real, live people I should fear.

At 8:30 PM, it was still too early for the house's residents to be asleep. I didn't know where Dr. Rivera and his wife had gone, but Lovely was downstairs making noises. Opening and closing drawers, clinking silverware, and shuffling her feet around.

I passed the time by devising a plan and texting Samuel emojis and a question. *Hey, I forgot to ask you, do you remember the first day of my last period?*

Not really. Why?

Just curious.

I didn't want to bring up the possibility of being pregnant over the phone, but I couldn't remember the first day of my last cycle. I usually got my period on the first day of the New Moon, but the last couple of months, my period had been out of whack.

Pinching the quartz between my fingers, I stared at the crystal and thought about what I would do if I were to actually find Bibi trapped in a room. Obviously, I hoped she wouldn't be, but what if?

I closed my eyes and imagined a white light of love and peace surrounding the house, filling each room, and especially covering Mrs. Rivera and Lovely. Hell, I threw one around Dr. Rivera, too, just in case my instincts were operating on overdrive, and he was nothing but a quirky old man with nothing to hide.

Couldn't hurt to envision good energy.

But I couldn't shake the feeling that there wasn't. Too many strange things about this house didn't add up. Like, who was the rosy-cheeked young woman in the photo with Dr. Rivera? Was he really that much older than his wife? Not that it was impossible. Young women married older men all the time, but…she couldn't have been old enough to leave Cuba as part of the Pedro Pan Operation of the 1960s, if that were her.

I was lying there, nearly falling asleep, the downstairs noises finally quiet, overwhelmed with the hellacious day when I heard it. From far away, at first, like from a dream.

Then closer. In the house.

Wake up, Queylin.

My eyes popped open at the sound. First, a baby crying. Then—a bloodcurdling scream.

SIXTEEN

Stepping into stillness and darkness of the upstairs hall, I stood at the top of the stairs, assessing where the sound had come from. It could've been downstairs, or a bedroom, or the ether itself. The house was quiet now. I must've fallen asleep.

All the bedroom doors were closed. I narrowed my eyes to see if there was another I might have missed when performing the cleansing, but from where I stood, there wasn't.

Five bedrooms in total upstairs.

Maybe a room existed *behind* the master? A connected sitting room, or office, or other space accessible only through that bedroom perhaps?

I waited for another scream, met only with silence. Unsettling silence. What did they do at night that the house sounded heavily unoccupied of human noises? Regular non-kitchen sounds, like coughing, or the TV, or toilets flushing, or God forbid, actual conversation?

But there couldn't be, I reminded myself. Because Dr. Rivera lived practically by himself with two women who couldn't speak. If I lived in muteness like that every day, I couldn't imagine how alone I'd feel. After a while, I'd start talking to inanimate objects like Tom Hanks to the volleyball, Wilson, in *Castaway*.

From somewhere in the distance, I heard the crying again, the one I'd detected in the master bedroom when I'd seen Mrs. Rivera staring out the window earlier, when Lovely scared me away. God, that felt like an entire week ago instead of half a day.

But that was the thing about the Harding Estate—reality, dreams, and dread all blended together. It was hard to tell where one started or the other began.

The crying came again, deeper, as though coming from the entrails of the home. It drove me insane with need to find out. I had to locate where it was coming from, knowing fully well I might not ever find out. As Bibi said, I might just have to accept that. Some ghosts would never be ready to move on.

I descended the stairs slowly, my eyes adjusting to the darkness as I went. A few candles were lit, flickering on their sconces, wax drippings collecting in bulky tails. *I know I heard a scream. It wasn't a dream.*

Determined to be fully awake, I was pretty sure that had been an actual scream. Dr. Rivera only wanted me to think otherwise. He loved messing with my mind. He'd wanted me to think these hallucinations were creations of my own brain, entities of my own madness. There was no doubt that was a possibility, but I had to follow my instincts.

Samuel told me they were good instincts.

And I believed there was darkness hidden in these walls.

Another cry emerged from the stillness, this one of a woman and more of despair, of subdued hopelessness, than physical pain. A helpless sobbing. My every nerve burned like individual fuses ready to detonate. I followed the sounds through the hallway, the servants' kitchen, and paused.

I closed my eyes for better calibration. The ballroom—the crying seemed to be coming from that direction. I stepped out of the kitchen, through the dining room, glad I had forgotten to put on my sandals. This way, I could silently wade across the wooden floors like a ghost in my own right.

I stopped at a china cabinet aglow on the inside with a soft nightlight. For a moment, it almost seemed like the crying was coming from behind it. Checking the wall behind the cabinet, I saw an electrical outlet and some dust bunnies but nothing out of the ordinary.

The crying stopped.

"Hello?" I whispered.

And waited.

No reply.

I was getting used to this house of no replies, no verbal ones anyway, but the home itself spoke volumes. I threw my hands into the action, letting my fingers slide across the cabinet and along the smooth, waxed dining table. I was always a tactile child who loved to touch everything, even got into trouble for it multiple times for accidentally breaking things my mother had been working on.

For years, I learned to keep my hands behind my back as my mother had asked, to stay out of trouble. But maybe that had been a suppressed natural instinct. I needed to touch things to hear them. I moved into the ballroom and touched the walls there.

A slight vibration coursed through me.

Energy.

No music played, no people danced, no servers roamed around offering hors-d'oeuvres, yet I could almost see them. See the parties, the hosts and hostesses over the years, the feathers, the dresses and tuxes, the delighted guests. I could almost feel the envy, the passions, the secrets of every person in the room, and yet the room was nearly empty, except for those stacked chairs and round, naked tables leaning against a wall.

And an armoire across the room.

A great big armoire that probably contained silverware, party platters, and tablecloths in every color. Or it could've been completely empty. I stepped across the beautiful parquet floors, imagining dresses, a slow waltz, gentlemen bowing, women laughing, drinks spilling. All the while, my eyes were riveted on the armoire.

The armoire.

It was a gorgeous, old, secretive piece, ignored, but intricately carved—loved at one time. I wanted to touch it, feel what it had to say, see if I could validate these odd impressions once and for all. All my life I'd had lucid dreams, instincts, only to find I'd been wrong or simply imagining things.

Had I been right—had I been right, just a few times, I might've cultivated my psychic abilities earlier. But I'd always been wrong. Which led to envy, jealousy, resentment for those who had them. For people like my own staff. In many ways, I hated them—hated my own employees. Women who were friends.

Fear. Fear of the unknown was the source of all problems.

Yet my friends, my witches, my *coven*, if you will, had accepted me, even though they knew I wasn't one of them. Not 100%. Yet they were supportive of my learning, of this spiritual journey on which I'd embarked three years ago. I had to get at least one impression right—if only for them. I didn't want to disappoint them.

Touch the armoire, Queylin.

From the corner of my eye, I saw a shape. A humanoid figure. My vision snapped right to it. Best to directly confront the ghosts.

But no one was there. I resumed my slow walk to the armoire and stopped right in front of it, staring at it. It was larger than it seemed from across the room, a heavy, vintage piece of carpentry.

Did you see him?

Did you really see him?

I turned slowly. Someone was talking to me, not with a real voice. I didn't hear the words in my mind either. More of a whisper from somewhere inside my soul. I felt like I was in a waking dream.

Who? I asked.

Roger.

Julia was here with me.

"Yes, I did," I spoke aloud, my own voice sounding odd and echo-y in the emptiness of the ballroom. "He said he'd wait for you. You should go to him."

Maybe I could fulfill my purpose here after all and help these spirits find their rightful place in the cosmos. I used to think that haunting a home was romantic, gothic, even glamorous. I used to think how, when I'd die, I'd haunt a beautiful house such as this myself, but now I knew better. This poor woman was a prisoner.

A prisoner of her own fear.

"He's waiting for you," I told her.

She contemplated it. I couldn't see her or hear her anymore, but somehow I knew, she was contemplating leaving this existence, this plane that had given her nothing but a century of solitude.

They are barren, she said.

"Who?" I asked the emptiness. "Who's barren?"

For a moment, I questioned my own sanity. Here I was standing inside an empty ballroom at the infamous Harding Estate of Miami, talking to the air around midnight, using words I rarely ever used, like "barren," and hearing voices and cries.

I didn't know how long I stood there, but it might've been an hour. I listened with more than my ears, trying to gauge what it all meant. Was she gone? She seemed gone. Maybe Julia had moved on after all.

But then, her voice returned.

All of them.

Because of me.

And then, the armoire doors yawned open by themselves. Slowly creaked open, exposing a gaping, dark interior, no shelves, a few things on the bottom covered in dust. My heart beat fervently in my own ears. I heard the swooshing of my own blood through icy veins, as the armoire called to me.

As in many of my dreams, I was paralyzed.

But why? I'd sought this room out, this armoire. I'd made a conscious, waking decision to come here, to solve a problem, to experience firsthand what I'd always imagined I could never. Coming here had been my choice, and now that a ghostly armoire had opened its doors to me all by itself, now I was going to freeze?

No.

This paralysis, this fear of *success*, would not control me. Yes, Dr. Rivera, the mind was a powerful thing, so powerful, in fact, that we could do whatever the hell we wanted in this life, but first we had to get past the enormous obstacle of our own damned selves.

I could do this.

I took slow steps toward the armoire. The cavernous interior was hard to see, but there were platters, serving dishes, a row of dusty champagne flutes, and a stack of cloth napkins. When I blinked, the napkins were stained—in red. Bright drops of red on ivory satin, spreading through the fibers. Inside a silver serving dish, something moved.

I got closer and held my breath.

Barren.

Who?

All of them.

Because of me.

Inside the tray, something moved. Something covered in dark red, something congealed in fleshy lining and blood, something with tiny limbs giving into their last impulses, pumping and gasping and trying to survive, wrapped in its own umbilical cord.

I drew a breath and covered my mouth, suppressing a scream. My stomach writhed in a tight knot, as I sucked in deep breaths of stagnant air, fighting down the warm saliva pooling in my mouth. But then, the pain, the anguish of having lost this child, of having built my dreams around him, all came crashing inside my chest, and I dropped to my knees.

But I'd never had a child.

I'd never built dreams.

These thoughts did not belong to me.

But these women had. All of them—the ones who'd lived in this house. I had to snap out of it. Julia and the ghosts of this house, and

Dr. Rivera himself, were all messing with me. I was stronger than this. I couldn't let one vision bring me down.

Gripping the armoire, I hoisted myself up to standing and faced the silver tray again, the baby taking its last breaths. There was nothing there. Just folded napkins and platters and fondue forks and dust. Lots of dust over it all. This armoire contained the expired dreams of countless women.

And at the very back was the oddest thing I had ever seen. Connected to the back wall, sticking out like a spout of the same dark brown color as the wooden armoire was a knob with a handle turned vertically. I reached out and touched it.

Vibrant energy sizzled through my fingertips.

Yes.

Wrapping my fingers around it, I turned the knob, and when I did, I felt the whole of the large piece of furniture lunge, squeal under its own weight, and let out a massive sigh. Hissing on hinges I couldn't see, it moved toward me, swiveling outward, the house's own doorway into another world. Slowly, it swung out, hovering over the floor, and I hadn't noticed that its feet never actually touched the ground.

And then there was a tunnel.

Dimly lit and long, tall enough to walk through but one would have to crouch to navigate it. Interior walls were paved with brick, and the air whooshing out the tunnel felt cold, but it was the music, the music emanating from the bowels of the house, that drew me in.

Music from another time and era.

Un son cubano playing on a Victrola.

SEVENTEEN

Two choices presented themselves—turn back and pretend I never saw this, or walk through the tunnel. If I turned back the way I came, I would never find out who was crying or why, might discover on the news that Bibi had gone missing then regret abandoning her for the rest of my life.

I could also proceed but find myself trapped, same way she might've been. There really wasn't a choice. I could never desert someone who needed my help. Holding my breath, I proceeded carefully, slowly. If I saw something potentially dangerous, I could always turn back, try a different method of helping, run back to my room to call the police.

I would've called by now, but I didn't have evidence, and I couldn't exactly tell the officer I'd been having "gut feelings" all day. One broken necklace wasn't exactly evidence. Finding out what was at the end of the tunnel would at least let me know what action to take.

Lowering my head, I took slow steps and followed the sound of the music. The air grew cooler as I went, and the warm light at the opposite end grew brighter. Enough to light my path and keep me from feeling like I was entering a dungeon.

This tunnel or vent, or secret passageway, or whatever it was, looked like it'd been here a long time. Probably built with the house, possibly to hide the cellar from law enforcement during the rum-running days. It wasn't common for Florida homes to have basements or cellars. Our grounds consisted of water-logged limestone, but some old homes had them for that exact reason—bootlegging.

A soft breeze cooed through the tunnel. I stopped several times to listen. I didn't want to simply appear at the exit and find myself face-to-face with disaster. I prepared several excuses in my head just in case Dr. Rivera should discover me here.

I was sleepwalking.

I heard a noise.

Wanted to make sure everyone was okay.

The ghosts told me to find this room.

None of them sounded convincing enough, and I knew, if caught, I'd anger the man of the house.

A few feet from the end of the tunnel, which must've run about twenty feet at a slope, I stopped, inching forward, wishing I could send my eyeballs ahead of me to peer into the room first. When I reached the end, I listened. For human noises, throat-clearing, footsteps, anything, though it was hard to pick up subtle sounds over the music. I was scared of what I might find but pushed through the fear.

I reached a sort of metal sliding door, closed over the tunnel exit, but not locked and with cut-out holes to let in light. This allowed me to see into the room from behind the relative safety of an ajar door. The room was well-lit—an art studio, from the looks of it, which relaxed my fears considerably. Even through limited visibility, I could see dozens of paintings set to dry all over the room, a few more up on easels in various states of completion, art lamps, and dozens upon dozens of cubbies along the walls.

I waited a long time before moving, and it occurred to me that I'd left the bedroom a couple of hours ago. I must've been moving through the tunnel at the careful rate of five minutes per inch. I couldn't mess this up. If I was going to trespass in private rooms, I was going to do it right.

When I did finally move, it was to slowly slide the metal door to one side, wide enough to creep through. I pushed my head inside and checked the room from one side all the way to another. The room was U-shaped, the center part being what seemed to be a dark, defunct fireplace. Fireplaces were about as useful in Miami as basements and cellars, but the first millionaires to move here from Chicago and New York City didn't know that at first, so the historic homes all had them. Also, a hundred years ago, the average air temperatures here were way cooler.

In the corner of the room was the old record player with the fluted bugle, just like I'd pictured it in my mind. I couldn't imagine

Dr. Rivera playing music like that off a digital device and was happy to see the real vintage deal. But I hadn't come for the Victrola; I'd come because I'd heard someone crying, but one glance around the room showed it was empty.

The lingering smell of cigar smoke told me that Dr. Rivera did use this room, however, and could be back at any given moment. I had to explore quickly. Another smell permeated the space, but this one was harder to pinpoint. Something chemical. A cleaning product of some kind. Could've been turpentine for the paints.

The paintings were all of naked women. Beautiful women. Young women but also mature ones. All in various states of undress. Some younger ones folded their arms over pregnant bellies, some lounged on chaises like Rose in *Titanic*. All of them were elegant and tasteful and looked like something that should've hung in a museum gallery.

Barbara Rivera was a talented woman, no doubt. It was sad to see her so disengaged. I was glad to know she at least had art to keep her going. But why were these works so hidden? Why not keep her studio out in the open where I'd imagine it'd be easier to wheel her in and out? He couldn't navigate the wheelchair through that tunnel. There had to be another entrance.

On the far wall was the current work in progress, a large painting about eight feet tall, four feet wide, big enough to hang on a great room wall of a mansion such as this one. A main showpiece. The woman on the canvas was stunning, with lanky arms and legs, long brown hair, and the face of a porcelain doll. I felt like I'd seen her before. A movie star from days past.

She stood with her knee up and resting on a bed's edge, a pose which covered her most womanly areas. The model was nude like the others, both arms cradling a pregnant belly, but the belly itself was not finished yet. Not the belly, nor the legs, nor the lower right quadrant of the work.

The subject's eyes gazed into mine, as if expressing how incredibly happy she was waiting for this child, and I wondered if creating scenes like this helped Barbara deal with her loss. As I crept closer, I realized it wasn't really a painting at all, more of a bas relief carving or something involving sheets of crepe paper layered over each other to create a sense of depth and texture. Whatever it was—it was exceptionally beautiful. On a table facing it were the layers themselves laid out for the next part of the process, and scattered all around were tools—scissors both large and small, a sharp poking tool, a blunt one like a hammer.

I heard a whooshing, like wind traveling through cracks in the walls, or through the cubbies themselves. Upon closer inspection, the cubbies were actually the deep slots used for wine bottles in a cellar. Well, well, well. So, this was the room that didn't exist? The one filled and sealed after Hurricane Andrew.

Sure, I could see that, Dr. Rivera.

What was so secretive about it? It was an amazing room, probably the most interesting of the house, and this collection was simply stunning, as he'd said it was. Maybe he'd felt bad about barking at me earlier which was why he'd offered to show it to me, but then he would've had to admit that he'd been lying about the cellar being closed.

Many of the wine cubbies contained what looked like rolled-up sheets of paper scrolls. I cautiously stepped over and pulled one out, unrolled it, and stared into a sad pair of eyes. One after another. More beautiful faces, these captured in charcoal. Each sketch of a gorgeous face was covered by a sheet of wax paper to protect from charcoal smudging. But each also had a paper clip attached to the top right corner. I turned the sketch around to see what the clip was holding—a cutting of natural hair.

One after another, the rolled-up sketches all held wisps of dark hair, blond hair, auburn hair, straight hair, shocks of curls clipped to the back. Did his wife really keep mementos of the hair of each model she drew? Why would she do that?

I shuddered and put the scrolls back, rubbing my arms in the chilly room. My goal wasn't to check out her weird art anyway, in the studio built into the room that supposedly didn't exist—it was to find Bibi. I searched each corner, looked inside the cubbies—for what, I wasn't sure. I even checked the fireplace, which reeked of remains of charred wood.

Something glittered from underneath one piece of wood. I reached in and pulled it out. A necklace—a basic thin gold chain with a cross hanging from it. I dropped it right where it was and stepped away, trying to come up with any number of reasons why something like that would be there in the fireplace. Next to the dark opening was a short stack of wood.

I almost didn't hear the sound that came next because of the music that was playing loudly, and by the time I saw the front end of the wheelchair and pair of legs being pushed into the room from behind the current painting, I ran back to the tunnel, climbed inside, and slid the door over me.

My heart pounded. I prayed that nobody had seen me. Through the small slits of the metal door, I watched as Dr. Rivera wheeled his wife in and placed her in front of her painting. He spoke to her in Spanish but so quietly and lovingly, it was hard to hear, especially with the Victrola playing near me. But he kissed the top of her head, turned to admire her work so far, and spoke to her at length about what she was creating.

Maybe now I'd finally hear her speak.

As I watched with my a ball in my throat, I realized what had been strange while glancing around the art studio at first. I hadn't seen any paint. Even now, glimpsing through my limited field of vision, I saw none of the usual paint tubes, bottles of turpentine, paint thinner, or trappings one might expect to find in an art studio. A canister contained paint brushes in various sizes, but aside from that, all that was being used for this piece of work were the layers of crepe paper.

But when Dr. Rivera lifted one up and held it up to the belly of the subject in the painting, I could see how thick it really was. Not crepe paper at all. In fact, the woman was made up of patches of flesh-colored bits of leather. I was having a hard time reconciling what that might be, when Dr. Rivera's hand stopped caressing his wife's hair.

He tilted his head at her, said something about her appearance, something quiet that my brain imagined might be, *Your hair is crooked today, amor.*

He proceeded to yank off her hair right off the top of her head. A wig. The old woman wore a wig, and he was fixing it for her. No wonder her hair had seemed too shiny to be real for a woman her age. No wonder she wore hats every time I saw her.

Dr. Rivera proceeded to put the wig on the table, lift one of his sharp tools, then begin scratching the top of Mrs. Rivera's skull with it, like one might scrape off stickiness, like extra adhesive or caulking. What the hell was he doing? And why did the back of this poor woman's head have the biggest scar I'd ever seen in my life?

EIGHTEEN

When you witness something you thought was true completely unravel and expose itself as a lie, you don't know how to react at first. What to think or feel.

No, was my first thought.

Denial. Denial that anyone would do something like this. That anyone would fake their wife. The more I watched the doctor fix the dummy's scalp, apply more glue to her head, then affix her hair back on, the more incredulous I felt. Also, the more attached to this hiding spot. Because the next thing you feel is fear that the same might happen to you, and right now, this hiding spot was my saving grace.

I could not let the old man find me here. From what I could tell, he'd created a doll. A doll, of all things, and told people it was his wife. How long had he lived this lie? Had he put her together just for me because I'd shown apprehension at coming here alone? Somehow, I doubted it. He treated her with such loving care, I had to think he'd had this wife replacement for quite some time.

Did this mean that Barbara Rivera never existed in the first place? Was she an imaginary wife he created? But, who then, was the woman in the photo with him?

Either way, I had to get out of here, use this opportunity that he was in the studio-cellar to run through the house looking for Bibi. How had he gotten in? Another door must've existed on the other side if he'd managed to wheel Barbara in here. This house was full of secrets, twists, and turns. I could stay here for weeks and not discover them all, I was willing to bet.

In horror, I watched Dr. Rivera kiss his creation on the cheek, pick up a paintbrush, pull open a drawer, and dab a palette of colors—eye shadow, blushes, and other types of makeup, like foundation and mascara—onto her face. I wished I could get a good look at her from my vantage point, to put two and two together and see for myself that it'd never been real to begin with, to prove to myself that it had always been an illusion, but her back still faced me.

He touched up Mrs. Rivera—or the doll of her—and stood back to assess his masterpiece.

Satisfied, he put the brush back in its container but then noticed something about her dress that he didn't like. He reached behind her, and, leaning her forward so her face mashed up against his stomach, unzipped the back of the dress. He pulled it off her slender arms with some degree of difficulty, and tossed it aside. The doll wore a bra from what I could tell, and I tried to get a good look at her skin. Where her spine was, I spotted a massive scar from base of neck to base of spine where it disappeared into a pair of underwear.

I couldn't see anymore.

Just that enormous scar running vertically along the back of her body like a wicked set of railroad tracks. A doll wouldn't have that. What the hell was she made of?

As she sat there nearly naked, I bristled at the thought of what he might do next. When I saw him heading my way and whistling, I lay down under the exposed slots in the metal door and prayed to the Universe that he not discover me. I shook so hard, I thought he would hear me trembling inside the tunnel.

Please, God, Universe, please…

The music stopped, and I heard the puttering noises of someone taking a record off and flipping it over. After he changed the record, and a scratchy sound began, he opened a door that creaked and closed it again. His footsteps disappeared to the opposite end of the art studio.

I was safe for the moment.

The music that started this time was a piano concerto, something slow and melancholy. On shaky hands, I raised myself up, my whole body trembling, just so I could place one eye at the bottom corner of the metal door's slot. The doctor was back with Barbara, a freaking doll, dressing her in a new outfit—a black dress. This one also slipped on easily and zipped behind her back.

"We can't have the girl seeing you in the same dress again, can we?" I heard him say in Spanish this time, thanks to the quieter piano selection.

I knew I needed to exit the tunnel and seek what I'd come to find instead of watching this bizarre unfolding of events, but it was hard to tear my gaze away. I was riveted watching Dr. Rivera treat this figure with utmost care, talk to her, love her like she was real. Had he made it himself or ordered it from one of those creepy sex shops, because damn, some of those dolls really did look like the real deal.

But did they make old ladies?

I doubted it.

This one of Barbara, if such a woman ever existed, looked like a middle-aged woman who had aged significantly in a short amount of time. Like a person who had undergone a great amount of stress with lines around the eyes and mouth and all. No wonder he covered her face with hats. No wonder Lovely protected her at all costs, as she'd done earlier when I'd snuck into the master bedroom. She was the doll's bodyguard, to make sure I didn't uncover this weird truth. Or maybe Lovely had been hired to aid him in his delusion.

Did he think she was real?

Was the doctor really a patient himself?

Once Barbara was dressed and the old man seemed satisfied with her appearance, he turned toward the painting and considered it. Picking up one of his tools, he stepped up to the piece and dabbed areas coming off, used a different brush to apply what I guessed was adhesive, and pressed the lifted corner down.

Then, unfolding a stepstool, he stood on the first step and reached up to the subject's face. "She's got Elizabeth Taylor's eyes…" he sang, replacing the words about Bette Davis in a song from long ago.

He laughed to himself, applying a small piece of material to the canvas. Its eyes came to life with a purple hue, just like the famous Hollywood starlet with violet peepers.

It really was beautiful. But all this time, had Dr. Rivera been the artist, not his wife? Had he created *all* the paintings in the house or just this one?

He lifted a larger piece of material from the table and used the scissors to carefully snip off a smaller piece, all while humming to himself. Then, using his other hand, he reached for a bottle of clear liquid, poured some into a metal pan, then dipped the piece of material into it. The liquid had to either be an adhesive or cleaning solution.

Patting it dry on a blotched towel, the doctor resumed his position on the stepstool and added some more violet fabric or leather to the subject's other eye. Little by little, the woman's expression came to life with each added layer of this material. In one particular section of the painting, he tried bringing depth to the woman's hand by creating shadows underneath her fingers. Having a hard time creating the effect he wanted, he went back to the table and fished around a metal bin for a piece that would suit his needs.

When he lifted the bin and carried it to a sink to rinse off the pieces, my eyebrows drew a knot, as I watched the water drain from the edge. Red-tinted water that thickened the more he poured. He rinsed the pieces again and fished around for the right piece. When he picked one up, and I saw the way it flapped around, caught the back of it, the deep redness of the underside, my stomach took a dive.

I threw up onto the tunnel floor.

The material was skin.

In retrospect, I should've seen it was skin, but I never imagined it. Never thought it would be possible for a man I'd been speaking to for two days to be capable of using human skin in art. I didn't know for a fact that it was human skin, but it had to be. The pieces patched together to create the impression of human skin in the painting, so what else would it be?

But the eyes.

If he was using skin, then certain parts of the image, such as the eyes, had to be something else. Unless he painted the skin in the various hues that irises came in. But no, that looked like purple skin, and it all came at me at once, rendering the tunnel too warm to almost breathe in, as my stomach heaved again.

That was Bibi's skin.

Port wine stained skin was dark pink or purplish in color.

Jesus Christ, I had to get out of here. Just then, a door slammed and a bucket flew across the room, hitting the wine bottle cubbies and knocking to the ground. The doctor exclaimed in surprise then covered his head, as another item flew across the room. This time, a few of his metal tools.

Carving tools.

Tools he used on people.

Women.

Bibi.

Where was she? Where was my friend in this house of horrors? Had he killed her, and if he had, had he done it mercifully at least? Or had he simply removed the port wine stain and she was still here, alive somewhere in the house?

The cries.

Another item flew across the room by disembodied hands, and the doctor yelled at whoever was causing it. For a flash, I caught sight of the pale dress lady standing in the corner, angry fists balled, stringy hair hanging over her face. I wanted to join her in throwing things across the art studio. Part of me wanted to bust in and scream, show the doctor that I knew his secret, that he hadn't counted on one thing—my psychic sight.

That's right—*my* psychic sight.

I'd found this room purely because of it. I'd never have thought to look inside the armoire and locate a hidden latch that undid the back of the *mueble* without them. Never would've found this hidden tunnel or this awful room. But was it too late?

Now that I'd figured out the truth behind Dr. Rivera's strangeness, it'd mean nothing if I couldn't find Bibi. Alive or dead, I had to locate her. Just to know.

Spirits, where is she? I thought. Where is my friend, the one who was here with me this morning? Please tell me.

If they could talk to me about other things, perhaps they could tell me where Bibi's body was hiding. The ghost responsible for the poltergeist activity, the one right now plucking all the charcoal sketch scrolls out of the cubbies and making them fly for seconds before landing on the ground, stopped and stared at me.

As the doctor yelled at the ghost to leave him alone, muttered curses in Spanish at me for not being able to get rid of the nuisance spirits he'd hired me to rid, the pale blue dress lady zeroed in on me.

No, don't, I tried telling her. Don't give me away.

But before I could back up in the tunnel or scramble away, she lifted into the ceiling like a Palmetto bug in the corner of the room, drew in for momentum, then flew straight at me. Through the sliding metal door, she flew with her force, hurrying past me in a rush of frigid air that made me flinch inside the tunnel and gasp out loud.

She is in the house, the ghost said

Then disappeared.

Slowly, I turned my eyes to see if the doctor had heard me. And there he stood in the middle of the studio, tool in hand, cigar hanging from his lips, staring at me through the metal door slits with angry impatience.

NINETEEN

"*No te me vayas!*" he screamed, running at the door that provided me with minimal protection. "Don't you leave."

I scrambled the way I'd come, head ducked low, quickly through the passageway despite the awkward posture.

"Quey*lín*!" he shouted.

The way he insisted on saying my name this way said it all. He did things however he damn well pleased, just like he'd insisted on drilling Bibi about her port wine stain. No respect.

My terror magnified, my breath charged and echoed through the tunnel, my gasps loud in my own ears. He was behind me, keeping up, running with his head low. I looked back so many times, I didn't realize when I arrived at the end of the tunnel and found the armoire flush up against the wall.

I punched at it.

Stuck.

The old man was almost at me, and I was ready to turn around and kick him if I had to.

"Why are you running?" he asked, changing his screaming tone. "I'm not mad at you, Quey*lín*. Come here. Let me show you the collection."

Yeah, sure.

"I don't want to see anything of yours." I punched against the armoire that wouldn't budge and furiously scanned the walls for another way out, but I'd reached the end of the line.

I just want out of here.

"But you came in the wrong way. This door is one-way. You have to come out the other side. Come."

He slowed a few feet from where I stood, and for a second, I thought he was actually being nice, and I'd been running for no reason. Then I saw the scalpel or X-ACTO knife in his right hand and remembered he was a crazy mother-effer who used skin to create paintings.

I had to get out of here.

At that moment, I spotted the dangling end of a cord slithering up the wall, held in place with brackets across the ceiling. I yanked on it, and the armoire unlatched with a hiss. With everything in me, I shoved against it to get it to move until it finally swung open with its own weight.

Dr. Rivera reached me and grabbed my sleeve, pulling my arm toward him, but I twisted out of his grasp and stepped out of the tunnel, booking it across the ballroom. He might've been older but he wasn't slow and walked after me using long, aggressive strides that scared me more than if he'd jogged.

I'd reached the dining room by then, opening random drawers in the china cabinets as I went, hoping to find a useful knife.

The doctor appeared in the doorway from the ballroom to the dining room. "I don't understand why you are running. I'm not going to hurt you."

"You mean like you didn't hurt any of those women?"

"Which women?"

Playing dumb.

Buying time.

"The ones in the sketches. With their hair clipped to the back?" I backed out of the dining room, opening the last drawer on the way out and finding a cake server. As stupid as I'd look holding a cake server, it was pointy with a serrated edge and that was better than nothing.

He chuckled low and menacing. "You mean my patients? Barbara used to love sketching them back when she could still draw. She only kept their hair as an example for when it came time to paint. So she could get the hair color just right."

In a charcoal sketch?

I wasn't buying it.

"Your wife?" I asked incredulously. "You mean that *thing* in the cellar that's not a living human? Is she a doll you made?"

Slowly, I backed through the service hallway, between the dining room and kitchen. I had to keep my eye on him, keep up the conversation to buy time while I found a way out. Once the space opened up, and I found myself in the middle of the service kitchen, I spotted Lovely in my peripheral vision. She clung to the cabinets, one hand clutching her chest when she saw the doctor and I engaged in a cat-and-mouse game.

"That is my wife, Barbara, as you already know, Quey*lín*. She cannot fend for herself, so I have to do everything for her. Bathe her, dress her…"

I shook my head. "Are you serious?"

"You don't believe me?"

Did he actually believe Barbara was real?

I couldn't tell what was worse—that he was lying or that he believed his own lie.

There was no way that woman in the cellar was a real human being, yet he insisted on lying to my face. All the more reason not to believe a word he spoke. I had to go without finding Bibi, unfortunately. I regretted having to leave her behind, but it was time to save myself.

"Come. I'll show you," Dr. Rivera insisted. "She is incapacitated and depends on me and Lovely for everything."

Yeah, because she's not real, she can't move, and she has a giant track of staples going up her back.

The moment I made it safely out of the kitchen, I emerged in the living room and made my move. I bolted for the front door, praying it'd be unlocked. I'd be leaving my things behind, including my phone upstairs, but none of that mattered at this point. All I could hear was Samuel in my mind telling me he told me so, asking if I was *sure* I was alright. Because he could come home if I needed him to. He could call the police for me.

No, and no, and no.

I'd turned him down on every point.

My hardheadedness had gotten me here.

When I slammed into the door, the doctor turned the corner, coming quickly out of the kitchen, and sliding toward me with such resolute steps, I fumbled with the lock. It wouldn't open. I heard a series of electronic beeps and a whine and knew he or Lovely was controlling the door through an alarm panel, which made sense, because I turned my vision at that moment to see him touching the wall.

The door was locked.

He was coming right at me.

I stepped backwards over a low potted plant, nearly tripping, then again as my sandal caught on the corner of an area rug. Keeping my eyes on the doctor who wore a peculiar expression, one of amusement and pure annoyance, I navigated through the living room back toward the kitchen in this circle dance that seemed to never end.

Where would I go from here?

I tried my hand at the French doors—locked. I could run back the way I came, make it to the armoire and run into the cellar to find the "other" exit he'd mention, but this man knew his house better than anybody. Chances are he would appear in the cellar faster than I could.

The upstairs. I could escape through a window. I seriously doubted an eighty-year-old man would follow me, and even if he did, assuming we both fell, I'd have a better chance of surviving broken bones than he would.

"I don't know why you are you doing this, Quey*lín*. Let's discuss it. You're frightened, but I can explain. I told you there was no cellar, because my wife is very private about her art studio. She's—"

"There is no wife, Dr. Rivera!" I yelled, inching for the stairs. "What I saw in there was a doll, something you made, or…"

A corpse.

Why the idea hadn't occurred to me before, I wasn't sure, but I was certain it had something to do with positivity, my annoying proclivity to thinking the best of a situation, giving the benefit of the doubt. The same trait that had made me a good person in the real world made me a naïve fool inside the Harding Estate.

I didn't want to say it out loud, because that would only give him the chance to confirm or debate it, and I didn't want to discover that I was stuck in a house with a corpse wife glued to a wheelchair.

What would that mean for me?

I ran upstairs, saw the nameless ghost blocking the door to my guest bedroom, so I hooked a left into the master bedroom, locking the door behind me. Catching my breath, I pressed my ear to the door and heard the doctor giving Lovely orders to lock all exits and windows and make sure something I couldn't hear was guarded.

My hands and body shook so hard, I worried I might not be able to go on. This couldn't have been happening. And God no, I couldn't faint again, so I focused on my breath like I did in yoga class. Deep breaths, just this moment, nothing else. Deep breaths would deliver much-needed oxygen to my muscles and keep my heart rate even. Deep breaths would keep me focused on what I had to do.

Nothing else.

As doors slammed and more electronic beeps checked the status of exits around the house, I backed up slowly, the backs of my legs touching the bed. I turned and saw the window where I'd seen "Mrs. Rivera" sitting, "watching" the outside world. How could he insist his wife was real unless he was truly a sick man? A sick individual, living by himself in this corner of the world with nobody but a terrified, mute housekeeper to look after him. No wonder nobody had been able to learn much about the new owners in years.

Hearing his footsteps slowly coming up the padded stairs, I reached for a large dresser and slid it along the wooden floor it until it blocked the door. Then I ran to the back of the room and prayed there was some other way out. There had to be a back room. I'd seen from the outside. At first glance, there was no way of getting past the master bath area, but searching the doctor's closet full of nothing but men's suits, men's shoes, men's *guayabera* shirts, a door hidden behind the racks presented itself to me.

"Quey*lín*! Quey*lín*, open this door!"

Parting the suits, I checked for a handle. No handle but there was a latch. Removing the latch, I pushed open a stuck door and moved stealthily into a musty room, locked it behind me, and turned on the light switch, as the doctor continued to yell that he wasn't going to hurt me.

I looked around. It was either a private office or a storage room for keeping boxes and files.

"Bibi?" I whispered. "Bibi, you here?"

This was where I'd seen movement in the window when I'd been down in the garden, but there didn't seem to be anyone here. Furthermore, the windows were locked, bolted shut. I checked the only closet, found it to be full of cardboard boxes. There were many of them piled on top of each other, file crates on the floor, also sitting on top of a big wooden desk.

A cockroach, startled by the sudden company, skittered out of a box. I moved the cardboard lid off one of them and spotted lots of old files.

Pulling one out, I read:

Jazmin Echevarría, 2000.

Lillian Inez, 1999.

Hope Weatherford, 1999.

I put the lid back and reached for another box. These files were even older, from 1995 and earlier. With each box I opened, the more

I went back in time, the more bugs would crawl out. Each file had a red tab in the corner. When I flipped open one file to see what the red tab indicated, on the back was a typed label—*no local family.*

Apparently, these had all been patients of Dr. Rivera at some point, before he retired, I guessed, and behind his desk, sitting by itself in a metal file sorter was a purple file folder. Pulling it out, I read Barbara Boudine, a file from 1976. She also had the red tab indicating no local family members, and when I opened the file, I recognized the woman's photo.

Barely recognized, but the resemblance was there. The doll? The framed living room photo?

In this pic, she was smiling and beautiful and fresh and alive, like in the "painting" he'd been working on in the cellar. It was the same woman as in the framed photo downstairs. I could see that now, the one I'd thought maybe was his daughter.

But I knew her from somewhere else.

The file contained all sorts of private information, including the type of medication he'd prescribed, all the symptoms of trauma disorder she'd experienced, and lots of envelopes. Greeting card envelopes. I opened one up, saw two little blue birds of an old greeting card proclaiming his love for her—neat handwriting in blue pen. Letter after letter of hearts and love and affection for this one woman.

Dr. Rivera was in love with his patient.

"But did he marry you, or take you prisoner?" I asked the photo. I brushed her face with my fingertip, feeling sad all of a sudden for whoever she was, as I got the sense that things had not ended well between them.

Both.

I looked up.

Who'd said that? Someone had spoken just now. One of the files sitting on the top fluttered in a breeze, even though the window was locked.

Another file moved, then another, softly lifting then settling down again, as though a rogue gust were moving them.

"Who's here?" I swallowed my fear. I had to face and speak to them. They weren't the ones who could hurt me, and it was about damn time I got over that.

He cared for me.

A woman spoke so softly, I almost couldn't hear her. She was reticent to speak, as if making any noise would cause her to give herself away.

I closed my eyes and did as I always tried to do when meditating—push away all thoughts, negative distraction, and live in the moment. *Just this.* I rolled my eyes up to the space between my brows and hoped that my Anja chakra would kick in.

"Speak to me," I said.

I waited, all the while aware that doctor's footsteps were pacing the hallways with greater urgency, doors opened and closed, and the old man was losing his patience looking for me.

I loved him, because he cared for me.

I had no one.

So I married him.

A woman appeared in front of me, filling the room with a cold so profound, I felt it in my bones. Felt my internal organs shrinking in an effort to stay warm. The windows froze over. Her features were familiar, a face I'd seen all over this house in different ways. Her eyes blazed with a violet inner light.

"I know you," I said. "You're from the bedroom. You came to me and Bibi last night." The young, beautiful woman with the luminous eyes. She was the one who watched me silently, who'd come to me with jewelry in her hands. The one in the "painting" made with skin.

Yes, she said.

"Was that yours? All that jewelry?"

Mine and every woman he's kept.

He keeps their personal items.

Kept? My skin prickled with anxiety.

"Did you really lose a child?" I asked. "He said you were pregnant." I wanted to make sure it was true, that he hadn't killed her instead. Part of me wanted to believe that it couldn't be all bad.

I did. I died giving birth.

And you will, too, if you don't get out.

TWENTY

My hands instinctively touched my midsection, shaking fingers splayed across my belly. I stared at her, trying to make sense of her words. How did she know? How could the ghosts know I was pregnant?

I had no time to ask her about it.

As the doorknob and door to the master bedroom shook with Dr. Rivera's rage, I had only a short time to figure out where to go from here. With the windows locked and no other rooms to enter, from what I could tell, it was a matter of time before he reached me. If not through the hallway door, then somewhere else, as this man must've had secret passageways to every part of the house.

The ghost cowered in the corner, squatting like she did in the guest bedroom. *He's coming*, she said. Did she not realize she was dead and could go anywhere she wanted?

"You don't have to stay here," I told her. "He can't hurt you."

He hurts everyone.

Shivers pricked up my spine. The man outside the master bedroom door really did intend to hurt me. I couldn't believe a word he said. So this had been his wife at some point, not just because he thought her to be. First she'd been his patient, then she'd married him, then she'd passed away while having his baby.

Not his baby.

He took me in.

"You're Barbara?"

Yes.

So Barbara Boudine had gotten pregnant, and the good doctor, in love with her, feeling the need to care for her, had married her out of goodwill. Her child had not been his.

The door rattled again.

Ven conmigo, she said in Spanish, urging me to follow her. She floated straight through the wall into the master closet. I hesitated going back the way I came, but being trapped inside a corner office wasn't helpful either. There was nowhere to hide.

Following a spirit into a closet, your mind starts to doubt itself, and everything about this house made me question my sanity. I was being led by Mrs. Rivera herself—the guest bedroom ghost had been my hostess all along. So who was that woman in the cellar? Was it really a doll?

No.

"No?" I questioned, even though I hadn't spoken aloud. Our minds were as one, same with Julia. I connected. I connected with spirits the way I always wanted to.

I cannot leave, she said.

"Yes, you can, Barbara. You're free!"

Not as long as he keeps me alive.

I understood.

He was keeping her "alive," wheeling her corpse around in a wheelchair, touching up her makeup, pretending she still existed. Barbara had been the patient? Seemed to me that Dr. Rivera needed a mental evaluation more than she did. Anybody capable of embalming a corpse to keep it around as a souvenir, all because he refused to accept the death of a loved one, was apt to do anything to keep his illusions going.

"The painting," I said.

With the flesh of others, she said, he is bringing me back to life. You must jump through.

Suddenly, a square door in the floor of the master closet flew open on hinges, and the ghost jumped into it, feet first, again as though she refused to believe she was dead. As if she possessed a flesh-and-bone body. If only I possessed a fraction of her same ability to float through walls and hang from the ceiling like a spider, I would've left a long time ago.

But ghosts didn't always know when they're dead, and Barbara was earthbound for a reason. A good reason. Someone would have to give her a proper burial and dispose of that flesh painting in order for her to be free, but not before handing it over to authorities for DNA testing.

A lot of women had suffered to bring that painting to life, no pun intended, and I was sad to think that Bibi may have been one of them. Looking down the open hole in the closet, it seemed like a narrow laundry chute. I wasn't sure I would fit the entire way down, but I also didn't have any other alternative.

I jumped.

And fell feet first into a dark room about ten feet below the ceiling, landing on my side. I would be bruised and battered if I survived this, but at least I'd be alive. The question was, would I make it out of here? There were only so many secret rooms a house could have, but I supposed it was better to be trapped inside the Harding Estate, where at least there were a million places to hide.

With the ghost of Barbara Boudine-Rivera apparently gone, I lay in darkness a minute, refusing to make noise or give away my hiding place. After all, the chute door above was still open, and the master of the house could peer down at me any moment. I should've closed it behind me, as I jumped.

I decided to crawl to the corner, so that if he did aim a flashlight or any light source into this room where I'd fallen, I'd at least be out of immediate sight. In a corner, I could cower while figuring out what to do next. Luckily, Dr. Rivera seemed to have left the master doorway. Maybe the dresser blockade had worked after all.

The moment I began navigating the dark, it was clear I wasn't alone. I couldn't see them, but I could feel them. I could also smell them, as I stumbled over limbs, legs, arms, and torsos, all of them cold and stiff. I covered my nose with my hand. No way. No damn way had I jumped headfirst into a room full of…

God, Universe, please.

I couldn't believe I was trapped in a room with the mother lode. Part of me still wished I would wake up from this dream, this nightmare, more like it, soaked in sweat, but at least it would not be real. I could laugh it off as that crazy hallucination I once had.

Not a chance—it was real, and those were legs that I'd tripped over. I reached around me for things to hold onto, my fingers gripping metal shelving units, water heater tubes, and other utility room things.

There was crying again—whimpering more like it.

It may or may not have been the exact same crying I'd heard earlier, but nonetheless, someone was alive in this room with me. One person, at least, possibly more. The faces of all the charcoal sketches haunted me in the darkness. I could see them all staring at me, begging me to help them, or crying because I hadn't.

"Who's in here?" I whispered.

My hand felt the wall for a light switch. If I could turn one on for only a moment, I might see where the door was, maybe be able to get out—get us all out—whoever was in here with me, whoever was crying in the stifling heat and darkness.

The sniffling continued. Whoever was here, she was too weak for words. But at least she was alive, assuming that was real crying, not ghostly tears. I fumbled in the dark, felt my foot touch a body that seemed warm and pliable compared to the others and reached down with shaking fingertips.

"Who's this?"

A woman moaned. She didn't seem to be aware of her surroundings. The slippery bottom of my sandal slipped on a slick surface, and I gripped a shelf to keep from falling. Metal items and aerosol cans rolled to the floor. My hand felt out the shape of a doorknob. I turned it, found it locked, and instinctively turned the lock. The door opened without any effort.

I kept it open slightly to let in just enough light to see without alerting anyone to the fact that I was in here—that *we* were in here. And then I saw her, writhing on the floor, moving her hands slowly, trying to wake up. Short, blond cropped hair, blue fingernails…

"Bibi!" I whisper-shouted.

Weak eyelids looked up then, narrowing as they adjusted to the fresh rays of light, and I saw her face—half of it had been removed. Half her skin was gone. Completely gone. And her face was red, raw, oozing with blood, bone showed through, but she was alive and shook her head softly from side to side.

I slipped in beside her.

"Bibi, you're okay, you're okay," I told her. Even though she wasn't, I wanted her to believe that she was, so she could get up, get out of this house, and run. "Did he hurt you besides here?" I touched a spot on her forehead still intact. "Shit, Bibi…shit."

Damn it, this had happened to her because of me, because I'd dragged her into this. I was so freakin pissed at myself, but this wasn't the time. This moment wasn't about me, and if I really felt all that remorseful then I would get her out of here and stay to deal with the doctor myself if it came to that.

But I had a general idea of where I was, had explored the house enough during the house cleansing to believe that the kitchen was to my right, and if we went out those doors, I might be able to unlock the back patio French doors, and run outside to the garden.

From there, we could find our way out.

"Queylin."

"Bibi, I'm going to get you out of here, okay? You have to walk, though. Can you stand?"

She winced in pain. "They're dead. They're all dead. What do we do?" She looked over her shoulder before squeezing her eyes shut.

I could see what she referred to, but holy shit, there was nothing we could do for those women. I squeezed out tears that rose and burned my lids. I gave them good thoughts. I prayed for their souls. But I could do nothing for them. I doubted any of them were alive anyway, but just in case, I used what little light filtered in to go around, one by one, touching each body to see if any were alive. I must've counted five bodies in the closet, but only Bibi felt warm. Only Bibi responded.

"They're dead, Bibi. We can't… I'm going to walk out and check who's out there. When you see me nod, you follow me out. We're going to get out of here." Grabbing her by the shoulders, I looked into her eyes. "You hear me? We're going…to get….out. Ready?"

She nodded.

God, she looked terrible. She'd be scarred for the rest of her life, in more ways than one. "I'm so sorry for this. But I'm so glad I found you." I threw my arms around her and cried into her shoulder, pulling back, forcing myself to stop. This wasn't the time for tears, and yet I was overcome with raw emotion.

"Wait for my signal."

Slowly, I stepped into the kitchen, my back against the wall. I tiptoed quietly into the room, squatting along the lower cabinets so as to avoid detection from the other side of the counters. All we had to do was make it to the French doors. Alarm or not, we could run outside into the coastal wilderness. Let the alarms sound. Let the police come. We'd be free.

We'd never be the same again.

But we'd be free of this horror.

I was halfway into the kitchen, almost to the other side, when the light snapped on. I stopped cold, blood draining from my face, and looked up. Lovely was there, waiting.

TWENTY-ONE

Our eyes met.

All this time, I hadn't been able to figure Lovely out. Was she frightened? Was she captive? Was she Dr. Rivera's loyal servant…what? She watched me carefully, and I saw the wheels turning in her head, wondering if she should report my presence to her employer? Doctor? Master?

As someone's footsteps headed up the living room near the kitchen, I shook my head. *No, please don't tell him.* Dark eyes flickered from me to her peripheral vision where I could hear Dr. Rivera heaving for breath.

"Have you seen her?" he asked, his voice deeper than usual.

Lovely stared at him, her hands clenched into a fist just under her breasts.

"Tell me, have you seen her!" he shouted. I felt his anger mounting and worried for the woman. For God's sake, Lovely, tell him yes or no, but answer him if you can. He wouldn't demand she answer if she couldn't speak, would he? At this point, I put nothing past him.

If he would've stepped into the kitchen right this moment, he would've seen me crouched next to the end cabinet, hiding in plain sight.

"Lovely?"

She wouldn't reply.

He stepped closer to her, reached into the kitchen where the butcher block stood on the counter and slipped out a large kitchen knife, pointing it at Lovely's chin. "I will only ask you once again, dear lady. Have you seen…the girl…in the house? *Eske ou te we ti fi a?*"

If Lovely's eyes widened any more, they'd have pushed out of her skull. Her whole body trembled. Couldn't he see that she was incapable of replying with even so much as a nod? The woman was so terrified, it was hard to watch.

Finally, the doctor gripped her face with his free hand, pushing her cheeks against her face bones, and pressed the knife into the corner of her mouth. With a swipe, he slid the point of the blade across the seal of her lips with a swift movement that had me wincing and looking away.

"Have…you…seen…her?" he asked through gritted teeth. "SPEAK!"

But Lovely couldn't. Even as her mouth gaped open, and she gasped for air. Her voice had escaped her, or she'd forgotten how to vocalize, or she was simply too scared of him. The doctor grabbed her by the hair and shoved her aside, slamming her against the French door.

Lovely's chest heaved, as a thin line of blood dripped from her mouth. Like a fish out of water, she gasped for huge breaths. Had he really glued her mouth shut?

"Useless," Dr. Rivera muttered and peered out the window, scanning the grounds. "I'll be back. Watch this door." He pressed a button on a small panel by the exit, disarming the alarm, and stepped outside.

Lovely looked at me again. It was hard to look back at her. He'd hurt her because of me. She'd taken a beating because of me. I didn't know how to thank her or what to say. I looked at Bibi lingering just inside the laundry room doorway.

"I'm going to move now. Wait for me," I whispered.

I crawled to the kitchen entrance closer to Lovely and peered outside. The doctor stood on the back porch smoking his cigar, knife dangling in his left hand, a smear of blood along the edge. Losing my nerve, I was about to go back the way I came. It was too close for comfort, as he could've re-entered the house at any moment.

But Lovely let go of the wall she was holding, took a few steps backwards, keeping her eyes on me the whole time, and bumped into an adjoining kitchen door. Opening it, she stood off to one side to show me it was a pantry. On its opposite wall was another door leading to the outside, complete with old jalousie glass windows.

If I thought about it too long, I'd lose my chance. "Let's go," I told Bibi, darting for the pantry, scampering across the short expanse of floor behind Dr. Rivera's field of view. We whisked past Lovely into the pantry, and if I'd had a moment to spare, I would've hugged her for this act of pure bravery.

But a second later, she'd closed the door gently behind us, and now we huddled together inside the closet just barely big enough for two people. I threw my arms around Bibi and couldn't help it—lost my shit and cried into her shoulder. I had to contain my stress, though, or the old man would surely hear us outside the door.

Straightening up, I looked Bibi in the eye and mouthed as quietly as I could, "The moment he comes back in, I open this door. You run out. You find the side gate. If it's locked, you run into the woods. Do not stop for anything until you've reached a person who can help you. Understand?"

She nodded but I could see that she was only half with it. Heavy eyelids told me she was coming out of being drugged, and the pain wasn't making its way back again. The left side of her face looked abysmal. Tons of surgeries would be required to help her look normal again, but I couldn't think about it right now.

I would never live this down, though.

Slowly, gingerly, I turned the lock on the knob, looking out the dirty jalousie windows. There stood Dr. Rivera spitting tobacco flakes from his tongue before turning and pulling on the French door again. This was it, our chance for escape. With a deep breath, I yanked on the door knob to set her free, but it wouldn't open, and that's when I saw a slide latch on the top part of the door that hadn't been unlocked.

Shit.

I reached up and undid it, but the sound had already alerted Dr. Rivera. Through the pantry door, I heard him asking Lovely what the noise had been.

The door was stuck with years of layered, thick paint, but I wrenched it free and stepped aside to let Bibi out. "GO!"

"Come with me," she said before darting out like a doe released into the wild, thin arms and legs pumping like mad, just as the pantry door opened, slamming me in the shoulder.

I cried out, scowled, and tried slipping out the door but the doctor's arm had reached around the door and grabbed my upper bicep. "There you are. Come here." His grip squeezed my arm.

I bit into his hand.

He let go.

Pulling the door towards me for momentum, I slammed it against his arm, and he cursed in seven languages. Now, he was pissed, more than I'd ever seen. It always amazed me how gentle some people could seem at first though dark clouds roiled just underneath their surface. He kept the door ajar wide enough that it pinned me against the escape door, not allowing me to access it.

"Give me that stool," he ordered Lovely.

I couldn't see her, but she must've handed him whatever he'd asked for, because suddenly, he wedged a wooden counter stool into the pantry, and any pressure I put onto the stool locked it even more firmly into place. I was stuck—couldn't open the escape door, couldn't step out of the pantry without someone's help.

With one eye in the pantry and one peering around the side of the door, I watched Dr. Rivera step back and let out a heavy breath, pushing his hands through his head of gray hair. Now that he had a moment to catch his breath, he reached out, nabbed Lovely by the edge of her skirt, and reeled her in like the catch of the day.

She fought against him, still without words, slapping her meek hands against his chest, catching him in the cheek. I knew right then that she needed to stop resisting, because I could see the impatience all over his face, and a far worse outcome than his annoyance awaited her.

But she kept flailing. She had lost her patience, too. Maybe years of frustration all built up inside her, but her attack grew stronger, and she drove her fist into his face, clipping him in the chin a few times before he finally plunged the kitchen knife deep into her belly.

I bit my lip.

Lovely collapsed into a heap spilling wider per second with dark red blood.

"Why?" I cried, resting my head against the door frame. I sobbed at the insanity of it all. How had it all degenerated so quickly? "Why did you do that? She didn't do anything to you. You're the monster."

I should've remained quiet, but there was nothing to lose at this point. It was just me and the doctor, and I was pretty sure I was done hiding from him. My fate now rested in his mercy and any ability I had left to sneak my way out of this.

"She betrayed me, *niña*. Or wasn't that clear?" He wiped his lip of blood from the cut Lovely had given him.

"She was scared of you."

"She was a child, she didn't listen," he spat like a father defending his violent disciplinary actions against his family.

I wasn't going to argue the obvious—that Lovely had been a middle-aged woman, not a child. But if he could think of his wife's corpse as a pseudo-living thing and his art studio as a place to reanimate her, his delusions were the least of my problems.

"You should've told your husband to come get you," he snickered, shaking his head in amazement. "But you women now, you feel like you don't need anybody, not even the men here to protect you."

I wanted to spit in his face for suggesting anything about my gender when he had no idea what it was like living as a woman in this world, but a part of me knew he was right. I *should've* told Samuel to come home to Miami, to call the police. Why hadn't I listened to my instinct? Why insist that everything was fine?

Why put my need to prove myself above my own safety?

Now, I was stuck inside a freaking pantry while the old man who'd lured me here searched through drawers in a cabinet for what, I had no idea. But he kept talking about young women, how they'd changed from when he was a young man, how they'd gotten stupider with time.

I ignored him. If I could somehow twist my hips, I might be able to angle them in such a way to climb over this stool. But then I'd have to run past the doctor and try every door as he chased me. No matter what, I was screwed, unless I leaped from a window.

"So, now you know about my secret room. My cellar that's not a cellar," he said, pulling something out of a drawer and holding it up in the darkness. A ball of string or twine or something. He came over and fumbled with it, using the knife to cut himself a length. "Don't judge me, *niña*. I gave those girls a good life before I expired them. It's no different than your generation taking in stray dogs or cats."

"Except we don't kill our dogs and cats after we rescue them," I said. Maybe there was something in the pantry I could use to disarm him, but all there was were cans of spaghetti sauce and boxes of pasta.

Dr. Rivera's tone was flippant. "Eh, I guess you're right. But your generation is way too compassionate. The more you care about others, the less you care for yourself. That's why you're in this predicament to begin with. Your compassion makes you weak."

"Screw you. It beats being a psychopath with no regard for life like you."

He regarded me with a raised eyebrow. "You think so?" He chuckled. "I rather thought of myself as a charming caregiver. I helped quite a number of patients in my time, *señorita.* Cured many."

Reaching into the pantry, he gripped one of my wrists and pulled it toward him. I winced, as he nearly broke my elbow. Resisting him only threatened to break my forearm, so I let him wrap the length of twine around my wrist while I stared at the pantry. Grabbing the first thing I could—a glass jar of pickles—I hurled it backwards hoping to smash his forehead with it, but he swerved in time and the jar broke on his tile floor.

"Look, why don't you stop resisting. Just let me do this and get what I need from you, and maybe I'll let you go. I promise."

He lied, and I knew it. I had no chance to do anything from this position, and at least he was looking to tie me up, not reach into the pantry with his knife and slice me up. He was strong for an older man. He found my other wrist and tied the two together so hard, I lost feeling in both hands. Yanking back the stool, he fished me out of the pantry.

Stumbling out, nearly slipping on the pool of Lovely's blood, I had no choice but to let him lead me through the house, hands bound behind my back. He pushed me through the front door into the darkest night and around the house.

The warmth of the outside air might've been the last I'd ever feel.

Swinging me around the side of the house, he reached a door opposite the garage, unlocked it with a key from his pocket, and pushed me inside. The room was musty and dark, but he flipped on a switch and showed me down a ramp that twisted a couple of times before he pushed open a heavy wooden door, and we were back where we started this chase.

Inside the cellar.

I could've made a crack about the cellar being real after he said it didn't exist, but he still held the knife in his other hand, and I didn't want to suffer Lovely's same fate. From this side of the room, I saw many things I hadn't from the tunnel side.

Mrs. Rivera's corpse, for one. Up close and personal. From this angle, I could tell she was definitely dead, a hard, drying body that'd been spectacularly painted using elements of trompe l'oeil with highlights and shading to look hyper-real. Her eyes were fake, though. Two, glistening real-looking orbs like small billiard balls with purple irises.

Purple irises.

Bibi's port wine stain.

A holding cell, for two. It looked almost exactly like the one in the Pirates of the Caribbean ride at Disney, complete with iron bars and a padlock, and I knew in a heartbeat that he was about to throw me in there before he did, and the door clanged shut, catching my ankle in the process. I screamed, because of how much I hated him.

And the pale dress ghost, for three.

Standing behind him.

TWENTY-TWO

My foot burned with pain. *Damn it.*

Why did he have to slam the door on me before I was all the way in? Now I was in a cage and hurt. In a freakin' cage. A thought of Samuel came to mind asking if I was all right, if I needed him to come home. I'd said no, I was fine.

Damn it, damn it.

Why?

Why had I insisted to be fine?

I'd been taught that we were all born with intuition, a mild form of sixth sense. That we were all psychic to a certain degree. I knew everything wasn't okay, yet I'd pretended it was, so Samuel wouldn't worry. What good was intuition if I habitually ignored it? What good was keeping peace if it led to chaos?

The ghost in the pale blue dress had floated all the way up to the cage bars. Curiously, she looked inside at me, regarding me like a trapped animal or a puzzle for her to solve.

I kicked at the solid bars. There was little chance of getting out of here, and the truth of that hit me hard. Random objects littered the cage—a hair tie, a shirt button, a sock—and the space smelled of urine.

Great.

I was going to die in here.

And my family would discuss how naïve I'd been to come to this house alone. In the end, my stubbornness had been my downfall. My need to feel special. I sobbed against the bars, pressing my forehead into them, letting the tears come. My only consolation…that I'd managed to get Bibi out. Through her survival, this torture would mean something.

But now, all of Samuel's and my hopes and dreams of one day starting a family, of growing old together, would never come. Samuel would mourn my death then move on, find someone else to love. Someone reserved, timid, with less sense of adventure. Someone who'd survive Life and not leave him wifeless.

I literally ruined everything.

The ghostly woman left the cage, reappearing on the opposite wall of the art studio. She looked helpless, like she didn't know what to do anymore to stop the insanity.

The doctor felt her presence. He shivered in the cold and muttered, "They won't leave me alone."

I wouldn't either if I was dead. I'd haunt him until his head exploded, until his brain melted from trying to figure out the "science" behind the haunting, and now I understood the pale dress ghost's motive.

From my cage, I had a clear view of it all—of the demented flesh painting, the doctor pacing the studio putting things in place. He needed order, or lose his mind. The doctor suffered some sort of overt obsessive compulsive disorder. And Barbara Rivera's corpse sitting in her wheelchair, staring into nothingness. A corpse. The doctor thought of his wife's corpse as real.

I shifted my stare to the painting's violet eyes and saw how they matched the corpse's fake ones. "Did you make those with my friend's…" I couldn't finish the question. It was hard enough imagining what he'd done to Bibi to get that patch of skin.

He glanced at the artwork then at me. "Her port wine stain? Yes, you like it?"

"You're sick, you know that?"

"I see how you think of me, but consider that I let her live, since I only needed her facial skin. Other subjects weren't as fortunate."

"Why not?" A tremor slipped into my voice.

He picked up a scalpel and ran his fingers along the blade. "Every part of this painting was made with corresponding parts of the body. The arms were made with skin from the arms, the legs were made from skin with the legs. Except for the eyes and hair, of course, since I decided to go with a unified crepe look."

I was flabbergasted. I kept imagining what he did to other women to get the "unified crepe look" that he wanted.

He stepped up to the painting and touched it gingerly, lovingly. "My wife started it while pregnant and never got to finish it. I've done my best to keep her vision going, but I'm not half the artist she used to be."

"I doubt her vision was to use skin."

"No, that was my addition, but it does give a unique texture, *verdad?* Almost like it was scraped together with oils using a spatula. I love it." He touched the pregnant belly, mostly empty except for the original painting underneath. "I thought you could go right here."

Me?

He planned to use my skin. "You say I'm pregnant, but you could just be saying that for your own purposes."

"I assure you I'm not. Julia Harding has never been wrong. Why do you think I bought this house?"

So he could seek out pregnant victims? He was mad as hell.

"All this, and this…" He pointed out huge sections of the subject's pregnant belly. "All pregnant skin."

Pregnant skin? He was talking like they'd been objects instead of victims. I held back a sob. "I'm not going to be a part of your painting, Dr. Rivera."

"Oh, but you are. I waited so long for pregnant skin to come along so I could use it for my beloved's *barriga*."

"I'm not 'pregnant skin.' I'm a person. My name is Queylin, and I'm not part of your twisted art project."

"You'll feel differently when you realize a part of you will live forever this way."

I didn't want to live forever. I wanted to live temporarily, freely, happily with my family and friends, not forever in the cellar of this crazy man's malevolent home.

He pulled out a small vial of clear liquid and a syringe and I knew that injection was meant for me. Behind him, the pale dress ghost stood by his ear, screaming without making a sound. Her mouth formed an O, and as she shouted at him, veins burst from her forehead. Her thin arms swiped away tools from his table.

One vial flew across the room and landed against the brick wall, smashing into pieces.

"See?" He sighed, shaking his head. "This is why I hired you. They don't leave me alone. They torment me, even though they can travel anywhere in the cosmos, but no, they stay here to taunt me."

"Because you ruined their lives. They want you to pay," I said.

"I won't pay. I live alone. Nobody bothers me, and nobody gets out once they know what I do here." He cast me a quick smile.

I swallowed.

"My friend did."

The smile on his face dissipated. "Yes. And whose fault is that? I already took care of Lovely. Now you."

The jab reminded me that there was still hope for me. By now, Bibi might've reached civilization and alerted the police. Then again, she was so weak when she left, she might've hit pavement unconscious or be out in the garden somewhere, face first in a ditch.

"God willing, none of that will happen."

"For someone who doesn't believe in God, you talk a lot about Him," he said, preparing another injection then wiping his hands on a paper towel.

"I never said I don't believe in God," I said. "I don't believe in organized religion. I pray my own way, but I do believe in a higher power."

"Yes? Well, you're going to need Him. Let's see if He appears for you. Lord knows, he didn't appear for me. He took my wife. He took my child…"

It wasn't your child, I thought.

"I can make her live again," he said, turning to the painting. He nodded, proud of his work.

"You can't play God," I told him. "Nothing will ever bring her back, not even what you're doing here. You know that, right?"

"I'm cursed, Quey*lín*. Cursed by *La Dama de Blanco*."

"I thought you didn't believe in curses." Two could play this game.

"Touché, but we shall see. So far, the curse lives on. No children, no babies, no viable pregnancies."

"Coincidences," I said.

Now I was being the rational one. I didn't believe Julia Harding had actually cursed this house. I thought her legacy had prevented good things from happening over the years, but that was to be expected from a home filled with so much negative energy.

Something buzzed in the doctor's pocket. He pulled out a phone—*my* phone. "Oh, I have this, by the way. You left it alone in the room."

"Let me have it."

"You're in no position to make demands of me, young lady." He laughed. "Besides, I've been answering your texts for you."

"What? No. Give it to me."

"Your husband asked if you were okay. I told him you were fine and didn't need any help. You know, because that is how you women are now. You demand knights in shining armor, then when you get them, you demand they give you space to conduct your own lives."

"That's not true."

"You want to know why I preserve my wife's body? Because she was one of the last true women. She knew her place and she respected mine."

"She was a prisoner," I said. "Who suffered from Stockholm Syndrome. Even now, she's scared of you. I would hardly call that respect."

"What do you mean *even now*?" His dark eyes flickered at me, eyebrows drawn into the center of his forehead.

Wait, he didn't know? That his wife haunted this house? That all he had to do was reach out to her and she might come to him? I had to use this amazing new revelation to my advantage somehow.

"Your wife is here."

"What do you mean? Who told you that?"

"Your wife did."

"But my wife is here." He gestured to the wheelchair.

I couldn't with this man. "Her ghost lives in your guest bedroom. Or didn't you know? Oops, I guess you shouldn't have set me up in there. Her spirit haunts this house, Dr. Rivera. I've seen her. I've seen her many times."

He flew to the cage, fingers gripping the iron bars. "Why do you say this?"

"Because it's true."

"What does she look like?"

"Like that painting, only more beautiful. With bright violet eyes. But she's in deep emotional pain."

"Why in pain?" His eyes filled with tears, and for a second, I actually felt sorry for him.

"Because she hates what you are doing. She hates that you torture and kill people." I didn't know if she did or didn't, but it couldn't hurt to say it.

"But I am doing it for you, *querida*," he begged the air, his eyes turning pink with tears. Before my eyes, the doctor's stony expression turned to heartbreak. "I do it so you can live again!" He broke down and sobbed, his fluffy white hair shaking against the iron bars.

I might've reached out to grab him had my hands not been tied behind my back.

I closed my eyes and went with my intuition. "She says to take the rope off my wrist."

He cleared his nose with the back of his hand. "She would not say that."

"Yes, she wants to take possession of me. She wants to use my hands."

"For?"

"So she can caress your face. She misses you. I won't escape, doctor. I'm in a cage, for shit's sake."

He thought about it for a split second. He lifted his tear-stained face to gauge mine. I almost felt bad lying to him. Almost.

"Turn around." He sniffled, standing to grab something off his table. I turned around, pressing my tied hands against the iron bars. Using one of his tools, he carved at the restraints until my wrists broke free.

"Now come back the way you were," I instructed. "She wants so much to hold you again."

Behind him, the pale dress ghost laughed.

Pressing his forehead to the bars, he resumed his sobbing. "I'm sorry, *querida.* I'm sorry to disappoint you. *Como te extraño, querida. Por favor, discúlpame.*" He begged for his wife's forgiveness and waited to feel her touch, the touch I was about to give him.

Reaching out slowly, I slid my fingers into his thick, white hair. The moment I did, he broke down even more, crying against the bars.

My heart pounded so hard, I thought he might detect it in the stillness. I wished this moment could've been different. I wished I could've actually delivered a tender message from beyond the grave for this mourning man.

But I couldn't.

I had to live.

Grabbing fistfuls of his hair, I yanked him against the iron bars with every ounce of force I had, slamming his forehead into the metal. I did it again and again, smashing him several times, as his hands tried to wrench mine free, but I wouldn't let go, not even as he used the scalpel in his hand to swipe at my hands over and over.

I would not let go.

Finally, he fell onto his side, knocking into his table, his pans and cups and vials and tools of torture all come crashing onto the floor, rolling every which way. Reaching out between the bars, I tried to get the one item I needed—the key—from the old man's pocket, but I couldn't extend far enough.

"Come on…" I muttered, gritting my teeth.

The pale dress ghost, watching my struggle from the ceiling, dove toward me, used what little energy she had left to hoist the old man onto his side. Then, the key slipped out of his pocket and onto the hard stone floor.

I reached for it again, bruising my armpit in the process. Just another inch and I would be able to reel it in with my fingertips, but I didn't need to. The pale dress ghost rolled in like a soft fog, nudged the key the last inch toward me, and quietly disappeared from this world.

TWENTY-THREE

I had only a moment.

The old man was moving, albeit slowly while muttering nonsensical things. From the blood loss, I thought he'd be passed out a while, but now I wasn't sure.

Taking advantage, I took the key and pressed it into the lock, giving it a twist, which was hard to do from the angle behind the bars, but the lock popped open, and I pushed my way out of the holding cell.

The iron bars pressed against Dr. Rivera's side, and I thought he would awaken from the pressure, so the first thing I did was grab my phone. For some reason, I felt compelled to pause and stare at Barbara's dehydrated mummified body one more time. I felt her sadness and desire to end the pain.

I wished the ghostly Barbara, wherever she was in the house or the ether, a peaceful passing into the other life. *I'm sorry for everything that happened to you,* I thought.

Wedging my way past the doctor, careful not to step on him or brush any part of his body with my feet, I stepped quietly all the way to the door, pushed down on the crank, and entered the outside world. It was still dark, though early morning, and I could feel the energy of the sun ready to rise over the horizon.

There was something about this time of day that always unsettled me. It was when I'd lie beside my husband having my craziest dreams, when the veil between the worlds felt the thinnest, when I'd often see shadows shifting up and down the walls.

I'd never experienced true magic until I stood beside Harding Estate at six in the morning, staring at the deep orange tones of the horizon, facing the guardians of the east, watchtower of air, facing the great Mother Ocean, knowing I'd just escaped the worst situation of my life. That full breath of air that came with freedom.

I tucked behind a coquina wall and fumbled with my phone. In stressful dreams, I often couldn't punch numbers, press buttons, or remember simple things like 911. But I breathed deeply, remembering to stay calm and texted Samuel first, knowing if I made an actual call or spoke aloud, the old man might hear me.

Not okay. Need help. Police.

Thank heavens autocorrect was on, or none of the words I texted with shaky hands would've come out right.

WHERE RU?

Samuel was both pissed and worried. I hoped he would some day forgive me.

Harding Estate, I replied, but autocorrect did not recognize my trembling message, so I tried again… *Send help ASAP—*

I couldn't send it. My phone was suddenly yanked from my hand, and the doctor, agile and persistent as he was, smashed it against the rough crushed shell exterior of the house. Glass pieces crumbled to the ground.

"You're not leaving," he panted, mouth gasping for air. In his right hand was the fucking syringe.

"You're not making me stay." My gaze burned at him.

He still managed to chuckle under his breath. "You're so confident. Your generation sure is determined…if tremendously foolish."

I wasn't going to insult his generation in return. They had raised my parents, who, in turn, had raised me, so if anyone was responsible for the way we horrible millennials had turned out, it'd be his.

I stared at him, urging my brain to think of a way out of this.

"I need you in order to complete the painting," he said blankly, as if such a thing were even an option.

I had to remember that this man was totally insane, that he didn't think rationally like regular people. In his mind, he probably thought I would be fine with sacrificing my skin for the pregnant belly of his fucked-up skin art.

"It's not going to happen, doctor. And I already alerted my husband. The police will be here soon. You may as well give up."

Inject yourself, you piece of shit.

"No. No, no, no." Wearing an odd expression of disbelief and amusement, he encroached on me slowly across the back patio. I stepped backwards and tripped on every rocking chair along the way. There was only one thing to do at this point—outrun him.

I turned and ran.

He chased me.

The old man chased me.

We were only as old as we felt. The asshole caught up with me and twisted the hell out of my arm. I screamed, fairly sure he had broken something. His syringe brushed against the crook of my elbow, but there was no way I would let him fill me with chemicals or any of his wicked ideas.

I kicked him hard, causing him to fall backwards against a rocking chair. He stumbled, and I set off running again, but he reached out, pulled on my shirt, and brought me to the ground. I slammed my head against one of the wooden columns of the back porch and for a moment, all I saw was blackness and stars that exploded into a radiating pattern.

Stars.

And blackness.

Coming to, I saw that my leg was being pulled by my ankle by a strong hand. My shirt had slid up along my upper back, my whole bra and stomach was exposed, as the old man dragged me along the patio floorboards back toward the side of the house with the cellar door. Even without seeing them, I knew my back was full of bloody scratches.

As he dragged me off the porch, however, I reached out to the last object I could get my hands on—a last flailing attempt—and caught a wide wooden coffee table between two rocking chairs. My nails scratched and I nabbed one leg and took the damn thing with me. As the doctor tried to drag me off the porch, the table wedged between the columns, stopping his efforts.

He turned, annoyed to see what was causing him so much trouble, and the next thing he saw was a flying rocking chair coming straight at him. I'd stood and grabbed the nearest one, and while I never thought I'd ever be strong enough to lift a rocking chair above my head, adrenaline was an amazing thing.

So was the will to survive.

So was the human brain.

And so I hoisted that chair over my head and whirled it through the air straight at him. He tried blocking his face with it, but it clocked him in the temple, and a gash opened up, releasing a thin line of blood seeping into his eyes.

"*Coño! Me cago en…*" he cried out.

Though I'd little energy left, I found the last of my reserves and ran. Ran as fast as I could across the back patio, coming out the other end and tripping to the ground right at the angel statue's feet.

"Shit."

I scrambled to my feet again, and the lantern turned on, glowing brightly in the early morning hours, but the doctor came running around the side of the house and tackled me like a linebacker. Together, we stumbled and hit Julia Harding's tombstone, tumbling into the tall grass.

I wasn't sure how I knew this, but Julia was here now, watching us struggle, and the old man's hard grip wrenched my waist, as another hand slipped around my neck. His fingers dug into my throat, I saw the syringe come up over his head, and watched it come down, almost in slow motion, toward my neck.

His arm, so close to my cheek, was in the perfect position for me to swivel my face and sink my teeth deep into his wrist. As he screamed out, letting go of the syringe, it flew into the grass, and I tasted blood and hated it, hoped to God and the Universe that I wouldn't catch something from this foul man's life essence. He let go, brought his hand to his chest, and cradled his wounds.

"*Puta*," he spat, eyes filled with hate.

Ah, yes, *puta*. Bitch. Whore. The word women the world over had to endure through centuries of humiliation anytime they dared to defend themselves. I owned that word with full pride.

"Your own fault, asshole."

And then he flew down on me again. I had no time to roll out of the way, and a split second later, I felt the pressure of his entire weight on my body, crushing me. Ribs cracked and internal organs buckled under his weight, but I kept my core muscles tight to fend him off as long as I could.

Full of anger, he struck my face with his fist, over and over, then twisted his hands around my neck and began choking me. I nearly blacked out again. I was pretty sure this was it. I could only muster up enough energy, and my muscles were officially giving out. My weaker body mass was no match for his larger one, and this position left very little for wits or defense strategy to accomplish.

Worse, with my head twisted to one side, I had a direct view of Lovely, dead against the inside French door. His faithful servant, simply wasted. That woman had risked it all so Bibi and I could escape, could survive. Maybe deep inside, she knew she'd never be able to leave even with the doors wide open.

Some women made no attempts to leave their shitty situations, and I could only surmise that a crushed spirit had to do with that.

Well, this crushed spirit had given of herself selflessly, and I was only sorry that I never got to thank her. Flitting in and out of consciousness, as the doctor unleashed his rage on me through fist pounds and punches to the chest, I imagined myself joining Lovely in another world.

Maybe it was better this way.

Maybe my unborn child and I would find Julia and her unborn child, and this way, I might escort her to the Light. Maybe I'd already completed my job on this earth, same way Lovely had, and now my time here was done. I only wished I'd had the chance to say goodbye.

My vision turned black.

In my mind, I fought back. I punched the old man, pushed him with newfound force, and found victory in Julia's garden. I imagined the French doors opening, Lovely standing on her own feet, and reaching for her summoning stick.

In my mind's eye, she struck the end against the ground while uttering a prayer in Creole, all while the ghost of Julia Harding knelt by my head and cried over me.

But it was all in my mind.

In this dream state between life and death.

In the ashen area between worlds.

But then, why, when I opened my eyes slightly to see how bad reality was, how close to dying I might actually be, did I catch a glimpse of Lovely, eyes rolled back into her head, white glowing orbs of fierce anger and determination in the middle of her face, holding her mighty wand?

She stood at the open French doors, fingers gripped around her summoning stick.

Striking the ground with it.

Over.

And over.

And when she was done, he stood next to us, and Dr. Rivera saw him too, stopped beating me to death to stare at him, even fell back onto his hands. Roger, looking down at his beloved Julia still cradling my head, lifted a foot above the old man's chest and stepped his ghostly self right into the doctor's body.

TWENTY-FOUR

Roger, or the doctor possessed by Roger—I wasn't sure anymore—wrenched himself off me, struggling to his feet. I gasped for breath, wavering in and out of consciousness, as oxygen found its way back into my lungs. A prickling spread through my skin, tickling my throat.

Running his hand through his hair, the doctor, with Roger standing inside of his body, looked nervously to the ocean.

"They're coming," said a voice full of watery reverberation. It was the doctor who spoke, but his voice sounded different, a composite of two or more voices, none of which belonged to him.

"Who is?" I asked.

"Coast Guard." He pulled something out of his pocket, but nothing was in his hand. "Nine o'clock. I need to get past Bimini and the Rum Line before they find me. Julia…love…I have to leave, but I'll be return soon."

Julia.

I'd forgotten she was behind me. I craned my neck to find her and saw her still kneeling and crying on the ground. Could she not see Roger? She wouldn't look up or acknowledge him.

"Julia…" Roger called to her.

Julia, I tried to speak but no sound came out. *He's here. He's waiting for you.* Did they exist on separate dimensions?

I couldn't move. All I could do was lay here and feel everyone's pain at once. They say that empaths become drained of energy after absorbing emotions of those around them. Well, I absorbed Julia's—her tormented soul waiting for her lover, wondering if she would ever see him again, torn over how on Earth she would survive the next year, if she could deliver this child at all, if she would survive an attack from her husband or the community once they saw…

Once they knew.

But I also felt Roger's anguish over the Coast Guard's pursuit, how he hadn't meant to fall into this line of work, but recent laws had created the perfect storm for making a fortune illegally. How else was a boat captain supposed to make a living? He never should have laid a hand on Julia, but she was the only one who understood him. A kind, loving woman. Yes, she belonged to another man, but that man did not appreciate what he had on his hands.

Some possessed diamonds but only saw sand.

I even felt the doctor's emotions—confusion, fear of death, isolation, misunderstanding, hatred, and revenge. In this dreamlike, trancelike state, the sentiments all swirled around me, through me. They used me as a conduit, the way I'd always asked for.

Now I understood when psychics hated that I called them talented, never understood why I envied them. Who would want this? Who would want to be bombarded day and night with the energy of others? I wanted to shake off the thoughts, rip my head off, end the voices.

Scrambling to my feet, I stood looking at the angel statue, flipping and flipping my lucky bracelet. They stared back at me, solemnly communicating all the sadness they'd seen over the century. The lantern dimmed to nothing then glowed again, its power dying.

Was I dying?

Was this death?

My ability to discern between life and death, dreams or reality was growing increasingly harder. In the distance, the great banyan tree awaited me, its branches etching sharp thorns into early morning sky, puncturing layers of rose and tangerine clouds. The tree could help me end things, it seemed to communicate. All I had to do was press my bare feet into its massive roots, climb, and soon it would all be over.

The sadness would end.

I'd loved this tree for so long. But I'd only seen it at night during the urban exploration of my teen years. In the morning, it was even more beautiful, a different animal altogether. I had to see it up close, even at the risk of watching Julia hang there again.

I stepped past the statue, aware that Roger was following me. Roger always followed me. Roger understood me like no other, but the Coast Guard captain told me…he told me they'd shot him point blank. He would never be coming back for me. He would never seen his own child, and even if he could, how would we ever create a life together?

An impossible situation.

There was no other way to deal with it than to end it. After they'd arrest my husband, there'd be nothing left for me here in Florida. I never thought I'd miss the cold winters of New York City and the harsh ones of Ohio as much as I did right now.

Queylin, wake up.

Julia—they were Julia's thoughts, yet they were mine also.

I felt as though I'd lived them myself. Maybe I had. All I knew was that I had to climb this tree and finish things once and for all. I couldn't take the pain anymore. Reaching the tree, I pressed my hands into the thick trunk and tangled roots as the doctor or Roger followed me. I knew he wanted to prevent what I was going to do, but this was the only way.

The tree's energy was older than all of us put together. It called me home.

"Why do you follow me?" I asked Roger.

"My life is yours, Julia," he replied. "And that of the life growing inside of you."

The life growing inside of me.

If the doctor had been right, and the statue indeed detected those imbued with new life, I couldn't climb this tree, yet it continued to pull me in, lull me to eternal rest. I had to climb it—and did. All the way to its first branch high in the air, about twelve feet off the ground, where Julia had once taken her life and was about to take it again.

Through me.

Because time was not linear as we thought it was, and never had been. Our souls could choose any time period we wanted to be in, live inside of any body, because souls were energy, and energy could not be created nor destroyed. So, our spirits repeated moments like these, over and over, until we freed ourselves and moved on.

Julia never freed herself.

Maybe I could help her.

Now that Roger was here, maybe he could help her too. Unable to rip myself out of this reverie, I climbed across the giant branch like I had this morning, or yesterday in Queylin-time, and reached the hanging roots that made this banyan look like a prisoner of its own misery.

The doctor followed me.

Though he was old, he was fit and pressed his shoes into the roots, bobbled a little unsteadily, but rose into the tree nonetheless. He followed me along the branch. If I were to snap out of the trance and remember that I was Queylin Sanchez-Gold and nobody else, now would be the time to panic. Last thing I needed was to become uber-aware that the murderer who'd chased me all night and disfigured my friend, was now in the tree with me. I tried to keep calm and tune into Julia's thoughts instead.

No death by doctor.

I'd rather take death by choice.

Any moment now, dawn would break on a new day, and I'd be gone from this world. I'd be reunited with Roger, once and for all, and we might be happy in Heaven if I didn't become stuck in this miserable half-existence.

"Come back here." It was the doctor's voice, snapping me back to reality. "I need to finish the painting, Quey*lín*. You must do this for me."

I must do nothing, old man.

I looked down. There was no way out of this situation except by dropping from the banyan, and the ropes were already in my hands. I looked down at a tangle I'd created—a noose. I had to fulfill this destiny and place it around my neck. I never quite belonged in this world anyway.

Were they my thoughts?

Or Julia's?

It all blended into one. I'd never suffered serious depression. This was how it felt.

I shook my head, trying to pry the evil thoughts from my mind. "Get it together, Queylin. Snap the hell out of it. Come on…"

In the distance, I heard sirens wail. The police had been alerted. Bibi had reached the highway. I could jump to the ground and run to them, break several bones, but at least I'd be alive. Leave Dr. Rivera up in this tree for the police to find, and it would've been a fine decision had I not been so trapped in this otherworldly pull.

Julia's energy overwhelmed me, tugged at my will. Of course it did—she was filled with pain and bringing everybody down with it. That was her curse—her legacy.

Around my bare feet, I watched white wisps of fabric blow around in the breeze. I saw the thin line of blood seeping into my toes. The Lady in White—*La Dama de Blanco*—was me, inside of me, using me. She'd haunt this house and garden forever. She'd look for a way out, trapped in this lonely existence. She'd use however many warm bodies she could until she found Roger.

"Julia, he's here. Don't you see him?" I begged. "Roger is there, coming at us." If she could only see him, she wouldn't need me anymore, she could go with him into the Light, and I'd finally be released from this trance.

"Roger?" I spoke through a different voice. "Roger, I'm coming to you, my love."

For a moment, I thought she might snap out of it, but I could hear what was in her mind clear as a bell. She'd been abandoned. By another man. Again. She could not redeem this life, so she would escape it and start all over in a new one.

"It doesn't have to be this way," I told her. "Julia, go towards the light. You're already free," I tried explaining again.

She listened, holding the banyan's roots limply in her hands. My hands. We were one and the same now. I touched my bracelet, imagined its power emanating and surrounding us with love. With light. Of course I believed in God, because we *were* God, created in His image. We all held the power to create our own destinies, exactly like Him.

This was not my fate. It couldn't be.

The sirens approached, just as Dr. Rivera inched toward me, reaching for me and side-stepping to avoid losing his balance. "Julia, don't. Don't jump," he said in Roger's voice. Julia's lover's features were superimposed over the doctor's.

Handsome.

Worrisome.

I wanted this nightmare to end, this inability to control my own body and mind. My rational side told me to throw this noose over Dr. Rivera's head and let gravity decide his fate, but I knew I couldn't do that. Even after all that had happened, I couldn't kill a man.

"Julia, stop!" Roger cried out.

She paused, looked at Roger/Dr. Rivera, our eyes connecting for the first time since Roger appeared. Finally, she saw him. I knew because I suddenly felt my heart ache turn to beating recognition and elation.

He came for me, after all.

I threw my arms out to reach for him—Julia reaching for Roger, yes—but also Queylin reaching for the man who wanted to kill her, nearly losing my balance in the first place. But I stopped and pulled back.

No, I couldn't.

"I'm sorry, Julia, but I can't let you take us both down," I said. If I was pregnant, which I was, I knew I was—I could feel the fluttery sensations inside of me. "I'll name my baby after Roger," I told her.

I would help them both live on in some way, but I couldn't take this fall.

That would be lovely.

She smiled. Julia Harding smiled, lifting my heart which smiled for her in return. I felt her pure happiness at my words, but I didn't have time to fully enjoy them, because Dr. Rivera reached me on the tree limb, grabbed me by the shoulders, and tugged on me to make me fall.

Which I did.

But I held on at the last moment, stomach rubbing against rough branches, my legs dangling below me. At that moment, Julia slipped from my body and fell into Roger's arms, taking the noose with her. Together, the three of them plummeted off the limb. I turned my face, wincing to avoid it. But I heard it loud, clear—the crack of Dr. Rivera's neck punctuating the morning stillness.

Julia and Roger evaporated from Harding Estate. The fervent glow of the angel's lantern died to a buzzing thrum before going dark altogether. And the police cars arrived.

TWENTY-FIVE

A curtain of darkness spread open, as soft fluorescent lights filtered through my lashes and silhouettes of multiple people looked down at me.

I'd been dreaming again.

I closed my mouth and rehydrated my lips.

The dreams were always about wine bottles and paintings and rooms decorated with the jewelry from women who'd never made it out of the house, women extinguished before me. In some dreams, I made it out into the light, ran toward the highway, and found people, the way I'd told Bibi to do, even though Bibi never made it that far.

She'd been found passed out on the side of the road, barely alive. It hadn't been her who'd called the police. It'd been my husband who'd had the good sense to realize I always ended my sentences with periods, never dashes or semicolons. He'd left the dental conference and boarded a late night flight as soon as he could, arriving at MIA around the same time two police officers helped me down from a banyan tree.

A banyan tree I couldn't get out of my head.

In other dreams, I never made it out at all. I'd wake up in a cold sweat, screaming about the dead women surrounding me on the floor or of yelling for help from a holding cell for days at a time without anyone to hear me.

One day at a time.

One day at a time, and therapy would help me forget. But for now, I had great distractions. Like these fantastic people at my bedside. Bibi was here, half her face in a bandage, along with Rain, Lorena, and Maggie. They'd only been allowed in, four at a time to see us, and it was so nice to see Bibi smiling, even if she'd been disfigured. I loved her and loved that she was still here.

"You look good," I mumbled, trying to sit up.

"So do you." She gazed at me with her good eye, and I knew she'd forgiven me long ago. That was another nightmare—the stress of not finding Bibi in the house. In other dreams, Bibi was dead.

I reached up and dabbed my fingertip along her gauzed cheek. "Did it go well?"

"Yeah, they took the graft from my inner thigh. Doctor says I should be able to take this thing off after a few weeks."

"Amazing," I said. I still couldn't hear the word "doctor" without it conjuring up images of that monster's face again.

One of my nurses walked in, the older lady with the gray hair in a ponytail, happily greeting my visitors and hovering over my line of vision. "Good morning. How are you feeling?"

"I'm good." My back hurt, and I felt like a truck hit me, but otherwise, all was A-okay. "Better than most people."

She raised an eyebrow. "So, you're the Queylin." She eyed me with a sneaky smile.

"*The* Queylin?"

"Yes, I saw your segment on the news. I didn't realize you were the lady who found out all that stuff that went down at the Harding Estate. My goodness, you've been through a lot."

"You think?" I said, and the whole room broke into laughter. Where was my husband?

"Well," she said, cocking her head. "Pretty impressive. I bet you never want to see another ghost again in your life, though, huh?"

I sighed, watching her check my IV bag. "Actually, ghosts aren't the problem. People are."

"I hear you. I can't believe that man was living there with that poor woman, and oh, my God, a corpse in a wheelchair? You can't make that stuff up."

"Yeah, no kidding," I murmured.

Though the stories about my harrowing experience had made it onto multiple news networks, and even Oprah's offices had called to invite me to come on and talk about it when I was ready, I couldn't.

Not yet.

In fact, I didn't even want my nurse bringing it up and was hoping nobody would ever talk about it while I was trying to recover. Maggie narrowed her eyes at the nurse when she turned around, and unsurprisingly, she changed the topic.

Because Maggie equaled magic.

"Daddy's coming now. He was showing family the new addition in the nursery," she explained. "All your levels are good. I'll have them bring your lunch in now."

"Great. Thank you." I smiled.

"Queylin," Rain said, her eyes filling with tears. "She's so beautiful. Oh…my…God. Like, seriously beautiful."

My water had broken at five in the morning. By six, I'd been wheeled into an emergency C-section thanks to the staff losing the baby's heart rate, and for the longest five minutes in the world, I thought I would lose her—my sweet angel.

But she'd had what the obstetrician called a true knot, a complete, tight knot in the umbilical cord, which cut off her heart rate until they pulled her out safely. It occurred in about 2% of all births.

Luckily, they'd given me an epidural shortly before it happened, so I was ready for surgery, and they had her out in five minutes, her Apgar scores coming out at all perfect 9s. Healthiest baby ever.

Speaking of which…

A little plastic hospital bin rolled into the room decorated with pink ribbons, followed by another nurse and then my husband, all smiles. Tired but in a great mood. This event was just what we needed. A distraction in our lives.

My staff—friends, really—all *ahhed* and cooed, and Maggie was already washing her hands so she could hold the little girl. But no way on Earth would she be first. Because Lovely Julia Gold was the most beautiful baby in the world, and Mommy needed her so very much, exactly as much as she needed Daddy, and everyone else could wait.

The bin wheeled all the way up to my bedside, and I sat up through my pain, getting ready to hold her for the first time since the birth. Had it been a boy, I would've stayed true to my word and named him Roger, but when we found out I'd be having a girl, I had the privilege of naming her after the two women who'd saved my life.

My life and Bibi's. I still suffered from the guilt of involving her, something that would take years to get over, the therapist said, but we would work it out together, as Bibi had her own therapy to get through as well.

As the nurse pushed down the safety bar at my bedside, Samuel slipped his hands underneath the little burrito bundle with the pink-and-blue, standard-issue beanie and placed Lovely in my arms. She had perfect skin, so smooth and soft, her nose was turned up like a button, and her little breathing noises melted my heart.

The tears curled over my cheeks.

I couldn't stop them. Nor did I want to.

I'd cried a lot over the last six and a half months. Out of fear, out of worry, out of guilt, out of panic, out of low self-esteem, out of love and appreciation for my husband, out of many things. But this was the first time I'd cried out of pure elation. Because while everything wasn't perfect and never would be again, it sure as hell came close.

Surrounded by friends.

Kissed by Samuel.

Holding my newborn.

Brand new path, new opportunities. Lovely had it all ahead of her, and I would do all I could to make sure she stayed safe in this world. Maybe my bracelet could pass on some of that good luck and energy. Because despite all that had happened, I still thought I'd turned out blessed in the end.

Still, more blessings couldn't hurt. Opening her swaddling just a bit, I slipped the monk's lucky bracelet off my wrist, doubled it up and slipped it onto my daughter's wrist.

Brand new beginning.

Brand new life.

Just in case.

About the Author

GABY TRIANA is the bestselling author of *Island of Bones*, *Cakespell*, *Wake the Hollow*, *Summer of Yesterday*, and many more, as well as 40+ ghostwritten novels for best-selling authors. Gaby has published with HarperCollins, Simon & Schuster, and Entangled, won an IRA Teen Choice Award, ALA Best Paperback Award, and Hispanic Magazine's Good Reads of 2008. She writes about ghosts, haunted places, and abandoned locations. When not obsessing over Halloween, Christmas, or the paranormal, she's taking her family to Disney World, the Grand Canyon, LA, New York, or Key West. Gaby dreams of living in the forests of New England one day but for the meantime resides in sunny Miami with her boys, Michael, Noah, and Murphy, her husband Curtis, their dog, Chloe, and four cats—Daisy, Mickey Meows, Paris, and the reformed thug/shooting survivor, Bowie.

Visit Gaby at **www.GabyTriana.com** and subscribe to her **newsletter**. Also, check out her blog at: **www.WitchHaunt.com.**

Also by Gaby Triana

Paranormal Young Adult:

WAKE THE HOLLOW

Contemporary Young Adult:

CAKESPELL

SUMMER OF YESTERDAY

RIDING THE UNIVERSE

THE TEMPTRESS FOUR

CUBANITA

BACKSTAGE PASS

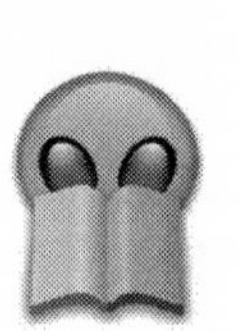

Made in the USA
Columbia, SC
01 February 2021

32133420R00286